Timmy's Ticklish Trials

First Edition

Christopher Trevor

Timmy's Ticklish Trials

Published by The Nazca Plains Corporation
Las Vegas, Nevada
2006

ISBN: 978-1-887895-74-3

Published by

The Nazca Plains Corporation ®
4640 Paradise Rd, Suite 141
Las Vegas NV 89109-8000

PUBLISHER'S NOTE
Timmy's Ticklish Trials is a work of fiction created wholly by *Christopher Trevor's* imagination. All characters are fictional and any resemblance to any persons living or deceased is purely by accident. No portion of this book reflects any real person or events.

Cover Art by Neil Bruce
Art Direction by Blake Stephens

Dedication

In Memory of Jack and his tickle website: "RopeJock.com"
We will always remember you with a smile and laughter...

Timmy's Ticklish Trials

Christopher Trevor

Contents

Introduction

Timmy's Ticklish Trials is the story that started it all. Well, it's the story that started Timothy Backman (star of my previous book "Timmy and The Hong Kong Tailor") on his sometimes perilous yet always titillating tickle journey. Before Timmy (as he is called in the story) wound up tickled at "The Leather Bar", before Timmy negotiated a business deal for his sexy rival Valerie and once again wound up tickle tortured and long before Timmy wound up in the clutches of the tickling tailor there was this story, "Timmy's Ticklish Trials." It is a story that was created by two guys (Timothy Backman and me) e-mailing their tickle fantasies back and forth over a number of months. It wasn't until the pages really started piling up that I realized we had the makings of a novel-length story here, perhaps even room for a sequel. Timmy Backman is my best ever online tickle buddy and I have the Internet and a gentleman named Jack (sadly, now deceased) who hosted a website called "RopeJock.com" to thank for bringing us together. When "RopeJock.com" was still in existence it was the best tickle website out there and it still hasn't been equaled. It consisted of many true and fictional tickle tales told by men (straight, gay and bisexual men) throughout the country. Jack did a wonderful job of categorizing the stories into sections such as "Tickle Wagers", "Cum Control", "Caught by Surprise" and even a section on "Tools of the Ticklish Trade" which featured pictures of devilish devices that could be used to tickle torture a guy with. (Re: my story "Mr. Kujman's Device" which appears in my book "Don't!! Stop!! That Tickles!!") I myself was fortunate enough to have two of my stories appear on Jack's site, "RopeJock.com" and it was because of those two stories that my friendship with Timmy Backman was born. Timmy had read my two tickle stories and contacted me via the site. When he told me that he was a mostly straight guy who enjoyed being tickled by sexy women we started throwing ideas back and forth for a fantasy where he could very well wind up tickled by a guy (or guys) and come away equally as aroused as when tickled by sexy women. With those thoughts in mind we started building a friendship and also started to mingle our erotic thoughts and fantasies together where tickling a guy was concerned. As stated above after we had been e-mailing each other our most erotic and deep fantasies concerning tickling we realized that we had the makings of a story here. When I suggested to Timmy that he let me use the e-mails to create a novel-length tickle story he happily agreed. What you are holding in hand (book-wise) is the finished result of part one of "Timmy's Ticklish Trials."

Happy Reading!!! And may all your tickle fantasies come true...

Christopher Trevor

A Boner Book

Prologue

"HA, HA, HA, HA, HA, HA, HA, HA, HA, HA, HA, HA, HA, HAR, HAR, HAR, HAR, HAR!" was the sound that filled the latest room that my so called buddy Ronald had me trapped in.

The sound was my own agonizing laughter, my uncontrolled laughter, my louder than loud laughter bursting from me faster than I could breathe as Ronald tickle tortured me in one of his many rooms that housed what seemed like a never ending array of tickle torture devices. Yes, you heard me correctly, tickle torture. I was being systematically and methodically tickle tortured. Actually, it was his latest device that was doing the work of tickling me as I lay there stretched out and tied down on a slab of wood that hung from the ceiling, held that way by heavy-duty cables. Ronald simply stood nearby enjoying every goddamned second of my jolly agony. Each room of the immense house housed a different tickle torture mechanism of some kind. It was a house of horrors that he had me in to put it quite bluntly.

"HAR, HAR, HAR, HAR, HAR, HAR, HAR, HA, HA, HA, HA, HA, HA, HA, R-Ronald, HA, HA, HA, HA, HA, HA, HA, HA, HA!" I blubbered, trying to get some under-standable words out of my mouth in between laughing and laughing myself nearly to death. "HA, HA, HA, HA, HA, HA, HA, HA, HA, t-turn that cr-crazy thing off man!"

The crazy thing that was presently tickling me, or to be more precise that was tickling my (nylon) black socked feet was a windmill sort of device with soft bristled hairbrushes attached to each slat of the thing. My socked feet, pushed together, dangled off the end of the slab of wood that I was tied down to on my back, my feet tied to the wood at the ankles as they dangled there to be exact and the windmill device spun fast against the bottoms of them. Ronald had the windmill device set up in just a way so that it spun and spun and spun against the soft and meaty bottoms of my poor trapped socked feet.

"HAR, HAR, HAR, HAR, HAR, HAR, HAR, HAR, Ronald, you bastard, ha, ha, ha, ha, ha, ha, ha, ha, ha, ha, ha, ha, turn it off man, pl-pleeeeeaaase man, please turn it off..." I garbled crazily, struggling helplessly under the tight and binding ropes, my muscles flexing involuntarily in my tree trunk like legs, my sinewy arms and broad shoulders amid my fruitless struggles.

"HAR, HAR, HAR yourself Buddy boy," Ronald said from where he stood near me, watching intently as I sweated my guts out atop that slab of wood, clad most humiliatingly in just my goddamned black nylon dress socks. "I told you before I started those brushes spinning against your feet that you had exactly three hours of tickle time on that slab. You haven't even completed the first half hour man..."

"OHHHHHHHRRRR GAWD man, I'll be fucking laughed to death by then," I ranted and clenched my hands into meaty sized fists at my sides, lifting my head up to see those infernal brushes as they spun and spun against my socked feet.

At the sight of my poor feet being tickle tortured my hard manhood throbbed like a thing alive between my legs and dribbled a goodly amount male of pre seed and beads of yellow piss as well. I could not believe that after all I had already been through that I was able to maintain a steel-like erection, but then again with all his tricks and conniving Ronald was making sure I stayed good and hard and worked up in the area of my goddamned meat pole.

"Lets go over it again okay buddy?" Ronald asked me, stepping over to me and placing a hand on my forehead, pushing my head back down. "Three hours of tickle torture from the spinning brushes with your sweetly scented and steamy black socks on and then..."

"And, and then, ha, ha, ha, ha, ha, ha, ha, ha, ha, ha, ha, ha, ha, and then you said two hours with my stinking socks off...HAR, HAR, HAR, HAR, HAR, HAR, HAR, HAR! GOD almighty man, not with my socks off too! HA HA HA HA HA HA HA HA HA HA!" I screamed out, finishing the sentence for him.

"Good boy Tim, it seemed you were listening to me after all," Ronald chuckled and squeezed one of my jutted up man nips, mashing it between his fingers, sending sexy chills and thrills through me. "The way I'm cooking your feet in those socks I'm sure they'll be beyond ticklish for round two of my latest machine that you're experiencing here."

My erection twitched and I could actually feel my balls cooking up a good batch of ball juice in my sweaty and stinking scrotum.

"R-Ronald, y-you bastard, ha, ha, ha, ha, ha, ha, ha, ha, ha, ha, ha, when, when the fucking fuck are you going to let me go man?" I garbled through the bouts of loud laughter erupting from me.

"Let you go?" Ronald asked me, sounding as if I had just asked the stupidest of questions. "But we're just getting started here bud..."

"J-just getting started? HA, HA, HA, HA, HA, HA, HA, HA, HA, HA, HA, HA!" I blurted crazily. "JUST GETTING STARTED? Holy fucking fuck man! Ronald, ha, ha, ha, ha, ha, ha, ha, ha, ha, ha, ha, from my calculations y-you've had me here now for three whole days! HA, HA, HA, HA, HA, HA, HA, HA! OH GAWD in his heaven man, you've been tickling torturing me for *three goddamned days...*"

My eyes filled with tears and I hooted and cackled and looked upwards at the ceiling as Ronald's infernal windmill machine with the brushes on it did its dirty work against the bottoms of my socked feet...

Three whole days had gone by, I could not believe it at that point; three whole days and I had spent the better parts of those days tied up and being tickled tortured in an uncanny variety of ways, all courtesy of my so called good buddy Ronald. That is what was the most mysterious part of all this, Ronald, a buddy of mine for more than a few years now was subjecting me to all of this. Why would a buddy do this to a buddy I had to wonder while in the throes of hysterical laughter. And the way that my so called buddy had acquired me for this experience went against every fucking thing that would entail a long friendship between two guys. I've actually known Ronald for almost ten years now. I worked with him for five years at Chase Bank. That was where we met as CO-workers. After I found the new job at Sidney Bank Ronald and I remained in touch. He's still at Chase. He's been to my home countless times with women he has dated to have dinner with me, my wife and our ten year old son. God, just thinking about my wife and son breaks my heart. If they saw me now and what Ronald was subjecting me to they would not believe it. Hell, I still didn't believe it actually... You see, Ronald, the fucking guy that he is had the audacity and the conniving nerve to kidnap me right out of my own goddamned house during the wee hours of the morning and bring me to this house of tickle horrors. And, to add insult to misery he managed to snag me at one of the moments when a guy is at his most vulnerable... If you need me to spell it out for you Ronald captured me while I was taking a wee morning hour piss, something that most guys suffer from during the night... GAWD, of all things...

Let me backtrack a bit and tell you about it okay? Like I already told you it had been three days already that Ronald had me trapped in his house of tickle tortures, a remote and isolated place he had purchased and rigged up over time just so that he could do this to me... Three days since the guy had kidnapped me, his good buddy right out of my goddamned bathroom while I was taking a much needed piss... I had to wonder for just how long Ronald had been planning all this; since we had met at Chase? Since we had become good buddies even after I left Chase and we kept in touch? As I looked down at my black socked feet as they were tickle tortured my mind drifted back to that fateful night and I also recalled all the times Ronald had been over my house and how after dinner we always relaxed in the living room, and I would take my shoes off while we were relaxing...

Chapter One

My name is Tim, Timothy Backman to be exact. Some of my buddies call me Timmy B. I'm thirty something years old, married for the last fifteen years and my wife and I have a ten year old son, Tim Junior. I have short cut black hair; my hair is actually cut in a classic banker's style, crystal blue eyes and no facial hair whatsoever, a real clean cut Wall Street type executive, that's me. I stand five feet nine inches tall, give or take an inch and my body is pretty muscular and well toned from the daily workouts that I put myself through at the Wall Street gym three to four times a week after working hours. As I pointed out I have known Ronald for a lot of years so when he did what he did in kidnapping me you can imagine how it came as a total shock. I mean, lets face it, how many poor guys out there get kidnapped by one of their best buddies? And right out of their own bathroom? And for the purposes of tickle torture of all the blasted things? I realize of course that all this sounds totally preposterous and I agree, it certainly is, it's totally fucking outrageous, but it happened, *and it happened to me*, yours truly, one of the most tickle sensitive guys on the planet. When it comes to my being tickle sensitive I have to say that God was real mean when he created me. I learned very early on that I was more tickle sensitive than most average guys out there. And I have had enough experiences that I can share with you to back up what I just said. But for the moment, let me tell you about Ronald and how he captured me. It happened three nights ago, and as far as I know my wife thinks that all this had to do with a joke being played on me by my fraternity brothers from my past college days, although my son did see me being taken by Ronald, so I wonder if he told her and worse, if she believed what he claims to have seen, *if* he did tell her... Okay, let me backtrack some more because all of this probably sounds like something out of the "Twilight Zone" of erotica to all of you who might be reading this...

It was the middle of the night like any other, what some people call the wee hours of the morning.

"Ohhhhh," I groaned softly as I awoke at 2:30 AM with a raging piss filled hard-on, next to my still slumbering wife. "Ohhhh, every night it's the same thing, every goddamned night..."

I threw the covers aside and carefully slid out from under them, sitting on my side of the bed, the need to urinate extremely intense, more intense than on other nights it seemed. My manhood was so piss filled and hard that it tented my boxer shorts like it was trying to break free of them. As I sat there trying to clear my head of sleep I chuckled with pride as my cock throbbed in my white boxers before I would stand up and pad on my (nylon) black socked feet to the bathroom diagonally across the hall from our bedroom. As I sat there in the moonlit room I rubbed my eyes gently and smacked my pasty feeling lips together.

"You okay honey?" I then heard my wife murmur from her side of the bed, more asleep than awake obviously.

"Yeah, I'm okay, I'm just fine babe, just the usual middle of the night time piss that needs to be taken care of," I replied, reached down to pull my socks up just a bit and then stood up, stretching my muscular arms above me, my big hands clenched into tight fists, still trying to shuck off sleep. "Go back to sleep babe, I'll be back in a minute or so..."

"It's all that water you drink at the gym and then all the juice you drink with dinner when you get home," Stephanie said softly.

"Yeah, you're right babe, you're so right," I said agreeably.

That said, my wife rolled over facing away from the bedroom door and I padded slowly out of the bedroom in the dark, across the hall and toward the bathroom, leaving the bathroom door slightly open. We have lived in that house for more than a few years at that point so walking in the mostly dark bedroom to the bathroom is not a difficult chore at all for me. I have to laugh when I say that my hard cock in my boxers pointed the way to the bathroom for me, as if it knew where to go for the much needed relief it was craving. As I walked my erection started to subside which of course would make it easier to piss. In the bathroom I flicked on the overhead fluorescent light and allowed my sleep filled eyes to adjust slightly to the glare as I positioned myself standing over the bowl. I then proceeded to take my semi hardness out of the fly opening of my boxers and I let loose with a long, thick, frothy stream into the water of the bowl, relief filling me as I piddled and relieved myself.

"Ohhhhhhh better, much fucking better," I murmured, chuckling deep in my throat as I pissed and pissed, even the sound of my stream as it plodded into the bowl somehow was filling me with relief.

Looking off to the side at the mirror over the sink at one point I could have sworn that I saw in the reflection the shower curtain over the tub move slightly. Thinking that I was more asleep than awake I thought that I must definitely be seeing things. I chuckled again and holding my manhood in my fingers to keep it steady I continued my wee morning hour piss. It seemed as if it would go on forever and forever, like as if I would be standing there for the rest of my life in just my boxer shorts and black dress socks, pissing my life away, hardy fucking har! When I was finally done I shook off the last droplets of beads of piss into the bowl and looking in the mirror's reflection I again saw the shower curtain move. This time I was sure I was not seeing things...

"What the hell?" I said softly, terror suddenly engulfing as I reached to flush the toilet.

As the sound of the water flowing in the bowl carried my generous deposit of piss to the sewers and as I was about to pack my very much relieved manhood back into my white boxer shorts it was at that moment that out of the corner of my eye I saw my buddy Ronald bolt like a fox from behind the shower curtain and right up behind me, directly from out of the bathtub he came. Before I could pack myself into my boxer shorts Ronald grabbed my upper biceps right where they curled real sexily and yanked my arms meanly behind me. I gasped in disbelief and a certain amount of terror as well, and being more asleep than awake there wasn't much that I could do except to murmur the words, "R-Ronald, here? In my house? At this time of night?" He held me super tight; I suppose all the workouts that he had put himself through at the gym had paid off real well at that point. The guy was a stack of hard iron-like musculature bud. Holding my arms real taut in his vise-like grip he yanked me away from the flushing toilet, my semi hardness dangling and swinging real provocatively in front of me, my balls doing a swing-type of dance as well. He gripped my arms tighter yet and whispered softly and almost lovingly in my ear "Nice socks buddy, I'm real fucking glad you sleep in your leftover dress socks from the workday because it's going to be my ultimate pleasure to see just how ticklish those feet of yours are while you're wearing those black nylon numbers…"

"Ronald, what the fucking fuck hell are you talking about buddy?" I garbled softly, thinking how this has to be a dream, a goddamned nightmare. *"You're going to tickle my socked feet?"*

"Sure as shit buddy boy, you heard me right," Ronald said into my ear. "We'll even have some sessions with those black sexy socks of yours off your feet as well… How does that sound?"

How did it sound? It sounded monstrous let me tell you. You see, I know just how very ticklish I am just about everywhere on my body, my sensitive pressure points as I call those areas, but my feet, *oh good God*, my *feet* are the ultimate ticklish part of me let me tell you. It was at that moment that Ronald held me tight in his grip that I felt I should somehow assert myself, but at the same time I didn't want my wife or kid to wake up to what was happening in the bathroom. I still didn't know exactly what the hell I was dealing with here. I mean, I had always thought of Ronald as a friend, a real good buddy and now I was starting to feel very threatened by him right here in my own bathroom in the middle of the night with my wife asleep in the very next room for crying out loud. I began to resist, trying to break free of Ronald's tight grip on me, but it was right at that point that he quickly changed his grip on me. He released my arms but before I could do anything he swung an arm around my neck and pulled me into a reverse head-lock.

"ACCCHHH, Ronald, what the fucking fucks are you doing man?" I jibber jabbered as softly as possible.

He yanked my head down and aimed it at the hanging hand towels. Ronald moved me forward on my socked feet and the top of my head connected slightly hard with the dangling towels. The towels absorbed most of the blow but I was still stunned as my head hit the wall behind the dangling towels and then I was thrown into a stupor of sorts. Ronald let go of my neck and yanked me to a somewhat standing position by my sleep mussed hair. Actually I sort of tottered about stupidly on my socked feet, my black socks rumpled a bit around my calves, just thought I would mention that for whatever the fucking fucks of the reason. As I tottered there in a stupor Ronald, in a very fast and blinding motion slid a spandex black hood over my head and cinched the ends around my neck…

"R-Ronald, wh-what?" I said, only able to see very slightly through the thin spandex material.

The inside of the hood smelled sweet somehow, sickly in way, I realized with mounting horror as Ronald again grabbed my arms that the inside of the hood was laced with chloroform or some kind of ether mixture. My head spun and then so did I bud. Ronald began spinning me like a top on my socked feet, the tile floor feeling cool under them I noticed. Round and round I went man, faster and faster, I becoming more and more disoriented with each passing moment because of the chloroform I was inhaling and the round about motion being heaped on me by Ronald.

"R-Ronald, st-stop, I'm getting dizzy here," I blubbered softly under the spandex hood but my so called buddy went on and on spinning me round and round and round.

It was obvious to me at that point how he intended to subdue me with the chloroform that was laced in the hood and there was no way I could fight the awful fumes, I mean, I had to breathe after all, right? I felt myself weakening and at that point I could not even scream out to my wife to get the kid and get the hell out of the house. What an awful and maddening feeling for a guy let me tell you. As my body went limp Ronald finally stopped whirling me around and yanked the hood off me. He held me by my arms then facing him. I looked into his eyes and saw that he was smiling very fiendishly at me, but there was also mischief in that smile. As I felt myself drifting toward blackness I could have sworn that Ronald pulled me close to him and pecked me on the lips, making a snide comment as to how my breath smelled from sleep...

Although chloroform does not render the recipient totally unconscious, as movies would have us believe I was still very docile and disoriented after Ronald had slid his spandex hood over my head and spun me like a goddamned top. As my head spun out of orbit Ronald then tugged my arms behind me again, crossing them at the wrists behind my lower back.

"Ron-Ronald, what is this?" I asked him, speaking very softly now as I felt the ropes being wound over and over my crossed wrists. "Fuck, *you're ty-tying me up buddy*. How did you get in my house? Fuck that, how did you get in my bathroom? Why are you doing this to me?"

As he tied me my so called buddy chuckled meanly and said "Everything will be explained to you soon Timmy boy, now keep your voice down, we wouldn't want you waking up your wife or son would we?"

I realized at that moment, at the mention of my wife and son just how terribly awful my predicament was. I began to feel panic surging through me at the thought of my wife and son. Fuck, how was I to be of any use to them I wondered if Ronald decided to harm them? I figured I would try to reason with Ronald, thinking this as he looped a good length of rope around my biceps curls and forced my big arms further behind me. Looking in the mirror over the sink I watched in horror as I was tied tighter and tighter with each passing second, my cock betraying me by getting hard and stiff again outside my goddamned boxers, I was hard as a rock and throbbing and not to mention that I was sweating in my socks. It's funny how a lot of times a feeling of helplessness or desperation mixed with outright fear will give a guy a raging hard-on. The time for reasoning with Ronald was now, *now or never*.

"Now look Ronald, if this is some kind of joke I really don't think its funny at all, not at all buddy," I said through trembling lips. "Who's in on this with you man?"

"No ones in on it with me Timmy, what do you think this is some kind of movie?" Ronald asked me, sounding sarcastic as hell. "You think this is like a conspiracy of some kind between me and someone else? No way man, this is just you and me buddy boy!"

"Wh-what was that you said before man?" I asked him, trying to sound calm and reasonable. "You, you plan to tickle my feet while I'm wearing my silky dress socks?"

My head was still spinning from the dose of chloroform or ether or whatever the fucking fuck was laced in that spandex hood but I had to somehow overcome that and reason with this guy. Tickle my feet while I was wearing my nylon dress socks? Horrors man, total fucking horrors! I mean just to let you all know that I am extremely ticklish, very ticklish actually. I wasn't one hundred percent sure if Ronald knew that for certain but I started to feel even more panic surge through me.

"Ronald, you can't have been serious about that, is that what this is all about?" I asked him.

Gods, just the words tickle torture were enough to send chills down my spine. Like I said I am extremely ticklish bud. But, no one, with the exception of my wife (and maybe some special folks from my past) knows just how ticklish I really am. Once my wife found out just how ticklish I was she used it against me whenever we had a disagreement and she was not getting her way. In the privacy of our home she would tickle me into a state of total submission until I promised to do whatever it was that she wanted. She uses it sparingly, but there are times when she uses it not so sparingly. So, since she's the only person who really knows how very ticklish I am I just cannot imagine Ronald wanting to tickle torture me, or worse, going so far as kidnapping me, his good buddy to do so. This was just so fucking bizarre. He finished tying my upper arms real tight and grabbed a handful of my hair, yanked my head back a bit, his lips very near mine as he spoke, all the while I was trying to balance myself in the awkward position I was now in.

"You heard me right buddy, tickle torture, *tickle tortures* in ways that even your executive imagination cannot fathom," Ronald said, sounding very unlike the Ronald I knew at that moment. "You see bud, while I was on that month long vacation from my job recently I bought a place, a huge old house in a very rural area. I turned that house into my own private tickle kingdom Timmy boy. It took me a lot of time and a shitload of money, and a lot of workmen needed to be hired, but it was worth every penny and every minute of my time to put it all together. And then when it was done all I needed was a tickle torture participant, and guess what bud? You're it! I have more than a few tickle torture devices that I plan to subject you to buddy..."

"S-subject me to?" I grunted miserably, my head still spinning. "Ronald, man, you can't mean that, *you mean to say that you're going to kidnap me right out of my own house?*"

By then I was stammering and watching as Ronald sifted through the clothes hamper that my wife and I kept in the bathroom to stockpile our dirty laundry in. At that point I knew I had no choice. If I were to be kidnapped I had to at least warn my wife. But before I could yell out to her to call the police Ronald had fished one of my white stinking sweat socks out of the hamper, probably it was one of the sweat socks I had worn while working out at the gym a couple of days ago, which meant it would be real stinky and ripe. Most times my wife Stephanie makes me put my socks directly from my feet into the washing machine, but somehow this pair of my sweat socks had found their way into our hamper. Ronald quickly crammed the foul and very moist sock deep, as deep as it would go into my mouth...

"MMMFFFF..." I gasped at the awful taste as Ronald's fingers did their work of filling my mouth with the rancid sweat sock.

He secured the sock in my mouth good and tight by wrapping some duct tape over it and around the back of my neck, insuring my silence I supposed.

"Rhy neee?" I asked desperately as Ronald filled my craw with the sock, me trying to actually say "Why me?"

Before Ronald answered me he squatted down to next get my black socked feet tied. It was those size elevens of mine in their black socks that seemed to be the reason for all of this. God's almighty, how many times had Ronald been to our house and how many times had he seen me with my shoes off after work? Did my showing off my dress socked feet somehow trigger all this in him? As he tied my feet he playfully snapped the elastic in my socks against my legs, pulled my socks the rest of the way up to my calves and began looping more rope around and around my sexy muscular calves. I was feeling like the captured super-hero or the damsel in distress in those old time movies made from comic book publications. As Ronald tied me my cock jutted up real hard outside my boxer shorts. Fuck, I had to admit that all through the feelings of panic there were also feelings of excitement, mostly in my groin it seemed, where my cock was showing off its tricks and massive girth by getting so overly hard and dripped pre seed from my wide sexy slit. Gods almighty and fucking fucks, I was totally panicked but somehow turned on all at the same time. With my mouth filled with my awful tasting sweat sock Ronald could hardly decipher what I was trying to say anymore and I couldn't even make much noise either. But as the guy then displayed his strength by hoisting me up onto one of his shoulders like a hunting trophy I wondered in horror what was next? God almighty, what the fuck was next?

Now before I continue on here let me just take a moment to say this, that gagging a poor guy with his sweaty and stinking sweat socks has to be one of the meanest things you can ever do to him. It truly sucks! But there I was man, tied up and gagged with one of my own rancid sweat socks, involuntarily chewing on the damned thing as Ronald hoisted me up to his shoulder. My wrists bound tight behind me, my big biceps tied up as well, the rope on them was snugly and tightly wrapped around my upper torso and right under my big nipples, rubbing them, teasing them somehow. Oh, did I mention my big nipples? They're of the jumbo sized let me tell you, what I call my man tits. They're that big, that fleshy and plump. To call them tits would imply womanly type of tits so I call them man tits. They are man sized tits and they are also extremely tickle sensitive. I thought of the words "Tickle Torture", the words that Ronald had said to me earlier and I started thinking, as the ropes rubbed against them, just how very ticklish my man tits really are! My wife proved that to me as well on various tickle occasions. Well, I moaned miserably through the foul smelling and awful tasting sweat sock crammed into and duct taped over my mouth. As Ronald lifted me higher to his shoulder I had another fleeting thought where my socks were concerned. I thought of the times when my wife had complained about my smelly socks, both my dress and sweat socks. She said how my dress socks always stunk when I took my shoes off after work when I would get home. She often wonders why I leave them on after getting out of my suit and changing into gym shorts and a tee shirt. I have no explanation for that just that it's a guy thing I suppose. Fuck, she even said how she wanted me to put them in the hamper or the washing machine myself, seeing as she hated handling them, that's how bad they were scented. And my sweat socks after the gym were no better bud. Now, as I chewed on my sweat sock crammed in my mouth I knew for sure just what my wife's complaints were about, and how justified they were. Ronald carried me to the bathroom door and put me down on my tied up socked feet for a moment. I tried desperately to balance myself on them as he slowly opened the bathroom door. He peeked out of the bathroom and into my bedroom where my wife Stephanie was soundly sleeping. She had no idea that her husband who had excused himself to take a piss was now about to be kidnapped right out of our bathroom, in his smelly socks no less, hardy fucking har!

"Okay buddy, now to get you out of here without that pretty wife of yours hearing us," Ronald said softly, dashing back over to me.

"Prease wron't," I said through my sock gag, trying to say the words "Please don't" as my so called buddy again prepared to hoist me like I was a sack of laundry or something. This time he slung me up across one of his big strong shoulders, wrapped an arm under my thighs and lugged me slowly and carefully from the bathroom. I thought about just how strong this fucking guy really was, I mean, *he had to be* in order to be carrying me the way he was. I'm no lightweight, let's face it muscle really weighs. All those times working out at the gym had really paid off not just for me but for Ronald as well it seemed. A look of misery was etched on my face as I looked into my and my wife's bedroom as Ronald carried me past it, the moon light on Stephanie's face as she lay there looking so peaceful filled me with woe. I couldn't make a sound not even a peep and she didn't rouse at all as I was kidnapped right under her nose for God's sakes. I mean, lets face it though, even if I wasn't gagged there was no way I would have made a sound to wake Stephanie. Being tied the way I was there would have been nothing I could do to help her if Ronald decided to take his anger out on Stephanie…or worse, our son Tim Junior. No, at that moment I figured it best to just let things take their course as they were. Once more I looked at Stephanie as I was lugged past our bedroom.

"Good-bye my sweet," I said to myself, sounding pitiful even to myself. "Will I ever see you again?"

My cock throbbed against Ronald's chest as he carried me slowly down the short hallway to the stairs that would lead to the front door of the house. Over and over I wondered if I would ever see Stephanie again. But then, horror of all horrors, my thoughts were suddenly cut off when I saw my son's bedroom door open and he peeked out, his cute face such a combination of mine and Stephanie's, his face one of innocence still. His young eyes tried to focus on what he thought he was seeing in his sleepy state, his dad being carried toward the stairs? I shook my head "NO NO", willing him to "Go back, *go back*!" and relief filled me a tad as I watched him retreat back into his room, silently closing the door behind him. A glimmer of hope I thought, thinking how Tim Junior would perhaps tell my wife what he saw transpiring, if he didn't think he was dreaming that is… Ronald lugged me carefully down the stairs, taking each step slowly, bouncing me playfully on his shoulder as he carried me and then quickly out the front door to a waiting van which was parked in my driveway behind my wife's and my car.

"mmmmffff…" I groaned miserably as Ronald lowered me off his shoulder and put me down in the back of the van by sliding me into a hammock harness of some kind that was hanging in the back of the van for the ride to come.

I looked up at him miserably as I dangled in that harness-like device, realizing at that moment that he really had kidnapped me. He buckled a few straps on the harness to keep me dangling safely and then with that look of mischief on his face he thumped my hard leaking cock. My cock throbbed long and hard and dribbled more pre seed. This time Ronald pressed a rag socked with the chloroform ether mixer against my face. I slipped into another sleepy stupor and then heard the van start as Ronald made his way into the driver's seat up front. I felt the van start moving.

"Tickle tickle, *tickle tickle,*" I heard Ronald musing in the driver's seat as he pulled out of my driveway. "Tickle, tickle…"

Chapter Two

Fuck, fucking fuck! Double fucking fucks I said to myself bitterly and in my sleepy stupor as Ronald drove me, his precious cargo from my house to a still unknown (unknown for me that is) destination. Fucking fuck man, I was trussed up like a goddamned Thanksgiving turkey and I was finding out that I might (definitely?) have some kind of twisted masochistic side to me as well. (My trussed up body swayed in the harness as the van moved down God knows what roads to God knows where. That was the magic word of the moment, *where. Where the fuck was Ronald taking me?*) Because this feeling of total helplessness was giving me feelings that I had never felt before, feelings between my legs mostly oh okay, I had felt these feelings before; I always knew that when it came to my sexuality I always had what would be referred to as a submissive side. But I never thought that those yearnings would manifest themselves during one of the direst moments of my life, when I was being kidnapped and by one of my best buddies of all people. My cock just seemed to continue getting harder and harder as I focused on my predicament. And to add to these new feelings were the nylon type of ropes that Ronald had tied around my biceps and over my chest. Fuck, they were pinching and rubbing my nipples, just adding to my stimulation. For a guy I have really sensitive nipples let me tell you, as I pointed out I call them my man tits. Other nicknames I've given my nubs over the years are my man nips, or my big fat man tits, or sometimes I call them the control knobs for my cock. My wife found out years ago, even before she had discovered just how very ticklish I was, was that she could tease me silly by playing with my man nips. She would rub and tweak and pull on each bulbous nipple, increasing my sexual arousal, hence the reason I call them the control knobs for my cock. Once I thought she had teased my nipples all she could with her fingers, then she would use her very educated mouth on them. Her sweet lips would fully engulf the nipple and she would suck like she was nursing, or like a vampire, or like she was siphoning my man nip. But, she also used her teeth and tongue as well. Oh man, her tongue would strum across my nip-tip, making it harder and harder, more erect with each swipe across it. Then she would use her teeth to give me a little taste of pain, just to get me in motion as she would call it, and then she'd start all over sucking and tongue strumming my nipple, playing it like it was a musical instrument. All the while when she would be doing this to one of my nipples her free hand would keep my other nipple stimulated until she was ready to switch. She became very adept at teasing and working me over this way for what seemed like hours. She would tease me to the point that I thought I would lose my load. But, alas, it was only a tease. There was never quite enough stimulation there to actually make me cum. She could be very mean this way let me tell you, but I love her, God, I love her and Ronald had taken me from her. These were the thoughts and memories that were flooding my foggy chloroformed brain as the ropes stretched and moved across my smooth, hairless chest and my sexual tension knobs, my ever-loving man nips. God almighty, Ronald, *Ronald*, of all people had managed to get my cock hard, and now I was beginning to leak. No man had ever caused this reaction in me, only girls I had dated and only my wife in recent history. What oh what the fucking fuck was going on?

And to top all these feelings and yearnings off Ronald had one of my rancid sweat socks stuffed and taped meanly into my mouth. Gods, that has to be the worst fucking way you can gag a poor guy, if you feel the need to gag the guy that is, hardy fucking har har. The musky smell and taste seemed to somehow add to my stimulation. And tickle torture, goddamn it man, TICKLE TORTURE, the awful seed that Ronald had planted in my mind…TICKLE TORTURE! I know, man do I know how very, very ticklish I am, extremely fucking ticklish. My wife has proven that to me. But, tickled, TICKLE FUCKING TORTURE that is beyond unbelievable. My wife has always used tickling against me to get what she wanted, as I pointed out, but the tickling always stopped when I gave in. The very idea of *tickle torture* raises thoughts of tickling going way beyond the "I give" point, beyond the point of screaming, "Uncle, I give up!" But for me, tickling has always been a sexual stimulus too! Even when my wife used it to get her way we would end up having great and rousing sex, but somehow Ronald's TICKLE TORTURE ideas aren't fitting into that mold for me… The scent of chloroform in my nostrils suddenly felt overpowering somehow and I drifted back into the arms of sleep. I suppose the movement of the van and the smell in my nostrils combined put me back to sleep…

What a sight this was when you really thought about it, and what a sight I was to put it quite bluntly. *And* what a bizarre and cruel twist of fate to befall a poor executive guy just because he got up in the middle of the night to take a much needed piss, nothing unusual there. And now look at me, strung up in my good buddies' van, dressed in just my white boxer shorts (with my erection sticking out of the fly opening I might add) and my silk black office socks from yesterday's workday. (What kept going through my chloroformed and fogged brain was that Ronald had said that he planned to tickle my silk socked feet… WHY? OH GOD WHY?) And kidnapped, *kidnapped* right out of my own house, literally carried off and out of my own bathroom. (Where I work we've had executive meetings and been instructed on being very careful while on business trips, the security chief of my company pointing out how high profile executives are always kidnap targets where ransom from big companies is concerned. But what the fucking fuck is an executive to do if he is suddenly kidnapped by a good buddy?) If a man's home isn't his sanctuary then what is? God almighty, what's gotten into my good buddy Ronald I wondered as the van plowed along and I half slept in the harness I was strapped into. He had been over our house for dinner any number of times, he had double dated with me and my wife when he had met different women here and there, wanting to see what we thought of them. Ronald always said he wanted to someday be married so he would ask my and my wife's opinion on most of his dates. We were always very kind where Ronald's dates were concerned but we often wondered if he just loved the bachelor life too much and if he would ever truly settle down. HOLY SHIT! Could Ronald have been planning all this all that time?

All these thoughts churned in my fogged mind as the van sped along a very dark and deserted road. As I lay strapped into that harness I finally managed to open my eyes and I looked straight up. I was still dizzy and disoriented from the chloroform that I was recently dosed with and my head was spinning also from the rancid sock I was chewing on. I suppose the chloroform would wear off and then snag me again, being that I had been given a couple of good doses of it. But the van had a skylight window. I looked up at the stars as they seemed to be passing by as the van literally stole me away to an unknown destination. I saw the night sky, the movement of huge trees, power lines and highway lampposts through the skylight. At the sight of these things a strange feeling of loneliness seemed to engulf me. My cock throbbed outside my boxer shorts, humiliating, and my balls were being hugged by the lower section of those same boxer shorts. I wiggled my toes under my silky nylon black socks and suddenly a thought came to me, a memory actually, a memory of a pleasant night out in a restaurant and what I at that moment realized was a damning conversation. It was the memory of me and my wife having dinner with Ronald and one of his many girlfriends that he had introduced the two of us to. Tim Junior was a baby at the time and we had left him with a babysitter so we could enjoy a night out with Ronald and one of his many conquests as he sometimes called them. I recalled how the conversation had gone to all of our college days and the antics we had engaged in back when we were very young. I remembered Ronald telling of how he had pledged a fraternity and how he had been tickle tortured during Hell Week. I remembered at that moment in the van how I had then made the mistake of telling Ronald that I had also pledged a fraternity and suffered some of the same evil antics back then. As I said that to my good buddy my wife and I looked at each other knowingly across the table, her foot caressing mine under the table. I smiled at her slyly as her stocking foot slid under my pants and up against my socked calf. I realized in the van that Ronald had definitely picked up on that look between my wife and I and I surmised that the plotting to kidnap me must have started there. Yes, that was it for sure, because in the restaurant that night after my wife had nudged me under the table I again looked at Ronald. He had cocked his head and he had this strange look in his eyes. Fucking fucks, I disregarded that look man! But now, in retrospect I think he was beginning to plot my TICKLISH demise then, all the way back then buds! And while he was having dinner with my wife and I and his girlfriend; what kind of a guy plots to kidnap a buddy and tickle torture him while he's out on a double date? I again wiggled my toes under my black socks and moaned miserably into my sock gag... I figured that that answered my question as to how Ronald knew how very ticklish I really was... I was tied up, gagged, totally fucking helpless and it looked like Ronald was going to make me his plaything whether I liked it or not. But fucking double fucks, my cock was leaking, just as if I were enjoying all this somehow...

A while later the van came to a slow halt on the deserted, dark and very scary looking road. I heard Ronald step out of the driver's section. I guessed I was awake at that moment. The back doors of the van swung open and I looked up to see my so called buddy climb up into the back section of the vehicle, lighting a thick cigar as he entered.

"Okay buddy boy, we need to talk a bit, plus I want to give you a preview of what you're in for once I get you to my secret domain," Ronald said and puffed his cigar.

I looked up at him helplessly and woefully...

A few moments later my musky sock was out of my mouth and I was now blindfolded, a white cloth tied over my eyes as I still lay trapped in that goddamned harness...

"Tickle, tickle," Ronald mused as he sat at my side, looking up at me, (even blindfolded I could feel his steely eyes boring into me) smoking his cigar. "Tickle, tickle buddy..."

He kept whispering those words and I cringed in the restraints, my cock hard, the nylon ropes teasing my erect man nips awfully, and blindfolded, not knowing yet that Ronald was holding a high powered battery operated toothbrush with hard bristles in his hand...

Pre seed dribbled from my wide sexy slit and the conversation between me and Ronald began...

"Secret Domain! Secret fucking domain?" I screamed angrily, my mouth still tasting of the awful sweat sock that Ronald had just extracted from it. "Ronald, what the fuck is this all about man?"

I then heard Ronald's voice directly next to my ear, "Tickle, tickle" and I smelled his cigar.

"Tickle, tickle buddy boy," Ronald chuckled and then I heard a small humming like an undersized electrical motor of some kind. "Tickle, tickle, tickle, tickle..."

My cock was super hard by then and pointing straight up like a goddamned flagpole and leaking, it was leaking just from being tied up and the ropes massaging my bare jutted up man-nips. But every fucking time Ronald said the words "Tickle, tickle" my dice jumped. I could not help it. And being blindfolded, not being able to see what was happening, and God, that humming noise, all of it combined just made my situation all the more intense somehow. I was wiggling myself in the harness, trying to get free somehow, but like earlier all I was able to do was move my toes under my socks, oh yeah, and my hard cock as it twitched and danced between my legs. I could feel the coolness of the night air as it moved across my slimy wet and still leaking cock. I could tell by the coolness that my pre seed was actually dripping down my thickly veined shaft, wetting more and more of my cock, no doubt making it glisten in the moonlight from the skylight window above me. Ronald hadn't even made the first move toward tickling me and I was almost beside myself already with anticipation.

"What the fuck Ronald? What are you doing to me?" I blurted out loudly. "What the hell do you mean your secret domain and how did you manage to get me like this? You could not have done this alone man. Please buddy; tell me this is all a joke of some kind. And don't you dare tickle me. Fucking fucks, I'll have you arrested for kidnapping and assault. My wife and family, *my boy*, they need me man! Come on, now turn me loose okay? OKAY?"

I babbled on and on but my cock was still leaking...

"Whoa man, slow down there, that's too many questions you're throwing at me at one time buddy boy," Ronald laughed, and from where his voice was coming from I could tell that he was now standing by my stretched out and tied feet.

Then I felt the palm of his hand running over the silky black bottoms of them.

"God almighty buddy, I've always wanted to touch these silk socked feet of yours," Ronald said breathlessly to me. "They remind me a lot of some of the women I dated who wore those erotic looking silky stockings man."

"BUDDY! You call me your buddy! Are we buddies Ronald?" I yelled at him then, the smell of his cigar filling the back of the van by then, me swaying in the harness and the agonizing darkness of the blindfold, the taste of my own rancid socks still in my mouth and the blasted scent of chloroform still in my nostrils, making my head spin. "What kind of buddy does what you've done to me Ronald? Oh God man, please, please don't touch my feet huh?"

"Now for the answers to your questions buddy, and we are buddies Timmy boy, I assure you of that, I'm just having some mean and sleazy fun with you," Ronald said to me.

I felt his nose against my toes and heard him as he inhaled.

"Oh fuck man, don't be sniffing my damned socked feet Ronald," I garbled miserably at him, remembering all the times my wife complained about how bad my socks stunk at the end of the day.

"Tell me something man, do you always wear your dress socks to bed or did I just get lucky tonight? Ronald asked me and I heard the humming of his electric tooth-brush, although I still didn't know what the fuck it was that was making that sound.

"I-I, oh man, like most business dudes out there I do tend to leave my socks on at the end of the day, I don't know why, its, its something my dad used to do, I don't know man, but *fuck*, what do my damned office socks have to do with all this Ronald?" I responded, sounding absolutely terrified.

I didn't really need an answer to my last question put to Ronald. I knew exactly what my silky office socks had to with all of this. I knew the horrors of having my feet tickled while I was wearing my thin silk socks, the way the thin material made the tickling sensations all the more maddening when being tickled on the bottoms of my feet. Stephanie had proved this point to me many times over in the past, and obvi-ously Ronald knew about it as well. So did two maids in a hotel I had stayed in years back while on a business trip but that'll have to be a story for somewhere down the line buds. With my lips trembling I asked and repeated my questions to Ronald.

"WH-what are you planning on doing to me man?" I asked Ronald

In between puffing his cigar he told me again that he had recently bought a huge house at a price that was practically a steal. He went on in the same breath and told me how he had all his inventions housed there in the many rooms of the house he had purchased, his house that he dubbed his "House of Tickle Horrors."

"I've always dabbled in inventing all kinds of strange gizmos," Ronald laughed and tweaked one of my big toes. "Fuck man, your feet smell real musty and clammy buddy…"

"I don't wonder the fucking fuck why, seeing as I've had those socks on since yesterday morning at SIX AM!" I replied sarcastically.

"Ronald, again, how the fuck did you get me like this? I still say you could not have done this alone!" I implored him.

He told me again that he did it all by himself, by listening to how I myself told him that I always got up during the night to piss, and citing what a damned nuisance it was. He pointed out how I also made the mistake of telling him how for safety purposes I and my wife always left a spare key in the outside mailbox for our son for when he gets home from school, just in case he should lose his key, you know how careless some kids can be. As Ronald spoke I realized miserably that he had simply let himself into the house, no doubt waiting till we had all gone to bed for the night, making it real easy for him to hide in the tub behind the shower curtain and then snag me when I awoke for my wee morning hour piss.

"And this is no joke buddy boy, although you will be laughing very soon," Ronald teased me then. "And you can forget about having me arrested for kidnapping, I mean, who the fuck would believe you after all?"

I prattled on how my wife would surely call the police when she woke up and saw that I was not there.

"She will tell them how I had woken up to go to the bathroom and then never came back to bed," I snapped at him as he continued to smoke his cigar and handle my socked feet.

Ronald simply laughed and told me that he highly doubted that she would even suspect that I was kidnapped out of the bathroom. More than likely if she reported my being missing to the police Ronald suggested that they would think that I was a guy who had snuck off to have some kind of illicit affair. I didn't mention to the guy how my son happened to see him carrying me off.

As Ronald and I spoke back and forth my cock remained hard and throbbing outside my boxer shorts...

But then, oh then, oh God then, a few moments later the deserted dark road and the wee hour were pierced by the sounds of my screeching laughter, as Ronald began the preview of my tortures by running the battery operated high powered toothbrush bristles over the bottoms of my silky nylon socked feet. As I laughed and laughed the van rocked up and down as I swayed madly in the harness...

"HA, HA, HA, HA, HA, HA, HA, HA, HA, HA, HA, HA, HA, HA, HA, HA, HA, HA, HA!" was the sound anyone passing by would have heard coming from the parked van along the road.

On that lonely and deserted road Ronald's van sat parked under a lamppost, with no one else around for miles upon miles it seemed, no one there to help the poor guy, *me*, who was being tickle tortured with an electric toothbrush in the back of that van. I guffawed, laughed, and cackled uncontrollably as Ronald ran that infernal vibrating toothbrush all over and over my silk socked feet.

"HA HA HA HA HA HA HA HA HA HA HA HA HA HA HA HA HA, hee, hee, hee, hee, hee, hee, hee, R-Ronald, stop, stop this buddy! HA HA HA HA HA HA HA OH GAWD I can't take it man!" I screamed in the blindfolded darkness, my toes wriggling like mad under my socks as Ronald played them like a harp with the toothbrush.

"Ah, this is truly music to my ears Timmy," Ronald said to me, holding me tight by my socked calf as he strummed the toothbrush across my toes, against my sensitive arches, over the bottoms of my feet, along the sides of them and then back up again over my toes. "Nothing sounds better than a good buddy laughing and having a good time, wouldn't you agree Timmy?"

"I-I am not, ha, ha, ha, ha, ha, ha, ha, ha, ha, ha, ha, ha, ha, har, har, I am not having a good time Ronald! Y-you've kidnapped me! HA HA HA HA HA HA HA HA HA HA HA HA HA and now you-you're tickling my goddamned feet, ha, ha, ha, ha, ha, ha, ha, ha, ha, ha, ha, ha!" I screeched loudly in the small back space of the van.

Chapter Three

"Ha, ha, ha, ha, ha, ha, ha, ha, ha, ha, ha, ha, ha, ha, ha, ha, ha, ha, ha!" came the sound of my insane laughter as Ronald ran his electric toothbrush over and over the bottoms of my silky nylon socked feet. "OH GOD NO, don't touch my feet man, don't tickle them Ronald! HA, ha, ha, ha, ha, ha, ha, ha, ha, ha, ha, ha, ha!"

As Ronald tickled me I thought miserably of the short conversation we had just had, how he explained how he had gotten into my house to nab me through my own careless talk. Damn, those loose lips really do sink ships! And what did he mean sleazy fun? I didn't call being kidnapped fun, not fun whatsoever let me tell you! And fuck, a huge house with inventions, TICKLE HORROR INVENTIONS of all things at that.

"OHHH GAWD RONALD, don't do this man!" I squealed, still not totally aware of what he was using on my socked feet to drive me tickle crazy. "HA, ha, ha, ha, ha, ha, ha, ha, ha, ha, ha, ha, ha, ha, ha, ha, ha, ha! St-st-stop, AHHHH, ha, ha, ha, ha, ha, ha, ha, ha, ha, ha, ha, ha, ha, ha, ha, ha, ha, ha, ha! WH-what the fucking fuck is that, HA, HA, HA, HA, HA, HA, HA, HA, HA, HA, HA, HA! Wh-whatever the fuck you're using on my feet is really push-pushing my tickle buttons like mad, ha, ha, ha, ha, ha, ha, ha, ha, ha, ha, ha, ha, ha, ha!"

I was still blindfolded and trussed up good and tight, unable to move as Ronald tickled the bottoms of my socked feet with his electric toothbrush. God, I was screaming so loud, I could not believe that there was no one around to hear me. *I mean, come on, somebody had to hear me!* Had Ronald taken me so far out in the country that there really was no one around at this time? Gawd let me tell you buds, I could not believe that he had snagged me and gotten me into this most outlandish of situations.

"Ron-Ronald, HA, HA, HA, HA, HA, HA, HA, HA, HA, HA, HA, HA, come on man, pl-please stop tickling me!" I begged through loud and screeching peals of laughter. "I-I can't take this! You're fucking driving me nuts man! HA, HA, HA, HAR, HA, HA, HAR, HA, HAR, HA, HA! And you're wrong man, ha, ha, ha, ha, ha, ha, ha, ha, ha, ha, ha, ha, ha, ha, ha, ha! There most certainly are things that sound better than a good buddy laughing his head off! HA, HA, HA, HA, HA, HA, HA, HA, HA! OH GAWD and this is just a preview? FUCKER man, ha, ha, ha, ha, ha, ha, ha, ha, ha, y-you can't be serious Ronald, you just *can't be serious!*"

"Oh Timmy my boy, this is just a little taste of what's in store for you my ticklish buddy," Ronald said with an evil tone to his voice. "What I'm using on your sexy socked feet is an electric toothbrush buddy. I brought it with me, you know, good old dental hygiene Timmy... Ha, ha!"

"AAAYYYYYYYYYYY OH FUCK RONALD, FUCKING FUCKS!" I screamed in the confines of the van. "HA, ha, ha, ha, ha, ha, ha, ha, ha, ha, ha, ha, ha! Dental hygiene is for the mouth and teeth man! Those are my damned feet you're using that el-electric toothbrush on! HAR, HAR, HAR, HAR, HAR, HAR, HAR, ha, ha, ha, ha, ha!"

The laughter and screams came up from within my gut after a while as Ronald worked the little vibrating device up and down and up and down the soles of my feet. When he went upwards he paid special attention to my wiggling toes as they tried to escape the tickling tormentor chasing them. But obviously they could not get away. All they could do was send their tickling signals to my brain by way of my throbbing cock, which was still hard, just for the record that is, leaking and standing tall at attention. I wondered how long this would go on, how much of this I would be able to take, and this being just the preview. OH FUCKING FUCKS, oh shit, I really was in a ticklish situation here...

If this was just the preview my mind whirled with thoughts, wondering thoughts of what the hell else Ronald could possibly have in mind for me. But then, suddenly, just as the tickle torture had begun it ended, it ended for the moment actually. Ronald turned off the electric toothbrush and I could still feel him staring at me as I tried to catch my breath.

"R-Ronald, let me go, *let me go* and I swear to you I'll forget about all of this," I murmured, trying to stifle the small spurts of laughter that were still erupting in my chest as it heaved up and down against the nylon ropes. "Th-thanks for stopping man, I-I really couldn't take anymore of that you know? I really am a very ticklish and overly tickle sensitive type of guy, just my bad luck when I was created I suppose, hardy fucking har and all that. Come on now man, this was some sick fun, but it's over now right? We're buds; we can just forget this ever happened. I won't even report it like I said I would. You could even drive me home and I'm sure that once I'm back in bed this will all have seemed like a bad dream. What do you say huh? Ronald?"

But Ronald was eerily quiet, I knew he was there looking me over as I lay in the harness babbling on and on. I could hear him breathing and man, let me tell you, it was not the breathing sounds of a calm man, it was the breathing sounds of an overly excited man. And this overly excited man had made my tied up body one raw nerve, one raw tickle nerve...

"Ronald, please, think about what I'm saying here man, you've got to let me go," I said insistently.

In response to my request however I heard the electric toothbrush turned back on.

"Shit, holy fucking shit," I garbled in panic anew. "What's that sound man? Oh no, now don't, don't you dare start that again!"

But this time the sound was closer to my ears somehow. I could hear it better, the mocking sounds of the electric toothbrush. I tensed my poor feet for another tickle onslaught, but that goddamned buzzing sound was, as I said, closer to my ears this time.

"Ronald, what are you doing?" I called out to him, trying to drown out the awful sound of that toothbrush with my loud voice, not wanting to hear it all, let alone feel it as it tickled my feet. Now wait just a minute here, let's talk about this rationally buddy. What, what the fucking fucks are you thinking about doing to me?"

As I spoke, pleaded is more like it, my feet were still all tensed up in anticipation for the tickling to come. But Ronald didn't say a word to me; he responded by pressing the vibrating bristles of the electric toothbrush against a new place, it was not my feet that he tickled this time. Now he was after my poor tickle sensitive man tits...

"FFFFUUUUUUUCCKKKKK!" I roared as I felt the contact of the bristles against one of my man tits. "EEEEEEEEEE! HA, HA, HA, HA, HA, HA, HA, HA, HA, HA, HA, ha, ha, ha, ha, ha! Y-you bastard, you're tickling my nips! HA, HA, HA, HA, HA, HA, HA, HA, HA, HA! Ronald, my feet were bad enough man, hee, hee, hee, hee, hee, hee, hee, hee, hee, hee, hee! But my nips, oh God, my man tits, NOOOOOOO! Oh FUCKING FUCKS, but my nipples are so fucking tickle sensitive."

Ronald tickle tortured my jutted up nipples. Once again the sound of my insane laughter echoed from the back of the van… And just to mention here, the fact that he had tickled my feet had only intensified the sensitivity of my nipples. God almighty, now that buzzing and tormenting thing was working on one nipple, then the other, then back to the first one and then back to the other. Ronald was moving his electric toothbrush back and forth and back and forth, working round and round my nipples, then up to the tips of them, really teasing the bejesus out of me. Fuck, but this was awful, having my man tits played like a push-button type of machine.

"OH NO, NO, YOU BASTARD, PLEASE RONALD, NOT MY MAN TITS, not my fucking man tits, ha, ha, ha, ha, ha, ha, ha, ha, ha, ha, ha, ha, ha, ha, ha, ha, ha!" I screamed. "Ronald, not my goddamned man tits!"

Those memories of my wife passionately and meanly playing with and stroking my ticklish nipples, her sucking on them like an out of control vacuum cleaner suddenly filled my mind. I swear there were times when Stephanie sucked my man-sized tits that I thought for sure they would start spurting milk. She was that intense about it let me tell you. Fuck, then came the memories of how she found out that my nipples could be a tickle playground for her and I laughed and I laughed like a hyena from what Ronald was doing to me and from the memories flooding my poor tortured mind. The vibrating bristles moving over and over my jutted up man tits was maddening and I laughed louder and louder, squirming like crazy in the harness prison. Yeah, my wife, my wonderful wife was the one who found out just how very sensitive my man tits could be when it came to tickle situations. I never realized it until my wife had put me through one of her "I'm going to tickle you until you agree to what I want" sessions. Once I had submitted to her desires we had cuddled and usually we had great and intense sex after she had tickled me nearly to death. This one time though we were going at it really hot and heavy and I was tweaking *her* nipples. Then she said something like, "Tim, you really like to play with my nipples don't you?" Well, of course I did, I mean which guy doesn't like to play with his wife's nipples? And I mumbled as such to her. "Well, have you ever had your nipples toyed with?" was her next question, which by the way I never got a chance to answer, because it was at that moment that she started going after both my nipples at one time. She had one in each hand and was pinching and pulling and scratching and twisting. All of a sudden I started chuckling, which turned into fits of laughter and it made me too weak to fight off her nipple attack, what we would have called a "purple nurple" back in high school. But, it did nothing to reduce the sudden swelling in my cock. In fact, although I hate it, tickling seems to really stimulate my sexual urges. (Just thought I would point all this out to you while Ronald was doing his dirty work with the toothbrush on me.) I was thinking and remembering all of this tickle history while I was still in the throes of the laughter that Ronald was causing me.

After a long while Ronald again turned off the toothbrush and said, "We best be on our way buddy, we still have a bit of a ride ahead of us…"

"R-Ronald, where the hell are we going?" I asked him miserably and in response he dosed me with his chloroform and ether mixture by pressing the cloth soaked with it against my nose and mouth. "MMMMmmmfff…"

In a stupor again, feeling helpless and disoriented again I heard the back doors of the van close and once again Ronald was driving. The scent of his cigar lingered in the back of the van...

Chapter Four

A Couple of Hours Later

The van finally came to a stop and to be perfectly honest nearly every part of my body was stretched and numb feeling at that point. I had to wonder just how long the drive from my house to wherever Ronald had brought me had taken. After all the times I had awoken and then slipped back into the chloroform/ether induced stupor I had most definitely lost track of time. But it seemed that he had finally reached his destination, *our* destination. I heard the back doors of the van yanked open and then my so called buddy unceremoniously pulled me out of the harness and got me propped up and standing on my tied up socked feet on what I guessed was the back ledge of the van. The surface of where I was standing felt to be on the narrow side so I leaned up against the doors of the back of the van real hard, pressing my muscular back against them, propped there like a trophy of some kind that Ronald had acquired. My buddy stood next to me holding tight to my upper arm, insuring that I would not slip and fall onto the pavement. Being that I was still blindfolded I did not know yet that the back of the van was facing the place that Ronald wanted me to see and to experience…

"Ron-Ronald, where the fuck are we man?" I asked him, my lips trembling as I spoke, feeling the warm gentle breeze on my scantily clad body.

Fucking fucks, fucking double fucks, my hands were still tied behind me, my biceps were still roped and yanked back meanly, making a real nice showcase of my chest and nipples and my socked feet were still securely tied up as well. Fuck, the way my upper body was roped really made my jutted up man tits stand out nice and inviting like. I could imagine any tit hungry individual, male or female wanting to feast on those big nubbies of mine at that moment. The white cloth blindfold tied over my eyes was maddening by then.

"Fuck man, some buddy you are, you got me outdoors in just my damned boxer shorts and socks!" I ranted, wondering where the fuck we were and feeling mortified to be on display like this. "What's the fucking point of all this Ronald? Kidnap a poor guy in the middle of the night just so you can tickle torture him?"

By now I was angry man, real fucking angry…

"You'll go to jail for this man, fuck what I said about not reporting it," I said through my now clenched teeth. "I will make sure of it, buddy or not, you will go to jail. I will have my attorney see to it that you rot in prison!"

"Hmm, your attorney huh?" Ronald asked me, sounding totally jovial. "Is he like most attorneys who wear long knee length black nylon socks?"

"FUCK that Ronald, and fuck you too!" I swore bitterly, wiggling my toes under my socks and trying to get my hands untied at the same time, but alas, it was useless, as Ronald had me tied real fucking tight. "You cannot just come into a guy's house and abduct him in the middle of the night… Fucking fucks man, I was taking a leak, something that all guys have to do at least once during the night and you kidnapped me!

What the hell kind of sick and twisted shit is that? And then, to add to the insult, you chloroform me over and over again, man, that shit stinks I got to tell you Ronald…"

Suddenly, to stop my jibber jabbering Ronald took the blindfold off me…

"And furthermore," I was saying as the blindfold was whipped off me, the sight of Ronald's huge tickle torture house cutting off my words.

I became truly silent for a few long moments and simply took in the sight before me, the sight of a huge and mansion-like house situated all by itself on a lonely road. Trees and well attended hedges surrounded the structure. Actually, the house bordered on the gothic, it was lit by the moon and two single lampposts. Standing on the van's back ledge against the doors of the vehicle I was high up enough to really take in the sight of the place, which caused me to take a long and gasping breath.

"Holy fucking fucks," I said softly, turning my head to look at Ronald as he grinned at me from ear to ear.

I saw that what he had been using on me in the van earlier was most definitely an electric toothbrush, because he was still holding it in hand, his stinky cigar however nowhere to be seen. At the sight of the electric toothbrush my cock gave an involuntary sort of jump, real comical looking if you ask me, but not so comical under the awful circumstances. And, even after all the chloroform that had been administered to me my cock was still hard, unbelievable but true buds. I felt a wave of utter humiliation when I looked down and saw my huge erect cock sticking out of the fly opening of my boxer shorts.

"Ronald, what is this place?" I asked him, feeling terrified now, the reality of this crazy situation really sinking in. "HOW, how the fuck did you afford this?"

"I date really rich girls buddy, a handsome so and so like me can siphon more than just sex from those pretty bitches you know," Ronald replied, holding tight to my arm as he spoke. "It took me over a year to put it all together, but now man, now it's ready for it's maiden voyage, and being that it was ready it simply needed a good tickle victim, and as I said and as I have obviously pointed out, you're it Timmy my boy. When you see my inventions you will not believe it!"

As Ronald spoke he chuckled meanly and rubbed the bristles of the electric toothbrush against my cock head.

"Now, stay well balanced buddy boy, because this is not going to be all that fun…" Ronald said

"OH GOD NO RONALD, NOT what I think you're thinking man, OHHHH please, no!" I pleaded and my buddy did the unthinkable, he turned on the electric toothbrush, tickling my cock head mercilessly, paying special attention to my goddamned piss slit.

"AAARRRRRRRHHHHH! HARRRRRR, HARRRRRR, HARRRRRR, HARRRRRR, oh you fucking fucked up fucker, harrrrrrr, harrrrrr, harrrrrr, harrrrrr, ha, ha, ha, ha, ha, ha, ha, ha, ha, ha, ha, ha, ha, ha, ha, ha!" I guffawed crazily, trying my damndest to stay balanced on my tied feet. "T-tickling a guy's cock, what a twisted, HARRRR, HARRRRR, HARRRRR, HARRRRR, ha, ha, ha, ha, ha, ha, ha, ha, ha! What a twisted thing to do to me man! RONALD, I demand that you stop this! HARRR HARRRRR HARRRR HARRRR HARRRR HARRRR HARRRR!"

He ran that damned toothbrush all around and around my poor cock head, teasing and skirting the helmet rim of my manhood. Ronald enjoyed every second of my misery, laughing at me as I tried desperately not to fall down off the ledge of the van, but also trying to get my poor cock away from that awful tickling toothbrush….

As I stood there tied up and helpless Ronald moved the electric toothbrush up and over my nipples as well, the sounds of my laughter seeming to be a welcome for me to the house of tickle horrors as it stared down and me and my captor. The only consolation I was feeling at that moment was that I was standing up so Ronald was not able to get to my feet to tickle them, at least not at that moment. Then it was away from my nipples with the electric toothbrush and back down to my poor cock head. My cock twitched and danced stupidly outside my boxer shorts as I laughed and cackled loud into the dark night…

"HARRRR, HARRRR, HARRRR, HARRRR," I screamed loudly, looking downward as my manhood suffered.

Ronald then proceeded to run that infernal toothbrush over my balls in the pouch of my boxers, it sending chills and thrills tingling through my very being…

"HARRR, HARRR, HARRRR, HARRRR, oh how very fucked up man, HARRR, HARRR, HARRRR, t-ticklin' my balls too!" I laughed and ranted madly.

After a good long while of making me laugh, squirm and nearly lose my balance Ronald turned off the toothbrush and pocketed it. He hopped down off the van's ledge, reached up, bent me over slightly and laid me across his broad shoulders, his arms wrapped over my thighs and upper body as he carried me, his tickle prize toward the house. My cock rested against the back of his huge neck and the need to cum was suddenly very intense… My cock was shiny with the slick, thick clear pre-seed and that pre-seed was most definitely slopping against my buddies neck as he lugged me toward his tickle torture palace. Gods, he had me on the brink of shooting my load, how fucked up was that I ask you. Outside of my wife and a few self inflicted hand-jobs I had never cum in front of anyone before, well, that may not be entirely true, but for the most-part, percentage wise it was true. Now, awful thought of awful thoughts, I was somehow wishing that Ronald would make me squirt, seeing as he was the one who had worked my cock over with that damned toothbrush of his. Fuck, being carried over his shoulders like a rolled up rug, humiliating as hell also let me tell you…

"Okay Timmy my boy, good buddy of mine, its time for you to meet some of my tickle inventions," Ronald huffed as he carried me. "I am sure that you will really get a charge out of them."

I whined miserably and Ronald simply laughed fiendishly. Man oh man, my nipples were rubbing helplessly against the ropes and my cock pressed harder against Ronald's neck. But those two things combined just were not enough for me to get any relief; it was not enough to make me shoot off… Oh woe of woes…

"Man, you should be flattered buddy, I had this entire place set up with you in mind," Ronald huffed as he lugged me toward the huge and foreboding structure.

"FUCKER MAN," I yelled at Ronald. "Put me down Ronald! Stop this insanity now! Flattered nothing, I am not flattered over having just been kidnapped from out of my own goddamned house!"

"Put you down Timmy boy?" Ronald asked me, his tone sounding like he could not believe what I had just asked him to do. "If I put you down you'll get your pretty silk socks all dirty, ha!"

Chuckling meanly Ronald pressed a palm over the back of my boxer shorts, gripping my sexy ass as he walked through the front door of the mansion…

The place was enormously spacious, freshly scented and very expensively decorated. But alas, there was no grand or guided tour for yours truly here. Instead, I was lugged to what would be the first of many rooms in this huge house of tickle horrors. As Ronald walked through the door of the first tickle room he reached over and finally untied my feet. He then set me down on my socked feet and as he closed the door behind us I stood there miserably, taking in the sight of the first tickle torture device…

"Oh man Ronald, NO, no, come on buddy, that thing looks like some kind of warped excuse for an octopus!" I babbled as my so called buddy sidled up next to me.

"That's actually a very good name for it buddy boy," Ronald said directly into my ear, his lips grazing my lobe as he spoke, sending chills through me. "And you can have the honor of knowing that you named it, "Timmy's Octopus", now…shall we begin? I'll need you in a spread eagle position so I'll have to modify your bindings a bit…"

Upon hearing that I thought that that would be my chance to escape all this lunacy, I mean, once I was untied I would be able to tackle Ronald, get the keys for his van from his pocket and get the hell out of this twisted house of horrors. While I was thinking how I would have to find something of his to wear, maybe even take his clothes, to my utter and total dismay the guy treated me to yet another good dose of the chloroform/ether mixture.

"RRRRMMMMFFF!" I snarled angrily and the room spun and eventually went black.

When I came to my so called good buddy had me hooked up, or more precisely strapped up and into what would be the first of his tickle torture devices, this very first one named so aptly by yours truly, hardy fucking har har, "The Octopus." I found myself suspended in a spider web like harness, spread out in an **"X"** position; my arms and legs spread wide, every goddamned part of me totally exposed and on view for Ronald's perverse pleasures. There were a number of strategically placed binding straps that held my arms and legs out wide and secure to prevent almost any movement. I struggled a tad just to test the bindings and sure enough they would not budge. The octopus was in actuality a motorized contraption with various arm-like metal rods protruding from the base of it. At the end of each of those arms was a cone shaped furry device, just so fucking perfect for tickling a poor guy with.

"What the fucking fuck," I heard myself mutter as the fog lifted from my brain and I again became aware of where I was.

Fucking totally fucks, I had been Ronald's kidnap-tickle victim now for what seemed like hours…and the last thing I remembered as I woke up was him bringing me into his big out of the way mansion and showing me the first of his tickle inventions. I shook my head to clear the cobwebs and then looked down at the "octopus" and saw next where I was, suspended directly over the monstrous thing, a ready but unwilling tickle target.

"Ronald, what is this man?" I asked him as I climbed slowly out of the recent stupor that I had been chloroformed into.

I quickly took in the fact also that my boxer shorts were now off me and I saw them sticking out of the back pocket of Ronald's pants. Fuck, I was naked as a jaybird, well, not really if you count the fact that I was still wearing those damn black silk socks that Ronald kept on talking about, my goddamned socks of all things! So actually the only clothing I really had that was worth losing were my boxers and now they were gone!

"OH FUCKS, FUCKING FUCK! OH GOD NO! OH SHIT!" I ranted over and over.

I began to become aware of the rest of that "octopus" thing. God, there were other arms on that thing, more than I realized at first, they were flexible looking and they arced in, all around my naked and vulnerable body.

"Ronald! GODDAMNIT RONALD!" I yelled as I became aware again of his presence, as he looked mockingly at me, standing nearby the device I was trapped in. "No more of this shit man! Come on! Shit, holy fucking shit! You've taken my underpants off me man! You've got me naked here, hey buddy, this is really embarrassing now!"

My hard cock pointed up at the ceiling, twitched a bit and dribbled a good dollop of pre seed. Although Ronald had teased and tickled me already, my cock was still hard as a rock and my balls were all sore from the overt sexual stimulation, without any release. My hardness proved that I was reacting to this awful situation in a very strange manner and also seeming to prove that my sexual subconscious seemed to enjoy being dominated and tickled and sexually teased, *even by another guy it seemed.* Fuck, I could understand all this with my wife, but another guy, this was all new territory in a way. But fucking fucks, I could not deny my sexual excitement, my barometer was rising right before me and right between my legs to be exact.

"Come on man, let me down from this thing," I pleaded. "Or at the very least, give me my goddamned boxer shorts! I've got my pride you know!"

But Ronald simply smiled and pulled my confiscated underpants from his back pocket and gave my hard cock a couple of good swats with them. You have no idea what that did to me buds, to see Ronald, or any guy for that matter, with my most private of garments in his hand, and teasing my cock with them of all things. Then, to my further horror I watched my buddy raise my worn boxers to his face and he inhaled deeply through is nose and mouth.

"Ah, I love the smell of sex in the wee morning hour's buddy," Ronald laughed at my astonished gawk as he stuck the underpants back in his rear pocket. "So, have you observed the rest of my "octopus", as you have so aptly named it? Have you seen what is on the ends of those other arms?"

Looking downward I saw those cone shaped furry devices at the ends of the arms on the "octopus" tickle device. Each arm had one of those fuzzies on it, God! And there was an arm with a fuzzy on it that seemed to be pointed at each of my socked feet. There were two more that seemed to be pointing at my crotch. There were a couple on each side generally pointing at my middle, my sides, my ribs and…my very sensitive nipples. There were two more that looked like they would happily find a home in my deep, smelly and hairy armpits. What I didn't know at that moment, only because I could not see them because of the way I was positioned in the device was that there was another of those fuzzy cone shaped devices under me, aimed directly at my exposed, gaping virgin bung hole…

"What I did to you in the van was only a rehearsal buddy," Ronald said to me, standing next to me with a remote control device in hand, looking up at me almost lovingly, if that were possible. "But rehearsal time is over as of now, now the real laughing will begin Timmy…" Ronald looked at me and laughed mercilessly at my facial expression of disbelief. My cock twitched some more. Damn, but that thing has a mind of its own.

"PLEASE RONALD, please don't," I whimpered, struggling fruitlessly in the bindings.

"These devices spin at a little better than the speed of old fashioned 78 records on old fashioned record players, and the longer they stay activated the faster they'll spin," Ronald told me, his reply not being happy news to my ears bud. "You're going to Tickle City buddy..."

"Ronald, my wife will call the police!" I bantered desperately. "She'll get you for this!"

"HEH, the real question here buddy actually is, *will she get you?*" Ronald asked me and pressed a button on the remote control device.

The cone shaped furry devices pointed at my nipples came to life first. They snaked forwards and I watched in horror as they spun like two tops against my nub tips...

"HA, HA, HA, HA, HA, HA, HA, HA, HA, HA, HA, HA, HA, HA, HA, HA, HA, HA!" was the sound that then filled the first tickle room.

"Man, those tits of yours sure are tickle sensitive," Ronald said and pressed a second button on the remote control.

The cone shaped devices at my socked feet came to life next and I howled my laughter now...

"HA, HA, HA, HA, HA, HA, HA, HA, HA, HA, HA, HAR, HAR, HAR, HAR, HAR, HAR, HAR!" I laughed raucously. "AAAARRRRHHHHHH HOUSTON, I've got a problem, ha, ha, ha, ha, ha, ha, ha, ha, ha, ha, ha, ha, ha, ha, ha!"

As those furry things spun against my man tits my nubs quickly hardened on my chest and became even more tickle sensitive. The result of that sent waves of louder and louder laughter through me and erupted out of my mouth. I could hear myself laughing crazily, as if I were laughing somewhere far away from me. The noise echoed in the big room and seemed to reverberate through the house and back again. My mouth hung open and I slung spittle most disgustingly while howling with laughter.

Chapter Five

"HA, ha, ha, ha, ha, ha, ha, ha, ha, ha, ha, ha, ha, ha, ha, ha, ha, ha, ha, ha! Turn...ha, ha, ha, ha, ha, ha, ha, ha, ha, ha, ha, ha, ha, ha, turn it off, Ronald, it, it's tickling me death! HA, ha, ha, ha, ha, ha, ha, ha, ha, ha, ha, ha, I-I can't take it, please stop it, I can't take it anymore, ha, ha, ha, ha, ha, ha, ha, ha, ha, ha, ha, ha!" I screamed and laughed and screamed and laughed, not really sure what the fucking fuck I was saying after a while.

I was going berserk. Those spinning fuzzies tickling my man tits were really working double time over my nipples, going around and around and around and around them, tickling me till I was in stitches. But oh good God, those two other fuzzies that were spinning up and down the soles of my silky nylon socked feet, oh good God in his heaven! By itself those fuzzies tickling my man tits would have been more than enough to have me in stitches, but, both, my nipples and my poor feet, fucking fucks, I was in double stitches! I was laughing, spitting, sputtering and writhing miserably, well, not really writhing you see. I really couldn't move all that much, not the way Ronald had me tied up in that spider web thing while his awful octopus device tickle tortured me. But what little I could move I did move, namely my toes under my socks and my splayed fingers, writhing those fractions of inches.

If my laughter could have been heard through the huge house and out into the dark night I could just imagine how the silence out there was being broken in the wee morning hours. It was the awful sound of a poor guy being totally tickle imperiled, his loud raucous laughter ripping apart the silence of the quiet night. I lifted my head a bit, another part of me that I was able to move and looked down and watched as the cone shaped fuzzies literally explored me like hunters or explorers, and they lapped at me, tickling me mercilessly.

"HA, HA, HA, HA, HA, HA, HA, HA, HA, HA, HA, HA, HA, HA, HA, HA, HA, HA, STOP, RONALD, STOP!" I cawed like a crow. "Th-those fucking things are in love with my goddamned man nips and my, my, ha, ha, ha, ha, ha, ha, ha, ha, my feet!"

Ronald simply chuckled at me and said "Stop Timmy? But like that song by the Carpenter's said we've only just begun. Just wait until you see, *and feel* the rest of the octopus when it comes into play. My, my, Timmy, just look at your cock; it's really standing tall again. Hmm, you say you want me to stop, but that's not what your cock says."

I could not believe this, he was tickle torturing me, *he was fucking tickle torturing me* and it was making my cock hard and then to add insult to injury he was taunting me with it.

"HA, ha, ha, ha, ha, ha, ha, ha, ha, ha, ha, ha, ha, ha, ha, R-Ronald," I ranted laughingly. "I can't help, ha, ha, ha, ha, ha, ha, ha, ha, ha, ha, ha, ha; I can't help what my cock d-does! You ought to know, ha, ha, ha, ha, ha, ha, ha, ha, that a guy's meat pole does what it wants to do, ohhhhhhrrrrrrr, ha, ha, ha, ha, ha, ha, ha, ha, ha, ha, ha, ha! I can't control my own cock, ha, ha, ha, ha, ha, ha, ha, ha, ha, ha, ha, ha, ha, oh Gawd, Ronald, please stop tickling me man, *pllleeeeeaaasseeee!"*

"Well Timmy my boy, seeing as your cock has a mind of it's own and it seems to be enjoying all this, let's just see if I can help your cock enjoy itself some more," Ronald said to me, grinning meanly, almost madly. "What do you say buddy?"

All I could do was reply with laughter...

And then, if I weren't laughing I would have cried with what Ronald subjected me to next. He pressed a few buttons on his remote control device and the two metal arms with the fuzzies on them aimed at my armpits came to life. They started spinning and moving toward my poor hairy and sweaty pits.

"OH NO, NO, RONALD, HA, HA, HA, HA, HA, HA, HA, HA, oh you bastard," I cackled.

They started rubbing and spinning up and down and all around the hollows beneath each of my arms.

"AAAAARRRRRRHHHHHHH, m-my tits, my feet, HA, ha, ha, ha, ha, ha, ha, ha, ha, ha, ha, ha, ha, ha, ha, ha, and now my smelly pits too?" I razzed loudly.

It felt as if the cone shaped fuzzies at my armpits were chewing at my moist and sweaty underarms, totally maddening buds, *totally awful.*

"RONALD, ha, ha, ha, ha, ha, ha, ha, ha, ha, ha, ha, ha, ha, you'll pay for this man, you will pay for this you bastard, ha, ha, ha, ha, ha, ha, ha, ha, ha, ha, ha!" I roared.

"Pay for it Timmy?" Ronald asked me in disbelief. "Pay for it? Man, I'm getting it for free.

Ronald chuckled and clucked with total satisfaction as he watched me suffer in his creation, and I knew that this would be the first of his many creations, MY GOD! But then, two more of the metal arms with fuzzies on them snaked upwards at my sides, criss crossed along my ribs and belly and began tickling those sections of me also. I found myself screaming in a tickle frenzy. I felt two more of those fuzzies swoon against the backs of my thighs as well, a real ticklish spot for poor yours truly here. I was beginning to lose my voice and I seriously thought I would lose my mind. Oh Good God, but it got even worse let me tell you. Even though I could not see them because of the position I was tethered into I felt more spinning fuzzies attack the backs of my stretched out legs, the cheeks of my sexy ass and a couple of them even snaked and trailed their way up and down the center of my back, really putting the tickles to me. When I felt all those arms moving their fuzzies over me and tickling the fucking fucks out of me I jerked my head up and down and from side to side and saw with a feeling of utter misery that there were still arms that weren't yet moving, arms that Ronald hadn't started using on me yet. One of them was pointed at my bouncing cock and balls, the other aimed at a place that no man should ever be tickle tortured in, his goddamned bung hole. While all this tickling was going on Ronald had me in a definite state of tickle terror, my cock was leaking again and looking for some kind of relief. I hadn't been given any relief when he had teased me earlier with his blasted electric toothbrush, all he had done was teased me to the edge and now he had me back on the verge of cumming again, ready to fall off the edge this time. But fucking fucks, there was nothing to finish the job, no friction to rub my poor cock against to make it spit to bring me the release I was so craving at that point. My balls were rumbling in my sac and hurting more and more. My cock was almost turning blue I needed to cum so badly. It was dripping at the end and bouncing, bouncing, bouncing in the air. I was going tickle fucking crazy, it was insane, but that's where I was going, tickle fucking crazy.

"Ha, ha, ha, ha, ha, ha, ha, ha, ha, ha, ha, ha, ha, ha, ha, ha, ha, ha!" I laughed crazily; watching as Ronald now stood at my being tickled socked feet.

While the cone shaped fuzzies were busy tickling my heels Ronald leaned down in front of me over my trapped feet, sniffed my sweaty socked toes and tweaked the two big ones under my socks, sending seductive chills through my very being again. Then, he watched in awe as the cone shaped fuzzies moved from my heels and spiraled themselves against the arches of my poor feet.

"Amazing, totally fucking amazing," Ronald said, watching as my socked feet suffered. "I chose so well where you're concerned buddy boy..."

Ronald then looked at me across my stretched out and tethered muscular body, a maniacal look in his eyes. He held up the remote control device and looked at the fuzzies aimed at my cock and balls.

"RONALD, no, NO, NO! You wouldn't man, ha, ha, ha, ha, ha, ha, ha, ha, ha, ha, ha, ha, ha!" I laughed, trying to sound like I meant what I was saying. "Oh God, not my meat stick and my, AAAAYYYYYYYYY, ha, ha, ha, ha, ha, ha, ha, ha, ha, my balls, you son of a ha, ha, ha, ha, ha, ha, ha, ha bitch!"

But before I could finish the sentence I felt the cone shaped fuzzies rubbing against my hard cock and dangling balls. I lifted my head to see the awfulness of it and laughed myself silly. Then, I felt something else under me as well. I felt one of those fuzzies at the end of a metal arm sliding and working its way into my sweaty and stretched open bung hole, my most private crevice was being brutally invaded and was about to be tickle tortured as well...

"OOOHHHHRRRRRRRR NOOOOOOOOOOOO!" I cried out. "HAR, HAR, HAR, HAR, HAR!"

"I call that one in your shit chute the diddler buddy," Ronald said to me as the warm furry thing wedged inside me and filled my sweaty and stinking anal canal.

It started spinning in there...

I pursed my lips, tried to stifle my laughter and watched in total horror of horrors as the cone shaped fuzzies near my cock and balls really worked me over in that area as well...

"AAAAAAAAAAAAHAHAHAHAHAHAHAHAHAHAHAHAHAHAHAHA!" I screamed in total tickle torment.

I had pleaded and begged Ronald to stop this madness, in between my bouts of laughter that is and instead he just laughed as well, at me, his poor tickle victim. And to my mounting horror the fuzzies at my cock and balls came to faster life and were now spinning and spinning against my private area. But if that wasn't bad enough, God, it even kills me to write about this, if that wasn't bad enough, having my cock and balls tickle tortured I felt another fuzzy spinning its tip upwards and further yet into my bung hole of all places.

"YYYYEEEEEEOOOOOOOEEEEEEEEE" I screeched, arching my body in a curved position as that invasive fuzzy made a home for itself in my goddamned anal canal. "AAAAAAAAAAAAHAHAHAHAHAHAHAHAHAHAHAHAHHAHEEEEEEEEHAHAHA!"

That spinning fuzzy sent me into a screaming, screeching, laughing fitful frenzy. Its little soft bristles just so playfully tweaked, scratched, teased and nibbled at the virgin flesh of my open and sweaty hole and it pressed onward buds, reaching deeper and deeper than just the rim of my stink hole. It felt as if it was going to drill itself teasing and tickling right up through my body. Fucking double fucks, I could almost feel it in my throat at that point, but inwardly I knew that that was just my sexual tension reacting. Then the thing in my bung hole pulled back, but only for a split second before it playfully and meanly re-entered me between my cheeks. God, it was actually fucking my sexy ass with its spinning tickling teasing fuzzy bristles. And while I laughed and screamed like a banshee Ronald enjoyed himself, listening to my noise...

As for the two spinning fuzzies at my cock and balls, well, lets just say this I was harder than ever before in all my thirty something years, or at least it sure as fuck felt that way. My cock was pulsing and jumping madly as I was now being tickle tortured all over my body and also being fucked like some cheap whore by the same type of device that was tickling me elsewhere and everywhere. Bug-eyed and screaming, I watched as the spinning fuzzies never really got to my cock per se, but just seemed to face it like another snake facing an enemy snake. It just spun there, mere and scant inches out of reach of my hard and very much in need of relief cock. But, *but*, the one at my balls, it moved right in under my sexy sweaty sac and spun its tickling bristles back and forth and back and forth across my scrotum, nudging my balls in there, tickling my sac, and cooking my man juice within, bringing it to a boil. Fucking fucks, they were cooking my balls and my balls, to put it plainly felt like they were at the bursting point. My juices were being boiled and building up in there and they were getting bigger and bigger. The only way to relieve the pressure in my poor balls was to spew my cum, and spew it in buckets. Fuck, I was in ticklish and sexual agony. I thought that Ronald had tickled and teased me all that he possibly could back in the van. But now I knew that this was worse and somehow I knew that it would only get even worse and worse...

"Man, this really does have a hell of an effect on you buddy boy," I heard Ronald saying as I screamed, cackled and reeled in the awful throes of laughter.

The diddler, as he so aptly called it, in my hole spun in a fast orbit-like manner and I realized with a sick fascination that it was spinning in two directions, clockwise and then counter clockwise, clockwise and then again counter clockwise. It would stop for a second every few minutes only to spin in the opposite direction. Fucking fucks, the spinning in my asshole had my head spinning as well, spinning far and away...

"R-R-R-RONALD, are, are you still here? HA, ha, ha, ha, ha, ha, ha, ha, ha, ha, ha, ha, ha, ha, ha, ha, ha, ha!" I screamed shrilly and uncontrollably, looking upwards through eyes filled with tears of laughter. "OH GAWD MAN! HA, ha, ha, ha, ha, ha, ha, ha, ha, ha, ha, ha, ha! DIDDLER, a fucking diddler, ha, ha, ha, ha, ha, ha, ha, ha, RONALD, are you here?" Th-that diddler is driving me ever-loving mad!"

It spun faster one way and then faster the other way, stopping only to give poor me a false sense that it was quitting, then it would start spinning faster again the other way. Spinning, spinning, spinning, Gawd, I felt as if it was going to spin my brains right out of my head through my stink hole.

"Of course I'm still here buddy," I heard Ronald call out to me, trying to sound reassuring from what I guessed. "Do you honestly think that I would miss even a moment of all this?"

"RONALD, please, please stop this thing!" I screamed out. "HA, ha, ha, ha, ha, ha, ha, ha, ha, ha, ha, ha, ha, ha, ha, ha, ha, ha, ha, ha!"

With a look of coyness on his face I saw Ronald then standing next to me. He was pushing buttons on his remote control and slowly, one by one the cone shaped fuzzies retracted away from my exposed naked flesh and ticklish parts and stopped tickling me.

"OHHHHHRRRRRRR, ha, ha, ha, ha, ha, ha, ha, ha, ha, ha, ha, ha, ha, ha, ha, ha, th-thank you Ronald, oh thank you man, thank you, ha, ha, ha, ha, ha, ha, ha, ha, ha!" I said as I lay there all sweaty and still laughing even though I was not being tickled any longer.

When the diddler retracted itself from my hole I felt a cool draft back there at my now devirginized bung hole. I farted loud and once as the thing slipped out of my shit chute, making Ronald laugh and wave his hand in the air, a look of mock disgust on his face.

"WHEW, nasty buddy," Ronald laughed as the cone shaped fuzzies were all turned off now, coming to a halt, no longer spinning.

"R-Ronald, enough of this," I stammered hoarsely, looking down at my hard, hard cock, hating Ronald for what he had done to me yet wishing that he would jack me off.

Jack me off? Wishing that my buddy would jack me off? What the fucking fuck was I thinking? But admittedly, now that the tickling had stopped my only agony was the sexual tension that had built up in my nuts and my cock trying to find something to trigger a gigantic orgasm. My balls were feeling really heavy and inflated with the sweet nectar called my man juices and my cock was one big sexual nerve. Gawd, I wanted to cum but how could I get release? There was no way that I could ask Ronald to jack me off, right?

"Ronald, look man, get my goddamned boxer shorts back on me and take me home now!" I grunted, clearing my throat as my voice slowly returned to a normal sounding monotone of sorts. "It's still night time man, my wife is more than likely still asleep and I'll be able to slip back in without her knowing I've been gone man..."

But as I spoke and prattled on and on Ronald looked at me in disbelief...

"Again Timmy my boy, we're just getting started here, and night time is nearly over," Ronald said to me and my heart sank as I heard the terrible news. "By now the sun is coming up and I didn't bring you here just so that I could use one device on you. By the way buddy boy, I think you should be made aware that besides chloroform this mixture that I've been using on you contains a very potent aphrodisiac."

As he told me this Ronald was pouring chloroform on a white cloth...

A-a-aphrodisiac?" I asked him and wiggled my toes under my black silky socks. "And man, you've already tickle tortured me more than I ever thought possible, how the fucking fucks can there be more? An aphrodisiac? You gave me an aphrodisiac?"

"A Spanish fly bud," Ronald chortled and pressed the cloth over my nose and mouth.

"RRRRRHHHHHHHHHHHH!" I reeled madly as I had no choice but to inhale and the awful fumes sent me into yet another stupor.

As my head spun and I entered a semi dreamland I felt myself freed from the tethers of the octopus and lifted in a prone position. I was carried out of the room in the manner of a bride being carried over the threshold on her wedding night by her handsome husband into the honeymoon suite. Fuck, I was realizing that no matter what I said to him Ronald was hell-bent on continuing with his plans for me.

"WHOOO, you're all sweaty buddy, I can smell your sweaty dress socks... ha!" I heard Ronald say as he lugged me huffing and puffing from the room. "R-Ronald, put me down man," I murmured helplessly.

"I think we'd better do something to clean up those stinky socks of yours huh? What do you say?" I heard Ronald ask me teasingly, his voice seeming to come from very far away, like through an echo chamber of some kind.

"F-fuck my socks, I-let me go bud," I whispered helplessly and then my head lolled back.

When I came to a short while later I found myself in a seated position, my hands were tied behind me and I was blindfolded, *again...*

Chapter Six

"AWWWHHHHH, this is no goddamned way to treat a guy you call your buddy," I said in the blindfolded darkness as my head again cleared from the latest dose of chloroform (aphrodisiac) that Ronald had so brutally administered to me.

Even though my eyes were covered with what I figured was that white cloth I could feel Ronald's steely gaze on me, penetrating me actually. Fuck, fucking fucks, I could feel him drinking in the sight of me. And what a sight I was at that moment let me tell you guys out there. Being blindfolded really intensifies a kidnap and bondage situation. I know it did for me, with what my buddy Ronald was putting me through, subjecting me to as he called it. Fuck, with buddies like Ronald who the hell needs enemies right? And fuck it all, I had already been through more torture, albeit TICKLE TORTURE than any prisoner I had ever heard of. And to add to my total humiliation I was on the verge of absolutely screaming until I burst a blood vessel if I could not cum soon. My cock wouldn't even go soft at that point. I woke up from those chloroformed naps and my cock was still as hard as when I was last awake. And my balls, damn, my poor balls. I felt like I had lead weights between my legs rather than testicles. I was seated on a chair that had a hole in the seat section, sort of like a toilet bowl ring. My balls were dangling low and feeling real pressured and heavy through the hole in the seat, chock filled with my thick and juicy pent-up Vitamin E sperm. My poor tortured balls were hanging in mid air buds. My cock was hard and fucking stiff buds, pointing straight up at heaven. I sat with my muscular back against the wooden straight-back chair, my well muscled arms pulled behind me and roped at the wrists. That blasted nylon rope circled my upper torso and was snugly pulled and tautly tight under my very plumped up and bulbous nipples. What a feeling! From the way my nipples had been tickle tortured it was amazing to me that they hadn't gotten so hard and burst right off my big chest. Maddening most of all though was that fucking blindfold impairing my sight. Knowing that Ronald had promised me some more tickle torture events sent chills of total trepidation through me, and totally fucking fuck, there was nothing I could do to stop him. My nipples, my armpits, the bottoms of my silky nylon socked feet and worst of all guys, my poor bung hole all felt the remnants of all the tickling I had already endured on this awful night. All those parts of my body that had been tickled were highly sensitized at that point and any more tickling would surely send me over the edge. My cock was throbbing and overly hard. Pre seed seeped from my piss slit and trickled down my shaft but no relief seemed near. My mouth dropped open in misery as I sat with my tree trunk like legs spread around the chair (the way Ronald had positioned me) and I thought of the "octopus", the awful and sinister first device that Ronald subjected me to since having so cleverly kidnapped and spirited me away to this secret hideaway of his...

"Hmm, looks like the sun is starting to come up out there buddy boy," I heard Ronald say then as he hunkered down next to me, brazenly taking one of my nipples between his thumb and first fingers of his hand. "I guess I'll have to give you something for breakfast pretty soon huh? Wouldn't want my good buddy to be hungry now…this is all in good sleazy fun after all…"

As Ronald spoke he squeezed and mashed my nipple real hard, twisted it too, sending even more chills through me… Fucking fucks, he's telling me about the sun coming up and feeding me breakfast and what I'm thinking about is the overpowering need to shoot my load of ball juice so I can empty my goddamned testicles. But I couldn't beg Ronald to make me cum. Gawd, he's a guy. As all these thoughts went through my head I wished that I could just roll over and bed and fuck my wife till lunch time. God knew I had enough good stuff in my balls to keep her busy all morning. God almighty, I would fill her up so much that she would have cum dripping out of her ears, hardy fucking har har guys.

"R-Ronald, Th-this is insane man, you've carried this AND ME far enough at this point!" I stammered and blurted through trembling lips. "If the sun's coming up then I should be getting into my goddamned suit and ready for the workday, not be here, wherever the hell *here* is!"

"Well, you've got your dress socks on buddy, so it's a good start for your suit huh?" Ronald mused and twirled my nipple in a fast motion with his mangy fingers.

"OOOOOOOOO, FUCKING fucks man, but I got sensitive man nips," I muttered, looking upward into the blindfolded darkness. "But fuck my socks Ronald, untie me man, *take me home!* NO MORE TICKLIN' me huh? Gawd man, playing with my man tits like that you're driving me crazy. Stop tweaking my nubs huh? That's just making my cock more stiff, Ronald, stop, you're making my cock frustratingly hard."

Actually, he had me so fucking hard that it had started to hurt at that point but all he did was talk about my damned socks. Fuck, he had me naked as the day I was born, except for those socks he was obsessed with, talking about and messing with.

"Well, like I said when I was lugging you in here bud, I was able to smell just how very sweaty those dressy socks of yours had become since I started working you over," Ronald said and let go of my nipple.

He then stood right up next to me…

"So, with that in mind and the smell of your socks in the air I figure that a good thorough cleaning is in order for those socks wouldn't you say?" Ronald asked me, sounding totally mocking as he tugged at the knot in my blindfold.

"I-I don't know what the fucking fuck to say at this point man," I stated sternly but miserably as well. "I don't know what you're talking about. What I do know Ronald, is that you've kidnapped me from my home, and you've tickled and teased me to the point that my cock won't go soft, and Gawd in heaven it hurts buddy. So, whatever the fuck you mean about cleaning up my socks, I have no damned idea what you're talking about and…"

That said Ronald whipped the blindfold off me. I looked around and then down to where he was looking. Positioned directly in front of the chair I was bound to was…

"HOLY FUCKING SHIT!" I reeled loudly and in terror once again. "A goddamned high powered, high spinning executive shoe shining machine!"

This time it was Ronald who was laughing loudly as I sat there helplessly choking on my tears. My cock seeped more pre-seed and my dangling heavy nuts churned…

I looked down at the usual, everyday device, but knowing how Ronald planned to use it on me sent awful chills though me from toes to my head. Looking down at the machine as it mocked me I took in the sight of the damned thing. You know the kind, the ones with the highly polished chrome body. Fuck, I could see my beleaguered naked tied up image in the chrome of that thing. My cock was sticking up and into my line of vision and bouncing as I looked past it at Ronald's next device of torture. On either side of the chrome body was a big fuzzy/fluffy cone, one red and one black. The big end of each of the fluffy/fuzzy polishing cones was near the chrome body and each tapered down to a point out at the ends. But unfamiliar to me where these shoe shine machines were concerned was that in the top of this one I saw two hatches with handles on each of them. I had to wonder what those were for... I figured I didn't need to ask as my host would more than likely explain it all to me in good time, Gawd! I looked up at Ronald with my mouth gaping and wide open.

"It, it's a goddamned high speed executive shoe shining machine!" I repeated and my cock twitched as I said those words, those awful words.

I think that the little brain in my cock was already anticipating all the ticklish sensations that would soon be traveling up from my feet, before traveling upward to my whimpering brain in my big head. My cock lurched again, and more clear pre-seed leaked from my wide sexy slit and trickled down the domed head, before it curled under the dome and trickled still farther down the already sticky sides of my vein marked shaft.

"It, it's a fucking shoe shine machine," I said again.

"HA, HA, and hardy har har for you buddy," Ronald laughed at my realization of what was sitting on the floor in front of me. "That is exactly what it is, (he winked at me then as he spoke) a very high speed executive shoe shining machine. But Timmy my laddy, you've lost your shoes or so it would appear, ha, ha and hardy fucking har again for you buddy boy!"

"FUCK me, you're really enjoying all this aren't you man?" I asked him miserably, my head lolling back and looking up at him helplessly.

"Timmy, I really want you to benefit from this machine by having your shoes, er, in your case your sexy, stinky silk socks polished."

"B-but you can't polish socks," I whimpered. "Fuck Ronald, if you put that thing on it will, it'll, oh God, it'll tickle my feet. OH FUCK RONALD, it will tickle my socked feet, not polish my socked feet! There is a difference man! (I was nearly crying now.) There's a fucking difference Ronald!"

As I spoke and pleaded my balls actually shifted in their sack and my cock bounced more and more. Fuck, it felt like my poor balls were actually changing positions and rolling around in my dangling sac.

"Ronald, you can't do this to me, now come on man, you've done enough to me already," I choked. "Come on now, you don't know what this will do to me..."

"HA, ha, why yes I do Timmy, I do know what it will do to you, it will tickle you," Ronald said to me in a mocking high pitched tone of voice as he squatted down next to me. *"It will tickle your feet, ha, ha, ha."*

It looked like there was to be no getting out of it for me, unless I tried one other tack, and at that point I was ready to try just about anything buds.

"Y-you're right Ronald," I whimpered very hoarsely now. "Th-that infernal thing *will* tickle my feet, but you're missing a point here *buddy boy, a very important point by the way...*"

"And what might that be pray tell?" Ronald asked as he hunkered down next to the straight backed chair that I was seated in and tied to as well.

"Y-you didn't invent that shoe shining machine, you told me that all the tickle torture devices in this place were *your* inventions!" I said to Ronald almost sounding mocking myself now, watching helplessly though as he proceeded to move my socked feet close together, handling them gingerly by my socked calves.

"You're right bud, I didn't invent this device, another man did, who he is I guess we will never know, but my good buddy, Timmy my laddy, I did ADD to this high speed executive shoe shining device," Ronald said, just as mockingly, as if we were trying to outdo each other.

"You, *you* added to it?" I asked him.

"Yes Timmy, I added to it, you see, instead of tickling your socked feet from the sides, the way it was made to polish shoes, it will tickle your feet from the inside," Ronald said and pulled open one of the hatches that I mentioned earlier, the hatches that were in the topmost part of the shoe shine device.

I looked down again with my mouth hanging open, a feeling beyond sheer terror engulfing me. I saw that there were two very wide openings inside the device, big and wide enough for a guy's feet to fit into just perfectly, in this case it would be *my* socked feet fitting just perfectly in there. And further in the device, inside those wide openings I saw what looked like hundreds of round, definitely motorized soft shoe cleaning bristles.

"Getting the picture now buddy?" Ronald asked me and I felt my poor feet sweating in my silky black nylon socks, the erotic and musty scent wafting up to my nostrils, it was also the scent of terror that I smelled.

My hard cock twitched in fear and became even more erect as my poor balls churned with the mess of gobs upon gobs of pent-up sperm that was stored up in them as they dangled from the hole in the chair.

"Ronald, no, no, *oh God, please no,"* I whimpered. "What do I have to do to get through to you buddy?"

"Now, once your sexy socked tootsies are in there I'll close the hatch, that way you won't be able to pull your feet away from the machine," Ronald said and gripped my socked calves now, hefting them off the floor and moving them over the two openings in the shoe shining device.

"Ron-Ronald, you bastard," I said, nearly in a whisper that reeked of terror by then. "What a twisted thing to do to that machine, you've turned a normal everyday executive device into a fucking *torture device!* And, and, oh man, and not to mention what a twisted and really fucked up thing you're about to do to me! OH GOD MAN, let go of my feet Ronald, *please man, let go of my damned feet..."*

I cringed in the chair, watching as Ronald ignored me and slid my socked feet into the two holes in the shoe shine device, plunging them in there to be more precise. My socked feet felt as if they had been swallowed up. Before I could move to yank them out Ronald closed the hatch around them and slid the latches locked on them, thus trapping my sweaty socked feet in the shoe shining machine...

"Ronald, before you start tickle torturing me again and making me laugh my fool head off, at least tell me this man, what's the point of all this? I asked him miserably, looking down woefully at my poor feet in the device now, only the very tops of my socks showing, somehow I found that to be sort of comical looking. "Why man, why the hell are you tickling me?"

"First, because you're ticklish buddy, you are very, *very* ticklish; Ronald replied and placed his finger on a switch on the device.

Around that switch were inscribed the words "FAST, FASTER, and FASTEST."

"And second, comedy," Ronald continued in his reply to me, his finger resting on the control button of the shoe shine device teasing and mocking me awfully. "I love comedy. I just love to hear a guy laugh."

"Comedy? Comedy?" I ranted at him, looking down at him as he hunkered next to me. "Fucking comedy huh? Hey look, we can rent a movie, a really funny movie, and then we can both laugh. No one would need to be tied up, just two buddies watching a really funny movie!"

My feet were pressed into and sweating profusely now in that damned shoe shining machine buds and surrounded all around and at every inch by those bristles, soft but prickly bristles. Those fucking bristles were hugging my feet as though they were in love with them, hardy fucking har! I could feel them on the bottoms of my socked feet, against my arches, pressed up against all of my toes, over both sides of my ankles, on the tops of my feet and even under my heels. I realized with a sickening sense of dread that both of my poor feet were about to go to "TICKLE HELL... As Ronald and I spoke to each other the bristles were still, but with my buddies finger on the control switch I was afraid that that was about to change dramatically. And my cock, God, how my cock was pulsing, I was still leaking pre-seed. What had leaked out earlier had dried up and become very sticky and stiff on my cock shaft, but with all the tickling that I was enduring my poor tortured balls just kept pushing out my clear thick liquid that continued to coat my cock head and eventually my thick veined shaft as well. My hard cock had been stimulated but untouched for what seemed like hours now and to be brutally honest I had lost track of the time. My poor cock ached for contact, for friction, for something, *anything* to come to a climax and trigger his two heavy and aching buddies to start pumping out their massive overstock of sperm that had been building in them...for hours.

"Funny movie, a funny movie," Ronald said, laughing at me. "Yes, we actually could laugh at a funny movie. What title would you suggest Timmy me laddy? But I assure you, there is no movie that's ever been made that you would find as funny as all my tickling devices. And I so enjoy laughing at you while you're laughing so hard."

"Ron-Ronald man, please, I'm begging you now," I said, my voice coming back from the whispering it had done just moments ago. "You've seen how very ticklish I am. I am really awfully ticklish buddy!"

"Why Timmy, of course I know how ticklish you are," Ronald said, grinning at me and nodding his head. "That's why I chose you for this little adventure. And I for one am thoroughly enjoying this escapade, and, from the way you've been laughing I just know that you think all of this is sooooo very funny..."

Ronald chuckled one last time and then flipped the switch on the shoe shine device to the "FASTEST" position. Suddenly, the shoe shine machine came to whirring life, looking for shoes to shine and finding none it had no choice but to go to work on my socked feet. Inside that device all those bristles that had been hugging my socked feet before were now moving beyond rapidly across, over, around and under my poor socked feet. Good God, there was no spot on my devilishly ticklish feet that was not being tickled and teased by those spinning whirling bristles. It felt like my feet were being vibrated and tickled on by thousands upon thousands of tiny nibbling teeth...

"AAAAAYYYYYYYYYY HA, ha, ha, ha, ha, ha, ha, ha, ha, ha, ha, ha, ha, ha, ha, ha, ha, ha, RON-RONALD, YOU BASTARD, HA, HA, HA, HA, HA, HA, HA, HA,

HA, HA!" I screamed in laughter. "What-what a fucking fucked up way to clean a poor guy's smelly dress socks! HAR, HAR, HAR, HAR, HAR, HAR, HAR, HAR, HAR, HAR, HAR! Didn't you just think to maybe put my socks in a washing machine? HAR, HAR, HAR, HAR, HAR, HAR, HAR!"

Chapter Seven

"AAAAAYYYYYYYYYYYY HA, ha, ha, ha, ha, ha, ha, ha, ha, ha, ha, ha, ha, ha, ha, ha! RON-RONALD, hee, hee, hee, hee, hee, hee, hee, hee, hee, hee, hee, heee! It, it's tickling my feet!" I squealed loudly and crazily. "SH-shit man, stop this thing, ha, ha, ha, ha, ha, ha, ha, ha, ha, ha, ha, ha, ha, ha, ha, ha, ha, ha, ha, ha!"

So there I sat, bound up good and tight in that straight backed chair, my heavy sperm loaded balls swinging through a strategically placed hole in the chair seat. My goddamned cock was poking holes in the air above my lap and leaking more and more pre-seed than I would have ever thought possible. My God, my socked feet were being shined, no, not exactly shined, tickled, tickled and tickled and tickled and tickled. My poor socked feet were trapped in a warped version of a shoe shine machine and being tickled unmercifully. Then, in my total hysteria I felt something else, something on my feet besides the tickling sensations I was being so meanly subjected to. Please remember, I need to remind you here that I was naked except for my socks, my black silky nylon socks to be exact. The spinning tickling bristles was what I felt at that moment most of all. But, oh God, and this is humiliating just to tell but it happened buds, *it really happened.* Those fucking spinning tickling bristles started eating my socks, I mean, they were tickling my socked feet, yes, but then suddenly they somehow began eating my socks right off me, *right off my feet.* The spinning motion I supposed was what caused them to start pulling at my thin office socks. Looking down through tear filled laughing eyes I saw my socks begin to stretch and slide down my calves into the bowels of the shoe shine device that my feet were trapped in. Not only was that damned machine tickling me, but now it was fixing to strip off the last bit of clothing that I was wearing. There they went, another inch, down went my socks, little by little, baring my sexy lower legs. As I laughed and laughed and watched the machine just kept tickling me and eating my socks. Ronald saw what was happening and this just gave him more added sadistic pleasure and he was suddenly guffawing, sounding totally fiendish as he pointed at my socks. Together we watched and laughed, laughed for different reasons, as my socks inch by goddamned inch disappeared into the torturous shoe shining machine. Lower and lower went my socks as the device tickled and tickled my slowly being bared feet. Down they went and then the tops of them were gone, they had disappeared below the top part of the machine that my feet were encased in. I could not believe this; Ronald's damned machine was eating and stripping my socks off me. I could no longer see my socks at that point but I sure as hell felt the bristles as they attacked my bare flesh that was now uncovered because of my slowly receding socks. Those damned socks, the reason for my kidnap it seemed were now over my heels. The tickling was more maddening as the stripping went on. The socks inched toward my wiggling toes. God, then they were at my toes and then, *then,* they were gone, eaten right off my poor feet and down in the bowels of the shoe shine machine! That fucking shoe shine device had just stripped me of my last bit of clothing. Ronald thought that this was hilarious, I saw it as just more humiliation, and awful of all awful's the tickling went on and on and on. Now those bristles in the shoe shine device were able to get directly to my hot sweaty, steamed up naked feet, and fuck, it sure gave new meaning to the word "tickle."

"AAAAAYYYYYYYYYY, ha, ha, ha, ha, ha, ha, ha, ha, ha, ha, ha, ha, ha, ha, ha, ha, ha! RONALD, y-you're driving me crazy, ha, ha, ha, ha, ha, ha, ha, ha, ha, ha, ha, ha, ha, ha! IT'S still tickling my feet, stop, stop this thing, ha, ha, ha, ha, ha, ha, ha, ha, ha, ha, ha, ha, ha, ha, ha, ha, ha! RONALD!"

I continued laughing crazily and witlessly even long after my black silk socks were gone.

"RONALD, RONALD, holy fucking shit man, ha, ha, ha, ha, ha, ha, ha, ha, ha, ha, ha, ha, ha, ha, d-did you see that man?" I cackled out my words. "DID you fuckin' see that? HAR, HAR, HAR, HAR, HAR, HAR, ohhhhrrrr God man, y-your devilish machine ate my socks right off my tickled feet! HA, ha, ha, ha, ha, ha, ha, ha, ha!"

"Of course I saw it, that was hilarious buddy boy," Ronald chuckled and squatted down behind me as I sat tied to the straight back chair, my now bared feet still awfully trapped in the confines of the shoe shining machine.

The fast spinning bristles in the machine massaged and lapped hungrily at my bare smelly feet. They felt like a thousand and more tiny teeth on them, nibbling me as they tickle tormented every last part of my poor, poor feet. All this sounds kind of monotonous at this point huh? Well, I can't help it, it's not my fault buds. I'm just a poor sap of a guy relating to all of you other poor saps of guys out there what befell me. It was Ronald's fault. He and his device of the moment were making me laugh and laugh and laugh. But you know buds, you know what's funny? What's really funny? I don't think all the laughter that was being extracted so forcefully from me was actually funny at all. I was finding out the hard way that laughing and funny do not necessarily go together. Like right at that moment, that awful moment, I was laughing only because Ronald was tormenting me with one of his machines, his machine tickling the SHIT out of my now bare feet. And, it was funny to watch my socks be eaten right off my feet by that machine. Anyone in their right mind I am sure would have laughed their heads off seeing that. But to me, the poor sap that it's all being done to, to me, it's not funny! I mean, I'm naked and have been for hours. Alright, I had my socks on for a while so I wasn't totally naked, but now I am! My feet are now bare and courtesy of Ronald's sock hungry shoe shine machine no less, leaving my poor feet exposed directly to those infernal spinning bristles down in the fiendish device.

"S-so much for shining up my stinky socks huh?" I managed to garble. "HA, ha, ha, ha, ha, ha, ha, ha, ha, ha, ha, ha, ha, ha, ha, ha, ha, ha, ha, ha!"

"Yeah, I suppose so Timmy my boy," Ronald replied and grabbed my upper arms real tight, right above where the rope was lashed tight over and under my huge biceps.

The bastard hoisted me up a bit in the chair so that my dangling balls swung back and forth a few times and the rope over my upper torso rubbed against my very sensitized nipples. Oh fucking fucks, but Ronald knew how to play me. He really knew how to play me like I was his musical instrument that needed fine tuning. My naked feet now felt like they had thousands upon thousands of feathers brushing every square inch of the skin on them. Fuck, another monstrous way to describe it was that it felt like thousands of ants crawling all around and over my feet from my heels and ankles all the way to my ticklish toes, which, by the way were wiggling like they had never wiggled before. Not that I could see them at that moment being that they were locked in the annals of the machine, but I sure could feel the involuntarily wiggling they were doing down in there as the bristles kissed them all over and in between each toe as well.

"OHHHHHHHHHH, ha, ha, ha, ha, ha, ha, ha, ha, ha, ha, ha, ha, ha, RON-RONALD, let go of me man, and turn, ha, ha, ha, ha, ha, ha, ha, ha, ha, ha, ha, ha, ha, turn off this FUCKING machine!" I screamed through uncontrollable fits of laughter as my so called buddy adjusted me in the chair.

My poor heavy hanging balls swung back and forth in the chair hole. Up till then I had not had the time to wonder about that hole in the chair and Ronald had not offered any kind of explanation. I had been too busy being teased and tormented about the shoe shine device to really give any rational thought as to why my nuts were dangling the way that they were. But then, to my horror of horrors I soon found out buds. I looked up at the ceiling at one point and threw my head back. Screaming loud laughter escaped me, along with frothy spittle as it spewed from my mouth. As I looked upward I did not see Ronald as he squatted beside my chair and reached under it... I was still babbling, begging to be released as Ronald did his dirty work. As I looked back down again slowly I saw Ronald squatted at the side of my chair and reaching under it. I didn't have an iota of a clue as to what the fucking fuck he was up to and to be perfectly honest I really didn't give a rat's ass. My concern was for my being tickle tortured now naked feet and how much more I would be forced to endure. But then, all of a fucking sudden I felt something new, almost like I had just sat on a goddamned branding iron or something. MY BALLS! Oh Gods, now my balls were somehow being tickled...

"EEEEEEEEEEYYYYOOWWWWWWWWWW!" I howled. "HA, ha, ha, ha, ha, ha, ha, ha, ha, ha, ha, ha, ha, ha, ha, ha, ha, ha, ha, ha, ha! Ronald, RONALD, what, what, ha, ha, ha, ha, ha, ha, ha, ha, ha, what the fuck are you doing to me now man?"

There was most definitely something down there working my balls buds. Ronald laughed at me some more, God that hurt let me tell you, to see my buddy laughing at my torments like that, and I cranked myself over as far as the ropes would let me and I could just make out what was under my chair. It was an electric motor of some kind with a very fast spinning pole sticking straight out from the center of it. And at the top of that pole were feathers, *feathers!* They were spinning too fast for me to count them but to my tortured mind it looked like a hundred, but fucking fucks, it felt like five hundred. Those feathers spun and whipped against my cum engorged balls and it looked as if my poor balls were actually jumping in their sac like Mexican fucking jumping beans. My ball sac bubbled up in goose flesh; it drew up as tight as it could with big sexy bumps on it where the hair follicles were. But alas, they could not draw themselves away from those spinning, whipping and tickling feathers. This was an all new torment, and although it was not being touched, my cock was simply pumping in the air, trying desperately to find some relief. And it kept on leaking pre-seed buds, in what seemed like buckets. I was being tickled to death at my feet and at the same time I was being sexually stimulated beyond belief with no relief. Gawd, but Ronald had an evil mind. I looked at him through the huge laugh caused tears in my eyes and as I laughed myself silly he simply grinned at me, as if I were enjoying his twisted and sick invention...

After a long while later I realized that I was still laughing and laughing, even though the shoe shining machine and the feather pole had both been turned off. I had lost track of time and my sense it seemed and my cock was incurably hard, begging, pleading for relief by then. When I realized that the machines had been turned off I felt really stupid because I was still laughing. I managed to stop laughing and took a few even breaths. After I was again able to breathe somewhat normally I looked up at my so called buddy through hazy vision…

"Th-thank you man, oh God, thank you, ha, ha, ha, ha, ha, ha, ha, ha, ha, ha, ha, ha," I said, a few laughs still escaping from me. "Oh for the love of God and his angels you tickled my balls…"

"Uh yeah and now come on Laddy, even you have to admit that that was funny," Ronald said and again squatted down next to the shoe shining machine.

"Yeah, a real barrel of laughs, hardy fucking har, but I'm the poor fuck in the barrel Ronald," I replied miserably as Ronald opened the hatch of the shoe shining machine.

Before he could grab my feet to extract them from the machine I myself pulled them out on my own accord, not that I would be able to escape from Ronald, seeing as I was tied to the chair, but for whatever the reason it gave me a small sense of freedom to remove my own feet from the clutches of that infernal device. I saw that my feet were all red and shiny looking all over…

"Oh God," I whispered.

Chuckling sadistically Ronald reached into the shoe shine device and then he was holding up my black silk socks. They were all mangled, twisted and moist looking, but still intact. The machine hadn't ripped them at all. I watched and my cock twitched as Ronald held my stinking socks to his nose and mouth and said "Whew, your feet really are all sweaty and randy buddy…"

"So tell me, do you want your socks back on your feet for the next tickle device buddy?" Ronald then asked me and my heart sank like the Titanic at just the very thought of yet another tickle device of torture…

"Man that sure was something though huh?" Ronald asked me, still laughing at me. "The way that machine ate your socks right off your feet buddy? As you would say, fucking fucks, I didn't expect that to happen."

"FUCKER, fucking fucks is right Ronald!" I suddenly thundered, having lost most of my patience I would think by then. "I didn't expect any of this to happen tonight! What the fucking fucks is this after all? A guy wakes up to take a leak during the night and winds up kidnapped and tickle tortured?"

As I ranted madly, letting off all my steam Ronald rolled my socks back onto my feet and grabbed them at the calves.

"R-RONALD, what are you doing man?" I screeched at him. "Look, I'm sorry I yelled okay? Just don't, don't…"

"Timmy, Laddy, it was so damned funny the way that machine ate your socks off your feet that I thought we would give it another good go," Ronald said and began sliding my poor, again socked feet into the wide open holes of the shoe shining device.

"OH GOD NO RONALD, NOT AGAIN, please!" I squealed and then my buddy closed the hatch, locking my feet in again. "FUCKER!"

Ronald wasted no time this time. He turned the machine on for the second go round and once again my socked feet were being brutally tickle tortured. Ronald laughed meanly at my plight, watching as my socks were again eaten from my being tickled feet. And just for the hell of it all he switched on the motorized pole under my chair as well. You remember that pole right buds? The one with the feathers at the top of it, yeah, I know you remember that. As my feet were tickled in the shoe shine device for the second time and as my socks were slowly eaten from my feet by said device my balls were again tickle tortured relentlessly again as well.

"HA, HA, HA, HA, HA, HA, HA, HA, HA, HA, HA, HA, HA, HA, HA, HA, HA, AAHHHHHRRRRR!" I screamed my laughter again. "LOOKIT that shit man, my socks are disappearing again! And what a fucking good host you are Ron-Ronald, ha, ha, ha, ha, ha, ha, ha, ha, ha, to make sure that my sweaty balls don't miss out on the fun too!"

I chortled and choked and laughed as I spoke…

"You are going to be amazed at what the next device does buddy boy," Ronald whispered in my ear as I laughed and laughed…and laughed and laughed… and laughed…and laughed…

A good half hour or so later, by my best calculations that is, Ronald was leading me blindfolded and with my hands tied behind me out of the room with the shoe shining device in it. My feet were still bare and I felt that I was being escorted down a rugged hallway. My chock filled balls were aching profusely and my cock stuck out long and hard as a flagpole. In the next room Ronald stood me in front of his next tickle torture device and proceeded then to take the blindfold off me. Staring straight ahead I gulped hard in terror anew.

"Hey buddy, at least with this device you just might get to relieve that pesky hard-on you've got," Ronald teased me.

"Holy fucking fuck," I whispered as I took in the sight of the awesome and monstrous device in front of me.

As I looked at it, drank in the sight of it, I had to really wonder about the mind of the man who had invented it. Fuck, I never really knew Ronald at all it would seem, not from what I was seeing and what I was experiencing. Ronald took my by my upper arms and walked me over to his newest creation that he was showing me, and soon I would be experiencing it that was for sure. My heart thundered and my hard cock dripped oodles of pre-seed…

"H-how can I go on?" I whispered as I looked at the awful device in the room that Ronald had just brought me into.

My eyes were still adjusting back to the light as well since he had taken the blindfold off me. This third contraption of Ronald's was very ugly looking I had to say, at least from my perspective it was, since I was the one who wound up on these torturous devices of his.

"Oh don't worry yourself or fret all that much over that issue buddy boy," Ronald said to me. "I won't let anything bad happen to you, you'll go on. You'll go on just fine. Here, take a sip…"

Ronald held a bottle of cool mineral water to my lips and I without hesitation sipped it down vigorously. The water was refreshing and cold and soothed my sweaty naked body.

"Th-thanks man," I said sheepishly and I felt my hard cock twitch between my legs as I stood with my hands tied behind me next to my so called buddy. "I –I really needed that… I am so fucking exhausted from all the tickling that I can't believe I'm even standing here."

"See? I told you I would take care of you man, like I said, you'll go on just fine," Ronald said and again held the bottle of water to my trembling lips, offering me more.

"Th-thanks man," I said and wrapped my lips around the tip of the bottle.

I drank some more water, drinking real deeply this time. Actually, I drained the bottle and then I felt more than my cock twitch. I felt my balls churn unnaturally in their sac and then my cock oozed a massive droplet of pre-seed that landed on the floor with a plopping sound.

"R-Ronald, wh-what the fucking fuck?" I asked him breathlessly. "I-I feel so damned sleazy all of a sudden man...Naw, fuck that, I feel real horned and real sexy here!"

"Well, that same aphrodisiac that I laced the chloroform with was in the water buddy boy," Ronald informed me and my mouth dropped open in total shock. "But I honestly think that it will be much more effective through being swallowed with the water rather than it was via the chloroform. Although, I do plan to continue using the chloroform on you when it's needed bud..."

Holy totally fucks I thought, the curious feeling in my cock and balls starting to feel overpowering then, like as if I could possibly fuck three to four different women one after the other at that very moment. Ronald had fed me his potion and in doing so he had tricked me into teasing *myself* up to a rage hard-on. I felt as if my cock would never go soft. Ronald had teased and tickled me into a sexual frenzy. My balls were swollen with globs and gobs of my milky scum that my body has ginned up because of the teasing at my man nips, my cock and balls, my feet and all the other tender parts of me that had received the treatment from Ronald's devices. Teasing, tickling, teasing, but no fucking relief for yours truly here. My cock seemed to be permanently hard now. What a fucking fucked up predicament for a guy huh? My meat pole just constantly stood out at attention, looking for attention, begging for attention, sticking out from my body. So, I was already very sensitive in my crotch area, I didn't need any help promoting that huh? But, this new feeling, this sensation of sleaziness seemed to be coming from deep inside me, that's the only way I can describe it buds. Nothing was touching my cock or balls, yet they were reacting as if they were being stimulated by some hidden force. My balls tingled and boiled in their sexy sac and my cock tingled as well, lurched a bit and ejected more pre-seed that dripped down from its tip. As I stood there my cock pulsed and more and more sexy pre-seed drooled out of my piss slit, what a sight that was! When my pre-milk plopped to the floor I somehow found that to be so danged sexy. And then my cock and balls felt like raw sex nerves. GOD almighty, they really needed to be touched, caressed, squeezed, rubbed, ANYTHING! Any fucking thing that would cause an orgasm or two, or three, hardy har, har! Again, I was not even being touched yet I was tottering on a sexual precipice and very soon I would fall if relief didn't find me in some form or another.

"Wh-what the fucks are you doing to me here man?" I asked incredulously, my blood engorged cock waving out in front of my well shaped, well curved hips, me flinching like I was trying to fuck the air in front of me, but I received no response because it was at that moment that before I knew what was about to transpire that Ronald stepped behind me and slammed the chloroform soaked cloth over my nose and mouth...again.

"Nap time bud..." I heard Ronald laugh as I struggled fruitlessly.

"RRRRRRRHHHMMMFFFFFFF...RO!" I reeled angrily and fell into a sleepy and dopey stupor.

Chapter Eight

When I came to I found that I had been strapped up (down?) to Ronald's latest device of tickle torture. Gawd, it was starting to feel like this was going to be the longest night of my life. I found myself lying with my arms at my sides and securely strapped down to a dangling in the air sheet of heavy duty plastic, fiberglass of some kind I suppose you can call what I was lying on. The sheet was suspended up off the floor by heavy duty cables at each of the four corners of the thing. I was on my stomach, strapped down good and fucking tight. I quickly saw that there were two holes in the sheet of fiberglass that I was on, one large hole for my muscular well shaped pecs and nipples to fit through, and man, the way my pecs were stretched and wedged into that hole it sure made my big man sized nips jut out and feel real super duper sensitive under me. The other hole was what a lot of gay guys out there would call a glory hole. It was the kind of hole of sorts where your cock and balls dangle through, and buds, that's just what the fuck my cock and balls were doing, dangling down out of a glory hole! My feet were pulled up behind me, the bottoms of them pointing at the ceiling and they were lashed at the ankles, the rope extending upwards and tied off to a beam above me.

"R-Ronald, you son of a bitch," I reeled through clenched teeth. "You knocked me out again!"

I felt like I was coming to for the fucking umpteenth time that night since being captured and shanghaied into this most awful of predicaments. But then, thoughts of my moments of stolen consciousnesses were cut short as I realized where I was. I slowly took in the sight of myself hooked up to that device that had first taken my breath away in horror when I saw it earlier.

"OH GOOD GOD, no!" I bellowed in terror.

Underneath the fiberglass sheet that I was strapped down to was a large motorized tickle device, actually it could very well have been the big brother of the one that had been under the chair I was tied to earlier and had the pole with the feathers on it. This device however had two poles extending from it. Each of those poles had pointy feathers at the end of them and those goddamned feathers were pointed straight up and aimed at my exposed and very accessible man tits. GODDDDDDD!

Over my poor bound up feet were a similar device set up on a nearby shelf, the pole with the feathers on that one stretched out to my feet and those feathers aimed directly at the bottoms of my bare feet, my bare feet a ready yet unwilling tickle target. And, horror of all horrors buds, under my cock and balls was a suction device in a latex sheath... Looking through the fiberglass sheet I was on I can honestly say that that sheath looked hungry, and boy howdy was my meat stick the food it would feed on. HAR HAR and double fucking HAR!

"This, my good buddy has to be my most fiendish creation yet," I heard Ronald saying from below me, his words suddenly cutting off my thoughts as I took in the sight of his latest device and where I was.

I lifted my head and looked down at Ronald, him standing at a control panel of sorts, looking like a mad scientist of some kind. The control panel appeared to be adorned with numerous buttons and dials. It looked like something directly out of a science fiction novel.

"R-Ronald, get me down from here, OH GOD, look at me man, tied up like a goddamned Thanksgiving turkey," I shouted. "I feel like the virgin sacrifice on an altar!"

On the control panel, to my utter humiliation I saw that Ronald had my boxer shorts and black socks, giving me the feeling that he more than likely planned to use them again at some point.

"I must say, that's a very creative way of describing how I tethered you to that device buddy," Ronald called up to me. "Although if I had my way there wouldn't be any need to tie you to these things. If I had my way you would have willingly submitted to these inventions of mine and we could have dispensed with all the restraints on you…"

"Never mind all that! That's baloney! I would never submit to shit like this!" I shrieked angrily down at my so called bud.

"Just a thought man, hence the need to bind you up tight," Ronald said. "Now, I think we'll begin with those luscious man nips of yours buddy. Now watch very closely through the plastic."

Ronald pressed a button on the control panel.

"OH NO OH NO!" I roared as the motorized device under my nipples came to spinning life and the feathers started spinning against my poor nubs. "HA, ha, ha, ha, ha, ha, ha, ha, ha, ha, ha, ha, ha, ha, ha, ha, ha, ha, ha, ha, ha! AND oh fuck, here I go again to Laugh City!"

"How's the air up there Timmy me Laddy?" Ronald laughed and pressed another button.

The device over my bare feet came to life and feathers upon feathers spun against the very sensitive bottoms of my very on display feet.

"OOOOOOOOOHHH FUCKER," I whined miserably. "HA, ha, ha, ha, ha, ha, ha, ha, ha, ha, ha, ha, ha, ha, ha, ha, ha, ha, ha, ha, ha, ha, ha!"

Then, looking down through the fiberglass I was lying on I gulped hard in terror between laughing when I saw the latex sheath under my crotch area open like a mouth and it began moving upwards. Fucking fuck, that thing was hell-bent on devouring my cock and drinking the man made milkshake that I had cooked up in my balls…

"Timmy, you really want to cum don't you?" Ronald catcalled up to me, sounding totally mean as he said it.

I mean, how many guys out there have a buddy who asks them if they want to cum? But given the circumstances and what I was being put through it seemed only fitting that Ronald should be asking me that, seeing as it was him who had gotten me all worked up into this state to begin with!

"Y-yes, GAWD, yes, what a dumb fucking question, ha, ha, ha, ha, ha, ha, ha, ha, ha, ha, ha, y-you've teased me to the point that I feel like I'm going crazy Ronald!" I laughed down at him. "HA, ha, ha, ha, ha, ha, ha, ha, ha, ha, ha, oh GOD RONALD, that thing, its getting closer to my cock, get me down from here buddy!"

Suddenly, the latex sheath stopped its movement. I darted my eyes to Ronald and saw that he had a hand on a dial on his control panel.

"Almost buddy, almost," he said to me, grinning and holding up a finger. "Now, you're not going to get down from there just yet, you see, you have some more laughing to do for me up there…"

"Ha, ha, ha, ha, ha, ha, ha, ha, ha, ha, ha, which I hope you note that I am doing very well," I cackled down at him.

"Yes, yes you are Timmy, good laddy, you certainly are," Ronald chuckled. "Now, as I just said, you're not getting down from there just yet, but, if you want Timmy, *if you want,* I will get you off."

As Ronald said that he smiled a totally wicked and evil smile…

I looked down at him and in between laughter looked at him with both horror and disgust. But fucking fucks, no man had ever gotten me so sexed up. No man had ever touched my cock or balls, no man had ever gone into that territory.

"Oh God Ronald, I need to cum, I have to got to cum!" I called out to him, not believing the words myself that were spewing from my mouth. "Please jack me off huh buddy? Huh Laddy? Ha, ha, ha, ha, ha, ha, ha, ha, ha, ha, ha, ha, ha, ha, ha, ha, ha, ha, ha, ha!"

I was laughing, screaming and pleading to my chuckle buddy as he stood there looking up at my naked and tease/tickled body…

Smiling and in a condescending voice Ronald said quite sternly, "Timmy, you are aware that once a man has an orgasm, once a man spews his seed, that he then becomes extremely sensitive to say, tickling. That is actually to say that someone like you who is already very extremely ticklish, your ticklishness would fly off the charts, if you cum that is. Trust me on this buddy, you have never felt tickling like you'll feel if you cum…"

As Ronald spoke I listened in horror and laughed and laughed…

"Now, it's your call buddy boy, do you still want me to bring you off?" Ronald chuckled as he saw the panicked look of confusion on my face.

I needed to cum so badly it was *unbelievable,* but the thought of being made even more ticklish than I already was, oh Good God, that was maddening. I could not even think about that buds! I already couldn't stand the tickling that Ronald had put me through and I could not imagine it being worse than it already was. What in heaven's name would more intense be like? But then, looking up at me with a severe look on his face Ronald turned the dials and switches on the control panel to the "Off" positions. Then, the latex sheath started coming to life again, slowly moving upwards toward my hanging cock and balls. Oh God, I wasn't being tickled now *but* I was about to be jacked off by my buddy Ronald… And if that happened then I would be even more tickle sensitive than I already was! Horny as I was feeling *I could not* be made to cum now, OH NO, decisions, decisions!

"NO! NO! I changed my mind Ronald!" I called out loudly, humiliation having set in real big at that moment, thinking how I could not be jacked off by a guy who was my buddy. "I'll uh; I'll just jack off later sometime, when I get home that is, yeah, that's it, when I get home! I don't want you to make me cum Ronald, no need to trouble yourself bud!"

But as I spoke stupidly, prattling on and on to Ronald's unhearing ears the latex sheath seemed to yawn, open wider and made its way upwards some more toward my very vulnerable hard cock.

"RONALD, what are you doing man?" I squawked as he raised the latex sheath up to the very tip of my leaking cock head. "STOP THAT! I said I don't want to cum, leave me alone man, *oh please bud, leave me the fuck alone!"*

Looking down through the fiberglass I watched as a huge glob of some clear lubricant of some kind was siphoned into the sheath from under it. No doubt Ronald had a control on his panel of buttons and dials that caused that. The sheath was now slicked all around and well lubed.

"Now Timmy me laddy, lets see just who wins out here in this little upcoming contest of ours shall we?" Ronald said to me. "My suction device or your willpower not to cum so you won't be even more extremely ticklish than you already is."

That said Ronald grinned from ear to ear, reached forward, pressed a button on his control panel and I heard the pumping suction sounds emanating from the latex sheath.

"RONALD, no, no," I pleaded.

He turned a dial and the sheath raised upwards some more to finally meet the end of my cock and a seal was made, (GULP! ULP!) The sheath actually grabbed my cock head in a greedy and hungered fashion. It pumped up and down a bit and all around my poor cock and it literally gobbled up more and more of my meat pole, sucking it up and deeply into its soft pliable surfaces.

"OOOOOOHHHHHHHHH!" I gasped, my head raised up off the fiberglass sheet, a look of total disbelief mixed with ecstasy on my face. "OOOOOOOOHHHHHHH!"

It slipped and slid because of the lubricant it was coated with, yet it held good and tight to my hardness, just like a young girl out on her first date with the guy she's had a crush on for the last year or so. The inside of the sheath seemed to be heated, GAWD, it felt like I was being given an artificial blowjob.

"OH GAWD, NO RONALD, you can't do this to me, s-stop this thing!" I crowed. "IT, it's sucking on my cock, it's nursing on me man! OH GAWD, it's sucking me deeper and deeper! AAAAAGGGHHHH, ohhhhhhhh shhhhiiittt RONALD, it, it's sucking my cock!"

I had to do something. I could not cum. I could not give my buddy the satisfaction! And to top it all off I could not cum and make myself even more ticklish, God knew I was ticklish enough already buds! I had to stop Ronald now, show him that he could not win this round in this contest of wits that he had shanghaied me into. Besides having to shoot my load I had to piss too. Yeah, that was it buds, I had to piss. Pissing would make my cock go soft too. Let's recall for a moment that it was a much needed piss that started this entire drama that night. I clenched my teeth and concentrated as hard as possible, very pleased with myself for having come up with such a good solution to such an improbable dilemma. I let the piss rip and oh man, it felt so good to let the hot frothy yellow liquid spew from my cock. I looked down at Ronald with total confidence, thinking that I had won, I had succeeded. My cock was actually getting softer, but GAWD, not enough to be released by the sucking and suckling sleeve tethered to it. I hardy har harred and looked at the yellow stream of liquid flowing down and into the clear tube at the end of the latex sheath that seemed to be so in love with my goddamned manhood. My piss landed in a clear plastic container at the end of the tube and then I heard Ronald chuckling as he looked up at me.

"Timmy, please, go right ahead and relieve yourself," he said to me. "It saves me the trouble of having to bring you to the bathroom. "For as soon as your bladder is empty my little latex device here will suck you back to full tilt. So, you can look at this as just a little reprieve okay? As a matter of fact, I think you're done pissing, ha, ha. Now pump baby, pump it up!"

My confidence melted away as I realized that Ronald was one hundred percent exactly right. My pissing was done but my cock was still in the suckling sheath and that goddamned sheath was sucking my cock and my cock was plumping up again inside it. *Ronald was right buds*; the sheath was going to suck me back up to full tilt. FUCKING fucks, it was sucking and sucking my cock even more potently now.

"FUCK, this thing is sucking my cock again Ronald!" I cried.

But I was going to fight it. I would not give in. But let me tell you, tickled to the point of insanity and all doped up with an aphrodisiac of some kind not giving in was most definitely easier said than done. I tensed every muscle in my tied up muscular body. I was actually fighting it, determined not to give in to the sucking machine. I don't know for sure just how long this went on but I do know that I had created some kind of stalemate, amazingly…

But again Ronald looked up at me and chuckled…

"Good try Timmy my laddy, I have to give it to you bud, after all you've been through not many men would be able to hold out this long," he said mockingly. "So you can be proud of yourself, but now lets get this over-with shall we?"

That said I watched with dread as Ronald stepped from behind his control panel to stand under my dangling balls. My look of dread turned to total terror as my cock was being sucked deeper yet into the latex sheath, pulsing and pulsing in there, and I saw Ronald's grinning face leering up at me, but it was what he was holding in hand that had really caused that look of utter terror to be etched on my face. In his hand Ronald held up a stiff goose feather. He twirled it in his fingers before reaching further up to apply the tip of it to my ball sac. Oh horror of all horrors I thought as he pressed the feather tip against my sac and twirled it around and around my most private of areas. It tickled, yes, but more than that it distracted me from my mission of not letting that blasted horned up sheath suck me off. I chuckled once, twice and on the third chuckle the orgasm that had been pent-up in my balls was unleashed. Cum as thick as molasses started gushing from my cock slit. I felt as if my entire body was being sucked out and pumped and siphoned through my balls right through my cock and out the end. My eyes actually rolled back in my head. FUCKING TOTALLY FUCKS, this was the most intense orgasm I had ever experienced, and for a guy of thirty something years old that's really saying something.

"AAAAAAAAAAAAAHHHGGGGGGGGGG!" I screamed as my balls continued to pump my very being out of my cock.

After what seemed like minutes upon minutes of continual and forced ecstasy it was over and my body went limp. If left alone I would more than likely sleep for a week, given all I had been put through after all. But I was not left alone. In my ecstasy induced stupor I heard Ronald say, "And now for the tickling of your life." I saw through hazy vision Ronald step back over to the control panel and then I heard more than felt it, the whirring sounds of the feathers on their poles coming back to life. The latex sheath slid off my cock. It actually looked spent, hardy fucking har! It looked like I had given it a good run for its money. My mess of thick soupy sperm was in the plastic container at the end of the tube attached to the sheath, along with my piss, what a sight that was! But now, back to more important issues, because the spinning feathers attacked my exposed nipples and my now freed cock and hanging balls, plus my naked feet sticking up in the air. Oh yes, I started laughing and I remember thinking and screaming, this is worse…

"OHHHHHH FUCK, THIS IS WORSE! HA, ha, ha, ha, ha, ha, ha, ha, ha, ha, ha, ha, ha, ha, ha, ha, ha, ha, ha, ha, ha, ha, ha! EEEEEEEEEEEEEEEEEEEEEEEEEE

E!" I reeled. "RONALD, you fucking fucked up fucker! THIS IS WORSE!"

Oh God, I did get off, woe is me, woe is fucking me…

Ronald's Journal
Entry from the beginning of January, 1994…

I finally landed a new job. Since being laid off from that brokerage firm nearly eight months ago I finally found a new job. And since being laid off I haven't really made any journal entries, I suppose I was feeling depressed from what had transpired. I really had high hopes of making it big in that firm, but fate seemed to have other plans for me. But now that things seem to be going my way again I'll make sure to keep my journal updated. Who knows, it might come in handy someday. I can't help remembering my creative writing teacher all the way back in high school, Dr. Fenner. He always said how everyone should write down their thoughts, *everyday*. Well, now that I'm employed again and things are looking up for me I'll try to make sure and adhere to that line of thinking. A new job, new dreams, new hopes for making it big in a corporate company, and to make it even more worth my while I'll be earning nearly five thousand dollars more than what I was getting at the dinky brokerage firm right at the start. And then if I prove myself within six months time I'll get an early review and a raise based on my performance from my past experience. Yes, it looks like I'll have lots of good stuff to write about in this journal. At twenty-seven years old landing a job like this one isn't all that bad I must say. My new job is with Chase Bank, and at a branch right in the heart of the Wall Street area of Manhattan. I'm starting to realize how even the location of my new job was worth being laid off from the brokerage firm for. My commute time has been nearly cut in half and if things keep going the way they're going at present time I'll be able to afford a place in Manhattan soon as well. And then so much for commuting on the trains, I'll have a company car take me to and from work at that point! It looks like I, Ronald Greene, am finally going to get the recognition I deserve. Those years spent in college and business school are finally going to pay off for me. I'll be working as the assistant manager of two departments, both Credit and Loans. (I still haven't cast aside my dreams of possibly inventing some kind of gizmo that could revolutionize mankind. I only wish that my parent's had seen fit to send me to some kind of trade school as well. I seem to have a really wild talent for coming up with ideas for inventions, machines of sorts. Perhaps while working at the bank I'll earn enough money (and meet enough well off women) to find a place where I can actually put that talent to use as well.) My start date at Chase Bank is a week from now so that gives me some time to do some clothes shopping, seeing as I'll need to wear a suit and tie everyday for this job, not like it was at the brokerage firm where a pair of slacks or khakis and a shirt and tie sufficed. I think I'll treat myself from top to bottom, from some new suits, ties, shirts, shoes, all the way down to some new socks, *God knows a guy always needs socks*…

Chapter Nine

"HAHAHAHAHAHAHAHAHAHAHAHAHAHAHAHAHA OHHHHH MY GAWD!" OH MY FUCKING GAWD!" was the shrill and nearly ear piercing sound coming out of my mouth now as Ronald worked the controls of the latest device that he had me tethered to, him looking like a mad scientist at the control panel.

I squirmed miserably and helplessly under the binding straps as the feathers attached to the highly spinning rods worked and tortured my nipples, my cock and balls and the bottoms of my raised up feet.

"HAHAHAHAHAHAHAHAHAHAHAHAHAHAHAHAHAHAHAHA!" I laughed, screaming my insane laughter at that point.

"I warned you Timmy, I told you man, I told you that if you shot your load you would become even more intensely tickle sensitive, now look at you up there my laddy, laughing louder than a hyena," Ronald said to me as he upped the speed on the devices tickling my jutted up nipples.

"I-I-I couldn't help, ha, ha, ha, ha, ha, ha, ha, ha, ha, ha, ha, ha, ha, ha, ha, ha, I couldn't help it man, th-that perverted sheath on your monstrosity sucked me off like an overly horned whore on a Saturday night, ha, ha, ha, ha, ha, ha, ha, ha, ha, ha, ha, ha, ha, and not to mention that goddamned goose feather you used on my poor nuts to help me along, very thoughtful of you I must say!" I jibber jabbered. "HA, HA, HA, HA, HA, HA, HA, HA, HA, HA, HA, HA, HA! Gods, my man tits, my fucking, fucking man tits, they're buzzin' like bees Ronald, ha, ha, ha, ha, ha, ha, ha, ha, ha, ha, ha, ha, ha, ha, oh GOD MAN, you got my man tits buzzing Ronald!"

I wiggled my toes uncontrollably as the devices at my raised feet spun at what felt like a hundred miles per hour...

"Ronald, I will make sure you pay for this, ha, ha, ha, ha, ha, ha, ha, ha, ha, ha, ha, ha, ha, ha!" I shrieked, trying to sound as threatening as possible.

"Pay for it? Pay for it Timmy?" Ronald asked me, sounding incredulous. "Buddy boy, by snagging you the way I did I'm getting it all for free..."

I was sweating like a stuck pig as I lay stretched out on that sheet of fiberglass. Then, looking down at Ronald, my so called buddy, my good friend, my goddamned captor, I screamed a question at him that felt needed to be answered and answered right away, "How, just how long do you plan on keeping me here man? HA, ha, ha, ha, ha, ha, ha, ha, ha, ha, ha, ha, ha, ha, ha, ha, ha, ha, ha, ha, ha! I'm a fucking married guy with a kid you know...ha, ha, ha, ha, ha, ha, ha, ha, ha, ha, ha, ha, ha, ha, ha!"

"Of course I know that buddy, I was there with you in the hospital waiting room the night Tim Junior was born," Ronald said.

As I was tickled more and more Ronald pulled a lever next to the control panel and the sheet of fiberglass that I was on was slowly lowered toward the floor... And then, finally, Ronald started turning all the dials on his latest torture device to the "OFF" positions. I breathed heavily, catching my breath by gasping, my laughter subsiding as I lay there trying to breathe somewhat normally again... It was a strange feeling to say it bluntly, not being able to stop laughing even though I was no longer being tickled, at least not at that moment.

"And besides having been there the night your son was born how can I forget all the times I've been to your house for dinner?" Ronald pointed out to me. "I'll tell you what, after we're done here you and I will go out for dinner, just us, we'll leave your wife and son at home, I won't bring one of my usual female conquests and we'll make it just a night out for you and me. And we'll talk about what a great time all this has been…so far buddy boy, so far…"

From what he was telling me it was answering my question, the fucking guy didn't know how long he planned to hold onto me, oh Good God!

"GREAT TIME?" I reeled as the feathers retreated from my overly sensitized tickled parts, my spent cock and balls feeling totally numb and yet somehow I was semi hard, more than likely that fucking aphrodisiac was still wreaking havoc on me, even after I had shot that huge pent-up load of slimy ball juice. "GREAT TIME for who man? For you maybe, lets remember that I'm the poor sap of a guy that got his ass kidnapped out of his bathroom when he went to take his nightly piss, and is now being tormented and tickle tortured here…and what is this "So Far" shit? Again, just how long do you plan on keeping me here Ronald?"

As I ranted and raved in anger the fiberglass sheet that I was on lowered to Ronald's standing level.

"Feeling hungry buddy?" he asked me.

"Fuck, fuck, you aren't listening to me man, but yeah, I suppose so, I suppose I'm hungry, what with all that laughing I've been doing I've sure worked up an appetite I guess," I replied. "But man, I'm afraid to eat, if you feed me and then tickle torture me like that again, and I know you are planning to, I'm liable to hurl…"

"Hmmm, you do have a point there buddy boy," Ronald said, pursing his lips as if he were in deep thought, actually it looked like he was trying to solve the world's greatest mystery. "But all the same I can't have you starving on me now… You need your energy after all, you do have more tickling to endure and… I know, *I know*, we'll do one more tickle device and after that we'll have some food for breakfast. Man, wait till you see the eating area I had constructed for this place. And then, after we eat I'll wait a couple of hours before I tickle you again, how does that sound bud?"

"HOW DOES IT SOUND? FUCK, it sounds lousy man!" I replied, looking at Ronald as he snickered meanly, spittle again flying from between my clenched teeth as I raved. "I can just imagine that you're going to keep me fucking tied up while we relax! Ronald, I don't want to be tied up! I don't want to be tickled again! I don't want to be here with you *buddy boy*! I want to go home! What I want is to be out of here and out of this insane situation you've thrown me so unwittingly into! Some fucked up excuse you are for a buddy I got to tell you Ronald…"

Ronald then undid the straps holding me to the fiberglass sheet. I saw an opportunity, and I am one never to pass up an opportunity! I made a move to bolt off the fiberglass sheet but Ronald quickly pressed the chloroform soaked cloth against my nose and mouth…

"RRRRMMMMMMM…" I snarled as my cock tingled.

When I came to a short while later I found myself lying on a thin wooden bench, my arms stretched out at my sides real taut and tied off at the wrists to posts that were on the sides of the bench that I was splayed out on. My feet were raised up off the bench; my legs spread out as wide as my arms were, and tied off at the ankles to two more posts on the sides of the bench.

"Wh-what the fucking fuck?" I mumbled as I awoke and looked around miserably. "GAWD, this time I'm tied up like a goddamned chicken… What the fuck am I in for now? Holy fuck! Look at me here, holy fucking fucks!"

To my horror I saw two of those dratted motorized devices with the cone shaped fuzzies on both sides of me, and (GULP) both of them were aiming their fuzzies at my hairy, sweaty and very, very exposed armpits. And oh God of gods, my balls were dangling over the bench, all sweaty and randy, hanging there like two kiwis in my sac, my semi hard cock pointing upwards. I squirmed in the unforgiving and stretching bondage. It seemed the more that I struggled the tighter the ropes became and the more I was stretched out…

"Now its time for the REAL buzzer Timmy my laddy," Ronald said and I looked up to find him standing over me.

"Th-the real buzzer?" I asked and screamed in a very high crescendo when I saw the dildo shaped vibrating butt plug that my so called buddy was holding. "OH GOD RONALD NO!"

"Note the tiny pin holes on this thing buddy," Ronald said as if he was demonstrating the damned thing and trying to make a sale with it. "Once it's wedged up in your rectum those pin holes will emit what will feel like thousands of tiny rolling tips, actually that is just what they are, massage tips…"

I looked up at Ronald in sheer and total terror, knowing how my poor asshole and sensitive armpits would suffer very soon…

"Now, let's get you moist and ready for entry huh bud?" Ronald asked me and squatted down between my stretched out legs, his face directly in front of my stinking bung hole…

I thought to myself how this would be the second time since being captured by Ronald that the guy would tickle my damned bung hole. I gritted my teeth as he spit into my shit chute. When he spit it into a second time I felt the walls of my anal canal seem to slurp up Ronald's warm saliva. I looked straight up at the ceiling miserably when he spit a good wad into my hole the third time…

So there I sat, stretched out like a chicken ready for the barbecue. When I really stopped and thought about it that's just what Ronald was doing to me in a way, barbecuing me via tickle torture. This was the absolute worst though, all of it, the very absolute worst. Ronald had teased and tickled me for hours at that point, how many hours I really had no idea. As I said I had lost track of the time. And all of it having been time spent trapped on Ronald's evil tickle torture devices. Then, when he finally got me strapped to that fiberglass sheet and attached that fucking sucking latex sheath to my cock I thought for sure I would go crazy. While Ronald was spitting in my hole, moistening me up like some cheap whore I thought about that sucking thing on Ronald's previous device and how I had shot the mother of all loads, how I had fed that sheath real well buds. But then the fucking guy drops the bomb, telling me how I would be many times more ticklish after cumming than I had been before it. So what do I do? With the need to cum so badly I try to hold back then and not cum, what a fucked up predicament for a guy let me tell you, the worst case of blue balls I had ever known! But I tried guys, as you all know I steeled myself against that impending orgasm and I fought like crazy as that infernal latex lubricated sheath ate my cock like crazy. And damn it I was winning. Since having been captured by Ronald I was winning one of his contests.

"Ohhhhhhhhh…" I moaned as he spit in my hole again and by then I was really sopped and warm back there, almost ready for the entrance of his dildo shaped vibrator.

Yeah, I was winning that contest, thinking I would not shoot my load for a guy! But then Ronald pulled that awful trick on me with the goose feather! First he shows it to me to get my attention as I was still fighting the overwhelming urge to blow my load into his latex sheath, fighting the urge and winning, or at least I thought I was winning buds. GAWD, he twirled that damned feather and that made me stupidly wonder what the fucking fuck he was going to do with it. Was I stupid? I knew exactly what the fucking fuck he was going to do with it. Just looking at him twirl that feather I think I slipped a bit, but man, I was still fighting that urge to cum, swearing inwardly how I would not, could not let a guy bring me off. But then, he did it, as you know, he twirled that damned feather against my dangling chock filled nut sac, all while the current instrument of his torture was sucking me off, that sheath was just pumping and pulling relentlessly on my poor sensitive tickled cock. I strained guys, I strained to hold back, I really did, but when Ronald twirled that feather on my gonads, around my gonads and literally strummed my balls like a guitar I simply lost control and burst into the most wonderful and agonizing orgasm I ever experienced. Now, as Ronald was spitting in my hole and moistening me up back there I felt my cock again rising to the occasion, going from semi hard to very hard. When he slid a finger halfway inside my shit chute and prodded around in my now wet crevice like it was a pussy my head spun. Thinking about that orgasm at the same time as my head spun, man it was agonizing because I really didn't have all that much time for afterglow and to really enjoy it all. Once I had cum Ronald just had to prove his point to me, of just how much more tickle sensitive I would become after having shot my load. So he started that infernal device back up again and began tickling me again and boy howdy and oh Gawd had he been right! I was so much more ticklish, it was awful. He could really hear my ear piercing screams and laughter now and he truly enjoyed my ticklish misery. And now, tied up on a bench so soon after that last tickle device, so soon after having been chloroformed again, having my hole spit in and prodded, yuck! And then to have the fucking guy who kidnapped me taunt me with family memories, the night of my son's birth of all things, to taunt me with food…GAWD! And now, back to the present tickle plight that I was about to endure, tied up and spread out on a thin wooden bench, spread out totally spread eagle, just spread for Ronald's perverse tickle pleasures. Again I was totally helpless and totally vulnerable to whatever the fuck he planned to do to me, and I was sure that it would be something that I would not much like but would bring him great pleasure.

"R-Ronald, what the fuck are you doing to me now man?" I garbled as he spit a few last times in my shit chute and used his finger to again spread his saliva around back there, deep inside me and all along the sugar walls of my most private crevice. "OHHHHRRRR Gawd, stop playing with my canal man! FUCKING FUCK, those are some of those motorized fuzzy cones like on the octopus right?"

"That is right my dear Timmy, very good observation me ticklish laddy, but, those are not the same ones," Ronald said to me laughingly, finally yanking his finger from my sopped up hole. "My little tickling fuzzies here are very similar to the ones you experienced on the octopus, a very good name you gave it I must say. Now, these are just for starters. As you can see I have them aimed at your ticklish armpits. But man, this buzzer is going to give you an entirely new experience.

"Ronald, GOD, no man," I whined desperately, looking up as he held the vibrating dildo device. "Ronald, please tell me you don't have any plans on putting that thing…that thing, up my butt, do you?"

"Why yes Timmy, you really are so very observant and smart I must say," Ronald mocked me. "This little vibrating item with all its stimulating rollers will simply tease and tickle you from the inside, while my fuzzies will tickle you from the outside. It is going to be soooo much fun to see you with this thing wedged tightly in your rectum…"

"NOOOOO, NO!" I screamed then as Ronald squatted at my hole and pressed that fucking (literally fucking) ass fucker up what used to be my virgin hole.

I don't know how Ronald kept dreaming this stuff up, I swear, but at that point I wished that his mind would just go blank.

"Please Ronald, please man, take that thing out of my, OOOOOPPPP, ass," I ranted through clenched teeth as the thing entered me inch by inch, sliding seductively against my moistened anal walls. "Damn, I think you bumped my Adam's apple. FUCK MAN, no! Haven't you done enough to me already? What a fucking way to get your pleasure, to make me suffer this way!"

"Done enough Timmy?" Ronald replied in answer to me. "Why, we're just getting started here buddy. I truly want you to experience everything that this amusement park of my creation consists of. We still have many more rooms to visit…"

I nodded my head in disbelief…

As Ronald pressed that dildo further up my ass my cock was now at full erection again.

"Fuck, fuck, fucking fuck! My cock is swelling up again man!" I pointed out to my buddy, although I was sure he was totally aware of that. "RONALD, damn man, you've got my cock swelling up again, fuck, I don't need this man! Come on, you've teased me enough here."

But Ronald simply smiled his maniacal grin at me, let go of the dildo that was now wedged deep inside me and pressed a button on the motorized device. The fuzzies came to life and started spinning in my armpits.

"OOOOOOOOPPP, ha, ha, ha, ha, ha, ha, ha, ha, ha, ha, ha, ha, ha, ha, ha, ha, ha! Y-you fucker, you, you've got me laughing again!" I screamed.

"And now my dear ticklish laddy, for the crème de la crème, tell me how you like this Timmy," Ronald said and flicked a switch on the vibrating butt plug as it stuck embarrassingly out of my hole.

"NOOOOOOOO, NO, RO-RONALD, EEEEEEEEEEEYYYYYYY!" was how I told him how I liked that thing in my hole. "HEE, HEE, HEE, HEE, HEE, HEE, HEE! OOOOOOOOOO, ha, ha, ha, ha, ha, ha, ha, ha, ha, ha, ha, ha!"

My cock jumped to a full erection by then and it was ready to play. Fuck, I was laughing and squirming and dying and my fucking cock was bouncing around looking for a playmate. GAWD, Ronald really knew how to push my buttons and drive me crazy it seemed. I was going to need a rubber room. I continued to scream and laugh as the spinning fuzzies did their dirty work to my ticklish exposed underarms. But now, with that damned vibrating butt plug that was tickling and teasing me from the inside (as Ronald had so aptly put it) against my prostate and all around the circumference of my asshole I was beyond screaming.

And so it went, as those fuzzies spun and gyrated against my hairy smelly armpits and as the vibrating butt plug (dildo) emitted little round spinning beads through tiny holes against my ass walls my mind whirled in a reverse orbit. I heard the sound of some poor guy's insane laughter and realized that it was my laughter that I was hearing.

"R-RONALD! HA, ha, ha, ha, ha, ha, ha, ha, ha, ha, ha, ha, ha, ha, ha, ha, ha!" I shrieked, my head raised and looking down at my hard cock as it bobbed long and hard and fat in the wind. "TH-THIS IS TOO much man, AAAAAAAHHHHHHH, ha, ha, ha, ha, ha, ha, ha, ha, ha, ha, ha, ha, ha, ha, ha, ha!"

"Oh Timmy, it's not too much, I have so much more to give!" Ronald said and grinned, chuckling at my fucked up predicament. "And now my buddy of buddies, now for some real fun, I have something more for you, more fun for...*us, ha, ha, ha and ha buddy...*"

That said Ronald pulled a thin feather out of his pocket and squatted down next to my groin.

"RO-RONALD! NO! NO MAN! AAAAAAAAAHHHHHH, ha, ha, ha, ha, ha, ha, ha, ha, ha, ha, ha, ha, ha, ha you wouldn't, ha, ha, ha, ha, ha, you wouldn't dare, ha, ha, ha, ha, ha, ha, ha, ha, you couldn't, ha, ha, ha, ha, ha, ha, ha, COULD YOU?" I laughed and cried and pleaded as I watched my monster of a buddy press the very tip of that feather into the piss slit of my shaft of steel. "AAAAAAAHHHHHHHHH!"

I squirmed in the awful stretched out position that I was tied in, my bound hands clenched into fists, my toes curling back involuntarily.

"Y-you son of a fucking bitch, ha, ha, ha, ha, ha, ha, ha, ha, ha, ha, ha, ha, ha, ha, ha, ha, y-you're tickling my piss hole man!" I roared through my laughter, sweating like mad now.

I felt the feather tip dip into my piss slit a bit further and it was prickly, OH GAWD, was it prickly! I squirmed some more, as much as I could, but Ronald had me securely tied, so securely tied that I could not move at all to escape the newest onslaught being heaped on me. I was able to throw my head around and flex my toes and fingers but that was about it and man, I was wiggling and jiggling those parts as much as possible. Beads of piss and pre-seed emanated out of my piss slit as Ronald meanly twirled the feather tip in there.

"Oh Timmy my boy, this is definitely going to be one for the history books," Ronald chuckled and grabbed my hard cock with one hand as he went on tickling my piss hole with his other hand.

"OHHHHRR, what the fucking fuck?" I grunted throatily as my buddy grabbed my cock.

Ronald's Journal
Entry Dated During the Second Week of January, 1994

What a way to start the New Year. I've been at the bank only three days now but I have to say I love the job. I have my own little office off to the side so I really don't have to hob knob all day with my staff, although for the most part they are a good group. Three guys and four women report to me. And to really put a feather in my cap I already have a date with a cute little number from the accounting department for Friday night after work. Her name is Lucy and she sure is a nice piece of ass. I'm also hoping that she has a nice chunk of change in her bank account, seeing as I'm the new guy just coming off lay off and still have to re-establish myself financially. It always amazes me how so many women are desperate to help a poor guy out when he's financially strapped. My direct manager is a vice president named Jim Stone, nice enough guy but he sure could stand to lose about fifty to eighty of those pounds of his. I work sort of directly with another assistant manager in my department named Timothy Backman, a lot of the people in the bank call him Tim, and I even noticed how some of the people address him as Timmy B. That's all fine and good for Timmy the handsome laddy as I've come to secretly call him, (he has a very boyish quality about him that I really can't put my finger on just yet, but when I met him the word laddy just popped into my mind) but for me there will be no nicknames or slang's where my name is concerned. I'm just Ronald, plain old fucking Ronald, and perhaps someday, Mr. Greene. But I have to say that Timothy, or whatever the fuck he wants to be called sure is a nice enough guy. It was him who introduced me to everyone in the department on my first day of work this week. It was him who took me to lunch on Monday and Tuesday, just to show me around the area and the best places to grab a quick but really good tasting lunch. It was him who helped me get my office set up as well, helping me to hang some pictures on my office walls that I had purchased before starting at the new job. I didn't bring any of the pictures I had from the brokerage firm to hang on these walls. I wanted an entirely new start. And as I said Timothy was even helpful in getting those pictures hung up. It was that event, him helping me to put up pictures that seemed to have really sparked something inside me, but like his boyish quality, it's something about Timothy that I can't seem to yet put my finger on. But he helped me to get pictures hung up in my private office, he happened to be in my office after getting some papers signed off on and he saw the frames leaning against a wall by my desk. I told him that I was going to take a couple of minutes to get them hung up, to liven up my office a bit. I pulled a chair near the wall where I wanted one of the pictures to be hung up; it was a landscape by Monet, just for the record. (I love artwork by Monet most of all it seems.) As I got my suit jacket off, prepared to climb up on the chair to drive the nail into the wall with a hammer Timothy quickly said, "Here, I'll do that, it's no problem at all." As I was about to thank him and tell him that it really was not necessary I watched as the guy leaned against my desk and unlaced his wingtip shoes before slipping them off his feet. I guessed his feet to be in the size ten and a half to eleven range. He added how he already had his suit jacket off, having left it in his office and his shirt sleeves were already rolled up as well, the mark of a true banker boy if ever there was one. He placed his wingtips beside my desk and climbed up on the chair that I had placed by the wall. For some strange reason that I can't define my heart was thundering in my chest. Timothy got himself balanced up on the chair in his navy blue nylon socked feet and held a hand open down near me. He told me to hand him the hammer and a nail. I thanked him again and handed him the items he had requested. As he leaned up a bit on his socked toes he said, "Hold onto the sides of my feet for me Ronald, I don't want to accidentally fall off this chair and ruin the new rug they put down in here after you were hired." We both laughed at his silly comment but I did as he asked and gripped his socked feet at the sides. His arches were very much curved and very deep for a guy I have to say. He then said, "Just hold my feet tight buddy, and don't move your hands over them whatever you do, my feet are really ticklish." My heart thundered even more-so in my chest for some reason. I squatted a bit and gripped Timothy's feet real tight at the sides, they felt real warm and moist, that warmness emanating through his thin socks to be precise. I have no idea why my heart was thundering in my chest the way it was or why my hands were suddenly a tad cold and shaking as I held onto the guy's feet. When he started hammering the nail into the wall my heart thundering matched each pound of the hammer as he swung it. I gently moved my thumbs to the bottoms of Timothy's feet. He didn't comment on it so perhaps he didn't notice my thumbs exploring the bottoms of his feet. The bottoms of them felt even warmer somehow. I felt a blockage of some kind at my throat. When he was done hammering the nail into the wall he told me to hand him the picture frame to be hung up. I let go of his feet for a moment, handed him the frame and again quickly grabbed his feet, keeping him carefully balanced on that chair as he leaned up to hang the picture. I noticed for some strange reason how Timothy's thin blue socks creased around his heels as he leaned up on the chair and hung the picture. "Okay, I think that'll do it Ronald," Timothy called down to me. Just let me know if it's straight." I told him that it looked fine and thanked him again for his help. He hopped down off the chair and as I put the chair back where it belonged at the side of my desk I stole glances at the laddy as he got his wingtips back onto his feet and quickly laced them up. He told me that when he had a minute again he would come back to help me hang up a couple more. Glancing up at the picture on the wall he said that it was perfect and that it really dressed the office up a bit. Then he said that he'd better get back to his office before Vice President Jim Stone sent out the search parties for him. We both chuckled at that remark and Timothy exited my office, reminding me that he would help me soon to get the other pictures hung up. I looked up at the picture on the wall, I looked at the chair that Timothy had just stood on in his socked feet, I raised my hands to my nose and mouth, inhaled Timothy's lingering sock scent and as my heart thundered I felt a tingling somewhere else… I was totally confused at the moment but had to get back to work and concentrated on my Friday night date with Lucy from the accounting department…

Chapter Ten

"HA, ha, ha, ha, ha, ha, ha, ha, ha, ha, ha, ha, ha, ha, ha, ha, ha, L-LEGGO of my manhood you sleazy pervert!" I thundered at Ronald as he held my cock tight with one hand and twirled that feather in my piss slit with his other hand. "That's my wife's exclusiveness you got there in your hand, ha, ha, ha, ha, ha, ha, ha, ha, ha, ha, ha, ha, ha, ha, ha, ha, ha, ha, ha!"

"And if your wife could see you now buddy boy," Ronald mused and at the mention of my wife I figured that by now she had woken up and discovered that I had never come back from the bathroom last night.

I wondered what Tim Junior would tell her, being that he did see me being helplessly carried off by Ronald.

"EEEEEEEEEEEEEEEEEE, hee, hee, hee, hee, hee, hee, hee, hee, hee, hee Y-you fucking son of a bitch, hee, hee, hee, hee, hee, hee, hee, hee, hee! Of all things, ha, ha, ha, ha, ha, ha, of all things to be tickling, my poor piss slit!" I screamed shrilly. "Y-you're setting my cock on fire man, EEEEEEEEEEEEE, I can't stand this, ha, ha, ha, ha, ha, ha, ha, ha, ha, ha, ha, ha, ha, ha, ha, ha!"

My cock was pounding but Ronald managed to keep that blasted feather in contact with my piss slit and spun and gyrated it against its target and the effects were my screams and laughter and ever loving wiggling of my toes and fingers. Gawd, and he was brazen enough to have grabbed my meat pole in his hand and he was holding it tight buds, tight enough I thought that I would spew a second load right there! And even through all this tickle torture if I closed my eyes I could see my beautiful wife hovering over my naked body in our bed as she would toy with me and tease me there, *there at our home, in our bed.* I could see her full breasts hanging down over me as she smiled ever so beautifully and played with my cock under the covers. Her nipples in my face so tempting, so in need of being fed on and I just so happy to oblige her as I would feast heartily, causing her those beautiful sounding moans that I loved so much, but then I opened my eyes. And it was not my wife I saw, it was fucking Ronald who had my cock in his hand and holy fucking shit I needed to cum again.

"DAMN, ha, ha, ha, ha, ha, ha, ha, ha, ha, ha, ha, RONALD, are, are you trying to tease another load of ball juice out of me bud?" I ranted at him from my awful position on that bench. "Be-because I think I am going to cum again man!"

I felt myself getting real close to a second orgasm. I wondered about my wife, what she must be thinking by now, maybe she called the police to report her hand-some husband missing, and maybe like I thought a few moments ago, what my boy might have told her. OH God, they had to find me before Ronald killed me with tickling and teasing me sexually! As I laughed and laughed and laughed and as Ronald held my cock my mind drifted away somehow. I didn't even notice it when Ronald stopped all the tickle tortures. He slowly pulled the vibrating butt plug from my bung hole and he stopped tickling my piss slit with the feather as well. Oh God, Ronald was shifting gears again The need to cum though was again immense and I wondered as my mind drifted back to reality if my buddy planned on jacking me off himself, seeing as he did have my cock in hand just a few moments ago…

But instead of being given an orgasm I was treated to another face full of chloroform…

"Breakfast and conversation time Timmy my boy," I heard Ronald saying as he lifted me off the bench after getting me unfettered.

Conversation? Conversation? What the fucking fuck did Ronald feel the need to discuss with me under these weird circumstances? As the guy carried me toward what he called his eating area I murmured the words "Help, help, somebody, help me, help…" and then all went black again for a while…

Chapter Eleven

(Breakfast and Conversation Time)

As I climbed slowly out of the latest chloroform induced stupor that Ronald had sent me into I lifted my head and found myself seated at a table in an elegant looking sort of dining room. My feet were each pressed against one of the chair legs, keeping my tree trunk like legs spread out good and wide and my aching and sweat sopped balls were resting on the chair. I thanked God that this chair didn't have a hole in it for my balls to dangle through. My thighs were lashed to the chair, securing them down to it. As I came around a bit more, the smell of the chloroform still awful in my nostrils I was aware of Ronald next to me as he tied a good length of rope under my muscular male cleavage, causing my man tits to really jut out nice and sexily...

"Good morning bud, breakfast time, you must be ravenous by now, after what a long and challenging night it's been for you that is," I heard Ronald saying right into my ear, his lips grazing my lobe as he spoke and then he stepped away from me.

I realized that my arms and my hands were free, (I supposed that Ronald didn't plan on spoon feeding me like a child) but my legs, my thighs and upper body were all tied and secured thoroughly to the chair. Upon further investigation, when I looked down at my feet and how they were each tied to one of the legs of the chair I saw that my thin black dress socks were back on my feet.

"Jeez," I said sarcastically, looking at Ronald as he sat across from me at the table in the luxurious room we were in. "You put my socks on my feet for me, what a good buddy you are. But about it being a good morning, I don't think so Ronald..."

As I spoke I took in the glorious fact that my hands and arms were not tied and a look of triumph came over my face, but Ronald was onto me in a heartbeat and what he said next dashed my triumphant hopes to smithereens...

"If you touch the ropes securing your legs and chest to that chair I'll nail you with the chloroform so fast that you won't even realize what's happened," Ronald said, sitting there and holding up the chloroform soaked cloth. "Got it Timmy my ticklish laddy?"

"I-I got it man, *I got it*," I said dejectedly and looked down at the stack of wheat toast on a plate in front of me, along with a bowl of hot cereal beside it.

In a large mug was steaming hot coffee that smelled delicious, dark with no sugar, just the way I like it... Ronald knew my tastes when it came to breakfast, seeing as we had breakfasted together enough times when we worked together at Chase bank. He knew that I enjoyed a simple light breakfast and that's just what he was giving me now during the time he had me in captivity.

"Eat up bud, I get the feeling you need it," Ronald said to me, sounding almost like the buddy I knew from the past.

"Is, is this food laced with that damned aphrodisiac?" I asked him and my cock throbbed big and hard between my spread and tied up legs.

"Ah, now that's for me to know and for your cock to find out," Ronald chuckled in reply.

"I notice that you're not eating," I said, looking at the fact that there was no food in front of Ronald as I cautiously bit into a slice of the wheat toast, my hand trembling as I brought it to my lips.

"I ate while you were in dreamland buddy," Ronald said. "Now tell me something, your wife's name is Stephanie."

"Yeah, so?" I asked him and sipped the coffee, holding the cup tight in both my trembling hands.

"Well, while you were asleep you must have been dreaming because you whispered the name Linda," Ronald said to me and I almost dropped the coffee cup.

"I-I said Linda? I said the name *Linda*?" I asked Ronald, sounding totally disbelieving, even to myself.

"Right as rain, Linda," Ronald repeated. "Who is she buddy?"

Even though Ronald was not tickling me at that moment I felt as if I was being tickled, mentally that is, as my memory played awful havoc with me and my sensitive parts...

"I-I dated her when I was in college," I told Ronald. "Sh-she found that she could get her way with me by, by, by...OH God Ronald..."

"How buddy? How did she get her way with you?" Ronald pressed me.

"By, by tickling me man, she tickled me and she always got her way with me," I said, practically in tears, my cock rock hard by then.

"Well now, this I indeed want to hear," Ronald said gleefully, his eyes open wide in anticipation. "While you eat your breakfast and drink your coffee you'll tell me about Linda and about one of the times she tickled you, then after that I'm locking those sexy socked feet of yours in a set of wooden stocks, HA!"

I gulped hard in terror and said one word, "Linda..."

"Linda huh? That's what I said?" I mumbled out loud as I ate a slice of toast, the breakfast that Ronald had set out before me.

I just knew from the look on Ronald's face as he watched me eat that what I was stuffing my face with was laced with that same goddamned aphrodisiac that he had been using on me from the outset of all this to keep my cock hard and right on the edge of orgasm. I looked down at my lap and sure enough Mr. Happy was still all red and wet and standing tall at soldierly attention, looking back up at me with one tickle tortured eye. I almost laughed as I thought about telling my cock, "Sorry Mr. Happy, but I'm famished, I've got to eat something here, and I'm sorry that in just a little while I know you'll start to feel a whole lot more frisky. But Ronald has tickled me to the point of insanity and hunger and I need some nourishment here..."

"Linda huh?" I dumbly repeated. "Ronald, I haven't thought of Linda in years. I have a beautiful wife and boy. Linda is history, maybe some bad history, but still, she's history. Stephanie knows how very ticklish I am, and we have fun with it sometimes when we're having sex. It's all just for foreplay, I mean; sometimes Stephanie will use it against me to get her way, but not torture. She'll tickle me until I give in to what she wants, but then it's over. But Linda..."

I nodded my head with a mouthful of food...

"Yes Timmy my laddy of ticklish lads, I want to know all about Linda, you say she's history yet you mumbled her name in your sleep," Ronald said to me. "She sounds most interesting."

He smiled inquisitively…

After another bight I gave in and decided to tell Ronald about Linda, seeing as he and she had a lot in common when it came to tickle torturing me…

"Well, Linda found out I was ticklish the first time we went parking," I said. "We were in college together and we had parked out on an old dam road, and we were necking pretty heavily for this early in our relationship. She claimed that she had had a crush on me the first time she saw me on campus and I suppose that was why she kept kissing and hugging the bejesus out of me in that car that night. She was hot man, kissing my lips over and over, kissing my cheeks till they were sopped with her lipstick. Fuck, she kissed my eyes, my ears, she sucked my earlobes. Yeah, I could tell she had a crush on me man. We both got so worked up that we were almost wrestling in the small space of that car, and in her animal-like lust she grabbed me at the ribs with both hands. Well, that sure broke up the scene let me tell you. I was suddenly cackling and fighting to get her hands off my ribs. But, she just became more determined to tickle me it seemed. She seemed to like the way I tried to push her off me, it spurred her on so to speak. The more I laughed and fought the more she tickled me. Well, that session didn't last too long, but I suppose it can be said that it set the stage for the future. Like Stephanie, Linda used to use my ticklishness to get her way. Like, for example, we would be outside a movie theater and I would want to see something like "Star Wars" and she'd want to see some sappy chick flick. Well, right there in front of people she would grab my ribs and go at me right there, with everyone watching in public until I would relent and we would wind up seeing the chick flick."

As I spoke I ate my breakfast and I began to feel the familiar tingling in my balls and already hard cock. Although I hate being tickled, it does sexually stimulate me, as has been pointed out buds. So, just thinking about Linda and what the fucking fuck she did to me was causing some action in my groin, but then, add Ronald's aphrodisiac to that equation and that was also beginning to cause some action there as well. My cock was simply glistening…

"At some pint in our short college romance Linda turned evil, sort of like you Ronald old buddy old pal," I said to Ronald and I could tell from his facial expression that he enjoyed that remark. "Although she never kidnapped me, hardy fucking har! Nah, she just kept me in her sorority house room sort of against my will. Once on an away football weekend, when the campus was almost vacant, she lured me over to her sorority house. That was strictly forbidden and taboo, but everyone from the sorority seemed to be gone too, along with the house mother. So we went up to Linda's room and we started making out really heavy. To that point we had not had sex together, although I had done everything I knew to get in her pants. She had managed thus far to keep me out. Well, this one time it seemed that she was caving in, I was getting her hotter and hotter. She let me feel her up but she wouldn't let me take any of her clothes off her. But she kept working on my clothes let me tell you and we rolled around in her bed and kissed and fondled each other like mad dogs in heat. First she got my shirt off me, and then it was my pants, which of course required that my shoes had to come off too. So there I was naked as I am right now, except no socks, Linda had gotten my socks off me too, and she was still fully clothed. I guess this sort of played to my submissive side and subconsciously gave her the upper hand. There was something in me that was feeling real vulnerable to be totally naked in front of Linda while she was still fully clothed. Once she had me totally naked though I began trying harder to get her out of her clothes, but she distracted me by beginning to stroke my hard cock and to fondle my balls, Gawd, it seems that people just love my balls Ronald. When she did this I sort of just laid back on the bed, thinking that she was going to jack me off. And man, she did, but to a point, and that point was NOT an orgasm. She would pump and stroke and feel my balls and when my balls would start to retract she would quit. She did this several times, pushing me back down when I objected. But then, she took off her panties and flashed her pussy at me. I felt as if I had just seen heaven in front of me. She asked if I wanted her to sit on my cock. "HOLY SHIT YEAH!" was my answer. That's when she broke the news that that would require me to be tied to the bed, for her safety, before she would sit on my bouncing and rigid cock. I was so frustrated, so horny and so naïve that I foolishly agreed to her requirements. Fuck, at that point I think I would have agreed to anything. So, once she had me tied spread eagle to the bed, she did come up and she began to sit down on my aching cock. She eased her pussy down and just touched the tip of my hardness. I was breathless man, fucking totally breathless. Her pussy lips were moist and felt so awesome against the tip of my cock, but all they did was nibble at the crown of my cock head, like it was fixing to swallow me up, but then she started. I shrieked with sudden laughter as she sat back down on her haunches and reached back with both hands and started scribbling her fingernails all over my naked feet. Needless to say I was in an instant hysteria, seeing as my feet really are the most ticklish part of my body. But this had never happened to me. I had never been tickled like this before. I pleaded and begged for her to stop, just as I've been doing with you Ronald, but she treated me the same way you have been doing. She just kept on tickling me. It seemed the more I laughed the more she wanted to tickle me. She just kept at it, on and on tickling and tickling me. And in turn I just kept on laughing and screaming and she enjoyed herself and every minute of my torments. But man, she didn't just tickle my feet buddy, NO; she enjoyed tickling me everywhere and anywhere that she could find a ticklish spot. She worked up my legs, squeezing my knees and the inner sections of my thighs. She tickled that very tender area right in the crotch where the thigh meets the body and also right behind my balls. I screamed and laughed through it all. She squeezed and stroked my sexy hips, my sides, most of all on her favorite spot, my ribs and then in my belly button. Linda is also the person who made me realize how very ticklish and sexy my man nipples are. She had lots of fun with my big plump nubs and my armpits. She left no ticklish spot un-tickled... That Friday night Linda had her fun with me, alone. But come Saturday morning Linda introduced me to some of her sorority sisters. I don't remember the name of that sorority house, but it must have been a witch's coven of some kind. Those bitches had fun with me all of Saturday and well into Sunday as well. But by Sunday night they had to get me out of that sorority house before the rest of the female students and the sorority house mother returned from the football weekend. But for the time they had me there they were bad Ronald, *really fucking bad.* They ganged up on me and also tag teamed me and just kept me laughing and screaming in that room practically all weekend. Needless to say that was the end of me and Linda. Once I was out of there I changed schools. I couldn't face her or any of those girls on campus again. Sorority sisters can be really cruel sometimes, just like good buddies can be Ronald..."

As I spoke and ate my breakfast in between and sipped my coffee Ronald seemed totally enraptured by my tale of Linda.

"So she kept you there all weekend?" Ronald asked me.

"Y-yes, her and about six or seven of her bitchy and sadistic girlfriends," I stammered. "Now don't be getting any ideas about holding onto me like that Ronald.

I'm a corporate executive, a married guy now, and a dad, *and I will be missed*!"

Ronald looked at me intently across the table...

"What about food?" he asked me. "Did Linda and her bitches feed you?"

"V-very little man, mostly they made me drink water, lots of water, food was an occasional muffin or maybe some yogurt, just to keep my energy going for the tickling they were making me endure," I replied. "But they did keep me well hydrated."

"And your bathroom needs?" Ronald asked me pressingly.

"Come on Ronald, do you need to know every last detail?" I asked him angrily. "It was totally humiliating, just as this is. Isn't that enough for you?"

Ronald simply glared at me and being that I was the one who was naked except for his socks, being that I was the one tied up the way I was and being that he was the one with the chloroform I felt it best to give him what he wanted.

"When I needed to take a leak they kept me tied to the bed and held a cup under my flaccid cock to capture my stream in," I said dejectedly, having finished my breakfast and coffee at that point. "I only needed to take a dump twice while I was a tickle torture prisoner in Linda's sorority house room. Those bitches waited till I was ready to nearly soil the bed they had me lashed to and then when I was sweating bullets they untied me. The need to take a dump was so overwhelming that all I could think about was getting my sexy butt into the bathroom. I mean, you would think that being that I was finally untied I would grab my clothes and make a beeline for the door of Linda's room and freedom. Well, the first problem with that, other than the fact that I had to take a long awaited dump was that Linda had had one of her bitchy girlfriends store my clothes in her room down the hall. Those bitches laughed and catcalled at me as I scrabbled madly in my nakedness into Linda's bathroom... While I sat in there farting, stinking up the bathroom and grunting, cursing at them they all laughed and catcalled at me through the closed door. When I was done and came out of the bathroom they were all on me like white on rice. I struggled madly but when one of them gave my balls a mean squeeze and another of them tickled my ribs, well, it wasn't long before I found myself retied to that damned bed... You can imagine I'm sure how very humiliating all of that was for me, being a guy and all that, to be held captive by a bunch of bitches."

"Yes, almost as humiliating as being abducted right out of your own bathroom in the middle of the night eh?" Ronald asked me snidely.

I just looked at him across the table, not answering that question...

"Okay Ronald, now you know about Linda, and I guess that all the tickling and teasing that you've done to me brought back a lot of those memories from my subconscious and from my college days," I said to Ronald at that point. "I mean, lets face it man, being held as a tickle captive by a bunch of horned up bitches isn't something that I talk about all the time you know? It was sexy in a way, real fucking kinky, but it was bad too Ronald, it was real bad. But Gawd, Linda didn't hold a candle to what you've done to me man. I mean, she tickled and teased me and then she brought in the cavalry, their tickling and teasing was bush league (no pun intended there) compared to what you've already put me through."

As I spoke I felt my cock throbbing from the aphrodisiac and the thoughts of Linda, her friends and what Ronald had already done to me, and not to mention the trepidation I was feeling of what was still to come where Ronald was concerned. My cock was simply bouncing in my lap and leaking more and more pre-seed.

"So you see Ronald, *you see*, I've been through this kind of thing before,"

I stated woefully. "But YOU WIN, YOU ARE THE BEST. Now please, come on and let me go, let me go man, let me go back to my wife Stephanie, and my son, Tim Junior…"

Ronald's Journal
Dated Early February 1994

The bank scored big last week by acquiring one of the biggest overseas accounts in banking history. And being that my department will be very instrumental in setting up the account and getting things moving I think I can honestly say that I'll be sitting pretty from now on. The way I see it my future with Chase as a big-time corporate executive has now been cemented. We all received an invitation for a celebration that is being held at a real exclusive club in uptown Manhattan a week from this Friday. The bank spared no expense for this celebration. There'll be open bars all night long, appetizers will be served along with a three course dinner and dessert and coffee will top off the evening, and not to mention live entertainment. Too bad Lucy won't be my date for the night, seeing as her and I ended up on the skids last week. I'll miss dating her but hey, as that old saying goes, "There are other fish in the sea."

The Night of the Bank Celebration

What a party! That's really putting it mildly but fuck, we all had a great time! I figure I better get all this written down before I conk out for the night. I'm usually not up this late but the party went till nearly eleven thirty PM and it took me a good hour or so to get home by train. As I said recently, someday, someday I'll have a company car that will take me to and from work. With this major acquisition in the bank's pocket I'm sure to get a huge promotion and a huge salary increase to boot. The way I plan to work really hard for this will insure that. The party was nothing short of an extravaganza. I mean, okay, first we all had to sit and listen to the bank's presidents and vice presidents and senior managers and managers all make their pep talk speeches, about how we all have our hard work cut out for us going forward. That really got a good rousing amount of applause from all the ass kissers out there. After the speeches the bartenders served drinks to all of us like it was going out of style. Over dinner I sat next to Timothy and his lovely wife Stephanie. Stephanie wasn't drinking, seeing as she is eight months pregnant. It was great to meet Timothy's wife, seeing as he and I have lunch together a lot and he talks about her constantly, what a wonderful and loving wife she is, how thoughtful she is, how friendly and considerate, hell, he even told me how if it weren't for Stephanie he wouldn't have any matched socks on a daily basis. I have to admit that a chill went up my spine when the handsome laddy told me that, although I still can't put my finger on all of this where Timothy and his damned socked feet are concerned. He then told me that Stephanie works as a teacher but that she would soon be a stay at home mom, being that she was pregnant for their first child. I of course congratulated the handsome laddy and treated him to lunch that day for his soon to be a new daddy. I asked him what names they had picked out and after swallowing a hefty bight of his sandwich he said that if it was a boy they planned to name him Timothy Junior and that if it was a girl they planned to name her Samantha. I told him that I thought those were great names. Timmy went on to tell me how they hadn't wanted to know the gender of the baby while Stephanie was pregnant, claiming how they both wanted to be surprised at the moment when she gave birth. I met Stephanie for the first time at the bank celebration and as I said she was lovely, everything

Timothy had said she was and more. I was very flattered when she told me that Tim (that's what she called him) had spoken very highly about me since I had been hired. She said that Tim told her that I was a great lunch buddy and a good friend to talk to. I thanked her for saying that and she in turn told me that they would love to have me over the house for dinner some time, adding how I should bring a date if I wanted to. I thanked Stephanie for the invitation and I got the feeling that she intended to see me married... After dinner and before dessert and coffee was to be served the live entertainment took to the stage. The bank hired a five piece band along with two lead singers, one guy and one girl. They performed mostly old songs from the fifties and sixties and some up to date stuff as well, but mostly the old bank fogies loved what they called the oldies but goodies, I could have hurled hearing that. While the band was performing Timothy excused himself to the men's room, leaving me at the table with Stephanie. While he was gone we talked about how her due date was now just a month or so away and how she was very anxious to finally give birth. I asked her if she and Tim planned to have other kids somewhere down the line and she said that they weren't sure, how it depended on their expenses and other personal issues. She then asked me if I planned to be a dad at some point in my life and with a smile on my face I told her that I needed to find a wife first. While Stephanie and I were chatting amiably we realized that there was suddenly some kind of funny commotion going on up on the stage where the band was. Our attention was suddenly drawn to the sounds of laughter in the stage area. Stephanie and I turned to see what all the fuss was about and she said, "Uh-oh, he does this all the time," as we saw Timothy walking up on the stage as the male lead singer held out his microphone for Timothy. I looked at Stephanie as she got to her feet, telling me to follow her. I walked with her up to the stage. "He's such a ham after he has a few drinks," Stephanie said to me, but I could tell that she was really embarrassed as we made our way to the stage area. Being that Stephanie is pregnant people cleared the way for her very quickly, plus it was her handsome laddy of a husband that was on the stage preparing to belt out a song for all of us, jeez. But it was when we got right up close to the stage that I noticed what my buddy had done that really wracked my nerves. Timothy, my good buddy was up on that stage with the microphone in hand, his suit jacket was off, his tie was pulled down, (something that Timothy would never do) his first two shirt buttons were undone and his shoes were off. My heart thundered at the sight of Timothy's black nylon socked feet, GoldToe brand to be exact. Smiling stupidly out at the audience Timothy announced that he was going to sing the song "That's What Friends are For", by Dionne Warwick and Friends and that he was dedicating it to his loving wife, his soon to be born child, and to his buddy Ronald. I was beyond flattered and embarrassed, but at the same time I could not take my eyes off Timothy's feet in those GoldToe brand socks. Stephanie giggled as everyone in the place applauded. The band started playing and Timothy began singing horribly the opening lines of the song. Everyone was cheering and even I found myself encouraging my handsome laddy of a buddy, yelling out, "Do it Timmy! Sing out Timmy!" When he was halfway through the song I came up with a brilliant idea. I went over to one of our office buddies; a guy named Lester and whispered my idea in his ear. He smiled jovially and said, "Let's do it." Together, Lester and I made our way up and onto the stage; we nodded reassuringly at the band members as they continued playing and Timothy continued singing and sidled up next to our singing buddy on either side of him. "Sing out Timmy me laddy!" I hooted. It would be the first time I called Timothy by the nickname I had coined for him. Then, Lester and I squatted down at Timothy's sides, grabbed the laddy's muscular legs and proceeded to hoist him to a seated position up on our shoulders, the two of us sharing Timothy's muscular bulky weight. Timothy hooted loudly, raised his hands above his head in triumph, waved his arms in the air and continued singing horribly as the crowd laughed and clapped. Stephanie looked up at her hoisted husband adoringly. But then, my moment of truth arrived, the real reason I wanted Lester to help me get Timmy hoisted up onto our shoulders. One of Timothy's socked feet were dangling over my chest as he sat up on my shoulder, his other socked foot dangled over Lester's chest. Making like I wanted to keep the guy balanced steadily up on my shoulder I grabbed Timothy's socked foot and held it tight with one hand as I held his thigh with my other hand. I held his foot by wrapping my hand around the arch side of it, my palm at the bottom of his meaty soft feeling foot. I saw Lester take note of what I did and he followed suit, doing the same thing with Timmy's other foot as it dangled over his chest. In between singing Timothy looked down at us and broke in the song to tell us, "Hold me tight guys, that's cool, but whatever the hell you do don't tickle my feet, those stinkers are real ticklish!" The audience went nuts with that and Timothy resumed singing.

Fuck, I have to admit that I could have held that guy on my shoulders all night if it meant getting a feel of his socked foot. What was up with that? What is up with that? I mean, I love women, I love everything about them, up to and including their feet, so what the fuck is this sudden obsession I seem to have with my work buddies' socked feet?

After Timothy's rousing rendition of "That's What Friends Are For" was done Lester and I put the guy down, he thanked us for the lift, and he thanked the audience for applauding his bad performance. He quickly collected his shoes and suit jacket, walked off the stage and back to the table with Stephanie and me. He received claps on the back and shoulders for his wonderful performance, ha, ha. At the table Timothy got his shoes back on his feet and I overheard Stephanie tell him that his socks stunk already and that he was to put them directly into the washing machine when they got home after the party... Again a chill traveled up my spine...

Chapter Twelve

"So Timmy my laddy, I suppose that I can safely say that thanks to that story you just told me and thanks to Linda I've come to realize that besides your feet, your armpits, your cock and balls and your man nipples that there are *other* parts of you that are truly vulnerable as well and that will require my ticklish attention," Ronald mused as I sat there with my empty plate and empty coffee cup in front of me. "I would say that I have my work cut out for me buddy, and as you can see I just love the work I'm doing!"

I hadn't even realized that I had devoured and drank every bit of what Ronald had served me, realizing just how very hungry I was, thinking how being tickle tortured can really exhaust a poor kidnapped guy.

"And I'll tell you bud, I have the machinery here to really do the tickle job on those other parts of yours," Ronald went on, looking across the table at me totally fiendishly.

I could not believe what the fucking fuck I was hearing. After all he had done to me already, after the ways he had tickled me *so much* he planned to tickle me even more, and from the sound of things he planned to tickle me further intensely than he had already done.

"Ronald, please, *please man,* think what you're doing here, holy fucking fucks, I told you, when it comes to tickle torturing me you are the best, YOU WIN, YOU FUCKING WIN OKAY?" I said, trying to play to Ronald's sympathetic side, if he still had one that is. "Think man, think about what you've done, now please, and let me go, let me go back to my wife Stephanie and my kid."

As I spoke my hands were flat on the table, the knowledge that I could not untie my legs and upper body were totally frustrating and maddening as Ronald held that chloroform soaked cloth at the ready.

"Linda is past, she's history, hell, I don't even know what the fuck became of her after I changed schools," I went on. "Okay, what she did to me was not fun, okay, okay, if I have to admit it, it got me hard, it still does when I think about it, I grant you that, but it was still totally humiliating, just like this is, FUCK, sitting here eating my breakfast that's laced with an aphrodisiac, tied to a chair, wearing just my damned black socks! Please man, take me home to Stephanie, and take me home now! I cannot possibly endure any more tickle torture…"

"Timmy my laddy, like I said earlier you have so much more to offer," Ronald said. "And I have *lots* more to give. I have faith in you buddy; I know that you can endure lots more! And come on man, you know I'm not going to hurt you, I'm going to tickle torture you, but I sure as hell am not going to hurt you. And I'm sure that you've got other stories like the Linda one for me, so before I do send you home to your wife and kid I want to hear those tales buddy…"

"B-but Ronald," I whimpered miserably.

"No buts Timmy, I chose you because I knew that you could handle this,"

Ronald laughed and got to his feet, looking at me totally menacingly. "I could have chosen any of my female conquests for all this man, but I chose *you*. I want to hear those stories of your ticklish past and I want to hear about who else tickled you to the point of madness..."

"Ronald, think about this, and think about it real well, when you do return me to my wife and kid how will I explain my absence?" What am I supposed to tell them?" I asked Ronald challengingly. "My kid, he saw..."

But I quickly swallowed my words, realizing that I did not want Ronald to know that Tim Junior saw him lugging me out of my house like a sack of dirty laundry.

"You were saying Timmy my boy?" Ronald asked, standing directly over me now.

"Nothing man, nothing, my brain is tickle fried man, I just don't know yet what I'm going to tell my wife and kid when you return me to them," I said, wiggling my toes in my socks, my hard cock glistening and aching to shoot its load.

I was afraid at that moment that if Ronald knew that Tim Junior had seen him carrying me from the house that he might harm the kid. Somehow I knew that Ronald wouldn't do that, but at this point I wasn't taking any chances. And let's face it I really wasn't in a position where I could be of much use to my wife or kid if Ronald did decide to do something to them.

"Well, you could tell them the truth," Ronald suggested, sounding silly. "That your good buddy snatched you away from them for some time and that you and he really had a great ticklish time together."

"Nah man, that's too humiliating, I cannot possibly tell my wife that," I said miserably, making the mistake of looking down at my hard cock, wanting to grab the throbbing and hard guy and really stroke him a few times, just to get myself off again.

Whatever that aphrodisiac was that Ronald was administering to me, it truly was doing the job keeping me good and fucking aroused. Ronald chuckled meanly and suddenly, in a fast swooping motion he slammed the chloroform soaked cloth over my nose and mouth...

"GGGGRRRRRRRMMMFFFFF!" I snarled angrily and with my hands free this time I reached up to try to push the cloth away before another stupor claimed me.

"Didn't even see me coming that time huh buddy?" Ronald laughed and pushed my head back till I was looking up at the ceiling through blurred vision.

My struggles were totally in vain as I felt myself slipping into oblivion...

"GGGRRRRRRFFFFFF! RRRRHHHHH GAWD!" I seethed.

"There you go bud, it's totally harmless, just rest up a while, digest your food and when you wake up those cute socked feet of yours will be locked in a set of wooden stocks," I heard Ronald saying as I drifted away. "After that I'll take your socks off you again and let you soak your bare feet in warm oil. That'll really soften 'em up for what I have in mind for you after the wooden stocks. You see Timmy, like I said, we're having a great fucking time here..."

"N-no more ticklin' me Ronald, no more tickle, no more," I murmured incoherently, wheezing out the words as he slowly took the cloth away from my nose and mouth.

A few moments later I was snoozing fitfully as I felt myself lifted out of the chair after Ronald had gotten me untied.

"No more ticklin' me, please," I whimpered as my head spun in a reverse orbit…

Ronald carried me in a stretched out prone position, my arms dangling up and over my head, my fingers pointing to the floor. The way he was lugging me made me realize (even in my chloroformed stupor) that every part of me was in a very vulnerable and ticklish state at that moment… And just to mention it, my cock was hard and throbbing, sticking straight up and real invitingly…

"R-Ronald, you, you bastard," I groaned as the room spun and I swayed as my buddy carried me. "I-I want to go, home…"

Then, again, all went black for a short time…

When I came to a while later, once again coming slowly out of Ronald's last chloroformed induced stupor I found that I was still humiliatingly naked, except of course for those stupid black socks that my so called buddy kept taking off my feet and then putting back on me. (That has to be the most humiliating thing, to have a buddy take your socks off your feet and *then* put them back on for you, Gawd! I mean, in my opinion a guy's socks are like his underpants, real intimate you know?) I found myself now seated on a little bench with my socked feet stretched out at forty-five degrees in front of me and clamped into the holes of a set of padded stocks that were attached to a chair. My back was up against a pole and my arms were pulled straight up and over my head with my wrists tied off somewhere really high up there. Gawd, what a position for a poor sap of a guy to be in huh buds? I shook my head and I found that my cock was still as hard as ever, all red, bloated and sticky, bobbing alertly between my legs. My balls were resting on the bench but boiling up another good batch of sperm. I shook my head again as I became aware of Ronald moving about.

"Ronald, hey man, let's stop all this huh? Please, you've had your fun and I really don't think that I can take anymore," I pleaded as I came to. "You've tickled and teased me to the point that I don't know whether I'm cumming or going, hardy har fucking har. And I really do need to get back to my wife and my kid and my job, fuck Ronald, I can't lose my job."

"All in good time Timmy," Ronald said, smirking at my pleading face. "I don't think you will be fired from Chase Bank for taking a few days off buddy. When I worked there with you I was able to count on one hand how many days off you took. I'm sure you're still like that. Believe me Timmy my laddy, you deserve a few days off for rest and relaxation and to experience my tickle devices. I have a lot more tickling to do where you're concerned man and you've got a lot more tickling to endure and some good story telling to do. You know, you are going to tell me about the times in your past when you got tickle tortured, but nothing like I'm doing to you right buddy? What you were subjected to in the past where tickle torture is concerned I'm sure small potatoes compared to what's happening here."

"R-Ronald, a few days?" I garbled. "*Fuck*, you plan to do this to me for a few days? Okay look, I'll tell you what. I'll tell you about how I was tickled and you stop tickling me, at least for a while, deal?"

I looked for acceptance in Ronald's devilish face. I had to do something so the guy would at least give me some time off from tickling me and then maybe I could think straight enough to devise some sort of escape plan…

"Okay, that seems fair enough," Ronald said with an evil grin. "You tell me about how you got tickle tortured and…"

As Ronald spoke he scribbled and scrabbled his fingertips up the bottoms of my socked feet locked in those damned stocks…

"...and I won't tickle you, at least for the time being," Ronald chuckled and again scribbled his fingertips up and down the bottoms of my trapped feet.

"AAAAAAA, ha, ha, ha, ha, ha, ha, ha," I laughed as Ronald pulled his hands away from my feet. "Now, now stop tickling me bud. OOOOOOO, okay thanks. Now, let me think, where were we?"

"Your ticklish history Timmy me ticklish laddy, your ticklish, ticklish history..." Ronald "reminded me sternly.

"Oh yeah, okay, I'll tell you more about my college days..." I began.

Chapter Thirteen

"Back when I was in college, my fraternity brothers, those sons of bitches, they had found out just how ticklish I was," I said to Ronald. "I recall you telling me Ronald how you were tickled during Hell Week in your fraternity. Well, I made the same mistake of pledging one, knowing how very ticklish I was, Gawd. Anyway, this was the second college I went to, you know, after Linda. I suppose being held prisoner as a tickle and sex slave can really traumatize a guy huh Ronald? Well, one night my fraternity brothers and I were all sitting around the frat house shooting the shit, when one guy announced that a massage parlor had just opened up just outside of town and that they had an all Asian staff. Well, that intrigued us all, me especially, seeing as I always had a fetish for soft skinned beautiful Asian women. But none of us had money to get a massage and it was one hundred bucks, as the guy who had told us all about the massage parlor pointed out. All together, each of us had a little bit of money and we decided to pool that little bit of money together and then draw cards to see who would be the victim, as it turned out. We all drew cards and I came out the winner. What I didn't know at the time was that all of this was a set-up. They had let me win. I didn't see anyone else's cards, they just said things like, "Oh, you beat me Tim," and that was it. I also didn't know that they planned on telling the girl that I was ticklish and that they would give her a tip to really work me over."

As I spoke I saw Ronald moving his hands toward my trapped feet. It seemed that the fucking guy couldn't stay away from my damned feet.

"Ro-Ronald, now stay away from my feet man," I said as sternly as possible, given the position I was in and he looked at other parts of me as well. (I knew I was not going to be getting out of this any time soon buds) "Just quit even looking at them like that, and that goes for my man tits and cock too. I'm telling you what happened bud."

Ronald simply gave me that evil grin of his and nodded his head... I got on with it...

"Okay, so we all went down to the shop," I continued. "The idea was that I was going to get a massage from a sexy Asian girl and then come back to the frat house and give the guys all the horny details, and by that we meant good jack off information. That way, everyone could go back and lay in their dorm bunks and vicariously whip themselves off thinking about a hot massage. Well, we all went into the shop and met the madam; I guess that's what I should really call her. She was a thirtiesh looking rather sexy Asian woman who seemed to be in charge. We all pulled out our money and my buddies told her that I was the lucky guy. The madam rang a bell and as several girls came out I noticed that one of my frat brothers was whispering to the madam as he handed her the bills. She was smiling real sexily and seemed to be sizing *me* up. Three girls came out, one was rather plump, one looked like she couldn't be over twelve, although I was sure she was and the third was a knockout, long black hair, beautiful olive skin, bright red lipstick and nail polish on her fingernails and toenails. She was clad in a very brief thong bikini, which showed off her ample breasts and broad hips. Well, with our mouths hanging open we all chose her. Her name was, strangely enough Teek Lee (tickly). The guys patted me on the back and pushed me forward as the madam whispered to Teek Lee. Then, Teek Lee took my arm, told me to come with her and ushered me into the back area. My buddies all hooted and wished me luck. We went into a small room where there was a long padded massage table in the center. Oddly enough it had straps hanging all around the edges and there were all kinds of things hanging on the walls, forks, rakes, silk scarves, all sorts of brushes and feathers. I was standing there with my mouth open when I realized that somehow she already had me mostly undressed and was asking me questions in a real sexy sounding voice. She unbuttoned my shirt and away it went then my pants were down around my ankles. She squatted down and I had to balance myself as she got my pants off me along with my shoes and socks. I chuckled and commented on the wonderful service she was providing.

"Dis u furs massage?" she asked me and I nodded in the affirmative as she knelt in front of me as she grabbed the sides of my underpants with her fingers. In a fast stroke down went my underpants and I was now naked before this sexy Asian woman, Teek Lee. I grabbed the towel lying on the table and covered myself. "Dat's okay, Teek Lee sees lots of nekked men. But lot of them old wrinkly men. You young, you have nice body, up on table please," she said. I blushed at the situation and her words about my body as she directed me up and onto the table. Once I was on the table Teek Lee positioned me facedown and managed to take the towel away from me. I rested my face in the face cradle and I felt her hand on the back of my head as she stroked my hair for a few moments and I heard her whisper "Handsome college boy." So there I was totally naked on that table. "Teek Lee start now to loosen you up," she said and took her hand off the back of my head, reluctantly it seemed. She oiled up her hands and started massaging me at the shoulders and went slowly down my back and legs. Needless to say it felt awesome, but at the same time even while doing a traditional massage she managed to eek a few giggles and chuckles out of me as she massaged the backs of my legs. Then, after wiping off the oil Teek Lee removed her shoes and climbed up on the table and began to walk on my back. I groaned and grunted like a football jock. "Dis berry good Teek Lee feet and toes berry good on handsome college boy," she said as she did her work. Wow man, she was right and I was almost like a dishrag, I was so limp and relaxed, except my cock was rigid and at attention like a good admiral beneath me. Teek Lee walked up to my shoulders and then she slipped one bare foot on the side of the face cradle and pressed her toes into it, against my cheek. I raised my head from the face cradle and she pressed her toes next against my nose and finally, my mouth. She kept pressing until her toes went into my mouth and I found myself dutifully tonguing her toes and she wiggled them in there. "You like Teek Lee feet?" she asked me and I could actually hear the amusement in her voice as I mumbled "Muum Humm." "Okay, time now to turn over," she announced as she jumped down from the table and literally flipped me onto my back, man, she was strong. I missed her toes in my mouth already hardy fucking har. Needless to say I was surprised at the action but doubly embarrassed at the fact that my cock was standing tall and at full mast from my crotch. "Oh you really LIKE Teek Lee, yes!" she said and actually batted my cock with one hand, gently slapping it actually, giggling as she did it. My cock waved in the air like an old police car's antenna, swish, swish it went. My eyes rolled back in my head, behind my blood red embarrassed face and I gripped the sides of the table as Teek Lee began now working on my front. "Hee, hee,

hee," I giggled when she squeezed my thighs, although she had a great time it seemed when she had massaged my muscular chest and if I didn't know better I got the feeling that she had been looking at my plump man tits with thoughts of nursing going through her head. "Ah ha, handsome college boy teekleesh? No?" she asked me. She looked down at me with those deep dark almonds shaped eyes and smiled at me with her bright red lips, freshly wet from a licking. "Oh, uh, hee, hee, just a little," I giggled back at her and she playfully batted my cock again, making it swish some more. "Teek Lee bet you mo dan just leetle teekleesh, huh?" she asked me and then she jumped to my ribs and dug her fingers into my sides and at the same time she pressed her barely clothed tits into my groin area and rubbed her sexy titties on my hard shaft. "Oooo, looka Mista Happy! He like my tits!" Teek Lee mused and she continued to work on my ribs. I was beginning to kick and raise my legs and use my hands and arms to fend her off, but her body kept my legs mostly down and she managed to apply her tickling technique between and around my hands and arms. To my utter and total amazement she then started swirling her tongue in my belly button. OH MY GOD RONALD, that's all I can say. I almost lost my ability to breathe when she did that. I was already bucking and giggling and laughing with her fingers on my ribs, but man, her tongue working around and in and out and around my belly button just pushed me into total heaves and guffaws. All my air was going out and I could not inhale from the laughing. I was about to pass out by the time she quit. Although, quit was not the right term. She stopped what she was doing, but she changed to do something else. Teek Lee moved around to the top of the table and pulled my wrists up and along with her. Once she had my arms stretched above my head she used one of those table straps I mentioned earlier to secure my wrists in that position. Then, with me still giggling like a schoolgirl she yelled out, "Moon girl, Moon girl!" and the madam stuck her head in the door. "Ah, Moon Girl, Teek Lee thinks you like handsome college boy's feet. Him have pretty feet, nice toes, prus him reary, reary teekleesh! See?" Teek Lee said and with that she reached down along my stretched out arms and attacked my armpits, scribbling her fingernails in my hairy pits, and I was off and laughing again, jerking and laughing and jerking and laughing, cursing at her for having binded me the fuck up. The madam, whose code name was apparently "Moon Girl", smiled a great big smile, stepped into the room and gladly attended to my bare feet. I was kicking and squirming so she worked on one of my feet at a time. But, she then first strapped one of my ankles, and then the other to the two corners of the table. I was spread out real sexy like and this also eliminated my kicking, but not my squirming, nor for that matter, my laughing. And Mr. Happy was still swishing in the wind. There was no deflating him. He wasn't embarrassed at all Ronald, just like he's not embarrassed now, but granted you did help him along with your Spanish fly that you gave me. In fact he was looking for company. The moon girl started tickling my feet, first with her long fingernails, and then she pulled some instruments from the wall, forks, combs, brushes, and feathers. She was just having a ball man, working on my damned feet with all of those everyday items, which had been turned evilly into devices of tickle torture, except of course for the feather, all of this while Teek Lee continued playing with my upper body. Finally, Teek Lee took a silk scarf from the wall and fanned it over my face and upper body. At the same time Moon Girl took the toes of one of my feet into her mouth and she started sucking and working my toes with her tongue. It felt like magic as her tongue went in between and all around my toes, each and every toe. She spent an inordinate amount of time working each of my toes. It didn't really tickle, but then after a while it sure as hell did. But at the same time it was really exciting. Teek Lee then took that silk scarf and covered my hard cock with it, but she didn't let it lay still. She started pulling the scarf across the head of my manhood, which sent me up the wall. Gawd, I was trying to fuck the ceiling. Teek Lee kept doing this over and over, but she would pause between scarf torments so that I would settle down a bit. But Moon Girl all the while was still sucking and tonguing my toes, now on my other foot. "Yes, Moon Girl likes toes of handsome college boy," Teek Lee commented, looking down at me knowingly as I suffered erotically on her table. I smiled up at her through clenched teeth and was inclined to agree with her. Moon Girl sure as hell loved my college boy toes because she was devouring them, holding tight to my sweaty bare feet as she did her work. After about fifteen minutes of this Teek Lee stopped and went over to my pants which she had thrown on a chair after having gotten them off me, removed my wallet and returned to my side. She draped the silk scarf across my lap, creating a carnival tent of silk. She quickly found that there was no money in my wallet, but there was a credit card. She tapped me on the forehead with the card while Moon Girl continued sucking my toes and she pulled on the silk scarf. "What limit on card?" Teek Lee asked me. I moaned and groaned the words a thousand and realized how easily she had extracted that information from me. Gawd, she had just asked and I had surrendered. Then, she re-draped my cock and pulled the scarf across it again. After that, she stepped to the side of the little room and ran my credit card. I asked her through some deep gasps why she was running a charge on my card, seeing as me and my buddies had already paid for all this. Teek Lee said, "We give you bonus massage, toes sucked, and tickled, all cost extra. Mista Happy want Teek Lee to also have nice big tip you sign for me handsome college boy." She stepped back to my strapped down body, pulled the silk scarf across my cock again and then diddled my armpit with a sharp fingernail, repeating the words "You sign handsome college boy." I told her that I would not sign that and then I laughed and guffawed as she trailed the scarf across my cock once more. When she freed my hands by loosening the straps around them but keeping them somewhat secured I maneuvered myself a bit and signed the charge slip. "He sign!" Teek Lee told Moon Girl, who muttered the word, "sheet", seeing as I got the feeling that she was really, really enjoying my feet a bit too much. To top it all off Teek Lee then grabbed my hard cock in her strong right hand and started pumping and pumping and in just a few strokes she had me squirting my college boy juices all over my chest. I grunted, I swore like a marine and I came in what seemed like buckets. When I was done I lay there panting and Teek Lee tossed my credit card down on my cum sopped chest. Laughing as they exited the room Teek Lee and Moon Girl said, "Bye!" and were out the door. In just a second a really big and muscular Asian guy stepped into the room and said in perfect English, "You've got one minute to get your stuff, get dressed and get out or I will put you out just like you are." Needless to say I quickly got dressed and hustled out to meet my grinning buddies. They wanted to know all about it, but I never told them about the tickling or the one thousand bucks. Fuck, I had been tickle tormented and made to pay for it. But somehow their eyes told me that they knew all about the tickling. So that's how I got tickled by a massage girl and a madam Ronald. Thanks for not tickling me while I related all that to you. Now, if you would be so kind as to let me up from here…"

I looked up at Ronald with questioning eyes.

"Oh but Timmy my laddy, now that you've told me the story, now the tickling begins," Ronald chuckled and held up a hairbrush with hard pointy bristles on it.

"NOOOOOOOOOOO!" I cried miserably.

Ronald's Journal
Entry Dated April 1994

I joined the company soccer team a couple of weeks ago. It was while I was having lunch with Timothy that I let him talk me into it. I tried telling the guy that I wasn't much of a sports nut, hell I don't even watch baseball or football during the seasons for them. But Timothy went on and on about teamwork and how Chase bank had already beaten the competition two years in a row to become the champion soccer team. How I wanted to say "Wow, hoorah," in a sarcastic tone, but I was still basically the new guy in the bank so I kept my opinion to myself. I had to stifle a laugh when I thought about all those stuffed shirts out of their suits and ties and in soccer uniforms, all of them running around on a field and competing to kick the ball, God. But then the thought of Timothy wearing those long soccer socks up to his knees flashed into my mind. The thought of him sitting in a locker room and rolling those long numbers onto his feet, up over his calves and to his knees was suddenly paramount in my mind. After I swallowed a mouthful of food I asked him if he was a team member. With a schoolboy looking grin on his face he said that he sure as hell was. I nodded, pretending to be considering his suggestions and then followed up by asking him what color the team's uniforms were. Timothy told me that the uniforms were navy blue shorts with a white stripe on either side of them, a matching tee shirt and navy blue knee high socks with two white stripes encircling the tops of them, all supplied by the bank. The cleats we as players would have to supply on our own. As Timothy chewed a mouthful of his food I thought about my new buddy wearing that uniform, most of all I thought about him wearing those long navy blue socks up to his knees. God, what is it about Timothy and his socks that seems to have me so totally transfixed? I told him that I would join up. I told him that I would go to Human Resources and sign up as soon as we got back to the bank after lunch. Timothy reached across the table, clapped me on the shoulder, and said, "That's the spirit buddy! That's the spirit! We'll show those other banks just what Chase is made of!" I wanted to say the word "lame" to him but again I kept my feelings to myself. Instead I said something else; something that I could not believe came out of my mouth. I said, "It'll be strange to see you in that uniform along with those long soccer socks up to your knees buddy. I've uh, noticed how you always tend to wear calf length thin nylon dress socks with your suits." Timothy looked at me a bit quizzically for a moment at the mention of his socks and he nervously reached up to straighten his tie, which just for the record really didn't need straightening. "Well, like most married so and so guys out there my wife keeps me in good supply where my socks and even my underwear are concerned. Hell, Stephanie never passes up a sale where my socks and undergarments are concerned. I got a sock and underwear drawer stocked to the point that I can hardly close them anymore." I told him that that was real cool and how I hope to someday be married and have those kinds of services bestowed on me as well. As we finished our lunch I thought about Timothy's wife purchasing his socks for him and yet another chill crept up my spine... I was sure that the guy was wondering how I knew that he always wore calf length nylon dress socks, but he didn't mention or ask why I was so studious where his socks of all things were concerned...

The Day of The Soccer Game

We won the soccer game. Amazingly, we won the game. I never thought that we would pull it off, seeing as in my opinion most of the guys on our team were a bunch of office dorks, but we did it, we won the game. And to be quite honest and right to the point we won because of Timothy's final play in the game. My good buddy scored the win for us. Watching him running across the field, kicking that ball, him sweating and grunting as he went, all I kept looking at were those long socks he had on, and how one of them was pushed slightly down away from his knee. There was something real erotic about that for some reason. After Timothy scored the winning goal for us Lester, my good buddy who helped me hoist Timmy during his singing expedition at the company celebration and I made our way quickly across the field as the crowd of gathered friends, family and co-workers cheered from the bleachers. As Timmy whooped it up with other team members Lester and I looked at each other, an unspoken knowingness between us, and squatted down at Timothy's sides. "Time for a victory ride for you Timmy me laddy!" I said to him and Lester and I, for the second time hoisted our good office buddy to our shoulders. We got him seated on our shoulders, grabbed one of his socked calves each and proceeded to carry him around the field two times as the crowd cheered. Timothy waved his arms above his head and laughed jovially... The sound of his laughter was somehow hypnotic to me...

When the game was over and the crowd had dispersed Timothy's no longer pregnant (she had a boy back in March and I still need to relate that experience herein) wife and my present girlfriend, Cynthia, found Timothy and I waiting for them by his car. I had thanked Timothy for the ride to and from the game, citing how I would much rather shower at home than at a public locker room. Timothy was in full agreement with me and jokingly said how we would stink up his car together for the ride home. As Stephanie and Cynthia approached us Timothy thanked me for the victory ride across the field, saying what a heady feeling it was to be carried like a king of sorts.... Timothy helped Stephanie get comfortable in the back seat of the car with the baby in his carseat. As Timothy helped Stephanie get comfortable I opened the other side door for Cynthia to climb into the back seat next to Stephanie. When the two women were in the car Timothy got into the driver's seat as I made my way into the passenger seat. My mind was suddenly awhirl at my good fortune when I heard Stephanie say, "Tim, how many times have we been through this? You cannot drive with your cleats on. It'll ruin the pedals." Timothy gripped the steering wheel and told his wife that he had again forgotten his sneakers, and asked her sarcastically if she would like for him to drive with just his socks on his feet, reminding her of how awful his feet smelled after he had sweated in his socks for a good period of time. Cynthia and I laughed good naturedly, (the baby cooed a little at the sound of the laughter), at this conversation but Stephanie was relentless. She told Timothy to take his cleats off and to put them in the trunk of the car and how this would teach him to remember his sneakers the next time. Tim grumped, looked at me and said that this was no way for the hero of the game to be treated. I simply smiled at him, me wanting his feet out of those cleats so badly, but for different reasons that Stephanie wanted them off him. Timothy bent over to unlace his cleats and to get them off his feet. Stephanie said we would keep the windows of the car open for the short drive to my place where they would drop Cynthia and me off. I offered to put Timothy's cleats in the trunk, holding out my hand as he got them off his feet. Timothy thanked me and handed me the cleats and the key for the trunk. My hand shook as I took the guy's cleats in my hand, but I masked it pretty well and stepped out of the car, telling him, "Be right back." We were parked way back in a parking lot and no one saw what I did before I deposited my good buddies' moist and smelly cleats in the trunk. I got the trunk of the car open and just as I was about to drop Timothy's cleats into it I held one of them to my nose and mouth, inhaling the musty scent of it real deeply. A chill went up my spine and I thought how if the guy's cleats were scented this way then his socks must have been a hundred times more-so. I stole a sniff of Timothy's other cleat, dropped them both in the trunk, slammed the hood of the trunk closed and made my way back to the passenger seat. When I got in the car and closed the door I saw that all the windows had been lowered. Stephanie jokingly told me and Cynthia how it was necessary to drive with the windows down, seeing as her husbands socks always smelled real funky after he had worn them for even just a few hours. Cynthia and I both laughed and poor Timothy jokingly (but I could tell he was angry) told his wife that that was a terrible way for to talk about her loving hubby's socks. For the ride from the soccer field to my place I stared in awe at Timothy's socked feet as he drove…

Chapter Fourteen

"Ronald, NOOOOOO, no, you promised you wouldn't tickle me, we made a deal remember?" I asked my buddy desperately as he began running the pointy bristles of the hairbrush up and down and up and down the bottoms of my feet while they were locked in the stocks. "HA, ha, ha, ha, ha, ha, ha, ha, ha, ha, ha, ha, ha, ha!"

That blasted hairbrush mocked me and I laughed loudly.

"The deal, as I recall it Timmy me laddy, was that I wouldn't tickle you while you were telling me about your massage parlor tickle Asian lady," Ronald said sternly as he trailed that hairbrush faster and faster up and down my socked feet alternately. "I said nothing about not tickling you afterwards."

"OH GAWD man, okay, okay, so I'll tell you another story from my tickle history, how's that?" I asked him, thinking I had found another reprieve, another way out.

"Oh yes Timmy, I will definitely hear another story of your past tickle torments, there's no doubt about that whatsoever," Ronald laughed and snapped the elastic in my socks against my calf skin. "*Right after I've heard you laugh some more...*"

That said Ronald ran that damned hairbrush faster and faster up and down the meaty bottoms of my socked feet.

"AAAAAYYYYYYYYYY, ha, ha, ha, ha, ha, ha, ha, ha, ha, ha, ha, ha, ha, ha, bl-blast it all, here we go again!" I screamed. "HAR, HAR, HAR, HAR, HAR, HAR, HAR!"

Ronald then stopped tickling my feet and moved to the post where my raised arms were tethered tightly at the wrists above me. Standing behind the post Ronald reached around it and suddenly he had two hairbrushes in his hands. Like a twisted magician he'd made that second hairbrush appear as if by magic. My so called buddy reached around the post with two hands and started brushing the hairbrush bristles against my smelly sweaty and randy armpits.

"HA, HA, HA, HA, HA, HA, HA, HA, HA, HA, HA, HA, HA, HA, HA, HA, HA, HA, HA, HA, HA! OH NO, OH NO!" I blubbered madly, looking from side to side as Ronald skimmed and skammed those hairbrushes around and around in my armpits, those brushes practically making love to my damned pits it seemed. "N-NOT my armpits Ronald, not my goddamned, ha, ha, ha, ha, ha, ha, ha, ha, ha, ha, ha, ha, armpits!"

As Ronald meanly tickle tortured my poor armpits I wriggled my trapped and socked feet in the stocks, taking in the sight of my feet in those black socks, those black socks seeming to be a huge factor that had played in with my kidnapping...

Ronald pressed those hairbrushes harder into my pits, wiggling them meanly in there. God almighty, I never knew just how awful two hairbrushes could feel when turned into devices for tickle torture.

"OHHHHHHHHHRRRRRRRR, har, har, har, har, har, har, har, har, har, har, har, har, har, har, har, har!" I screamed my laughter, squirming awfully on my naked ass on the little bench Ronald had me on, my cock dancing long and hard between my legs, stalked up like a flagpole, all red and dripping pre seed and beads upon beads of piss as well.

"Aren't those stocks that I got your feet in just great Timmy my boy?" Ronald asked me. "I got them on E-bay, believe it or not."

"Y-yeah, just fucking great, ha, ha, ha, ha, ha, ha, ha, ha, ha, ha, ha, ha, ha, ha, ha, ha, ha, ha, ha!" I guffawed. "Just what the fuck every guy wants, a pair of stocks so he can lock up his buddies socked feet and ti-tickle, ha, ha, ha, ha, ha, ha, ha, ha, ha, ha, ha, ha, tickle him!"

"Admittedly I had to pay through the nose for those stocks, it seems that lots of people out there have tickle fetishes bud, but I would bet none as intense as mine," Ronald snickered and tickled my armpits harder yet with the hairbrushes. Then, he dropped the hairbrushes on the floor and went at my pits with his fingertips.

"YAAAAAAAAHHHRRRRR!" I reeled as Ronald dug in real deep at my armpits. "HA, ha, ha, ha, ha, ha, ha, ha, ha, ha, ha, ha, ha, ha, ha, ha!"

The bastard even tugged at the moist and sweaty armpits hairs in there...

"AAAAARRRRRRRRRR, har, har, har, har, har, har, har, har, har, har!" I laughed as he tugged at my armpit hairs in between tweaking and tickling my pits.

"Of course I could have built the stocks myself," Ronald mused from behind me. "But I wanted them quick because I knew that after I put this tickle palace together I would be acquiring my tickle victim, *that's you bud*."

"HA, ha, ha, ha, ha, ha, ha, ha, ha, ha, ha, ha, ha, ha, ha, well aren't I just the lucky guy?" I laughed and laughed harder and harder. "Ronald, ha, ha, ha, ha, ha, ha, ha, ha, ha, ha, ha, ha! If you keep tickling me this way I'll hurl my breakfast!"

"Nah, you will not bud," Ronald corrected me, accepting no excuses it would seem to stop the tickle tortures he was heaping on me. "You ate more than two hours ago at this point, you're well digested, on with the tickle session I say buddy..."

"HA, ha, ha, ha, ha, ha, ha, ha, ha, ha, ha, ha, ha, ha, ha, ha, ha, ha, ha, ha, ha, ha, ha, ha! T-two hours ago that was that I ate?" I blurted crazily.

Fucking fucks, I could not believe that that much time had gone by. Two hours ago I had eaten, that meant from my calculations of time that by then it had to be daylight out, and worse, by now my wife would have woken up and found that I was not there. I laughed crazily and saw her beautiful face and my sons in front of my tear filled laugh filled eyes...

And sure enough, an hour or so earlier while I was being tickle tortured, or maybe while I had been relating my story of Teek Lee to Ronald my wife had awakened.

"Timmy?" she asked, looking at the clock on my night table and saw that it was the time that I usually got up for work. "Timmy?"

She climbed out of bed and walked from the bedroom in her nightgown, calling my name as she exited the bedroom.

"Where could he be so early in the day?" she asked no one in particular as my son came out of the bathroom after brushing his teeth.

He looked at her sadly...

"Timmy, did you see your dad this morning?" she asked him.

Timmy Junior hesitated a moment before he said, "I saw a man carrying Daddy out of the house last night."

Stephanie laughed and wondered just where that son of ours got his imagination from, thinking how he must watch too many movies for such a young boy.

"Don't be silly Timmy Junior," she said to him sternly but laughing at what he said at the same time. "More than likely he left for work early and didn't want to wake us. He did say he's been very busy lately at work…"

"No Mom, I saw that man carrying Daddy, Daddy had a sock in his mouth and he was tied up," Timmy Junior insisted and my wife laughed again, but not half as hard as I had been laughing since my capture.

So now, where was I? Oh yeah, sitting on that little bench with my socked feet locked in the stocks, sweating and laughing and wishing that I could shoot another load of cum. God, but my cock was rock hard. This latest tickle session that Ronald was heaping on me was awful. First the fucking guy had tickled my socked feet in those stocks with a hairbrush and then, he left my poor feet in the stocks while he attended to my exposed armpits with the hairbrush and then his fingers and thumbs. Ronald had been merrily and sadistically tickling me using his tickle equipment on me for hours at that point and I had been merrily laughing my head off. Plus, between the tickling and all the sexy thoughts that it was bringing back was sure as fuck keeping my cock hard and leaking buds. Not to mention how Ronald kept administering ball churning aphrodisiacs to me via chloroform and food and water as well, God! So there I sat, laughing and looking straight ahead through tear filled eyes as Ronald tickled and tickled my armpits, and then as he tickled me he made yet another inquiry.

"Timmy, okay, so far you've told me about Linda and how she discovered you were ticklish and how she tormented you along with her sorority sisters, enough for you to change schools," Ronald said. "Then you told me about how your fraternity brothers at another college had set you up for a tickling session at the Asian massage parlor, and how they not only had you tickled but made you pay an extra thousand dollars for it to boot. Timmy, you really are one very ticklish laddy aren't you?"

All I could do was laugh as Ronald spoke; I could not even answer the guy at that point.

"Now Timmy, I have a question for you," Ronald said as I went on and on laughing like a hyena, wondering what the fucking fuck he wanted to ask me. "Now, I want you to tell me actually, just how, how did those fraternity brothers of yours know that you were ticklish? That's what I want you to tell me next."

That said he stopped tickling and stroking my now very soggy armpits and my laughter slowly subsided. I looked down at my feet still locked in the stocks and then looked up at Ronald through my still tear filled eyes.

"No, no, really, don't make me tell you about that," I said miserably, snuffling my words out. "It was too humiliating man."

"Ah ha, humiliating," Ronald said jovially. "All the more reason that I would want to know."

To hammer his point home even more Ronald stroked in one of my armpits again, making me giggle.

"Now, don't leave out one smidgen of a detail," Ronald said. "Let's get started."

"Please, no man, don't make me tell that story!" I grunted throatily, but to spur me on Ronald wiggled his fingers deeper in my armpit. "Ha, ha, ha, ha, ha, ha, ha, ha, ha, ha, ha, okay, okay, I'll tell you. If it will stop you tickling me again I will tell you…"

"Tell me everything, now!" Ronald demanded.

"Shit," I said as he stopped tickling me. "Okay, here goes. I had transferred to this new college, after the Linda episode. I had settled into a new life, joined a fraternity and was really enjoying college life. Well, the Greek organizations were having a spring competition among the fraternities and sororities. Since I had been a high school wrestling champion I volunteered for the Greek Wrestling competition. Well, I had been through several rounds and had easily defeated all my competitors. It was double elimination and a rather good wrestler I had defeated earlier was up again, this time for the championship. I was winded but still pretty confident, and it showed, making the other side pretty worried. I guess I should mention here that we were all wearing the same kind of wrestling gear, a latex singlet that dipped to mid abdomen in the front and just above the ass in the rear. Under that was nothing that a guy could wear but a jock. And yeah, we had our socks and sneakers on. This outfit really showed off our muscular bodies, what we had all worked so hard for in the weight rooms, but it sort of played into my demise as well. The match started and it was soon obvious that I had the upper hand. Although the other guy was strong and quick I was stronger and quicker, plus I was experienced. At one point I had him near a pin, but he was giving it his all to keep his shoulders off the mat. In desperation he reached around me with one hand and I found it right on my sexy ass. My wrestling outfit was cut so low in the back that his hand slipped under the material and found the back elastic to my jockstrap. Finding this, he pulled meanly, it stretched way out of the back of my singlet, but it also pulled really tight on my poor cock and balls that were now, just for the record being squashed in the front. This caused me to let up on my pin move and for him to more easily keep his shoulders off the mat. I let out an "OOOOO" sound as he pulled more on the elastic of my jockstrap. We were sort of at a stalemate, but the action of him grabbing at my jockstrap from behind had scooted us over toward the edge of the ring, and it just so happened it was the side of the ring where all his supporters had gathered, them leaning against the mat beneath the ropes."

"Ronald, can I stop now?" I pleaded. "Please don't make me tell you the rest buddy…"

"Okay Timmy, you don't have to tell me anymore," Ronald said and picked up one of the discarded hairbrushes. "I'll just start tickling your socked feet again with this hairbrush. How does that sound?"

He gave me that evil grin which I had come to loathe…

"NO, NO! OKAY, I'll go on," I squawked as he approached my trapped feet with the hairbrush. "Well, there we were, stalemated for the championship of the fraternities. I had had him in a near pin hold and now the bastard had hold of my jockstrap from behind, squashing and mashing my cock and balls. What a feeling, let me tell you. I was on my hands and knees as he dragged me along embarrassingly by the back elastic of my jockstrap, yanking upwards so my poor cock and balls suffered each time he did that. That was when I felt something at my feet. I was thinking that there was no fucking way this guy can reach that far, seeing as he still had hold of my jockstrap. So I turned my head and was able to peer under my arm back toward my feet, and there I saw one of his supporters pulling on my sneaker laces. This made me quickly look to the other side and sure enough there was another guy untying that sneaker lace too. I yelled, "HEY!" But they just laughed at me and each other and started getting my sneakers off my feet. As I struggled their good buddy who had me by the back of my jockstrap gave it a yank up, sending searing pain through me via my cock and balls, stopping my struggles so his buds could get my sneakers off my feet. And they soon did have my sneakers off and then my situation was even worse, seeing as I was now slipping on my sweat socked feet. The slipping made it easier for the guy to guide me along with my jockstrap as if I was a puppy on a leash. He moved me closer to the edge of the mat. I yelled to the referee for some help but he simply shrugged and smiled at me like he was saying, "I think I would like to see how this turns out." My yelling got my opponents attention and now he became aware of what was going on. Once he saw his buddies getting my sneakers off he started to pull and jerk even harder on my jockstrap, which caused me more discomfort and further reduced any chance of leverage I might have had. Then, it was as if he got another idea in his evil little pea brain and with his other hand he reached down and grabbed me bodily. I let out a yelping sort of sound as I left the mat and found myself lifted above his head. He had temporarily let go of my jockstrap. He spun me a few times and then amid the cheers of the crowd and his buddies he sent me plunging back down to the mat. I said "OOOFF" and before I could scurry away from him he grabbed the back of my jock-strap in hand again, tugging on it meanly. With his other hand again he managed to grab the little shoulder strap on my singlet and he pulled it off my shoulder. The tension and elasticity of the singlet caused the strap to snap all the way down to my bent elbow. I yelled something like "Hey, what the fucking fuck hell do you think you're doing?" I yelled and looked at the two referees who just continued to give me this, "Well, well, well, look at what's happening now," look." By now the two of the guy's mat accomplices were pulling on my thick white athletic socks and were stripping my feet bare. The way my opponent had dropped me on the mat just moments ago had caused me to land with my ankles now under the ropes, off the mat and hanging in mid air. This made the task of stripping my socks off my feet quick and easy. It also further reduced my leverage over my opponent, enough so he was able to reach over to my other shoulder and slip that strap off and down to my elbow. Well, now the hell had started. The two mat accomplices each grabbed one of my ankles under an arm and turned their backs to the ring for support. By then my feet had been stripped of my white athletic socks. The two guys started scribbling their fingers up and down the bottoms of my bare feet. I immediately started howling, but shit, I couldn't get my feet loose from their grips. They held tight to my ankles and worked meanly on my bare soles. They were also quickly joined by who knows how many of their friends that were crowded in. Laughing uncontrollably I looked up at the referee for help, yelling and laughing to him, "Those bastards are tickling my damned feet!" He just chuckled and said, "Well now, that's an interesting technique, don't you think bud?" So he was obviously not going to be of any help to me. I was still managing to hold onto my opponent, but just barely. Once he saw my reaction to the foot tickling, I mean, hell, how could he miss it, I mean, I was yelling and laughing loudly in his ear, he used his free hand to begin to explore ticklish spots on me himself. And oh God, he found my man tits, which had been totally exposed by the slipped shoulder straps. I was laughing, hooting, bouncing and holding on for dear life. But, once he started working on my man tits my cock started responding and it started getting hard. But no one, not even me was aware of it, yet. Then, another culprit from the crowd reached up onto the mat and snagged the edge of the low scoop of my singlet, right above my ass and right below where my opponent had my jockstrap stretched out, and this fucking guy pulled for all he was worth. Fucking fucks, the singlet stretched way below my ass, exposing the inner cheeks of my rectum and then everyone could see where the stretched jockstrap was pulled up between my legs, totally humiliating. Still laughing, and louder and louder with each passing second and weakening from the tickling I felt my singlet slip down. Fuck, it was already off my shoulders and now it was being pulled down off my ass. I released my hold on my opponent with the idea of rescuing my singlet, and my dignity. Well, the thing was already stretched so tight that when I lowered my arms to grab it the straps snapped instantly off my arms, leaving nothing to hold it up. They guy kept pulling and the singlet slid down my legs and stopped at the two guys holding my ankles. Released, my opponent quickly made a reversal and pulled himself up on top of me, but the perverted bastard maintained his grip on my jockstrap. Then, with coordinated help, my singlet was slipped past my naked feet by those two bastards tickling me, one at a time, without them missing a ticklish beat. To further my utter humiliation my opponent's fans started yelling, "Pin him, pin him, pin him", and that's what it looked like he was going to do. He yelled for the guys at my feet to turn me loose and he flipped my laughing ass over. Now, my laughing, giggling weak body lay on its back. And fucking totally fucks, all I was wearing by then was my stretched jockstrap. But, once on my back it became quickly obvious to everyone around the mat that I was sporting a huge erection, barely concealed in my stretched jockstrap. Now, the guys re-grabbed and started tickling my now upturned feet, further rendering me helpless. I was lying there on that mat, laughing, cackling and sputtering, in nothing but my still pulled and stretched jockstrap. Suddenly, my opponent was on top of me, holding my upper body and shoulders to the mat, but he was still pulling on my jockstrap, Gawd. At that point the crowd, including my supporters, (I could not believe that) began to chant, "Strip him, strip him, strip him!" and the referee began to count me out, because my shoulders were pinned. And the way I was laughing I was not going to be able to extricate myself. The referee counted, "One, two!" and then my opponent looked up at the referee, smiled and shook his head, "No", and with his eyes signaled for the referee to just look around. The referee passed on his count, glanced around at the assembled crowd, heard poor me guffawing and their chants of "Strip him" and backed away from his count. He sat back on his haunches and said to my opponent, "Okay, well, strip him!" Now this was a co-ed crowd Ronald, fraternity and sorority members, and the crowd had tripled since my laughter had rung out from the wrestling ring. I guess a lot of people wanted to see the champion bested for once huh? So, with encouragement, and even from my supporters, the bastards, my opponent jumped to his feet, extricated me from the foot ticklers, reversed the pull on my jockstrap, pulling it downwards now, and down my legs and over my feet, rendering me completely naked in the wrestling ring. I was still weak and still chuckling from all the tickling and not able to render a defense. So, my opponent reached down, picked my naked ass up off the mat and with a little help from his friends who stretched the ropes of the ring, he dropped me upside down through the four ropes, so my head and shoulders were pressed down on the mat and my poor feet flailed straight up in the air and the rest of my sexy naked body was held in place for all to see, even my bouncing and succulent looking erection. I screamed out "You bastards!" as I landed unceremoniously in the ropes and the guys laughed and the girls squealed, and I was turning red as a beet. Now, the two ticklers jumped up on the edge of the ring and again attacked my upturned soles. I was off and laughing again and heard myself begging them to stop. A couple more guys started working on my ribs and sides and still more held my wrists out while some took advantage of my exposed sweaty armpits. All that made me laugh and laugh fucking hard. But my son of a bitch opponent wasn't satisfied with all that. He sat down where my head was almost buried in his latex covered crotch and he started going meanly at my man nipples. The bastard twisted and pulled and stroked and tweaked, and as you know Ronald, that's a very sexy place for me. Well, all the tickling and nip tweaking caused my exposed cock to start throbbing and bobbing to the beat of the band. Fucking fuck Ronald, by then my manhood was fully erect, hard as a rock. I laughed and hooted and hollered and then to my total humiliation, I shot my goddamned load, my cock gushed a good glob of cum straight out, then another few globs of my good stuff, and then some more. The first glob actually hit my opponent right in the face. Then the next glob hit him in the chest and so on until I was just dribbling in my own face below. Everybody screamed when I shot my load, the girls ran off laughing and the guys laughed and pointed at me. Gawd, after that much humiliation they did show me some mercy and un-hitched me from the ropes and threw my singlet at me. I hid my face, pulled on the singlet and made a hasty getaway. My opponent jumped back up into the ring and waved my jockstrap around for all to see. It was like a trophy he had bested from his opponent. I sometimes wonder if that bastard still has my jockstrap. Fuck, I stayed away from school for an entire semester after that, and even when I came back I kept a very, very low profile. So, that's how those guys found out that I was ticklish. Now Ronald, after all you've put me through, can't you at least show me the same mercy those guys did, and let me go…huh?"

Chapter Fifteen

After going through the long and agonizing process of telling Ronald about how my college buddies found out about my being ticklish, instead of abiding by my pleas to be released Ronald first un-tethered my socked feet from the stocks. As Ronald handled my socked feet, lifting them out of the stocks my cock jutted long and hard in front of me. Fuck, what was it about watching Ronald handle my feet that so put me in erectile motion? He then untied my wrists from the post where they had been stretched above me. By then my arms were numb and tingling. Gawd, when all this was over (whenever the fuck that would be) I realized that I would have a lot to think about not that I hadn't thought about how being tickled and tormented always sent me into a sexual frenzy, boy had I thought about it over the years. Ronald then helped me to my feet, my hands still roped good and tight in front of me...

"Feeling okay Timmy?" he asked me and took my bound wrists in his hands, stretching my arms out gently in front of me.

"I-I'm physically and mentally exhausted buddy," I replied. "All the tickling you've subjected me to has sapped me I suppose. Plus, telling you the stories of my ticklish past also sapped my mind I guess, and not to mention the chloroform naps you've been giving me, Gawd man, that stuff really stinks. I must be the first fucking guy in history to have a raging hard-on from being chloroformed..."

"Well, if you cooperate with me now I won't be forced to use the chloroform on you this time bud," Ronald said and began untying my wrists, holding my hands gingerly up in front of me.

"Y-you're going to let me go right?" I asked him hopefully, a huge feeling of relief engulfing me as he untied my wrists. "Oh man Ronald; I knew eventually you'd come to your senses. Man, I promise not to tell anyone about all of this. It'll be our secret; just us buddy, sort of like when we were in college, fraternity stuff, stuff you never tell anyone you know, just between us guys..."

But as I spoke on and on I didn't realize that once the ropes around my wrists had been loosened Ronald moved in a fast and blinding motion, taking full advantage of my physical and mental exhaustions. When the rope fell away from one of my wrists and dangled from my other wrist Ronald quickly whirled me around on my socked feet, and fuck, before I could even react to being spun like a top he yanked my arms meanly behind me.

"RONALD, what are you doing buddy? What the fucking fuck are you doing?" I croaked miserably, fear filling me up again. "I-I thought that once I told you about my tickle history you would let me go and..."

"I never said anything about letting you go Timmy my ticklish boy," Ronald said laughingly. "And I am sure that you have lots more tickle history to tell me about. It looks to me like we'll be at this for a good while more man..."

As Ronald spoke he tied my hands tightly behind me all over again...

"Oh come on man, *come on Ronald*, you can't be serious here," I pleaded miserably as my buddy then squatted to tie my socked feet, snapping the elastic in my socks after he was done. "FUCK!"

Chuckling meanly as he got to his feet Ronald playfully hoisted me up off the floor like a groom carrying his virgin bride over the threshold to their marriage bed...

"Now let's bathe those sexy and ticklish feet of yours in some nice warm oil huh bud?" Ronald asked me as he lugged me from the room where the stocks were. "After those tootsies of yours have soaked in warm oil for a while they'll be even more tickle sensitive. And, while your feet are bared and taking an oily bath you can tell me still more of your tickle history..."

"FUCK, *fuck, fuck,*" I whsispered despondently as I was carried from the room, looking down at my socked feet, knowing how my buddy would wallow in again taking those silky nylon socks off them for me.

Double fucks, I knew that he would not give me the privilege of taking my own socks off my feet by untying my hands, oh no, Ronald was not taking any chances there buds...

"RONALD, put me down man, haven't you done enough tickling to me already?" I barked at the guy as he huffed, carrying me, his special prize to yet another room. "Man, I'm even losing track of the time here. You kidnapped me days ago it seems, but I know it was just last night! Fuck, I feel as if I've been here for eons! And man, you fucking fuck, you've tickle tortured me beyond belief! How can I go on buddy? You are driving me crazy with all this tickling, and all the talk of tickling, and all the thoughts of impending tickling, and worst, fucking teasing my cock to the point of cumming, but then not letting me cum! Alright, well, you did make me cum that one time, with that sadistic latex sucking sheath and that was just so you could make me more ticklish than I already was, Gawd, what a fucked up thing to do to a guy."

As Ronald carried me and I prattled on and on I took in the sights of the hall-ways in his immense mansion-like tickle palace... Shit, this was all so fucking crazy, totally insane actually. Now Ronald was carrying my fucking tickle limp body to another room so that he could soak my feet in warm oil and make them even more ticklish. GODDDAMN it all, how could my poor feet be made even more ticklish? As he carried me Ronald grinned at me, lugging me into the room where I saw a pedicure-like station set-up. Ronald sat me in the chair and in front of the chair was a large, deep motorized basin, filled with gyrating warm oil. As Ronald got me seated in the chair he strapped my naked waist to the back of it.

"This will keep you in position buddy boy," he said meanly as he cinched my waist to the chair.

Next, he untied my feet, stripped my black socks off them and crammed those stinkers in his back pocket, like he was going to use them again at some point, which I was sure he would. Then, he lifted my feet one at a time and submerged them into the warm oil.

"Oh man, that feels so good," I said, leaning back in the chair as the oil jet-tisoned over my bare feet. "That feels so relaxing Ronald..."

I wiggled my toes gratefully...

"Yes Timmy, it's very relaxing," Ronald said and dipped his hands into the oil to fasten straps aroud my ankles, straps that were tethered at the sides in the deep basin, lest I try to lift my feet out of it. "The warm oil feels very good and very invigorat-ing on your feet, and it will sooth and soften them up at the same time. The byproduct of the softening is that your feet will be even more sensitive than before, you know

Timmy me laddy, *more ticklish…"*

I simply groaned, torn between the luxurious feeling of the warm oil as it cascaded over my feet and the awful anticipation of what the ticklish outcome would be once my feet were softened.

"Now Timmy, I want you to tell me how your wife has tickle tortured you to get what she wanted," Ronald said, grinning down at me.

I looked up at his smiling face, my jaw drooping and said, "You don't really want to hear anymore do you?"

"Oh, but I do, and if you don't cooperate I can just go to work on those sensitive man tits of yours, as you call them," Ronald said and held up a feather that had been in his pocket.

He wiggled the tip of the feather against one of my jutted up man tits and my hard cock dribbled a dollop of pre cum…

"Ha, ha, NO, no, don't tickle my man tits, I'll tell you about my wife tickling me," I blurted crazily. "Just don't tickle me…"

Ronald pulled up a chair in front of the basin that my feet were strapped into. The warm oil soothed and softened my feet and my cock was still hard and pointing at the ceiling.

"Okay, my wife Stephanie, she has this friend Valerie who is an antique dealer," I began. "Valerie and I really don't get along. We just sort of tolerate each other. Stephanie is really the only reason that we have anything to do with each other. Well, Valerie had brought over this antique Chinese vase for Stephanie to look at. Stephanie fell in love with it and she wanted me to buy it for her. I didn't like the thing at all. It didn't go with anything we had, it was ugly and we didn't have any place to put it, and I told her so. I also pointed out that it was expensive and, NO, I was not going to buy the vase for her. I sort of glared at Valerie, silently asking her why you brought that thing over here. She seemed to get the hint and started wrapping the vase back up. But Stephanie stopped her and gave her a big grin and a wink. Hell, I was the man of the house. I had made a decision and I was standing my ground. She could wink at her friend all she wanted, it was not going to work, or so I thought. So Stephanie proceeded to put on her seductive face and slid up to me, giving me this pretty please chat. But, then she attacked my sides and started tickling me right through the shirt I was wearing. I immediately broke out in laughter, buckled and went into a stupid looking protective dance. But, Stephanie is quick and she stayed with me and quickly moved her probing hands and wiggling fingers in and out against my ribs, avoiding my protective hands and arms. The laughing and dodging her as she tickled me had caused me to scrunch my eyes closed, a bad move on my part, so I was trying to fend her off just from feel, and not succeeding. Stephanie kept moving forward and I kept moving backward until I stumbled over an ottoman and landed on the carpet with Stephanie right on top of me. I thanked God that Tim Junior was in school, seeing as this was real embarrassing for me. I was laughing and guffawing by now and I was really unable to get away from Stephanie's tickle attack upon me. I quickly rolled over onto my stomach and tried to keep my arms at my sides to protect my ticklish ribs. Stephanie was sitting on the small of my back, pinning me to the carpet, and saying "Pretty Please" "Pretty please, please buy me the vase, pretty please" over and over as she tickled me. Then, amid my laughter, I heard her tell Valerie, who had been standing there the whole time with her mouth open in total disbelief as to what was happening, that if she helped, Timothy would buy her the vase. So, Valerie asked Stephanie what she should do and my loving wife tells her that my feet are extremely ticklish. She then told Valerie that if she sat on the back of my thighs that she could take my shoes and socks off and work some mischief on my bare feet. I screamed out, NO, NO, VALERIE, don't you dare take my shoes and socks off me!" Well, Valerie, not really liking me, (or maybe she does in a sadistic sort of way) jumped at this opportunity and was on my legs and stripping off my shoes and socks in no time. At that point Stephanie was digging her fingers in between my arms and ribs and working up and down my sides and Valerie was now raking her fingernails up and down and up and down my naked soles and even tweaking my toes. I was weak from laughter and laughing was all that I could do. Then, Stephanie asked me if I would now buy the vase for her, or should she and Valerie continue tickling me, and maybe even worse. Well, knowing how ticklish I am and how ticklish I can be made to be I decided in a hurry, that the vase was a cheap price to pay to get those two tickling fiends off me, so I gave in, although they were *still* tickling me and I was still laughing. Stephanie quit tickling me and reached behind her and extracted my wallet from the back pocket of my pants. Valerie however, was still working on my feet like there was no tomorrow. Stephanie extracted the two hundred dollars cash for the vase and tossed my wallet on the couch. Valerie just kept right on tickling my feet and I just kept right on laughing. It seemed that the bitch was somehow transfixed by my feet. Stephanie actually had to get up and pull her good friend off me to give her the money, telling her that that was enough, that if she tickled poor Timmy past his limits he would become ultra-tickle sensitive, and she did not want that, although you do seem to want that Ronald, old buddy of mine. I was by then in a fetal position on the floor and rubbing my sides and scratching my bare feet, trying to relieve the ticklish feeling that lingered there. The two women gloated meanly at their success, Valerie counting her money and Stephanie admiring her new vase. When Valerie left I confronted Stephanie, telling her not to ever do anything like that again, as I sat there getting my socks and shoes back on. She smiled coyly at me and I knew that this would not be the only time that my wife would use tickling as a way to get what she wanted from me. So you see Ronald, Stephanie used tickle torture to get what she wanted, against my will. And to make it even worse she did it in front of and with the help of her friend Valerie. And the fact that this happened in front of Valerie did lead to another situation at Valerie's antique shop where the bitch used my ticklishness for another antique purchase, an antique purchase that ultimately led to even more tickle torture at the hands of my loving and beautiful wife. Oh shit Ronald, look at this man, between telling you that story and having my feet in this oil my cock is harder than hard and leaking like crazy. God, and just from talking about all this it's hard! Please man; can't you please turn me loose now?"

"Turn you loose buddy?" Ronald asked and squatted down at my feet as they soaked in the gyrating and warm oil. "Turn you loose, now that sure is a novel way of stating it I must say, turn you loose."

"Yeah, turn me loose, as in let me go, as in how about letting me the fuck out of here?" I said angrily.

"But Timmy, if I turn you loose, then why am I soaking your feet in this oil?" Ronald asked me, sounding totally bewildered. "Nah, I want to hear you laugh some more and after I'm done soaking those tootsies of yours in the oil I have a real treat in store for you."

Ronald grinned at me, looking totally evil and flicked his tongue in and out of his mouth a few times. I had no idea at that moment what that tongue flicking implied.

"Ronald, again, how much more can you possibly tickle me?" I asked, ranting my words miserably. "You've had me here more than seven or eight hours already, at least…"

"Oh Timmy, me ticklish laddy that you are, how unknowing you are also," Ronald mused. "With the size of this place that I've created I can most definitely subject you to at least a few more long *days* of tickle fun.

At the sound of the word "days" my heart hammered in total fear in my chest…

"Now, you said that the tickling that Stephanie and Valerie did to you in your home led to a tickle situation for you when it came to another antique purchase," Ronald prodded me.

"Yeah, that was just between me and that bitch Valerie," I said, glancing down at my feet as they soaked in the warm oil.

"I want to hear about that now buddy," Ronald said and reached forward to give one of my man tits a good squeeze and twist. "And you know what'll happen if you don't tell me…"

He squeezed my man tit again and without any further prodding I began jibber jabbering…

Chapter Sixteen

"Well, okay, the continuation of my ticklish subjugation by my wife Stephanie has *a lot* to do with her friend, that bitch Valerie," I went on miserably for Ronald. "As I said she owns an antique shop. And also as you already know Valerie was introduced to my utter and total helplessness when being tickled and how Stephanie had used it, in Valerie's presence no less, to make me do what she wanted and to get what she wanted, namely that vase that one time. But there was another time after that man, oh God, there sure as shit was another time. One day I got a call from Valerie at my office. She said that Stephanie's and my anniversary was approaching, which was correct and that she had an item that she was sure Stephanie would just flip over. (Man, little did I know at that moment how it would be me who would be flipped (literally) over the item.) The first thing I asked that bitch was how she had gotten my office phone number and the second question I asked her was what the item was. She told me that Stephanie had given her my office number in case of emergencies or other events, but she refused to tell me what the item she had was, indicating that I had to see it first-hand for myself. I hesitated, but Valerie used all her sales and female persuasiveness until I agreed to stop by her shop on my way home from work. Now, Valerie and Stephanie are friends from way back, but Valerie and I have never really gotten along, we just sort of tolerate each other, as I think I already mentioned. So, begrudgingly, I agreed to stop by her shop after work. I called Stephanie to tell her that I had something that I needed to take care of after work and that I would be running a little late. She told me she was fine with that because that way she could go to the mall and shop before all the stores closed. I told her to be careful with her spending and she simply laughed and teasingly told me how she was just tickled to spend my money, or that I was simply tickled for her to spend my money. A chill ran down my spine as I told her that that was not funny. She just giggled and said that she would see me later. I had the feeling that somehow she knew exactly what I would be doing after work. We said our "I love yous" to each other and hung up. So after work, I went to Valerie's shop, all spiffy in a navy blue pinstriped suit. Valerie's shop is in an old warehouse district, which is probably good for reduced rents and easy shipping and receiving, but it sure as hell was not good for a handsome lug like me in a suit which screams money. The way some of the passerby around that area drank in the sight of me as I made my way to Valerie's shop after getting off the train made me just a tad antsy. If you really want to know Ronald, I was sweating in my socks. The shop was locked when I arrived so I knocked and waited. I didn't wait long and before long Valerie opened the door, greeting me warmly. We exchanged cool hellos and I entered. Now let me tell you Ronald, Valerie is not an unattractive woman. She's very athletic and sexy in a very boyish sense. She has small breasts but great legs; I'd say they would be called dancer's legs. For a girl, she has surprisingly good upper body strength and needless to say, those great legs of hers are strong. I think she was a gymnast or something like that in college. If I weren't married, and if I and Valerie got along better, I could actually see myself having asked her out. So, anyway, I entered the shop and she quickly relocked the door behind me, putting up the "Closed" sign. She quickly ushered me to the rear of the shop. I was immediately drawn to her bare lower legs as she walked ahead of me. She was wearing a tight skirt and low heel sling back shoes and both her heels were out of the slings. So, as she walked her shoes slapped at her bare soles, making slap, slap, slap, slap, sounds. There was something real kinky and erotic about that somehow. Plus, what made it more erotic was how I could see the muscles in her calves working as she walked. I then realized that she was telling me about the Oriental desk that she was about to show me and that she thought that Stephanie would go ape over it. I cleared my head of the thoughts of her calves and feet and paid attention to what she was saying. When she stopped in front of this big desk and turned to face me I somehow sensed that she knew that I had been ogling her legs and feet. She smiled, gave me a sexy little pose and bluntly said, "Timmy, do you like my legs?" I then realized that I sure was staring. I cleared my throat and also realized that I had been set up in going to Valerie's shop. I didn't know what the bitch had in mind for me but I would not let her get away with it that was for sure, *right*. I cleared my throat again and looked away from her legs, saying, "Don't be silly Valerie, is this the desk you wanted me to see?" She affirmed my question and began showing me the desk. It was nice but it had a three thousand dollar price tag on it, which made it not so nice. That was much more than I wanted to spend for Stephanie's and my anniversary. I quickly told Valerie that, figuring that would end her sales pitch right there. But instead she said something like, "Oh, I think you'll come around and decide that it's worth it Timmy." She smiled, hopped up onto the desk and told me to take a really good look at the workmanship. So, I squatted down and I was looking at the desk when I noticed that the bitch had crossed her legs and was dangling her already loose shoes from her toes. She did have really great legs Ronald, and real sexy arches, and her shoes dropped, ker-plop, and man, she had sexy toes too! Now, as I squatted there I kept reminding myself that I was a married man. Valerie worked her feet up and down at the ankles and then splayed her painted toes. She then reached out with one foot and tweaked me gently on the nose. I could not help but stare again and inhale deeply the musty and sexy scent of her foot. I quickly realized that I was being mesmerized by Valerie's sexy feet. I stood up, straightened my tie and told her, "No, it's a very nice desk, but its way too expensive." Valerie smiled at me and said, "Okay Timmy lets see just how persuasive I can be." So, sitting there swinging her bare legs and feet in front of me she said that she would throw in this unique Oriental room divider at no extra cost. Hell, she said she would even throw in free delivery for both items. She started sales pitching how the room divider would be perfect in my and Stephanie's home, separating the large living space without being a wall. And she hopped down off the desk and quickly directed me to this ornate metal frame that was attached to the floor at the bottom and to the ceiling rafters at the top. It had been hidden behind the Oriental room divider. It was about eight feet wide with a large oversized door-like opening in the center that seemed to be two separate frames inside the larger frame. At the four corners of the inner frame were short chains with what looked something like manacles and the center had a larger version hanging on each side. Padding across the room barefooted Valerie directed me over to the Oriental room divider, saying, "Timmy come here, this is not only a good conversation piece, but it can add to entertainment at parties." Man, I should have been wary, since it was Valerie I mean. Fuck, we were always trying to one up the other, and at the moment she had this devilish looking grin on her face. I somehow knew that I was about to be one upped. "Entertainment, what in the hell kind of entertainment can this thing offer?" I asked her, stepping further into her spider's web while she wiggled her lure. She then said, "Well, its sort of participatory entertainment, the Chinese used to use these in many of their party rooms." She then directed me with a smile on her face, to step up on the little steps of the thing on either side of the inner frame. Without thinking about what she might be planning she then said to me, "Now, reach up and grab those little handles on either side of the frame top." I shucked off my suit jacket, tossed it over a nearby chair, reached up as she said to the handles and Valerie stretched up on her tiptoes behind me. As she rubbed her crotch against my sexy ass in my suit pants she said, "Yes, like that..." And then, oh Gawd of Gawds while I was stupidly grasping the handles, thinking that something big was going to happen as I tugged on them Val stretched around me and with blinding speed took one of the manacle-like looking things in her hands and snapped it quickly and efficiently around my wrist. Fuck, they were manacles; they were not just, like-manacles. They were the real McCoy. I quickly said, "Hey!" in a complaining sounding manner and Valerie simply giggled, reached over to my other wrist and before I thought to pull it away from the handle she got that one manacled as well. And while I was brainlessly inspecting the manacles that now held my wrists and as I was pulling on them, trying to free myself Valerie was busying herself by attaching the lower manacles to my ankles, securing my feet and legs to the bottom corners of the frame. As she began to attach the center harness securely around my waist I continued complaining and bitching at her, saying things like, "Valerie, what the fucking fuck are you doing? Unfasten me from this thing, now!" She simply gigged that giggle that I had come to hate and said, "But Timmy, you said yourself that you wanted to see how this was used for entertainment, and as the proprietor of this shop I'm just demonstrating for you. Besides, you need to know how to use this thing so you can show Stephanie." Oh man, Valerie really was enjoying herself at my expense, having tricked me into that spread eagled position in that iron frame. I shouted at her, "Valerie, I don't plan on buying any of this junk for Stephanie so you can just release me now!" She ignored what I said and asked me if I was comfortable. I gritted my teeth, clenched my fingers into fists and curled my toes back under my navy blue socks that I was wearing that day and spat my words at her, "What the hell do you mean comfortable? Let me out of this contraption!" And as I ranted miserably I continued struggling to get free, but man, it was no use. I was secure in that thing. While in that position I also became aware of the fact that my cock had plumped up from having looked at Valerie's naked legs and feet and the leg show she had been giving me since I had so dumbly walked into her shop, into her clutches. And admittedly I was concerned that it might become noticeably visible in my suit pants. I didn't think at that moment that Valerie had noticed but she sure as hell was enjoying herself, playing me like I was a stupid male. But, the fact that she had managed to trick me into that predicament was adding a tingling to my crotch somehow. She smiled as she looked me over in the thing and said, "I'll take that as a yes. Okay, here's some of the fun parts of this room divider entertainment center, the thing you're in is actually called A Spinning Chinaman. Let me show you. If I remove this pin..." and she pulled a pin out that was near the floor and then went on speaking, "...it releases the inner portions of the frame on a horizontal axis and the spinning Chinaman, in this case Timmy, *you*, can be sent tumbling over and over." I looked at her in disbelief, thinking she wouldn't do it. But with that Valerie grabbed the inner frame and pulled like she was playing

Wheel of Fortune and I went spinning head over heels inside that frame. I screamed like I was riding a carnival ride and Valerie just laughed in total enjoyment. She spun me again and again, numerous times as I screamed and yelled like a frightened schoolgirl. Finally, she stopped my spinning, but she stopped me upside down. As I hung there she slipped the pin back in and went on explaining how the spinning Chinaman contraption worked, "Now, the victim, I mean the center of entertainment can be spun either way." Valerie proceeded to pull out another pin which released the inner frame on a vertical axis. I screamed, "Now Valerie, wait a minute here!" but it was to no avail and she gave me a whirl, spinning me around and around. Fucking fucks, this time I was screaming and hollering even louder. And again, Valerie was enjoying herself at my expense. She spun me and spun me and spun me. Then, she again stopped my spinning and reinserted the pin, locking the frame down, but poor me, I was still upside down and somewhat dizzy and disoriented. Valerie said, "See, party games using this device can be played by asking the victim, uh, the central player questions. If he gets them right he gets a point toward release. But if he gets them wrong, well, he loses a point and goes spinning." And she took the pin out and gave me another few spins and I went around and around and around like I was spinning on my head. When I stopped spinning I was sort of in a diagonal position and Valerie said, "Say, since you're already in position, lets you and I play a short game, okay?" She grinned as if I could do more than object to all this horseplay, which I was still doing, but as I said it was to no avail. Valerie then asked me, "Okay, lets see, what shall I ask you?" She made like she was deep in thought, mulling something really big over in her mind. At the same damned time she adjusted me in the spinning Chinaman so I was again upside down, raised one of her bare feet and, leaning on the frame she pressed that foot against my face, stroking it, her toes dangerously close to my lips and mouth. She teased my nose and ears with her toes and then placed them back by my mouth. She slid her soles over my lips a few times and I found myself licking her damned foot, greedily sucking at her toes each time she would place them by my quivering lips. She looked down at me at one point and I stupidly said, "Yum" as she again inserted a couple of toes in my mouth. Valerie giggled and acted like she was still thinking while at the same damned time she was teasing me with her bare foot. And I got to tell you Ronald, this barefoot work was making me fucking hot. I just hoped that Valerie didn't notice, you know what I mean, the goddamned tent that was in my suit pants. Then she announced, "I've got it, I know what I'll ask you. Timmy, do you like women's feet?" She giggled and made sure to wiggle her toes under my chin. I sputtered up at her, "Uh, uh, of course not, of course I don't...I, uh," and she cut me off by saying "Wrong answer Timmy," and laughing Valerie gave me a big whirl and I went around and around yelling as I spun. The spinning slowed and she stopped the thing before it coasted to a halt on its own, making sure I was left in an upside down position. I was beyond irate and I hollered upwards at her, "Stop this nonsense now Valerie!" as my eyes seemed to keep spinning in their sockets. She ignored me and said, "Next question, do you find my feet and legs sexy Timmy? Well, do you?" and her foot returned to tease my face. My eyes stopped spinning and my vision was upside down, but I could see and taste her sexy foot. And God, I could see the coy sexy look on her face. I ranted again at her, "Valerie, I'm a married man. I'm married to your friend, in case you need to be reminded. How could you ask me such questions?" I tried to sound astonished and sincere but Valerie simply grinned at me and turned to the sizeable lump in my suit pants and thumped it. She said, "Well, I see a sign here that says you find my feet and legs very sexy. BUZZ! Wrong answer Timmy Backman!" And laughing even harder now she gave me another spin and I cried miserably for her to stop. After that last spin that seemed to go on and on she stopped me and said, "So you see Timmy, the spinning Chinaman can make for some really great in-home entertainment," and she laughed even more yet. I looked up at her, sweating now and said, "Valerie, this is not funny at all!" I was mad, totally pissed off that she had gotten the better of me and I was also feeling embarrassed that she had managed to get me turned on. But all she said was, "Timmy, the part of the spinning Chinaman that I think you and Stephanie will mostly enjoy will be entertaining your friends by showing them just how ticklish you are. You remember that don't you Timmy?" I shook in terror in the bondage and she pulled out a couple of stiff looking feathers. I screamed, "VALERIE! Now, what the fucking fuck are you up to? No! Don't you dare!" As I pleaded with her at that point she was busy rolling my suit pants down to my thighs. In my upside down position that made her task real easy. She took those feathers and ran them up and down my now bare legs, which were pointing toward the ceiling, working the feathers over my thin socked calves and all the way up to my tickle sensitive knees and a little above as well. She had me laughing and laughing. Then, she said what I was afraid she would say, "No tickling should ever be done without including the feet!" and no matter how I objected she simply continued in what she had deemed her demonstration. She stood close to me again and reached up to remove my shoes and socks. Once Valerie had denuded my feet she used those blasted feathers to torment my warm and moist soles and toes. I laughed like crazy as she worked those feathers up and down my soles and even pulled them between each toe. That really got me laughing loudly let me tell you Ronald. I was actually laughing, sputtering and guffawing for Valerie's entertainment. She exclaimed, "Wow, I know that Stephanie said you were ticklish, but does she know just how *very* ticklish you truly are?" All I could do in response was laugh and laugh. Then, she moved down to my head and teased my nose, ears and neck with the feathers. I laughed and sneezed a few times but the bitch was not satisfied with this, my shirt was in her way and she told me so by saying, "I know that Stephanie will forgive me for taking your shirt off you, seeing as its only for the art of tickling and for my demonstration here." I objected by saying that tickling a poor guy was not an art! Over my continued objections she unbuttoned my shirt, pulled it from my pants and let it drape over me. This exposed my belly and ribs and some of my armpits, and oh yes Ronald, I see you looking at them, my delectable man tits. My face was covered with my askew dress shirt and Valerie used those feathers like she was a buccaneer sword fighter. She really worked over my poor man tits, and man, you know how that affects me. Then, she finally stopped tickling me but she was giggling sadistically. She pulled my shirt back into my pants and I looked upwards and it was beyond obvious that I had a massive sized erection in my suit pants. Well, this was more than a massive sized erection, because she had caused it earlier when she had teased me with her feet, but now it was a whopper of an erection that was tenting my suit pants. And God, there was even a wet spot forming where the head of my cock would be. She asked me, "Did I do that?" giggling as she said it, pointing at my crotch. I turned forty different shades of red and told her that it was time to turn me loose, really meaning it this time. She continued to giggle but then she took my picture and quickly locked the camera away. She apologized by saying that she had no idea that I would get SOOOO excited with her tickling me. She righted me in the spinning Chinaman and finally released me. After I got myself put back together in my suit, namely rolling my suit pants back down and adjusting my shirt and tie and getting my suit jacket on she made me sign a purchase agreement for the spinning Chinaman on threat of showing Stephanie the picture of her darling husband in the thing. Quite honestly, I don't know what kind of difference that made because once Stephanie got the desk for our anniversary. Valerie had the spinning Chinaman installed as her gift for our anniversary. And again, under the threat of exposing my previous ride in the Chinaman she made me demonstrate it for Stephanie. Stephanie was ecstatic over both gifts, but played with the spinning Chinaman, her loving husband to be precise, for hours, with Valerie right there to enjoy it as well. Then, that damned bitch Valerie pulled out two feathers and told Stephanie that the spinning Chinaman, me, might be ticklish, to Stephanie's delight of course. And so I spun and laughed and spun and laughed and spun and laughed..."

Ronald's Journal
Dated May 1994

I never made an entry about the night that Timothy's son; Tim Junior, as they named him was born. I was at home relaxing when the phone call came at around eleven thirty that night. I was just finishing watching the news and was ready to hit the sack when the phone rang. I instantly imagined that it was someone calling with bad news, I mean the phone never rings that late so I figured someone was either very sick, or very dead, hardy har, fucking har. I answered the phone and all I heard was the sound of a guy hooting, cackling and laughing. I said "hello" over and over and asked who it was, although the guy's voice sounded very familiar. Finally, Timothy Backman said, "Ronald, it's me buddy! It's Timothy Backman! *It's me!*" and as he said that he was laughing and laughing. The sound of his laughter was somehow hypnotic, although if anyone were to ask me about that I wouldn't know how to explain it, just that somehow the sound of Timothy's laughter got under my skin and I wanted to hear more of it, lots more actually. I asked my work buddy what was going on, if he was okay, if everything was okay. He said that things could not be better and that Stephanie was in labor. She had begun labor pains two hours ago at home, he had driven her to the hospital post-haste and now she was in the delivery room delivering their first child. I congratulated the handsome laddy, wished him the best and then he asked if I would be so kind as to come to the hospital and keep him company in the waiting area while Stephanie was giving birth. I figured Tim was not a modern day hubby in that he was not going to be present in the delivery room when his wife gave birth. Tim said that he realized how late it was and how we did have work the next day but if I took a day off or even half a day he would make my excuses for me. He obviously would not be going to work for the next few days. I was sure that he would take at least a week's worth of vacation to spend time with his wife and newborn baby. I told him that I would be there after I asked him which hospital she was in. Being that she was in a hospital not too close to where I live it took me a while to get there. I parked my car in the visitor's section of the parking lot and then dashed to the waiting area outside the delivery room where Stephanie was still in labor. I found my handsome buddy sitting in a chair outside the delivery room and lo and behold he was snoozing. I stifled my laughter at the sight of him fast asleep in that chair. After all that excitement and hooting and hawing on the phone the guy had actually fallen asleep. By now it was after twelve thirty AM and the waiting area outside the delivery room was deserted except for the handsome sleeping laddy and me. But it was as I silently approached Tim that my heart thundered in my chest at the sight of him snoozing the way he was. He was seated in one of those traditional plastic waiting room chairs and I saw that his shoes, casual slip-on deck shoes to be exact were under his chair. Tim's black socked feet were propped up on a chair across from him. His head was lolled forward down by his chest as he softly snored. I supposed that the excitement of his wife being in labor had really sapped his energy at that point. Needless to say, and after all I've written in this journal already, I was somehow instantly drawn to Tim's socked feet propped up on that chair across from the one he was sitting in. I made my way over to him, being careful not to wake the sleeping laddy (beauty?). He looked real peaceful the way he was snoozing there and I thought how funny it would be if I decided to wake him by lifting him suddenly out of that chair and gave him a few congratulatory spins. It was something that a buddy would do after all. Or how about if I decided to wake him by trailing a fingertip over the bottom of one of his socked feet? Now that thought really got me thinking let me tell you. As I thought of those things, lifting my buddy and spinning him and tickling his foot and as I took in the sight of Tim's black socked feet propped on that chair I felt that familiar tingling in my crotch. Again, what was up with that? I decided not to lift the guy out of his chair and spin him and not to tickle his socked feet either. I would lift and spin him for when we heard that Stephanie had given birth. After having hoisted the guy at the soccer game and back at the bank celebration while he had been up on that stage belting out a song it was obvious that I was the handsome laddy's handler. As for tickling his feet, well, that opportunity would come someday too. But as I thought about that I realized what craziness I was entertaining. I quietly sat down in the chair next to the one that Tim had his socked feet propped up on. The second I sat down I was able to smell Tim's socked feet and at that moment I knew just what Stephanie had been talking about when it came to her handsome hubby's sock feet odor. I saw that the socks that Tim had on were the same black Goldtoe socks he'd had on at work that day. I surmised that even though the handsome laddy had changed out of his suit to khakis and a pullover shirt and deck shoes after he had gotten home from work he kept his dress socks on, not changing to more casual socks, say sweat or crew socks. But God, what was this obsession that I had with my work buddies socks and feet? And now, *now* the scent wafting up from those socked feet was sending me into some kind of funky orbit. I made sure Tim was really asleep, made sure no one was around to see what I was about to do and then slowly leaned my face down toward Tim's feet. He went on snoring peacefully and when my face was directly over those black nylon ribbed socks of his I inhaled deeply. The scent of Tim's socks was pure raunchy heaven somehow although I could not believe what I was doing. As Tim would say, "Fucking fucks!" I was in a hospital where my good buddies wife was about to give birth and I was sniffing his goddamned socks while he snoozed. Someone please tell me what was up with that! The musty odor of Tim's socked feet filled my nostrils and I had all to do to prevent myself from pressing my nose and mouth against the gold section of his Goldtoe socks. It was that area, his gold covered toes that really seemed to be emanating the most odors. At the sound of a door opening nearby where we were seated I quickly lifted my head up and away from Tim's feet and Tim stirred a bit, smacking his lips together as he slowly awoke. He slowly opened his eyes, looking across at me. At the sight of me he smiled from ear to ear, said, "Hi buddy thanks for coming. I can't believe that with the state of mind I'm in I fell asleep." I told him it was okay, that given the excitement he was feeling he must also be feeling drained, and without thinking gave his socked foot that was closest to me a quick squeeze. It felt all moist and warm in my fingers and thumb. Before he could say anything about why I had just given his foot a squeeze I asked him if there was any word yet on Stephanie or his soon to be born baby. "Naw man, she's still in there," Tim said and pointed over his shoulder with a thumb at the delivery room behind us. He told me how Stephanie had been in labor for over five hours now and that she probably would be in there for the next five hours or more. He looked really scared as he told me that and I tried to reassure him that all labors don't necessarily take that long. Tim reminded me that this was his and Stephanie's first child and that first-time labor could take even more than twenty-four hours. As he spoke he didn't realize (and man nor did I) that I was massaging one of his socked feet. I asked him if he wanted me to get him anything, maybe some tea from the hospital cafeteria, or some coffee. Tim laughed and said that he was wired enough, that he didn't need caffeine. He said that what he could really use was a beer or maybe something stronger. Seeing as he hadn't asked me to stop massaging his foot I squeezed it tighter. I laughed along with him and told him that they didn't serve hard liquor in the hospital cafeteria. While we sat there, while we talked and while I massaged Tim's foot the doctor came out of the delivery room and over to where we were sitting. He said, "Mr. Backman?" Tim looked up at the doctor expectantly, pulled his feet down off the chair and said "Yes Doctor Maxwell?" The middle aged doctor had salt and pepper colored hair and steely blue eyes and he was smiling at the about to be father. He told Tim that Stephanie was doing fine and that from his calculations it would be another three hours at least before she gave birth. Doctor Maxwell suggested that Tim go home and that he would call him when the baby was born. Tim shook his head and said, "No, no, no, I'm staying right here till Stephanie gives birth." As he said it he propped his feet back up on the chair next to me. The doctor smiled at Tim, patted him on the back and said that would be fine too. Tim quickly introduced me to the doctor as his best work buddy. I was flattered to say the least. The doctor smiled at both of us and returned to the delivery room. I asked Tim if he was sure he wanted to stay there all those hours, putting a hand around his foot as I asked him. He said that he certainly did and then surprised me by saying that it felt great the way I was massaging his foot, that it was totally relaxing him... He reminded me however not to tickle him, seeing as he had very, *very* ticklish feet. He even pointed out to me how the thin nylon socks he was wearing made his feet even more ticklish, something about the thin silky material that caused his ticklishness to increase somehow, chuckling stupidly as he said it, obviously embarrassed talking about his ticklish feet... As he told me that chills went up my spine and I was suddenly thinking the craziest of thoughts...

Stephanie had the baby three hours later, amazingly short labor for a first time pregnancy. The doctor came out of the delivery room and told Tim that he had a beautiful seven and a half pound son and that Stephanie was doing great as well. Tim and I bolted from our chairs, him in his socked feet of course and he whooped for joy, jumping up and down like a Mexican jumping bean at first. He then grabbed the doctor. He hugged the doctor and thanked him over and over again, tears spilling from the handsome laddy's eyes. Tim was shaking with the ecstasy of being a new dad and I have to say that I was glad to have been there for him. I was even gladder that I had gotten to massage the guy's one foot while we waited for Stephanie to give birth. He then let go of the doctor and turned to hug me. Instead, I grabbed Tim, hoisted him in my muscular arms and spun him in an airplane spin. The doctor laughed jovially, said that I must workout a lot and told Tim and I that he had to get back to Stephanie, congratulating Tim again. Tim reached out an arm and shook hands with the doctor as I held the laddy aloft. Tim rejoiced, "A son, oh man Ronald, *a son*, we're going to call him Tim Junior." I told Tim that that sounded great and as he whoo whooed I airplane spun him again… Tim hooked an arm around my neck for support, stretched his socked feet way out and whoo whooed some more as I spun the ecstatic new daddy laddy. When I put Tim down so he could get his shoes on and make his way to the delivery room to see Stephanie I sat back down and realized that I had a major-sized boner in my pants…

A Boner Book

Chapter Seventeen

After finishing my tirade of how Stephanie's bitchy friend Valerie had tricked me into the spinning Chinaman device in her antique shop I watched as Ronald squatted in front of my bare feet as they soaked in the warm gyrating oil. He reached into the deep basin of oil and un-strapped my feet before lifting them out of the thick slimy liquid. He set some towels on the floor in front of me so my feet could drip dry as they came out of the basin all slimy with the oil all over them. I crooned and swooned a bit in the seat I was bound to as my so called buddy massaged both my oiled feet with brute strength.

"OHHHHH man, that does feel great Ronald," I said with my eyes closed, a look of ecstasy on my face.

"Yeah, and I'll bet you were thinking that I was going to tickle you huh bud?" Ronald asked me and began wiping my feet clean of the oil with a warm towel.

"Well, it did cross my mind at that, I mean, it is what you've been doing to me since you captured me and brought me here and…" I began to say as Ronald gingerly lifted one of my bare feet and wiped it strongly with the towel, cutting off my words as the feeling was magical.

I enjoyed the feeling of my buddy massaging the oil off my feet with that towel but inwardly I was cringing, thinking that he would start tickling my oil soft feet at any second…

"I'm glad you like the way this feels Timmy," Ronald said. "Remember the night when Stephanie gave birth to Tim Junior how I massaged one of your feet while we were in the waiting area outside the delivery room?"

"Oh yeah, sure, man, even then you seemed to have some sort of fixation for my socked feet," I said, remembering that night very well suddenly, how I had propped my socked feet up on that chair so that I could rest a bit while Stephanie was giving birth.

"I suppose you could say that bud, a real fixation for your socked feet," Ronald said admittedly to me.

Looking back on it at that moment while he wiped the oil off my bare feet I realized with a sick knowledge how it had been right there in front of me all the time. Ronald always seemed to have some excuse or another for having to get at my feet, my socked feet to be exact. And he knew from our macho guy conversations that I sometimes slept with my dress socks on. Gawd, did I somehow invite all of this? Did my loose lips really sink my own ship?

When Ronald was done wiping all the oil from my feet and from between my toes and from my arches and heels (he sure took a long enough time bud) he moved the basin of oil away from my feet and sat down at the end of the bench next to me, my ever-present black socks in his hand as he began speaking to me.

"I need you to do something for me Timmy boy," Ronald said.

"What the fuck could I possibly do for you? I asked him in reply, seeing the intense look in his eyes as he twisted and stretched my socks in his hands.

"I need for you to call your wife and let her know that you're okay," Ronald said and my chin dropped and my mouth fell open in shock. "You see man, I'm planning to hold onto you for at least a couple more days here, it's going to take that long to put you through the trials of all my tickle torture devices and I don't want Stephanie sending the police out to look for you, or to even file a missing person's report."

I could not believe what the fucking fuck I was hearing. Hold onto me for a couple more days? Tickle torture devices that I had to be put through as in a trial? And call my wife? *Call my wife?*

"YOU HAVE GOT TO BE KIDDING ME!" I snarled. "And just what the fuck am I supposed to tell her that I'm doing man?"

"Oh, I'm sure you'll think of something buddy, after I've tickled you again," Ronald said and squatted down to get my socks back onto my feet.

"RONALD, no, no, Oh God no, don't tickle me anymore man, please," I pleaded as I watched him roll those smelly and god awful socks onto my soft oiled feet.

My cock throbbed long and hard as I watched the fucking guy roll my socks over my feet and up to my muscular calves.

"When you decide to call your wife and tell her that you're okay I'll reward you by taking one whole hour off your next tickle session, but no more than that buddy," Ronald said as he began untying me from the bench I was seated on, undoing the restraint around my waist. "Now, your next tickle session starts right away and it's going to take place in the room right next to this one."

Ronald stood over me with the chloroform soaked cloth in his hand, held up like it was a shield of some sort.

"And in the room right next to this one I have something real wild and sweet cooked up for you Timmy my laddy," Ronald said and moved the cloth toward my face.

"No Ronald, no..." I whimpered and then I was chloroformed into yet another stupor...

Chapter Eighteen

Chloroformed again, I was feeling totally helpless, totally frustrated at that point and now Ronald claimed that he was going to make me call Stephanie with some excuse for my absence so that she would not worry about me. Fucking fucks buds, this time as I came to I found myself again wearing a goddamned blindfold as Ronald did his dirty work of binding me up tight to the next tickle torture device that he planned to subject me to.

"R-Ronald, what are you doing man?" I called out miserably as I felt my wrists being tied up in front of me.

Though I was blindfolded I was able to decipher that I was lying on my stomach on a half table of some kind in a diagonal position. My arms were stretched out tightly in front of me and my hands were crossed at the wrists as Ronald was busily tying them. My legs were splayed behind me, stretched open in a **"V"** type of position and my socked feet were tied off to what felt like supports behind whatever the fucking fuck Ronald had me half laying on. My hard cock dangled underneath me, off the table I was on actually and I felt a sense of woe that a thin length of rope had been tied around the base of my cock and balls. Thoughts of my buddy having handled my most private region while I had been asleep infuriated me.

"Just getting you ready for the next tickle torture session Timmy me ticklish laddy," Ronald laughed as he finished tying my wrists in front of me and then tying the slack of the rope off to a support. "As I said before I brought you in here what I have in store for you now is totally wild and sweet bud..."

At that point I was stretched out and tied up good and fucking tight as a drum...

"R-Ronald, I cannot fucking move, what the hell are you doing to me here man?" I garbled miserably, wiggling only my toes under my socks and my fingers, the only parts of me that I could move actually.

"I suppose that now is as good a time as any to show you," Ronald said and reached for my blindfold. "I do want to get this show on the road after all..."

Ronald chuckled meanly and whipped the blindfold off me. I let my eyes adjust to the light and looked around, taking in the awful position I was now in...

"HOLY fucking fucks, Ronald, I'm no acrobat man, fucking fuck, you got me in a goddamned Superman flying position," I yelled, tugging on the ropes on my wrists and feet, my cock feeling awful with that damned thin length of rope tied around the base of it.

"Yeah, and it would appear that Superman has been snatched right out of the sky huh buddy?" Ronald laughed.

"WHAT IS THIS MAN?" I roared the sick realization that I could not get myself untied settling in hard and heavy.

"Well, I'm about to tickle a very, very special spot on your body Timmy my laddy," Ronald said and pressed a button on a wall mounting.

The half table I was tethered to rose a bit upwards till it, and I, was suspended up off the floor.

"LET ME DOWN, oh God, what is this shit?" I moaned as my legs and arms were stretched even tighter. "OHHHHRRRR FUCK!"

As I rose a tad higher yet I saw that one of Ronald's motorized devices was directly under me and the long rod on this one had a host of small feathers attached to the end of it. And oh Gawd of Gawds, the end of that infernal thing was aimed directly at that very tender, very ticklish spot between my balls and cock, that very special place that some men call their G-spot. Looking down at that device and where it was aimed at caused me to gulp real hard in total terror and I clenched my teeth to prevent the scream that was threatening to erupt from deep within me.

"OH FUCK, OH FUCKING FUCK RONALD, you can't do this to me man!" I screeched, rather than screamed.

"I beg to differ Timmy my good buddy of buddies, because you see, I can do it and I am doing it to you," Ronald snickered and turned off the device that was causing me to rise upwards and pull me tighter and tighter along with it. "Okay, that's perfect..."

"Perfect for you maybe, but not for poor old me," I grunted. "Ronald, if you tickle that spot on me I'll lose my mind for sure. You have no idea how sexy that part of me really is!"

"Tell me man, way back; did Linda tickle that spot on you when you were dating her?" Ronald asked me, stepping behind me and brazenly walking between my splayed legs and even more brazenly he caressed my hairy scrotum and tied balls, sending definite chills through my very being.

"L-Linda, *again with Linda*," I complained miserably. "But if you must know, and obviously you seem to *have* to know, yes, that bitch tickled that special spot of mine that you're about to tickle torture, *buddy*... When that bitch tickled tortured my special spot I had no fucking idea that years later a buddy of mine would be torturing me in nearly the same fashion."

Ronald chuckled meanly and sniffed at my sweaty and stinking balls like a pig in heat...

"OH MAN, don't be doing that buddy," I said as he stepped away from my crotch, but not before giving my scrotum one more good caress.

"Nice and ripe Timmy boy, real juicy and ready for the tickling to come," Ronald said. "It actually smells to me like those eggs of yours could use some polishing bud."

With that said Ronald took a remote control device from his pocket, held it up and asked if I was ready.

"OH GOD NO, Ronald please, *please let me go home man,* please, please take me back to my wife and kid," I pleaded to my buddies deaf ears it seemed.

Smiling from ear to ear Ronald pressed a button on the remote control he was holding, turning it on and the tickle device down below my splayed legs and suddenly that special spot between my cock and balls was being mercilessly and speedily tickle tortured by what felt like a hundred spinning feathers...

"OOOOHHHHHHH, OHHHHHHH GODS, OHHHHHHHH NO, ha, ha, ha, ha, ha, ha, ha, ha, ha, ha, ha, ha, ha, ha, ha, ha, ha, ha, ha, ha, ha!" I squealed. "RONALD, you fucking fucker!"

Being stretched out and tied tighter than a drum I could not even squirm that much as the feathers spun and tormented my special spot like mad…

"HA, ha, ha, ha, ha, ha, ha, ha, ha, ha, ha, ha, ha, ha, ha, ha, ha, ha! OH GOD, oh GOD Ronald! TURN IT OFF, please turn it off!" I screeched.

To add to my miserable ticklish torment Ronald stepped to one of my socked feet, grabbed it by the ankle, produced his electric toothbrush from another of his pockets and flicked it on to high speed. He pressed those vibrating bristles against the bottom of my meaty and oiled socked foot.

"NO, NO, NO FAIR!" I reeled. "HA, ha, ha, ha, ha, ha, ha, ha, ha, ha, ha, ha, ha, ha, ha, ha! OH GOD, no fair at all!"

"Okay Timmy, you're looking at a good three hours of this," Ronald said.

"A, a good three hours, ha, ha, ha, ha, ha, ha, ha, ha, ha, ha, ha, ha, ha, ha, ha, ha, what, what's so good about those hours b-bud?" I garbled, laughing and trying to speak at the same time.

Underneath me my cock tingled and dribbled dollops of pre seed and piss and my sac swayed a bit and churned, my balls filled to the max it felt like with my stored up sexy juices. But there was to be no relief, not even from Ronald's awful gizmo as it tickled my secret G-spot. That fucking thing with the feathers on it was nowhere near my dangling cock and balls. I was being tickled into a state of total erotic aggravation.

"AAARHHHHHHHHHHH, ha, ha, ha, ha, ha, ha, ha, ha, ha, ha, ha, ha, ha, ha, ha, ha, ha!" I screamed in laughter, the sounds that Ronald wanted to hear as he continued gliding that infernal toothbrush over my socked foot, holding me tight by my ankle.

"This proves what I told you earlier Timmy me ticklish laddy," Ronald chuckled and pressed the vibrating bristles harder yet against the bottom of my foot, gliding it up and down and up and down my soles. "That once your feet had been good and oiled and softened that you would be even more tickling sensitive on the bottoms of them. And this tooth-brushing that I'm giving them is nothing compared to the device that I have waiting for them in the next room I'll be taking you to at some point."

"OH GOD NO, NO RONALD!" I begged. "HA, ha, ha, ha, ha, ha, ha, ha, ha, ha, ha, ha, ha, ha, ha, ha!" I chortled crazily, my cock and balls now tingling, feeling just the way that buzzing toothbrush was feeling.

I could not even think straight enough to see in my tortured mind what Ronald had in mind for my poor feet in the next room he would bring me to. Although, I did wonder real stupidly if he would tickle my feet with my socks on or off, that thought causing me to sputter and laugh even harder as his feather device worked my G-spot and he worked my foot manually with his toothbrush…

"HAR, har, har, har, har, har, har, har, har, har, har, har, har, har!" I was laughing and did not even realize that my good buddy had switched spots and was now tickling the bottom of my other foot, holding tight to my ankle as he did his dirty work with the toothbrush.

Okay Timmy, now, as I told you, you can cut down this tickle torture session by one hour," Ronald reminded me. "But you need to do something for me first, *you must agree to it…*"

As he spoke Ronald glided his infernal toothbrush over the arch of my foot that he was presently tickling, all while his feather device seemed to press harder as it spun against my G-spot.

"OH GOD, what'll I tell her man?" I gasped loudly, before another laughing jag captured me in its clutches. "HA, ha, ha, ha, ha, ha, ha, ha, ha, ha, ha, ha, ha, ha, ha, ha, ha, ha, ha, ha! What in the fucking fuck will I tell my wife if I call her?"

"That's totally up to you buddy," Ronald said as he brushed my foot with his toothbrush some more. "You can go three whole hours while you think about it in your tickled state, or you can agree to call her and I'll take one hour off your tickle time right now. It's your choice buddy. I mean to keep you up there for three hours is no problem for me."

"Ha, ha, ha, ha, ha, ha, ha, ha, ha, ha, ha, ha, ha, ha, ha, ha, ha, ha, ha, ha, ha, ha, ha, ha, ha, ha, ha!" I laughed crazily. "And if tell you, ha, ha, ha, ha, ha, ha, ha, ha, ha, if I tell you that I won't call her at all?"

"Then I'll keep you on that device for four hours," Ronald said and finally turned off his electric toothbrush. "In a way you are in control here Timmy…"

My heart sank and I heard myself screaming, "I'll call her! I'll call her! Oh God, I'll call her!"

"Good boy Timmy my laddy," Ronald said and squeezed one of my socked feet. "Now you have only two hours of this to endure…and I'm sure you'll do very well at it…"

"I-I'll be, ha, ha, ha, ha, ha, ha, ha, ha, ha, ha, ha, ha, ha, ha, ha, ha, ha, ha, ha, ha!" I gasped, spittle flying from my fast moving lips as I laughed and laughed. "I'll be dead before that time, ha, ha, ha, ha, ha, ha, ha, ha, ha, ha, ha, ha, ha, ha, ha, ha, ha, ha, ha!"

I craned my head back a little when I felt Ronald's mouth at the bottom of one of my feet. I laughed even louder as he flicked his tongue over my foot and brazenly kissed it… I didn't know at that moment that Ronald was preparing me for his next tickle torture device. As I laughed and laughed and laughed I thought about what the fucking fuck I was going to tell Stephanie once Ronald had me on the phone with her…

There were actually a million and one ridiculous excuses I could offer her for my absence. The truth would be the most rational thing to tell her. And if I told her the truth I would also have to be able to tell her where Ronald had me, which was of course impossible, seeing as he had brought me there blindfolded and in a danged chloroformed stupor. No, telling Stephanie the truth, that her poor hubby had been kidnapped was out of the question. I would have to come up with something else. But what? What the fucking fuck does a guy in my ticklish position tell his wife when he's being tickle tortured to within an inch of his life by his best buddy? As I laughed and laughed louder and louder I tried to come up with some semblance of an idea of what I would tell my wife once Ronald had me on the phone with her.

Chapter Nineteen

Well, I didn't die from having my G-spot tickle tortured for an entire two hours. I was however a quivering, shaking and goose bump riddled laddy as Ronald unfettered me from the raised table I had been on while having my special sexy spot tickle tortured. Leaving my hands tied securely in front of me Ronald helped me off the table. As I stood next to him, still laughing a little my cock jutted hard and solid out in front of me and at that point I had the scariest case of blue balls in all of my thirty something years.

"Feeling good buddy?" Ronald asked me as he held my upper arm tight; I standing next to him totally mortified wearing just those silly black socks of mine that seemed to have caused me all this trouble. "You ready to abide by your side of our deal and call Stephanie?"

"I-I gotta fucking piss like a racehorse Ronald," I grunted. "And with this fucking hard-on I'm sporting I don't think that's going to be a very easy chore..."

"Okay man, I'll let you piss and whatever else you need to do, but after that," Ronald said, squeezing my arm tight.

"After that I'll call Stephanie," I said, looking at him from the side of my line of vision.

"Good deal, if you backed out of our agreement I was prepared to hoist you back up there," Ronald said, pointing at the half table that he had just taken me off of and my heart filled with woe at the sight of those feathers on that rod under that table.

"I'll stick to our agreement Ronald," I said through clenched teeth, barely holding my water at that point, fuck, barely holding my cum at that point. "Now, just get me to a bathroom so I can piss buddy!"

Ronald chuckled meanly, walked me out of the room where he had just tickled my G-spot and deposited me in a bathroom that was halfway down the hallway to the next room where he planned to tickle torture my poor feet somehow.

"HEY! How about untying my hands buddy boy?" I called out as Ronald closed the bathroom door after flicking on the light for me.

"Your hands are tied in front of you Timmy, you don't need your hands untied if all you're going to do is piss, and whatever," Ronald chuckled from outside the bathroom, obviously knowing fully well that I planned to jack off as well while in the bathroom.

Fuck, it was the only way I would be able to relieve myself...

"Now just get busy and piss till your heart's content buddy boy," Ronald said. "Unless you told me you needed to take a dump your hands stay tied just as they are! I'm giving you five minutes!"

Hearing that I quickly sidled up to the toilet bowl, lifted the ring and stood over it, my muscular body slightly arched forward due to the sexual urges I was feeling at that point. I clenched my teeth and grabbed my sticky pre-seed slicked cock with both hands...

"OOOOOOOOOOOO..." I groaned and looked up at the ceiling as I slowly began stroking. "Fucking fucks, *fucking totally fucks...*"

I stroked myself slowly at first, my whole body scented with sweat, the scent from my randy socks wafting up to me, causing me to stroke and choke myself faster with each passing second. My sperm filled balls swung real sexily between my legs and I felt that special spot between my cock and balls come alive as I stroked myself like I was a violin.

"OOOOOOOOOOO..." I groaned again and gripped my manhood tighter.

I looked down and the sight of the ropes binding my wrists sent a shiver of fear through me... The sight of my black socks scrunched down around my calves sent a shiver of ecstasy through me. I stroked faster and arched my body further back. I was getting close buds... I groaned again and then felt my juices beginning to rush from my chock filled balls through my tube...

"OOHHHHRRRR yeah, fucking fucks," I groaned and for a blinding moment saw four faces in front of me as I shot my pent up load of sexy juices.

I saw Stephanie, I saw Valerie, I saw Linda, and oh Gawd, I saw Ronald... Fucking Fucks, I saw Ronald... Four faces of people who had at one time or another made my life a tickle torture hell... I stroked and choked my good stuff out of me, pumping my cock for all I was worth, groaning in a real man's passion! The sounds of my thick slimy seed as it plopped into the cold water of the toilet bowl just seemed to egg me on even more, to stroke even more of it out of me. I recalled the last time I had cum at the hands of Ronald's latex cock hungry sheath as it siphoned a good mess out of me. Thinking of that I stroked myself still more buds, really cranking my crank if you know what I mean. It felt like it would go on forever as I came and came, the plopping sound of my cum mixed with my throes of passion in the bathroom echoing real sexily around me. Then, when I was done shooting my load, like most guys out there I pissed like a goddamned racehorse. My cock was finally semi soft and I felt some semblance of relief, although with what Ronald planned to put me through some more I knew that I would need to cum again real soon. Holding my manhood as it went more flaccid I pissed a long yellow stream into the bowl, my piss mixing somewhat erotically with all my sperm...

When I was finally done I flushed away both messes, reached down to pull up my socks and exited the bathroom...

"I bet that felt good huh buddy boy?" Ronald asked me, taking me by my arm as soon as I came out of the bathroom.

"Damn it all Ronald, were you listening?" I asked him with a grin. "Look, I'll talk to my wife okay? Just don't tickle me. This is all so fucking crazy man!"

"Well, while you're on the phone with her of course I won't tickle you buddy," Ronald said, smiling at me approvingly as he led me into yet another room where he quickly tied me to a chair, the only difference about this room being that it had a phone in it. "We wouldn't want her thinking you were being tortured now would we?"

I looked at Ronald and with a sarcastic tone in my voice said, "Hardy fucking har, har buddy boy..."

"Alright Timmy, I know I've called you countless times in the past on your home phone, but just for kicks, what's your phone number? Ronald asked me, lifting the receiver off the phone, listening for a dial tone and prepared to dial.

"Ronald, do we really have to do this?" I questioned him with a whining sound in my voice.

"No, not at all Timmy, we most certainly do not have to do this," Ronald said, sounding very unlike the Ronald I knew at that moment. "But if you don't your wife might, just might involve the police. And that would be bad for me, kidnapping and all that. I mean, okay, all of this is just in fun but I suppose I have to face the fact that *I did kidnap you*. I mean, would you have come here of your own volition knowing what I had in store for you buddy?"

I nodded my head, "No."

"And of course if you don't call her it would be extremely bad for you as well, in a ticklish sense, remember, four whole hours of having your G-spot tickled again," Ronald reminded me. "And that of course would be disastrous, seeing as you just shot your load and that made you even more tickle sensitive..."

As Ronald spoke I listened with mounting dread...

"And, *and*, just think Timmy boy, *just think* how long I could tickle you before anyone found us, man, both your heart and your cock might burst, ha, ha," Ronald laughed. "And that sure as fucking all fucks would be a sight to see..."

He sat there then with the receiver in hand, giving me that evil grin...

"But, you promised not to tickle me as much, I said softly. "...if I talk to my wife right?"

"That is totally correct Timmy boy, very astute and executive sounding I must say..." Ronald chuckled. "Now, the phone number?"

"Three seven four three four two, seven two two nine," I recited with fear in my eyes, still wondering what the fuck I was going to tell her.

"Ronald, what do I tell her?" I asked him desperately as I heard my phone at home ringing.

"Once you hear her lovely voice I'm sure you'll think of something," Ronald giggled meanly at my unbelievable predicament.

As the phone at the other end of the connection rang Ronald held the phone to my ear, but leaned in real close to me so that he could hear both sides of the impending conversation.

"Hello?" I heard Stephanie answer.

"Honey, Stephanie, it's me, Timmy," I said quickly, trying not to allow my feelings of fear to belie me as I spoke to her.

"Timmy? *Timmy*, where the hell are you?" she said, sounding concerned but irritated at the same time. "You had me worried. Its afternoon already and I haven't seen or heard from you since we said good night last night. And Tim Junior told me that he saw some man carrying you over his shoulder and out of the house last night. I told him that he must have been dreaming. *Where are you Timmy*?"

Two things she said caused my heart to plummet more than it had already, the fact that it was afternoon, which meant that Ronald had been tickle torturing me and mentally torturing me for beyond hours at that point and that Timmy Junior had told her that he saw me being kidnapped and that Ronald had just heard her say that. Oh God!

"Huh, uh, uh, yeah, well, you see Stephanie, the thing is, I'm really not sure where I am right now," I said stupidly and Ronald gave my thigh a warning type of squeeze.

"What? *You don't know where you are*?" Stephanie yelled into the phone, her tone bordering on panic.

"Well, yeah, that's right honey, I mean, you know those silly fraternity brothers of mine from my college days?" I asked her, not giving her a moment to reply right away. "Well, they uh, some of them are in town, yeah, and they playfully and as a joke kidnapped me last night. I just played along with it you know? That was one of them that Tim Junior saw carrying me out of the house last night. The joke was that they would get into our house and then snag me while I went to take my nightly piss..."

"You have got to be kidding!" Stephanie went on, sounding like she did not believe me. "Why, after all these years would they want to do something like that?"

"Uh, well, good question, but you see, they wanted to have a reunion," I said, thinking as fast as possible. "I didn't tell you about it because I really didn't plan on going so when they heard that I wasn't going to be attending they uh, decided to playfully kidnap me to the reunion, yeah, that's it honey, your handsome hubby was shanghaied. They had said they would do it but I didn't think they actually had the balls to carry it, or me, ha, ha, for that matter out. They wanted me at the reunion so they kidnapped me and now they have me here at the reunion."

"Timmy, they kidnapped you while you were taking your nightly piss?" she asked me then. "In other words while you were wearing just your socks and boxer shorts?"

"Uh yeah, honey, that was part of the kidnapping, to make it as humiliating as possible," I said. "But uh, don't worry; they had clothes for me here, wherever here is..."

"What does that mean Timmy, *wherever here is*?" Stephanie asked me.

"It uh, it means they brought me here blindfolded honey," I replied, trying to sound as jovial as possible.

"Timmy, I thought that you didn't like those guys, because they always got you into, how can I put this, ha, ha, ticklish situations?" my wife asked me.

"Uh, yeah, that's right too honey, and well, that's sort of why I didn't want to go to the reunion," I said. "I was actually afraid they might do just that, put me into yet another ticklish situation, and uh, guess what?"

I glanced at Ronald and saw the stern looking expression etched on his face...

"So let me guess, they have gotten you into a ticklish situation already," Stephanie said. "Since you don't know where you are, it would be my guess that those guys were definitely looking to revisit some of your ticklish college days, right?"

Stephanie was starting to sound more curious than mad...

"Uh yeah, you got it right honey, they really wanted for me to join them and to join in on all the fun from the old days," I said, sounding totally ridiculous even to myself. "...sort of just for laughs, just for a lot of laughs actually Stephanie, hee, hee, funny huh?"

"Timmy, hee, hee yourself, your fraternity brothers thought you were so much fun, that to get to tickle you again after all these years they created a mock kidnapping?" Stephanie asked me. "*They kidnapped you so that they could tickle you, like in college?*"

"Yeah, wild huh?" I asked her. "WHEEE! Ha, ha."

"Ha, ha, that is wild, I suppose, but strange and very funny too," Stephanie said, sounding a tad calmer now. "I am glad you called though. I was worried that something really bad did happen to you. I was about to call your office to see where you were. I thought you had gone into work earlier than usual, at least that's what I told

Tim Junior you had probably done."

"Oh, well, would you call Jerry; he works with me, and tell him that I decided to take an overdue but unexpected vacation?" I quickly asked her, needing to obviously cover my tracks at work as well.

I mean, while I was on the phone with her I may as well take care of everything and not losing my job was pretty important I would think...

"You see Stephanie, I'm basically all caught up on all my work so he shouldn't be mad that I'm not there," I said to her. "Just tell him that I had a last minute hunting trip that came up, okay?"

"Okay, sure, I'll tell him, I'm just glad to know that you're alright," Stephanie said, starting to sound real sexy and inquisitive. "Now tell me, have those mean old fraternity brothers of yours really tickled you a lot since they kidnapped you last night?"

"Uh, ha, ha, yeah, they sure have," I replied sheepishly. "They've really had a ball tickling me Stephanie, and I get the feeling I'm in for even more here. I'll uh; I'll have lots of stories to tell you when I get home."

"Well, I'm sort of jealous," Stephanie said, surprising me totally at that moment. "I mean, your frat brothers are tickling you and I don't get to see it. I would be really interested in seeing that Timmy. I don't think I've ever seen a guy tickle another guy."

Ronald stifled a laugh and signaled for me to cut off the conversation already.

"Well, it's just as bad as when a woman tickles me," I said stupidly. "Listen honey, I've got to go now. The guys want to get something to eat I think. But I will see you soon."

"Okay, I'll call Jerry for you," Stephanie said. "And tell those guys that I'm really jealous that I can't see all the tickling fun they're putting you through. I really would have loved to join in on the action but I suppose it's a guy thing..."

"Bye Stephanie," I said somewhat sadly. "I love you..."

I heard her tell me that she loved me and she hung up as well.

"Well, well, that sure as hell was an interesting phone call," Ronald said, smiling at me as he hung up the phone. "Your wife really does have an open mind when it comes to her handsome hubby being tickled. But, now that that's been taken care of we can get back to our fun and games here."

"Now Ronald, look, I did what you asked, so go easy on me huh?" I pleaded. "I really don't think I can take much more of this man..."

In response Ronald treated me to a nose and mouth full of chloroform, laughing meanly as he sedated me yet again...

Chapter Twenty

After the phone call to my wife and after the latest dose of chloroform wore off I found myself in yet another (Good God "another") ticklish situation, courtesy of my good buddy Ronald. With this particular session of tickle torture I would find out why Ronald had been flicking his tongue at me in such a suggestive manner lately. I found myself lying this time on a dangling slab of heavy wood that was suspended from the ceiling by heavy-duty cables. I was stretched out this time on my muscular back, tied down to the damned thing, blindfolded *yet again* and my feet were also tied down to the wood at the ankles, but the bottoms of my socked feet were dangling just off the very end of the slab.

"So Timmy my ticklish laddy of lads, your son saw me carrying you out of the house eh?" I heard Ronald asking me as my head cleared and while he was finishing tying my feet down to the slab of wood that I was now stretched out on. "That's rich man that is so funny, real sweet if you ask me…"

"It's not funny Ronald, it's awful, God, what was my boy thinking when he saw that? Have you thought about that? Fucking fucks, I can just imagine!" I reeled at Ronald, forcing my head to clear. "Hopefully my wife will tell him what I told her, that it was all part of a college prank, a joke being played on me by some of my old buddies!"

"Well, as luck would have it I do know a bit about psychology and I can say that he'll carry that memory around with him until he's an adult," Ronald said and squeezed both of my socked feet, inhaling their funky odor as well. "And then when he's an adult one of two things will transpire. Either he'll want to capture some guy and lug him out of his house, and he'll make sure, like me, that the guy he captures wears his dress socks to bed, or, he'll want to be the guy being kidnapped. All that will depend on which way his fantasy goes stronger."

"Neither of those things will happen if I talk to him about it, if and when you bring me home man," I ranted miserably, my eyes glaring and angry looking behind my blindfold.

"You mean to say that you plan to talk to a ten year old kid about what he saw that night buddy?" Ronald asked me. "In my opinion you would do well to wait till he's a lot older. You and your wife shouldn't bring it up to him at all…"

That said Ronald stepped to the side of the slab of wood and looked me over. Fuck, even blindfolded I could feel his steely eyes on me. I grimaced miserably now behind my blindfold, thinking of my son having seen my capture, and of course thinking that now that Ronald was done lashing me to the slab of wood it would soon be tickle torture time for poor me again.

"Okay buddy boy, I think we're ready for the next round of tickles," Ronald said and grabbed one of my man tits mashed it tight between his fingers and thumb and then let go of it as abruptly as he had grabbed it.

"OHHHHHHH…" I moaned in a mixture of ecstasy and total frustration as my cock twitched from Ronald's squeeze on my man nip.

Lets not lose sight of the fact that I had just shot my load and that made every part of me real sexy and sensitive feeling. And anyone whose been reading this memoir from the outset knows just how very sensitive my man nips are, Gawd!

"Fuck, fucking fucks, but my goddamned man tits really are the control knobs for my cock," I mumbled as I felt my cock growing rigidly stiff yet again.

I supposed that the aphrodisiac that Ronald had been using on me was still weaving its awful magic where my sexual organs were concerned. Ronald chuckled and said, "They sure are bud, they sure as hell are..."

"Now, I have a bit of a riddle for you buddy, do you remember that old Batman TV series where the villain called the Riddler always stumped Batman and Robin with his riddles?" Ronald asked me and I could not believe what the fuck I was hearing, the Riddler?

"Of course I remember that, I never missed that TV show," I replied. "But of course at the same time I never thought that I would wind up in a predicament like Batman and Robin used to wind up in..."

"Good point Timmy, very good point, okay, now, if you answer this riddle correctly I'll take five minutes off the tickle time that you earned when you spoke to your wife," Ronald said and again squeezed one of my nipples, causing the hardness between my legs to twitch upward even more.

"*And if I don't answer it correctly?*" I asked Ronald miserably.

"Then I'll just add ten minutes to the hour that I plan to tickle you for with the latest device that you're tied to," Ronald laughed. "Now, here's the riddle, and you only have a moment to answer it and you only get one guess at the answer. Are you ready?"

"Do I have a choice?" I asked him sarcastically.

"None whatsoever," Ronald laughed. "Now, here's the riddle, when does Timmy rhyme with bubble?"

As he asked me the riddle he gave one of my nipples a twist...

"WH-what?" I barked angrily. "What the fuck kind of riddle is that?"

"Again, when does Timmy rhyme with bubble?" Ronald asked me again.

"Okay man, I'll bight, I'll fucking bight, when does Timmy rhyme with bubble?" I repeated the riddle and pursed my lips together for a moment. "*When does Timmy rhyme with bubble? When the fucking fucks does Timmy rhyme with bubble?* I've got it, I think. Timmy rhymes with bubble *when he's in trouble!* Just like I have been since you captured me, *in trouble...* Yeah, that's it buddy, Timmy rhymes with bubble when he's trouble!"

"Wrong buddy boy," Ronald snickered and whipped the blindfold off me.

I quickly took in the sight of myself tied down to the slab of wood. At the end of the slab where my socked feet were tied down and dangling off the end I saw a mechanical looking device with two very mechanical looking pointy tongues sticking out of the ends of it. Those two mechanical tongues were aimed directly and precisely at the bottoms of my poor feet.

"Oh fuck," I whispered and then knew why Ronald had been sticking and flicking his tongue at me lately.

He was preparing me for a real foot tongue lashing buds...

"The correct answer to the riddle, When does Timmy rhyme with bubble is when he's double," Ronald laughed and held up yet another remote control device.

It was all so ingenious how Ronald had created all these tickle torture devices and had remote controls for all them, *simply ingenious*. It reminded me of the remote control that the men had in the remake of that movie "The Stepford Wives."

"*Double*, as in you are about to have your feet doubly tickled this time out buddy boy," Ronald said to me in a mocking tone.

"OH GOD RONALD, those things look like goddamned cow tongues," I murmured fearfully. "Y-you said that if I called my wife you would go easy on me..."

"And I am, I'm only going to tickle you for an hour with those mechanical cow tongues, as you so aptly named them," Ronald chuckled. "My original plan was to subject you to that for two hours, hell, maybe three, but let's not forget the extra tagged on ten minutes that you earned because you didn't answer the riddle correctly."

"Yeah, let's not forget those ten minutes," I said dejectedly.

Smiling fiendishly at me my so called buddy pressed a button on the remote control...

"Double tickle time buddy, with double devices," Ronald laughed as the mechanical tongues came to life at the bottoms of my feet. "Now Timmy rhymes with bubble, ha, ha!"

"HA, ha, ha, ha, ha, ha, ha, ha, ha, ha, ha, ha, ha, ha, ha, ha, ha, ha!" I screeched, once again trapped in the throes of laughter as the mechanical tongues came to up and down and up and down and up and down life against the bottoms of my trapped and socked feet. "OH GOD RONALD, th-those things are lick tickling the bottoms of my feeeeeettttt! HA, ha, ha, ha, ha, ha, ha, ha, ha, ha, ha, ha, ha, ha, ha, ha!"

"I told you that once your feet had been oiled that they would be even more tickle responsive," Ronald said and pressed another button on the remote control.

The mechanical tongues lick tickled my feet faster...

"OH MY GOD RONALD, this is the worst yet, ha, ha, ha, ha, ha, ha, ha, ha, ha, ha, ha, ha, I-I can't stand it!" I laughed through clenched teeth and my eyes squeezed halfway shut. "Th-the pressure from those tongues, ha, ha, ha, ha, ha, ha, ha, it, it's killin' me man!"

"You will find Timmy my laddy that each device will make you think that it's worse than the one before it," Ronald said, sounding like a college instructor of some kind. "However, they all have one thing in common; they will tickle the ever-loving shit out of you..."

"HAR, HAR, HAR, HAR, HAR, HAR, HAR, ohhhhhhhrrrrr GOD, an hour and ten minutes of this and I will pass out for real, not like when you use that rancid chloroform on me, ha, ha, ha, ha, ha, ha, ha, ha, ha, ha, ha, ha, ha, ha!" I guffawed real heartily. "Gawd, those tongues are lick tickling the bottoms of my feet up and down and up and down."

Smiling at my observation Ronald stepped over to the slab of wood that I was tied to and grabbed one of my nipples again, squeezed it a bit and twisted it. Fuck, it was bad enough that I was laughing from having my socked feet lick tickled but as Ronald played with my goddamned man tit I saw my cock growing harder again between my tied down legs. Fuck, how could I possibly get hard like that again after having just shot a monster sized load back in the bathroom? But then, I recalled Ronald's aphrodisiac and the constant tickling I had been subjected to. And lets face it folks tickling him really sets Timmy in motion, as even I have found out myself since being captured by Ronald, since being tickle tortured by Ronald and since being forced to reveal my ticklish past by Ronald.

"HA, ha, ha, ha, ha, ha, ha, ha, ha, ha, ha, ha, ha, ha, ha, ha, ha, ha, ha!" I laughed crazily. "Ronald, please stop this, please, ha, ha, ha, ha, ha, ha, ha, ha, ha, ha, ha, ha, I-I'll do whatever you want, just please, stop this! I can't take anymore!"

"Buddy boy, you are doing just what I want you to do, you're laughing and laughing and I see from the way I'm handling your man tit here that your cock is getting hard again," Ronald chuckled and tweaked the very tip of my man tit, sending true chills through me. "So I know that you really are enjoying yourself."

"*I AM NOT ENJOYING MYSELF*, ha, ha, ha, ha, ha, ha, ha, ha, ha, ha, ha, ha!" I spitted laughingly.

Chuckling meanly Ronald pressed yet another button on the remote control and the mechanical tongues started licking my feet faster yet, increasing the pressure on my feet at the same time. The tongues revved themselves from my heels and went all the way up to the tips of my socked toes and then back down again. What a sight that was that's all I can say buds. I could hardly breathe as the tickling was getting worse with each pass of the mechanical tongues on my poor ticklish feet.

"RONALD, ha, ha, ha, ha, ha, ha, ha, ha, ha, ha, ha, ha, ha, ha, ha, ha, ha, ha, ha, ha!" I laughed. "Y-you have got to turn off those tongues man! I-I can't breathe! HA, ha, ha, ha, ha, ha, ha, ha, ha, ha, ha, ha, ha, ha!"

Ronald pressed another button on the remote control and the tongues slowed down a bit and the pressure eased up a bit on my feet. I was able to catch my breath and breathe normally in between gasping and laughing still.

"You know Timmy, I think, that if I take one of your socks off you I can have one of those tongues lick tickle you between your toes and the other tongue can continue to lick tickle your socked foot, what do you think buddy?" Ronald asked me and my eyes opened in total despair.

"OOOOOOOOOOHHHHHHH, noooooooo, ha, ha, ha, ha, ha, ha, ha, ha, ha, ha, ha, R-Ronald, don't do that man, please, I cannot stand to have my toes or in between them licked!" I laughed out my reply. "PLLLEEEEEEASE don't do that!"

All of a sudden the tongues stopped and I looked up to see Ronald standing right next to me and looking down into my eyes.

"How do you know you don't like to have your toes and in between them tickled?" he asked me, sounding stern. "Has someone tickled you there before? Your wife or Valerie perhaps?"

"Oh, uh, no, no, I've never been tickled between my toes before, I just know that I won't like it," I said to Ronald, trying to convince him that I had not been tickled there before.

"Somehow I don't think you're telling me the entire truth buddy," Ronald admonished me, twisting one of my nipples real hard. "Before I take one of your socks off and turn the mechanical tongues back on why don't you take advantage of this unexpected break I'm giving you and tell me when you've been tickled at the toes and in between them before."

As he spoke he twisted my poor man tit harder and my cock pulsed long and hard between my legs.

"OUCH, easy with my man tit, Gawd that hurts, alright, I'll tell you," I said angrily. "This was when I was a teenager actually. My goddamned tickle history goes that far back, if you can believe it. My older brother would tickle me and my other brother to get us to do things for him. One time the miserable bastard noticed that I had a hard-on while he was tickling me. I managed to get away from him and didn't talk about it with him at all. Then, one night while I was in bed sleeping he somehow managed to get my hands tied above my head to the bed board, he stripped off my pajama bottoms and then as I slowly awoke he got me tied to the bed itself. When I awoke fully I was astounded to find myself in the position he had me. I quickly tried to yell for my parents but he stifled that real quickly by gagging me and told me that he was going to tickle me and watch me get hard again. Now Ronald, you can just imagine, I'm sure just how mortifying that was for an impressionable teenager. Anyway, he did just that, tickled me all over, but spent most of his time at my feet and he even licked and slobbered over them. While I made grunting helpless sounds into my gag he then sucked on my toes and licked in between them and man, that shit drove me crazy. I was laughing and cackling into my gag, sputtering like crazy and then embarrassment of all embarrassments I shot a gutsy teenaged load without my older brother even touching my cock. I writhed and slithered on my bed, the tight bondage holding me in check as I erupted rope after thick rope of teenaged sperm. My brother made me do all his chores for him and clean up his room and fix his bike and a host of other crap; and if I didn't do all that he told me to do he threatened to tell all our friends just how ticklish I was and what it does to me when I'm tickle tortured. So you see Ronald, you have to stop all this and let me go. I cannot stand to have my bare feet lick tickled and licking my toes and in between them is just over the top pure torture for me. If you do that to me the fun in all of this will stop. I have no doubt that you'll have to take me to a hospital."

Ronald smiled evilly down at me, more evilly than I had seen yet since all this began...

"Man, I'm so glad you told me that buddy," Ronald said sounding concerned for my welfare, or so I thought. "I didn't think your bare toes was that ticklish that you could actually shoot a load without me or anyone even touching your manhood?"

"Well, it has been a long time since *that* happened I will say," I said through trembling lips, thinking that for sure he was going to let me go now, seeing as I told him that if he tickled me in that fashion he would wind up having to take me to a hospital.

"I'll tell you what Timmy my ticklish laddy," Ronald said, now looking as if a light bulb had gone on in his head. "You still have about an hour and five minutes worth of tickle time up there on that slab and what I'm going to do is this. If you can shoot a load while you're being lick tickled on one socked foot and in between the toes on your other bare foot by my mechanical tongues before your time is up I'll stop the device and we'll go to the next room where the next tickle torture device is. If you don't shoot a load you'll still have a full hour and ten minutes to go with the lick tickling, the extra ten minutes of course being your penalty for not getting the riddle correct."

He couldn't be serious could he? I had just shot a load when he had allowed me to use the bathroom and now he expected me to shoot another one? *And without touching my cock at that?*

"Ronald, that was when I was a teenager man, I don't think I can pull that off, especially if I'm not pulling myself off, hardy har, fucking har," I said throatily.

"Well, we'll see what happens; all we can do is try right me laddy?" Ronald asked me jovially. "And this time I'm going to get the event on tape, so just give me some time to turn on the video camera and to get your sock off..."

"VIDEO CAMERA? VIDEO CAMERA? NOOOOOOOO RONALD, NO!" I blubbered at the total awfulness now.

I was about to be lick tickled on one bare foot and one socked foot and it was going to be captured on video, oh woe of fucking woes! Ronald proceeded to pull my left sock off my foot. Then, I saw a red light come on that was on a hidden video camera behind a partition in the present room where Ronald had me. Ronald aimed the camera right at me and my cock stood up and at attention. My manhood wasn't camera shy it seemed. Ronald then made a few adjustments to the mechanical tongues by my feet, he pressed a button on his remote control and the tongue at my left (bared) foot started licking on my bare toes and wiggling its way in between my toes. The tongue at my right foot, my socked foot to be precise licked up and down and up and down on that foot. Within seconds I was screaming with laughter. I closed my eyes tight, trying to control myself... Well, that was easier said than done, as the saying goes and once again, within seconds I simply erupted with laughter from deep within my stomach and my cock was rock hard now. Holy fuck, would I be able to shoot a load without touching my cock? Would I be able to shoot a load so soon after I had just cum? These were the questions going through my tortured mind as Ronald stood watching the tongues do their work on my poor ticklish feet. And to make the situation all the more worse he was smiling at me and teasing my nipples at the same time. The way I was laughing and screaming anybody else would have stopped those mechanical tongues from what they were doing to me. Why didn't Ronald stop? Why oh why did he continue to do all this to me? Fuck, I had to shoot a load before my hour and ten minutes were up! It was my only hope of getting off that slab of wood and for the mechanical tongues to stop tickling my poor feet!

Chapter Twenty-One

"HA, ha, ha, ha, ha, ha, ha, ha, ha, ha, ha, ha, ha, ha, ha, ha, ha, you bastard Ronald!" I laughed and screamed as the mechanical tongues did their dirty work on my one socked foot and my other bare foot.

The tongue at my bare foot seemed to be in love with the areas between my toes and it feasted and feasted there like a vampire sucking blood. Watching that thing force its way between my toes and then licking there was sending me into a higher and higher laughing fit. My other foot, the socked one, was not to be left out though, as the other tongue trailed itself up and down and up and down the bottom of that foot. Oh Gawd, Ronald's cow tongue machine was an evil thing let me tell you buds. And there was my good buddy, standing nearby with a video camera turned onto record, capturing all my torments and laughter on tape. Good movie watching I supposed for a cold and lonely night huh? I saw my other black sock sticking out of Ronald's pants pocket and for some damned reason that really made my cock harder yet and my erection swung in the wind as I laughed and laughed. I mean, how many guys can say that their buddy has one of his smelly socks in his pocket?"

"RO-RONNALD, I-I- ha, ha, ha, ha, ha, ha, ha, ha, ha, ha, ha, ha, ha, ha, ha! I-I think it's gonna happen man!" I laughed, snarling at the same time. "I'm gonna shoot my ever lovin' fuckin' load!"

Reeling crazily, I lifted my head up off the slab of wood that I was laying on, looked down across my muscular tied up body, concentrated on my dribbling and twitching erection and it stood rigid and stiff as I went on laughing and laughing and laughing…

"OOOOOOOHHHHHHH!" I seethed as globs upon globs of my creamy sperm erupted from my piss slit. "HA, HA, HA, HA, HA, HA, HA, HA, HA, HA, HA, HA, HA, HA, HA, HA, HA, HA, HA, HA, HA, HA, F-FUCKING FUCKS, lookit me cumming Ronald! FUCKING FUCKS again man, th-that hasn't happened in years! LOOKIT me cum…"

"Yeah, look at it, totally fucking amazing bud," Ronald marveled at my sexy display, watching intently and making a fast adjustment on the video camera, no doubt he wanted a close-up of my eruption. "Never saw a guy shoot his load without his cock being touched, and from being tickled no less. Timmy my laddy, its think it's safe to assume here that *you are* a true tickle fetishist."

"Ha, ha, ha, ha, ha, ha, ha, ha, ha, ha, ha, ha, ha, ha, ha, ha, no, *no shit Sherlock*!" I laughed louder. "OH GOD, it feels worse now, after I cum I'm always so much more tickle sensitive man!"

"I think we established that even before the outset of this buddy," Ronald laughed.

The mechanical tongues at my feet seemed to speed up as I laughed and laughed more and more…

"O-Okay Ronald, okay man, ha, ha, ha, ha, ha, ha, ha, ha, ha, ha, ha, ha, ha, ha, ha, I-I did what you said, I shot a load, *I shot a fucking load*!" I guffawed. "Now let me off this thing man, ha, ha, ha, ha, ha, ha, ha, ha, ha, ha, ha, ha, ha!"

As I laughed and spoke the sperm that I had erupted slithered over my chest and nipples areas, sending more chills through me.

"Just one more thing before I let you off that slab buddy," Ronald said, pressed a button on his remote control device, pointed upwards at the ceiling and told me to take a look. I looked up and screamed because what I saw was a pole with feathers on the end of it descending downward toward my crotch area.

"AAAAYYYYYYYYYYYYYYRRRR NOOOOOOO!" I screamed.

Ronald's Journal
Dated the third week of July 1994

What a summer it's been so far, hot, *miserably hot*, and real humid too, ninety to one hundred percent humidity the last few days. It seems that New York City really suffers when it comes to humidity. Shit and it's only July, with August still to look forward to. And to make the situation even worse the goddamned air conditioning at the bank broke down today. The Personnel department promised that they would have service technicians there as early as possible, but unfortunately for us yuppies they never showed. It seemed that the same problem was occurring all over the city and there just weren't enough air conditioner technicians to go around to satisfy all the sweating suits in the city. People had their air conditioners jacked up to the highest settings and because they were being run all day and all night they were breaking down. All of us used desk fans to try to keep cool, but when you have to wear a shirt and tie, well, a desk fan just doesn't cut it like an air conditioner. Basically a desk fan just blows the hot air around. But, I didn't start this journal entry to complain about the heat, however, the heat did bring me a bit of a stroke of luck today where my work buddy Tim Backman is concerned, or should I say where Tim Backman and his socked feet were concerned. I needed to get some papers signed off by him before I could send them out to the customers, so without calling the guy I trotted from my desk to his office. We've known each other seven months or so now and I was there the night his wife gave birth to their son so I simply figured that I didn't need a formal invitation to his office. I knocked twice and stuck my head in the door, saying, "Got a minute Tim?" Tim was on the phone as I stepped into his office, closing the door softly behind me. He looked up at me as I entered his office, smiled his killer smile, and waved for me to come in. I heard him mention the name Jerry and the name Mr. Maxwell so I figured Tim was on the phone with our vice president and one of the bank's biggest customers. Mr. Maxwell represents a company that we do huge dealings with. But as I stepped into Tim's office my heart instantly thundered in my chest at the sight of what I saw. There was Tim, sitting behind his desk, his suit jacket off, his white shirt sleeves rolled up to his elbows, the first two top buttons on his shirt unbuttoned and his tie yanked down and his feet propped up on his desk as he chatted and prattled on the phone. It was Tim's feet up on that desk that had captured my undivided attention, as the laddy had his shoes off. Tim's navy blue nylon dress socked feet were propped up on his desk and crossed at the ankles, his right foot sort of lying across the left one as he talked on the phone. He saw the papers in my hand, whispered, "Be right with you buddy," and returned to his phone conversation. Tim's office was just as hot as everyone else's, but unlike everyone else Tim didn't have a desk fan going to help keep him cool, instead he was sweating and toughing it out. I slowly made my way around his desk and sure enough there were the guy's burgundy loafers under his desk. He had obviously slipped his loafers off while talking on the phone and propped his feet up on the desk. Even though Tim's office was as stiflingly hot as everyone else's my hands suddenly felt cold and they were shaking. It was the sight of those size eleven's of his in those thin ribbed blue nylon socks that was driving me crazy. I still have not figured out this new and what seems like a fanatical obsession of mine. But I can say that it's a mania that consumes me. Sometimes when I get home at night I find myself thinking of Tim and his socked feet. I think of him at home getting his shoes off, padding around in his socks. Again I ask, what is up with all this? Tim and I grinned at each other, silently telling each other how comical he looked with his big ol' smelly feet propped up on his desk, and yes Sir, they sure did smell. But they didn't smell in a way that was repulsive in the way that Stephanie had talked about in the car that time, rather they smelled musty and inviting somehow, hypnotic, as if they could draw you to them. Still smiling at Tim as he spoke on the phone, saying things like, "Yes Mr. Maxwell" and "Sure Jerry I can look into that and take care of it for you, certainly," I propped myself on the edge of Tim's desk, sitting with my back to him, right next to his propped up socked feet on that desk while he spoke to Jerry and Mr. Maxwell. I decided to test the waters a bit and see just how much I could get away with here. While he talked and rattled on and on, on the phone I arched my head a bit and looked at Tim from a backward glance. I grinned at him, lifted his feet by hefting up the left one at the bottom of his crossed tootsies and slid my papers that I needed him to sign under his heel, quickly setting his feet back down. He smiled in a silly manner and gave me a thumbs-up signal. I smiled back at him at the fact that I had just turned his socked feet into a makeshift paperweight of sorts. He pointed to the phone and shrugged, silently telling me that he was sorry but it was our boss and a big client after all. I whispered that it was alright and to take his time. I was in heaven to say it plainly. As I sat there on the edge of Tim's desk I inhaled deeply, but silently, not wanting the handsome laddy to know that I was sniffing his socked feet. I made a ho hum kind of sound, as if I was bored listening to his end of the conversation that he was participating in and made as if in an unconscious gesture to have my hand find its way to his right foot that was resting atop his left foot as they sat there propped on his desk crossed at the ankles. I gently squeezed the top part of Tim's socked foot but didn't turn my head to look at him that time. He simply went on with his end of the conversation, not pausing and not telling me to get my hand off his foot. I decided to plunge in a bit more. I moved my hand upwards as I held his socked foot and then glided the palm of my hand over his socked toes. The scent wafting up from his toes areas was the most intoxicating it seemed, just like the night in the hospital when his wife gave birth, how the toe section of his GoldToe brand socks really were very scented that night. I played it off as if I was doing this without realizing it, as if I were just sitting there killing time, as if I had just picked up a knick knack from Tim's desk and started fiddling with it as he spoke on the phone. In this case though the knick knack was Tim's socked feet. With my fingers trembling I snagged a small portion of the toes section of his sock and turned to grin at him this time. He grinned back at me, shrugged, and pointed at the phone, seemingly unaware of what I was doing as I tugged the toe section of his sock slightly upward. I turned my back again, let go of Tim's toe section of sock and let go of his foot as I was able to tell from his end of the conversation that the phone call was winding up. Tim said, "Sure thing Jerry, yes Sir Mr. Maxwell, I'm on it, it will be taken care of before the day is out." He paused to listen once more and then said, "Okay guys, I have Ronald Greene here in my office and he seems to need my attention next. Looks like everybody is making Timmy sweat in his socks today huh?" A chill went up my spine as Timmy laughed into the phone in response to whatever Jerry or Mr. Maxwell had said about his statement concerning sweating in his socks. He politely said good-bye and leaned forward to hang up the phone. He said, "Sorry about that buddy, but you know how Jerry kisses Maxwell's ass, and he expects us too as well." We both laughed as I got up off Tim's desk and sat down in the chair facing him, his socked feet now in my face. I told him that I needed him to sign off on the papers I had just placed under his feet and he said that it would be no problem, lifting his feet and taking them off the desk. Tim then said, "Sorry that I had my feet up on the desk buddy, and to make it worse these damned smelly socks of mine are stinking up the office." I laughed good naturedly as he signed the papers and told him that it didn't really smell all that bad. My heart pounded and my cock throbbed in my pleated suit pants as I realized that Tim hadn't made mention of the way I had handled his foot and sock while he'd had those smelly tootsies of his up on the desk, interesting, *very interesting*. Tim disagreed with me about the smell wafting from his dress socks and said how Stephanie was right about how his socks smell when he takes his shoes off when he arrives home from work at the end of the day. He then said, "So a lot of times during the day here I take my shoes off so my feet can air out, but with the air conditioning broken today I guess I really wasn't doing such a great job huh bud?" I actually got the feeling that I was being somehow cock teased. Timmy went on to say, "I know it's not very professional for a corporate executive to be taking his shoes off at work during the day, but most times I keep my feet under my desk so no one is the wiser if they happen to come in here. In your case you caught me I would suppose Ronald." He pushed the signed papers across to me and we both smiled. I said, "Well, in my opinion your feet are okay and they don't smell all that bad at all and yeah, its okay to take your shoes off during the day while you're working, it helps to relax you I would think." Timmy couldn't agree more and I was glad I had just said that seeing as it seemed to have opened more doors. Timmy crossed his hands up behind his head and supposing that it was cool to do so he again propped those navy blue socked feet of his up on the desk. I stifled a chuckle when I saw how the toe section of his sock was still pulled away from his toes a bit where I had fiddled with it. He went on to tell me how sometimes during his lunch hour, if he eats in the office, he'll take his shoes off and walk around on the rug in his socked feet, saying how relaxing it feels. I softly said that I would try it some time. I collected the papers I had needed signed, gave Tim's feet a quick squeeze each and told him that I had better get back to work. He wished me a good day, said that if I found an extra fan lying around the bank to bring it to him, told me how he would cool his feet with it and then I walked out of his office, closing the door behind me. I thanked God that I had worn pleated and sort of baggy suit pants that day, seeing as the erection that I had at that moment felt like a rod of steel in there...

Chapter Twenty-Two

"OH MY GOD, RONALD, ha, ha, ha, ha, ha, ha, ha, ha, ha, ha, ha, ha, ha, ha, ha, ha" I laughed crazily. "Please, don't do that! That would be totally beyond cruelty for a poor ticklish laddy like me! OH MAN, you are driving me insane buddy! HA, ha, ha, ha, ha, ha, ha, ha, ha, ha, ha, ha, ha, ha, ha, ha, ha, ha, ha, ha!"

"Well, seeing as you were able to shoot that load so potently without your cock being touched just a few moments ago I want to see how quick you can get hard again," Ronald laughed meanly. "And it'll be good to capture that on video as well… Who knows, maybe you'll shoot yet *another* load for me here…"

"Ronald, you prick, ha, ha, ha, ha, ha, ha, ha, ha, ha, ha, ha, don't do this, I mean it!" I reeled through clenched teeth as the mechanical tongues were still doing their dirty work on my feet.

I managed to stop laughing long enough and I demanded that Ronald not tickle my crotch with the feathers that were on the pole that was slowly descending from the ceiling toward my very vulnerable, very tickle sensitive crotch area. The pole was attached to some kind of mechanical apparatus up there and obviously Ronald had the controls at his fingertips.

"Ronald, you, you said, that once I shot a load without touching my cock you would let me off this thing, now, turn off those tongues and, ha, ha, ha, ha, ha, ha, ha, ha, ha, ha, ha, ha, ha, ha" I said and was suddenly off and laughing again. "And please man, ha, ha, ha, ha, ha, ha, ha, ha, ha, ha, ha, ha, ha, don't tickle my cock and balls with those feathers! MAKE THEM GO BACK UP MAN!"

"Oh, I see you're not as ticklish when you're angry or feeling cheated huh buddy?" Ronald asked me. "Well, in that case maybe I can be a good friend and make it up to you okay?"

He stepped over to me, grinned that evil grin of his and proceeded to pull my other sock off me. I screamed "NO, NO, NO" over and over again as he made some quick adjustments to the mechanical tongues as they slithered and slathered over my now both bared feet. Ronald then pressed another button on his blasted remote control device and I suddenly felt that the tongues were licking my bare feet faster yet, and both of them now torturing me by tickling me between the toes on each foot. Fucking totally fucks buds, both of those mechanical monster tongues were now working my bare feet and licking my toes and working meanly in between my toes and I erupted into louder peals of laughter. Fuck it all, there was no way I could hold back from laughing like a hyena that had been given a massive dose of steroids. The feathers moved downward so slowly, teasing me with the knowledge of what they were sure to do at any second. I glanced at Ronald and now saw both of my socks sticking out of his pocket and again at the sight of that my sticky cock grew amazingly hard yet again. Seeing those damned smelly socks of mine sticking out of my buddies pocket made my hard cock twitch and I started laughing even louder as the feathers reached me and made contact with my crotch area, spinning around and around and tickling my cock head, my shaft, and my balls, and further yet all around the base of my poor manhood. Now there was no way to hold back my laughter, even if I wanted to.

HAHAHAHAHAHAHAHAHAHAHAHAHAHAHAHAHAHAHAHAHAHAHAHAHAHA HAHAHAHHAHAHAHAHAHAHAH!" was the sound that filled the room as I lay on that slab being erotically and unmercifully tickled at my bare feet and sensitive cock. "SSSSSSTTTTTOOOPPPP RONALD, turn it off, *turn it all off, you promised man!*"

"Now that's more like it buddy, that is exactly what I want to hear," Ronald said, sounding like a proud parent. "I want to hear you laughing your head off real loudly and look at that man, your cock *is* getting hard again. *Amazing!* Now I'm sure you will be able to shoot another load for me, proof to me of how much you really are enjoying all this! Shoot one more load for me Timmy me laddy, one more, *and then, I promise*, I'll let you off that slab of wood and we'll move on to the next room."

"RONALD, nooooooooooooooo, ha, ha, ha, ha, ha, ha, ha, ha, ha, ha, ha, ha, ha, ha, ha, ha, ha, ha, ha, ha, ha, ha, ha!" I crowed and cawed. "I-I can't cum anymore, PLEEEEAASSSEEE MAN, please stop, ha, ha, ha, ha, ha, ha, ha, ha, ha, ha, ha, ha, ha, ha, ha, ha, ha, ha!"

"Oh, but you're a strong guy Timmy my laddy," Ronald said to me in a disagreeing tone of voice. "That's part of the reason I chose you for this little adventure."

The spinning feathers at my cock spun faster and faster…

"I'm sure you'll be able to cum again for me, *eventually*," Ronald said mockingly. "And those feathers will help you along for sure…"

As my cock stood up straight as a stalk one of the feathers found its way to my piss hole and tickled it, slithering its way in there, just as Ronald had done to me earlier with a feather.

"HAHAHAHAHAHAHAHAHAHAHAHAHAHAHAHAHAHAHAHAHAHA" I guffawed crazily as the mechanical tongues tickled my bare feet and those danged feathers worked my manhood.

I again glanced over at Ronald and again took in the sight of my black socks sticking out of his pocket. Something about that, something about a buddy having such an intimate part of my apparel in his possession made my cock harder yet as the tickling feathers spun and spun.

"Ronald, please, please, ha, ha, ha, ha, ha, ha, ha, ha, ha, ha, ha, ha, ha, ha, ha, don't make me cum again man," I pleaded. "If, if, ha, ha, ha, ha, ha, ha, ha, ha, ha, ha, if I cum again I'll be even more tickle sensitive you bastard!"

"Good show Timmy me ticklish laddy, *you are so right*," Ronald said meanly and continued video taping my present torments.

"OOOOOOOOOHHHHHHHHHH, ha, ha, ha, ha, ha, ha, ha, ha, ha, ha, ha, ha, ha, ha, ha, ha, ha, ha, ha OOOOOOHHHHHRRRRR GAWD MAN!" I chortled madly and lifted my head up off the slab of wood. "HOLY FUCKING FUCKS, lookit those blasted feathers spin man!"

I grunted, I gasped, I think I farted and woe is me man, I felt my sexy juices boiling and being cooked up anew in my nuts.

"Holy shit Ronald, you fucking prick, ha, ha, ha, ha, ha, ha, ha, ha, ha, ha, ha, ha, ha, ha, ha, ha, ha, ha, ha, ha y-you're going to get my nut again man!" I laughed insanely. "I'm gonna need a goddamned rubber room when this is over! HA, ha, ha, ha, ha, ha, ha, ha, ha, ha, ha, ha, ha, ha, ha, ha, ha, ha, ha!"

The feathers spun and spun against my cock head, the one that was in my piss slit didn't seem to want to leave it and the mechanical tongues licked and licked my feet in between my toes. Ronald stood by watching intently and videotaped my anguish…

"RRRRRRRHHHHHHHH I cannot believe this, I really can't fucking believe this, but, ha, ha, ha, ha, ha, ha, ha, ha, ha, ha, ha, ha, ha, I think I'm actually gonna let fly with another load soon," I seethed. "Fucking totally fucks, I'm gonna cum again Ronald!"

"That is *exactly* what I want buddy," Ronald called out to me from where he was standing. "I want for you to shoot another load for me and like I promised, then we'll move to the next tickle room.

He video taped me, waiting for the combination of the mechanical tongues and spinning feathers to do their work and make me cum yet again while I laughed and laughed my head off…

"OOOOOOOOOOOOOHHHHHHHHHHH, I-I-I'm cumming, I'm fucking, ha, ha, ha, ha, ha, ha, ha, ha, ha, ha, ha, ha, ha, ha, c-cumming!" I screamed from deep within my belly, lifted my head up off the slab and watched in utter amazement as I spewed glob after glob of my sexy stuff from my cock. "OOOOHHHHHHHHHRRRRRRRR!"

The feathers on the pole ascended, they had done their work after all, and my poor hard and sensitive feeling cock erupted my juices all over my chest and stomach areas again.

"Ha, ha, ha, ha, ha, ha, ha, ha, ha, ha, ha, ha, ha, ha, ha, ha, ha, ha, ha, ha, ha, ha, ha, ha, ha, ha, ha, ha, ha, ha, ha!" I laughed crazily as I shot my load and the mechanical tongues continued tickling my bare feet.

"PLLLEEEAAAASSEEEE Ronald, ha, ha, ha, ha, ha, ha, ha, ha, ha, ha, ha, ha, make it stop," I pleaded laughingly. "HAHAHAHAHAHAHAHAHAHAHAHAHAHAH AHA, please man, I can't stand this any more, pllleeeeeaassssseee! HA, ha, ha, ha, ha, ha, ha, ha, ha, ha, ha, ha, ha, ha, ha, ha, ha, ha, ha!"

"Okay buddy, I did make a promise after all," Ronald said and used the hand-held remote control to turn off the mechanical tongues and slowly I was able to catch my breath.

As he turned off the video camera I watched my sexy juices again slither over my chest, over my man tits, (that really sent chills through me let me tell you) and off the sides of my torso. Laying there still tied down to that dangling slab I was breathing heavily in and out, still trying hard to catch my breath evenly when I felt Ronald put one of my socks back on my feet. I looked up and across my tied down muscular body and gasped as I saw him slowly pulling my sock up to my calf and smiling at me the whole time. Fucking fucks, the guy really was fixated and somehow in love with my socked feet. He then reached in his pocket, got my other black sock and put that one on my other foot for me, the same way as he had done with the first one, very gingerly and slowly pulling it up to my calf. My sensitive and flaccid cock tingled as Ronald pressed my feet together and kissed my toes a few times.

"Man, I just love your smelly socked feet Timmy my laddy," Ronald said to me, sounding totally lust filled. "And I can't wait to tickle you more and more…"

"Please Ronald," I said through trembling lips, able to speak now. "*You have to let me go. I cannot stand the tickling anymore. Please let me go!*"

"Come on buddy," Ronald said, sounding like we were football buds at that moment. "You know inwardly that you're really having a good time here. I mean, just look at all the times you just shot your load for me. Don't tell me you didn't enjoy that, you know you did. I would even be willing to guess that Stephanie has never made you cum that much in such a short span of time."

I glared at him miserably and angrily as he again held my socked feet together, sniffed them a bit and then kissed my toes again...

"And come on man, I put this whole tickle palace together just for you," Ronald said, stepping away from my socked feet and moving to the area of the slab where my upper body was tethered. "Would you cheat a good buddy out of trying out his greatest creation?"

"Some goddamned creation," I reeled as Ronald tied a blindfold over my eyes again. "I didn't ask you to create all this, nor did I ask to be made a part of it..."

"Well, you're here now and until we're done I want you to enjoy every moment of it," Ronald said, untied me from the slab of wood, grabbed my upper arms real quick, yanked them behind me and led me exhausted from laughter out of the room.

He brought me blindfolded to the next room, or should I say the next tickle torture chamber...

Chapter Twenty-Three

(Lunch Time)

Well, okay, when Ronald took the blindfold off me that time I didn't find myself lashed to, tied to, or strapped down (up) to another tickle torture device, at least not that moment I didn't. Instead I found myself seated at the same table that my buddy and I had sat at hours earlier when he'd served me breakfast. Now it was lunch time. And boy howdy was I hungry at that point. Being tickle tortured, being made to shoot my load those three times had really given me an appetite. I sat at the table with my socked feet this time locked in some kind of wooden cabinet that had padlocks on both sides of it. All that was visible of my feet were the tops of my black socks as I sat there. The box also weighed a lot so I was powerless to move my feet about at all. Once again, while I sat and ate Ronald sat across from me with the chloroform and the cloth ready. Just in case I try anything foolish, as he had stated while locking my feet in the wooden cabinet under the table. To tell it plainly I was beyond exhausted at that point and let's face it buds, even if I did try anything, foolish, as Ronald had named it, I doubted I would've been successful in any escape attempts. No, my good buddy seemed to hold all the aces in this card game that was for sure. Ronald told me that while we ate lunch he wanted to hear about another of my past ticklish experiences. I sipped purple grape juice and ate wonderful tasting meatloaf with boiled potatoes. I guessed that while I was being tickle tortured Ronald had had the food cooking. I mean, I didn't see any chefs around being paid to cook for the poor hapless tickle victim.

"Is that all we're going to talk about while you have me here?" I asked Ronald miserably, picking up my fork and filling my mouth with meatloaf.

"Well, unless you can think of something else that we have in common at the moment buddy I'd be glad to hear about it," Ronald chuckled. "But no, I want to hear more about your ticklish, ticklish past..." I sighed, sounding woeful and then began another tale from my, what Ronald called, ticklish past...

"Okay, I had another ticklish experience when I was young that was very humiliating," I began. "Actually, it seems that tickling a guy and humiliation goes hand in hand I would have to say. This took place at a family reunion when I was about fourteen or fifteen years old. As you know already my brother knew that I was ticklish and many times he tormented me with tickling for his sadistic pleasures. Anyway, my brother and I are the oldest of the cousins. At the time of the reunion he was about sixteen or seventeen and as I said I was fourteen or fifteen and all of our other dozen or so cousins were there, all of them younger than us, basically very innocent. Well, at this family reunion my brother, the conniver that he can be must have alerted our cousins to the fact that I was extremely ticklish. Even at fourteen or fifteen I was made to play with the younger group of kids in the family. We were all playing Tag and somehow several of my cousins ganged up on me and wrestled me to the grass. We were all laughing and playing and just having a grand old time the way kids will. Two of my twelve year old female cousins grabbed my arms and pulled them straight out, splaying me in a way. Then they each used their bare feet, you see, they had shed their shoes, to press against my head and face for leverage. Although they weren't aware of it, this was actually a fulfilled fantasy of mine, to have women's bare feet against my face. The smell was heavenly to me and their soft feet pressed into my cheeks and their wiggling toes played against my nose and mouth. Oh Man Ronald, it was so great, and my fourteen or fifteen year old cock stirred in my pants. Yeah, I enjoyed that let me tell you…"

I stopped in my tirade for a moment to consume more food and to gulp some grape juice…

"But then, as the girls held my arms down by sitting on them and with their bare feet pressed against my face and while I was secretly enjoying that kind of attention, I was pounced upon by the rest of the young cousins," I continued. You see, the rest of the mob of cousins was about to begin a tickle attack, obviously, and the girls with their feet in my face were actually part of the attack. I suddenly felt my sneakers being pried off my feet. I mumbled things like "Hey", and "What's going on?" as I licked the girls toes that were near my mouth, actually being forced to lick them as I spoke when you really stop and think about it. I tried to lift my head to see what was happening but the girls just pressed harder with their feet, especially against my mouth. It seemed that they were enjoying the sensations that my tongue was causing to their toes as I tried to talk. Then I felt my socks taken off my feet. There was no way that I could move my legs at that point seeing as there were cousins pinning my legs down too. Once my sneakers and socks were off my worst fears were realized and I inwardly knew that my conniving brother had manufactured yet another tickle torture soirée for me. I felt little hands and fingers begin working on the soles of my bare feet. Those little monsters even pulled up grass and used the blades to grass tickle my toes and of course in between them. Now you know why I didn't want to be tickled between my toes Ronald that has to be the worst for me bud. I broke out in loud gales of laughter, and through my laughter I could hear the gleeful laughs of joy from all my young cousins as they all began to join in on the tickle fun. Little hands worked on my knees and thighs through my pants, even venturing up and under my pants legs. And man, my cock got stiffer and stiffer. But, just let me explain here, there was nothing sexual in my cousin's minds, this was merely them getting their older cousin and having some mean fun with him. And tickling their cousin was a fun way to torture me, as they were finding out. But, even though they meant nothing sexual in their actions it was somehow serving to stimulate my teenaged cock into a full woody. Little hands went under my tee shirt and found my ribs and tummy and they also found just how ticklish those areas were as well. They used more grass blades on my belly button after having pushed my shirt up and out of its way. Then they pushed my shirt further up and tickled my armpits and what I at the time called my boy tits, but trust me Ronald, those boy tits were every bit as sensitive then as they are today. When they tickled the tips of my boy tits with those blades of grass I cackled so loudly I thought for sure that some of the adults at the reunion would hear me and come running and make us stop, but that didn't happen. Instead I was tickled more and more. The more they tickled me the more I laughed and the harder my cock got. Plus, let's not forget that I had those two girls with their goddamned bare and sweet tootsies pressing into my face. So, they were all having their fun and I was being tickle tortured and unbeknownst to them I was being sexually turned on. I guess more than anything it was the feet in my face and the grass blades being wiggled on my boy tits but I laughed and laughed and then I shot one of my first earlier teenaged loads. It was an earth shattering orgasm for me. My cousins just thought that I was laughing differently, the way that I was suddenly breathless. And fucking fucks of all fucks, they just kept it up until one of them noticed that I was laughing even louder, don't forget that after I cum I'm even more tickle sensitive, and he also noticed the wet spot on my pants. He called the others' attention to it and they naively thought that they had made me pee in my pants. Well, they all jumped up and ran off laughing at my utter humiliation. I was humiliated then myself and just ran off to hide. And after that I never went to another family reunion. But in all honesty I do think back on that day and wonder if those cousins of mine remember that day the way I do. I would think though that the difference between the ways that they remember it and the way that I remember it is that I jack off thinking about it and the situation I had found myself in..."

When my tirade was done I had also finished eating my lunch. I put my fork down and looked across the table at my good buddy.

"There are other stories I could tell you about of how my conniving brother got me into ticklish situations," I said glumly and burped gently after sipping down what was left of my grape juice. "It all wasn't while we were just kids after all. It seemed that he just reveled in putting me in ticklish situations."

After I was done eating and drinking the grape juice I felt the familiar tingling in my cock and balls. I had been duped again by Ronald it would seem. He had fed me and made me drink more of his aphrodisiac.

"Well, seeing as I want you to digest your food again Timmy and seeing as we'll need at least two hours time before I tickle you again why don't we kill those hours with you telling me just how very conniving that brother of yours could be," Ronald suggested with a vile look in his eyes as he stared across at me, finishing up his food as well.

Seeing as I had no choice in the matter I plunged right into another tirade about my older brother... I didn't even try to bargain with Ronald about getting some time taken off whatever would be my next tickle torture session, seeing as I was too exhausted both physically and mentally at that point it seemed...

"Well Ronald, this ticklish laddy that you captured has more tickle tales to tell you than anyone else you know I would imagine," I began again, sounding miserable as I spoke. "That wicked and conniving brother of mine just kept playing mean tricks on me by putting me into all kinds of ticklish situations. And I just kept on being naïve enough to fall into the traps he set. This one that I'll tell you about now was while we were in our twenties and at that time my brother had declared to all of us that he was gay. Well, that went a long way toward explaining why he delighted so in putting me in such sexually embarrassing and ticklish situations. And once he came out his antics just became more and more blatant and more and more sadistic and more and more humiliating for yours truly here. Although, I got to tell you Ronald, my brother himself never really participated in any of my humiliations, I suppose that he somehow got his jollies by knowing that I had been tricked and/or sexually humiliated. I think that it really bothered him that I did not understand his being gay and really didn't support him in it at that time. Perhaps setting me up for tickle torture situations was his way of getting back at me. But, he was, *is*, my brother and I kept giving him the benefit of the doubt, which of course was my big stupid mistake. One time I told my brother that my dentist was retiring and that I really needed to find a new one. My brother happily told me that he had a good friend that was a dentist and was eager to take on new patients. He swore to me that the guy, Doctor Teekle, was a great dentist. So, without thinking of the strange name this dentist had I made an appointment with him, through my brother. All Doctor Teekle had available was an appointment for Friday afternoon at three PM; so, I took off work that Friday early in the day and went to the address my brother had given me. The doctor's office was in a commercial section of town. I entered and found a nice looking young man working behind a sliding glass window. His nametag read "Willie Hard" and he greeted me as I approached the window. He gave me a "New Patient" form to fill out and said that Doctor Teekle would be with me shortly. There was one other guy in the waiting room and like me he was dressed in a business suit. He smiled over at me as I sat down across from him in the waiting room. I asked him politely if he was waiting for the doctor. He said "No", that his brother was in for some work and didn't want him driving after being "gassed", ha, ha. He went on to explain to me that he was there to drive him home, although I had to wonder at the "ha ha" that he had uttered at me. I told him that that was interesting and that my brother had recommended Doctor Teekle to me. I asked the handsome business guy if he came to Doctor Teekle as well. He said that he did, that actually both he and his partner went to Doctor Teekle as well as his brother and his partner too. He smiled real professionally and I thought that if all these businessmen and their business partners all came to the same dentist that the guy must be good. But the word gas had kind of unnerved me. I told the handsome businessman that I was there just for a checkup so I didn't think that I would need any gas. As I told the business guy that I finished filling out my "New Patient" form. Well, in response to what I had just said my waiting room companion added that Doctor Teekle used lots of gas when it came to his patients, adding that it tends to keep them happy. Then he said, "If you know what I mean, ha, ha." I sort of gave him a funny look and I thought that he was a tad strange. And man, little did I know that I myself was in for a very strange afternoon, uh, weekend. Just then, another patient came in. It was another handsome guy in a business suit. He approached Willie who greeted him by name, Mr. Feathers. He was looking to squeeze in an appointment. Willie told Mr. Feathers that the doctor had a patient in the gas chamber now and they both laughed. Willie then pointed over at me and said, "And Mr. Timmy Backman over there is our next victim." And they laughed again. All those people in that dentist's office had the strangest names and it was beginning to give me the willies, no pun intended Ronald. I actually felt as if I had entered the twilight zone. Mr. Feathers sat down and smiled at me. I nodded politely. Then Willie told me that Doctor Teekle would see me now. I was glad that I hadn't had to wait all that long. I hate waiting rooms. Anyway, I stood up and walked through the inner office door. Once I was on the other side Willie, a rather large and athletic looking guy, now that I could get a full look at him, directed me to an empty examining room. That was when I began to hear laughter. I looked at Willie and asked him what in the world that was. He simply chuckled and told me that it was Mr. Bristle. Willie told me that Mr. Bristle was cumming, and quickly corrected himself by saying that he was *coming* out from under the nitrous oxide, calling it the laughing gas. Willie told me that Doctor Teekle found it to be really helpful with patients, adding how he was sure that I would find out as well. I just looked at him blankly as he looked at me in almost a lustful manner. As I stepped into the vacant room I reminded him that I would not need any laughing gas. Willie said that we would just have to see about that, reminding me of doctor's orders and all that good stuff. Willie directed me into a large reclining chair with all the dental instruments positioned off to one side. I shucked off my suit jacket, placed it over a regular chair that was in the examination room and sat down in the reclining dentist's chair. Willie then attached a bib around my neck and pushed the seat way back to the point that my feet were actually almost higher than my head. I said "Whoa, is it really necessary to recline me back so far?" in a complaining tone of voice. Willie replied by telling me that it was his job to make sure that the patient was comfortable before the doctor arrived. He then handed me some headphones and asked me what kind of music I liked, citing that they had everything from classical to classical, ha, ha. I stupidly ha, haed along with him and said that I guessed it was to be classical. As I put the headphones over my ears I looked down at my feet and saw that Willie was busily undoing my shoelaces. I asked him what the hell he was doing. He explained that it was just part of their relaxation policy, plus it was not good to sit for long periods of time with your shoes on, circulation and all that. He proceeded to remove both my shoes and he placed them under the chair. He looked up at me as I sat there dumbfounded with the earphones in my hands. I was still holding them above my head. Willie then in an authoritative sounding kind of voice instructed me to put the headphones on and he added that Doctor Teekle would be right in. Still squatting at my now socked feet he tweaked one of my big toes, smiled evilly and walked out. As I sat there in that strangest of positions with my shoes off no less I wondered what the hell kind of dentist this was that my brother had sent me to. Or more to the point, what the hell had I gotten myself into? Or had my brother set me up again? When that thought entered my head I nearly freaked and said "Oh No" out loud, thinking that he had better not have set me up again… Suddenly, as I was thinking all these thoughts I heard a very sinister sounding voice say, "Well hello there Mr. Timmy Backman!" Obviously it was the dentist. He looked to be a guy in his thirties with a slick shaved head and a huge lustful smile. He walked into the examining room with two other guys who were wearing lab coats. Those two other guys looked like personal trainers from a gym. As they entered the room the personal trainers split up. One walked around the chair where my head was and the other muscleman stopped at my feet. While they did this the dentist introduced himself, saying, "I'm Doctor Teekle and may I say that I'm very glad you have come to be a patient of mine here." He went on to tell me that the two musclemen in the room with him were his assistants. He introduced the one behind me as Butch, him being the gas passer, we all chuckled at that. The other stack of muscles he introduced as Dash, explaining that he was the resident footman, going on to say that Dash dealt with anything that needed to be taken care of down in that part of the room, hence his nickname the footman. I quickly told Doctor Teekle that I was just there for a checkup and that I would not need any gas. He grinned at me with his eyes almost popping out of his head and asked me who the doctor was, who was in charge there. I suppose that all the training I'd had as a kid when I was taken to doctors came into play at that moment because I found myself (stupidly) obeying Doctor Teekle's orders. He then told Butch to get started while he took a look in my mouth. With that Butch placed a nosepiece over my nose and quickly turned on the gas. I immediately noticed a quick sharp, but sweet smell and then nothing. I heard Doctor Teekle tell me to open up wide and he began looking around in my mouth. I felt his latex gloved finger probing along my gums, under the roof of my mouth and even toying with my tongue. It wasn't long before the gas really took effect and I started to feel totally relaxed and found that I was fighting a smile. The doctor continued to probe and poke around in my mouth, looking intently at me as he did so. Then I heard him say, "Dash!" And Dash, who was stationed down at my feet began to massage my socked tootsies. Oh man Ronald, it felt so fucking good let me tell you man. Then I heard the doctor say, "Butch!" which I think signaled the brutish muscleman to up my dosage of laughing gas. Then I heard the doctor again say, "Dash!" and to my horror and excitement I felt Dash slipping my dress socks off my feet. I stupidly laughed a few hee, hee; hee's and drunkenly mumbled, "Doctor T-Teekle, he's taking my smelly socks off me." I heard Doctor Teekle call out "Butch!" one more time before he looked at me and said, "Why Mr. Timmy Backman, so he is, *he is* taking off your dress socks. *Isn't that just so funny*?" At that point Butch stopped gassing me and I felt like I was in La La land. I again laughed a few stupid sounding hee, hee, hee's and asked, "But why is he taking my socks off me?" Without replying to my most unbelievable question Doctor Teekle reached over and swung a clamp over my far wrist and secured it to the arm of the chair with a click. Then, reaching over in the other direction he did the same thing with my other wrist. While the dentist was clamping my wrists to the armrests of the chair at the same time Dash was clamping my now bared ankles into clamps of their own. Once my feet were secured Dash really started massaging them. I mean he *really* began to massage my feet, heel to toes, toes back to heels, pressing hard against my arches, working each and every toe by tweaking them hard, twisting them, pressing them. I hee, hee, heed again and asked the doctor what the clamps were for, mumbling down at Dash how he had magic hands and fingers. Butch again turned on the gas and I have to say that by then I was in full giggle mode. But, to add to the scene that was unfolding in that dentist's office I found that Dash's foot massage was making my cock plump up, which of course made my suit pants begin to tent. Doctor Teekle told me that the clamps were to keep me in place, calling me his friend and dear boy, and then adding that my teeth looked fine. He said that we just needed to schedule me for a routine cleaning, say by the following week. I wanted to garble at him that I could have told him that, that I had only come in for a routine checkup and now he had gassed me into a state of oblivion of sorts, clamped me into that infernal chair and had my shoes and socks taken off my feet. And I also wondered why I had to wait till the following week for a routine teeth cleaning. I mean, he had me in the chair right? Why not just get it over with right then and there and spare me the trouble of having to come back the following week? But as my head spun I received the answer to those unspoken questions when I heard Doctor Teekle then say, "So now I think you're ready for some fun don't you Mister Timmy Backman?" I looked up at him through hazy vision and he grinned down at me with these "Gotcha bud" looking eyes. I murmured the word "fun" a few times and heard myself stupidly giggling a few hee, hee, hee's. Then, I wasn't sure if I was seeing things at that point but I could have sworn that Butch was reaching over me and unbuttoning my shirt at the same time that Dash was running his magic fingers up and under my pants legs. I said, "Oh ho, ho, ho, ho, Doctor T-Teekle, this muscle head of yours here is unbuttoning my shirt, hee, hee, hee, hee, hee, and Dash is running his fingers up my pants, hee, hee, hee, hee, hee, legs…" And Ronald, my cock as usual had a mind of it's own as it just kept firming up in my suit pants. Doctor Teekle simply joined in the fun of my humiliation and began unbuckling my belt, unfastening my pants button and lowering my zipper. I laughed stupidly, ho, ho, hoing and asked the doctor just what in the hell he thought he was doing, slurring my words as I spoke. Then, I saw Willie stick his head into the room and heard him ask Doctor Teekle if he was ready for him and the others. Well, at the sight of Willie I mistakenly thought that help was on the way. WRONG! I called out, "Weeeeelie, help me, thhhheeeesse, hee, hee, hee, these guys are starting to tickle me! And I'm a veryyyyyyy ticklish guy Weeeeeelieee!" I could barely make out what I was saying but then what Willie had said registered in my gassed and tortured mind. I cried out to Willie, "Wh-what do you mean ready for you and the others, what others?" And so, in reply to my laughed out question in walked Willie, the other guy from the waiting room, Mr. Feathers, the late arrival, and one other guy who I assumed was the patient who had been ahead of me. Now there were seven guys huddled around my reclined and very vulnerable body and I was stupidly giggling to the beat of the band. And now that Doctor Teekle had opened my suit pants my growing erection was even more obvious. I heard Doctor Teekle say, "Ah yes Willie, I do think we are ready for all of you. Let the party begin." I quickly spat out the words, "What, ha, ha, ha, ha, ha, ha, what party?" laughing in between my words. Doctor Teekle then jovially said, "Why Timmy, to reward you for such good dental hygiene, we're throwing you a tickle party. Won't that be such fun, and, since this is Friday after- noon, we have all weekend to entertain you." Upon hearing that memories of Linda and being held all weekend in her dorm room being tickle tortured flooded my mind. I screamed out, "Noooooo, oh God no, hee, hee, hee, hee, ha, ha, my, my brother put you up to this, hee, hee, hee, he tricked me again…ha, ha, ha, ha, ha, ha, ha, ha, and, and it looks like I'm going to pay for it by losing a weekend…"

As I laughed and haw, haw, hawed, the rest of Doctor Teekle's brood gath- ered around my reclined body and they each began to work at removing my clothes. In my gassed and weakened state they were able to unclamp my arms and legs just long enough to remove my shirt and pants. They left my underpants on me for a while and then they really got down to tickling me in earnest. They were also apparently intent on teasing me sexually and seeing just how hard they could make my cock and yet, not let me shoot my load. Ronald, man, let me tell you, those guys were really good at tickling and teasing. Once I was naked they no longer needed the laughing gas. They just used fingers, feathers, brushes, and oh Gawd, spinning dental equipment to tickle and tease my very naked, my very sexy and my very vulnerable ticklish body. I fucking laughed and screamed all weekend. Sometime late on Sunday evening I finally shot a load, which actually felt like it ripped my nuts out when I finally came. Fuck man, it was earth shattering. Then of course it was back to tickling me some more in my now very overly sensitized state, because at this point Ronald my man, we all know what the fucking fuck it does to me to be tickled after I've shot a load… And man, I kept telling myself that I had to quit listening to my brother, he just kept tricking me into more and more predicaments.

I stopped speaking and simply stared across the table at Ronald, my captor, my so called good buddy…

He had a look of utter and total amazement on his face. When he finally spoke he said, "That dentist kept you there all weekend just like Linda did to you in college Timmy? Exactly how many times have you been kidnapped and tickle tortured laddy?"

Ronald's Journal
Dated January 1995

It's a new year. New goals, new dreams, new opportunities, as Jerry, our vice president at the bank said it today in our monthly meeting in the company boardroom. And to start my new year off right I've been elected to accompany my good buddy Tim Backman on a business trip to Washington DC. It seems that the bank landed yet another new corporate client and the business is based somewhere in Washington DC. I have to say that I came to work in the right place, business is booming. As the expression went back in the 1940's, Bully for me! At the meeting Jerry stood up at the conference table and announced the new acquisition. Of course all of us brown nosers erupted quickly into applause. Once we were done applauding Jerry announced that he was sending two of his best managers to Washington to meet with the CEO's of the company that the bank would now be doing business with; without stopping to come up for air the robust guy pointed to me and Tim and said, Timothy Backman and Ronald Greene. Once again all the brown nosers in the room erupted into applause. Needless to say I was very glad at this turn of events. I've been at the bank for a year at this point and I feel that I more than deserved a promotion months ago. I mean, okay, I was given a nice hefty raise back in June for my first half year there, but that was just a raise, a raise along with a promotion is bound to be even heftier. Maybe going on this business trip with Timmy the handsome laddy will secure a nice new and higher position for me, *maybe*. Jerry said that it would be a three day trip, that it would be two weeks from today and that he would brief both Tim and I in his office privately on what to expect down in Washington. He told me how Tim had been on these kinds of business excursions in the past and that he wanted me to start getting my feet wet now. As Jerry said that Tim clapped me on the back and a chill crawled up my spine. Get my feet wet? How about getting Timmy's feet wet? That sounded like a much better plan to me. God, why oh fucking why do I think of these things where my buddy Tim's feet are concerned? I mean, on one hand I was thinking how it would be great to meet some female piece of ass down in Washington when all the business mumbo jumbo was over at the end of the day. Not for Timmy though, that guy is totally faithful to his wife, which I see nothing wrong with mind you. The times I've seen them together I can tell how crazy they are for each other. But I'm sure that the laddy wouldn't mind if I hooked up some pussy action for myself while we're in Washington. Actually, being the buddy he is I was sure he would encourage it. He would be glad that I wasn't skirt chasing at the bank at least. But then on the other hand there's that part of me that seems to actually lust (lust, can you believe that shit? Lust!) after my handsome buddies' socked feet. I'm sure that a psychiatrist would have a field day with that one! Jerry wished everyone in the room a happy and prosperous new year and wound up the meeting. Over the next two weeks Jerry met with me and Tim every morning before the day began to brief us on what he expected when we got to Washington. Tim and I had lunch every other day or so to go over the preliminaries and finally the day of the trip arrived. We would be riding Amtrak out of Penn Station and the trip would take approximately two and a half hours. We arrived at Penn Station in a company car and got our luggages situated in the lower compartment of the train along with our garment bags with our suits for the next three days. As we walked along the platform toward the car of the train where we would be sitting, carrying our attaché cases I couldn't help but notice that Tim was walking a little funny, limping almost. I asked him what was wrong, both of us glancing down at his feet as he plodded along. As we walked onto the train he told me that he had just bought the wingtips he was wearing the previous day and added what a mistake it obviously had been to wear new shoes on a business trip. Like most guys it takes Tim a few days to really break in a new pair of shoes. I asked him if he brought an extra pair of shoes with him and he said that he had; his loafers, and that at the moment they were in his luggage. We both laughed a bit good naturedly at the fact that poor Tim's comfortable shoes were in his luggage, totally out of his reach at the moment. We found our seats, hung our suit jackets on wall hooks in our compartment, loosened our ties, and as we sat down the look on Tim's face was one of relief, relief at getting off his poor aching feet that is. As we settled in our seats I asked Tim how he was going to be able to get to the meetings in Washington if his feet were hurting him so badly, citing the fact that he could not wear his loafers with his suits in the corporate atmosphere. He gave me a look that sort of said, "No shit Sherlock" and said that hopefully by the time of the first meeting he would have broken his new wingtips in. If not he would just have to deal with it. We were sitting across from each other with our attaché cases on the floor between our legs in a compartment that was actually for four people. As we got ourselves settled in I wondered if we would be the only two riders in our compartment or if we would be sharing. I asked Tim if he felt like working on some stuff while we rode to Washington or if he just preferred to relax. He said that he wanted to do neither, grimacing in the anguish he was feeling at the pain in his feet as his shoes obviously squeezed the bejesus out of them. (It's funny, I read recently in GQ magazine how a new pair of shoes should not hurt when a guy first wears them, if they're really good shoes that is. Timmy obviously bought shoes that were not very good quality or the article I had read was erroneous in their advice.) Suddenly my heart raced as I came up with what I thought was a brilliant idea. I innocently looked down at Tim's wingtip shoed feet and suggested that he either loosen the laces a bit or simply take his shoes off for part of the ride to Washington. He looked across at me, chuckled a bit and said "Hardy fucking har buddy, the way my socks smell you know that's not a good option to consider here. You remember what Stephanie said about my smelly socks that day in the car right? And get this, I just put my socks on a few hours ago and believe me I'm sure they stink already. Most guys, it takes them all day to work up a good foot stink, but not me man. Timmy's socks smell good and rank after a short time in my shoes." We both laughed real loudly at the conversation we were having, two business buddies talking about one of the buddies' smelly socks. I told Tim how I didn't mind the smell of his socks and even if I did why the hell should he be uncomfortable? I also reminded him of the hot day in his office when the air conditioning was on the fritz and how I didn't mind his scented socks that day either. He seemed to consider what I had suggested; he shrugged, smiled and then leaned down and began unlacing his wingtips. As he undid the laces on his shoes he said that he hoped no one else would be sharing the train compartment with us. The train started moving out of Penn station and my heart thundered in my chest. As he unlaced his shoes I told him that at least his feet would be a bit soothed after a while if he rode with them off. I even went so far as to suggest that he prop his feet up on the vacant seat next to me. God, but I was becoming pretty bold here where my good buddies feet were concerned. Timmy slipped his shoes off and the look of relief that came over his face that time was even more pronounced than when we had sat down. The laddy was wearing a pair of what I had come to call my favorites when it came to his dress socks, GoldToe brand navy blue nylon thin ribbed numbers. He sighed, propped his socked feet up on the vacant seat next to me, stretching his legs out and said that that was better, *that that was much better.* I smiled over at him as he wiggled his toes in his socks and he sniffed the air like a dog, getting a good chuckle out of both of us. He said, "Man, when the conductor comes in here to collect our tickets he's not going to believe how it smells because of my damned smelly socks!" Again we both laughed and I quickly told Tim how his feet really didn't smell all that bad, I even went so far as to say that Stephanie had been exaggerating that day in the car after the company soccer game. Tim agreed and we both laughed at how women just don't appreciate a guy's funky foot odor. To keep the conversation going I told Tim about dates of mine who had complained about my sock odor when I would take my shoes off after arriving back at my place or theirs. Tim quickly said, "Oh yeah, speaking of that, no skirt chasing at the company where we have to meet with the CEO's Ronald. We're going there for business, remember that." As he lectured me he lifted one of his feet and with a silly looking expression on his face he jiggled his big toe under his sock at me, wagging it as if it were his index finger. I smiled coyly, gave his wagging big toe a tweak and he lowered his foot back to the seat next to mine. Needless to say I was plumping up in my suit pants and hoped that Tim wouldn't notice. A few moments later as the train picked up speed the door to our compartment opened and a real handsome guy with dark hair and steely blue eyes popped his head in. He said, "Excuse me, is this compartment number eleven?" Tim and I looked up at him and in unison said, "Yes." The guy smiled, stepped into the compartment and said that he was in the right place. He was wearing a charcoal colored business suit and like us he was carrying an attaché case. I could not help but notice that his steely blue eyes were momentarily riveted on Tim's socked feet propped up on the seat next to me. Tim quickly apologized to the handsome young guy and lifted his feet off the seat. The guy said that it was fine, that he would take the other vacant seat next to Tim. Tim put his feet back down on the seat next to me and as the newcomer sat down in his seat what he said sent an icy chill up my spine. He said, "I always hope to have a vacant seat across from me as well. I love takin' my dang shoes off and just letting my socks breathe a bit for the long ride." That said he sat down next to Tim, got his shoes off and propped his black socked feet up on the seat next to Tim's. God, now I had two pairs of handsome guy's socked feet next to me... To try to keep my mind off the fact that the train compartment was being smelled up by handsome guy's funky sock odor I picked up my attaché case and made like I was going to be doing some office work. "My name is John by the way, John Edwards," the handsome guy with the Southern accent said….

Chapter Twenty Four

"I didn't look at it as being kidnapped back then Ronald," I said glumly after Ronald and I had finished our lunch and I had finished telling him my tickling dentist story.

I sat at that table feeling totally helpless with my socked feet still locked in the padlocked wooden cabinet-like thing that was in front of my chair.

"I was a lot younger then, a lot more on the adventurous side," I went on. "Back then I looked at my tickle captivities as just college pranks, sadistic games that we played on each other, games played by brothers, mostly my brother though who played jokes on me, hardy fucking har, and har. But looking back on it I suppose that I did spend a lot of time kidnapped and tickle tortured huh buddy?"

Ronald just kept staring at me across the table, our empty lunch plates in front of us, and nodded his head "Yes."

"But Ronald, what you've done to me is hundreds of times worse man," I said miserably, my palms flat on the table as I spoke, leaning forward a bit. "I mean, *you really* did kidnap me man! You forcefully took me from my home! And unlike years ago it's not fun and games this time, *this time* I really am suffering and *this time* I have a wife and a boy who depend on me..."

As I leaned forward some more, only wanting to look beseeching Ronald grabbed the chloroform soaked cloth and held it up threateningly. I quickly sat back in my chair and said, "No, no, don't, I was just stretching man!" Ronald slowly lowered the cloth back to the table and I looked miserably down at my socked feet locked in that infernal box under the table, keeping me immobilized...

"So tell me man, exactly how many times did you fall for your brother's antics and games?" Ronald asked me as I raised my eyes from the box my feet were in and looked across at my captor.

"Gawd, at this point I would have to say I lost count," I replied. "I mean, you would think that the games and the tricky nonsense would have stopped when we were kids, but that brother of mine kept it up even while I was in college, *and,* he even played a trick on me when I graduated college. He tricked me into becoming the tickle victim of a sadistic tailor that he knew..."

"*A sadistic tailor?*" Ronald asked me.

"Yeah, you know the person who does the alterations on your clothes," I said sarcastically.

"I know what a tailor is buddy boy, I just never heard of one being sadistic," Ronald said.

"Well, it seems that my brothers' wiles knew no limits," I said to Ronald. "And I'm sure you want to hear about it..."

"I sure do," Ronald replied, glancing up at a clock that was on the wall. "We still have some time so that you can digest your lunch and then we'll get to your next tickle session."

I groaned miserably...

"In the meantime I'll hear about this sadistic tailor of yours," Ronald prompted me, glaring at me threateningly across the table.

"Okay," I said, figuring at this point that I would tell Ronald anything just to keep from being tickle tortured for any amount of time. "I had graduated college, business school to be exact and my brother, as a gift, had purchased my first custom made suit for me. My brother told me that I should begin job interviewing as soon as possible with at least one really nice suit, and my brother very gladly made the purchase *and* he even set up an appointment for me with the tailor who would fit me for the suit that he had purchased for me. I arrived at the tailor shop at four PM on a Friday afternoon. (Looking back on it I realize now as I tell you these things Ronald that it was amazing to me how my brother always made these appointments for me on Friday afternoons, leaving the whole weekend ahead of me for my tickle torments and his fun.) The tailor was a rather dapper looking guy in his mid forties. He was beginning to show the distinguished wrinkles in his face and grays in his hair. But, he was a fairly large and fit looking man, broad shoulders and slightly taller than me. He was wearing a two piece suit with regal looking cufflinks and pointy wingtips. At the moment his suit jacket was on a hanger off to the side of the fitting area and he was busy finishing up with a gentleman while I waited in the outer room flipping through a GQ magazine. After a short while the tailor emerged from the fitting area with the other gentleman. The tailor made a couple of notes in his appointment book as to when the gentleman's suit would be ready. I watched as they shook hands, some kind of sinister look passing between them and then the tailor saw the gentleman to the door. Strangely, at least it was strange to me; the tailor locked the door after he had closed it. But he quickly disarmed my apprehensive feeling with a warm friendly greeting, saying, "Hello there young man, you must be Timmy Backman. Your brother has told me all about you. Going to be a banker or something and you need a fine suit to get your career started off just right? Well Mr. Backman, I am your man. I will see that you have the finest suit that money can buy for your very first career suit. Your brother said that money was no object and that you should follow all my instructions to the letter." I grinned sheepishly and shook hands with the tailor, or, to be more precise I received a shaking by the tailor while he held my hand in a firm grip and vigorously pumped my hand. He practically hauled me out of my chair and shook me bodily up and down as he greeted me. He told me that his name was Dan Marteen, but that I should simply call him Dan and he said that he would call me Timmy, if that was okay with me. I told him that that was fine and he clapped me on the back in a friendly manner and said that we were going to have a lot of fun fixing me up. I stupidly beamed with Dan's friendliness, told him to please call me Timmy and I had no idea just how much trouble I was in at that moment. So Dan escorted me into the rear fitting room and had me stand up on a platform in the epicenter of the room. The room was virtually surrounded by mirrors and I could hardly look anywhere without seeing my reflection staring back at me. So anyway, Dan set about doing all these measurements and checks on me, asking how I liked to wear my clothes, where I kept my wallet, etc. and on and on. Once Dan seemed to have completed the measurements of my legs, arms, neck and other areas of my body he announced that that was the preliminaries. He then said, "Now I need to get some really refined and exact measurements. But I can't do that through your clothes." He looked at me as though I knew what he was talking about. It was obvious I didn't know what he was getting at until he looked at me expectantly and questioningly. I asked him, "You mean you want me to take my clothes off? You expect me to strip right here in front of you?" I was amazed and appalled and excited at the situation, all at the same time I was feeling all those emotions. The tailor looked at me in disbelief and said, "Exactly Timmy, there is only one way for me to have your *exact* measurements for your new suit and that is to make those measurements without the hindrance of your clothes. Otherwise you might just as well go and pull a suit off the rack and buy it from a department store. I'm an artist and I make custom fitted clothes and at the moment you're my model. So come on Timmy, let's get you out of those clothes, right now!" By then he was speaking emphatically and it was plain to see that he was taking control of the situation, and me, as it unfolded. I really did want a custom made suit after all. I mean, how many guys fresh out of college have a custom made suit for job interviews? So, I watched as Dan stepped forward and onto the platform that I was on and he brazenly began unbuttoning my shirt. He first undid the button at my collar then the next and so on down toward my waist. He worked quickly and impatiently at getting my shirt unbuttoned. I simply stood there in total astonishment, not making a move to assist him in getting me undressed. I just figured that this was all part of the services as the dapperly dressed tailor unbuttoned my shirt. Once my shirt was fully unbuttoned Dan pulled it up and yanked the tails of it out of my pants. He then unbuttoned my cuffs, grabbed my arms, spun me around and pulled the shirt out from the back of my pants, slipping the shirt finally off my arms and tossing it on a nearby chair. When he was done with my outer shirt Dan pushed my t-shirt up and over my head, turning me once more to face him again. Now I was naked from the waist down. Fuck, I stood there in awe over all of this as Dan began working at my pants; first the belt, then the pants fastener and "Zip" down went the zipper. My pants slid down my legs as Dan squatted before me. I wanted to tell the guy to stop, that I had changed my mind, but I found myself supporting myself on Dan's shoulder as he popped each of my shoes off my feet, followed by getting my pants off me, one leg at a time. Thoughts of that custom made suit danced in my head so I figured I would just do what the tailor said. At that point I was stripped down to my under shorts and socks, and I was standing up on that platform openmouthed. The tailor then in an insisting tone of voice said, "Come on now Timmy my boy, all of it. I can't have some little piece of BVD or GoldToe socks causing me to error in my measurements. Make like this is the locker room in the college gym and off with those shorts and socks." I looked at him in disbelief as he chucked my pants onto the chair with my other clothes and said, "But Dan, then I'll be naked," whining from my perch on the central platform. The tailor said, "Exactly my lad, and once you are naked I'll be able to do my work and make all the crucial measurements for your suit." I thought how this would be a suit fitting that I would never forget as I said over and over, "But, but..." Dan chuckled and said, "But nothing. Come on now. We're both grown men here, *adults* Timmy. There is no sense in you acting like a baby. You're going to be a big time banker or businessman, so you must learn to be decisive. So now, get out of those underpants and socks." He was even more than emphatic. It seemed that he really cared about how my suit would look once it was tailored for me. What I didn't know was that the tailor was thinking that I was real pliable. I found this out later from my dear never loving brother. The tailor was thinking that it was obvious that there was no telling what he could get me to do. In his eyes I was a handsome and gullible college boy. What he wanted more than anything at that moment was to get me totally naked and strapped up for a good tickling session. The tailor thought of my brother and how right the guy was, that I had a nice muscular body and getting me stripped was making his cock twitch. He figured that once he started on tickling me he would be really horned up like a bitch in heat. So, I, and unbeknown to me what the wicked tailor was thinking, *I* reluctantly complied and pulled my socks off one at a time and then slowly lowered my white under shorts. The tailor snatched the little pieces of clothing from me and tossed them on the chair with my other garments. Now I was standing there totally naked as the day I was born before Dan the tailor who was still in his shirt and tie and suit pants. I tried to cover my semi hard cock with my hands. Dan quickly swatted my hands away so that he could get a good look at my equipment, although he of course didn't let me know that. He told me that I should keep my hands at my sides at all times during the measurements, unless otherwise instructed, and man, would I be instructed. Then, he had me assume all kinds of peculiar positions while he used his measuring tape to take his measurements. Dan also had a still camera set up with a remote activator and he would position me, handling my arms and legs, step to take some measurements and then step back and fire the camera at me. I felt like a goddamned porn star. I whined at him, "What's the camera for man?" He explained that he would need to compare my measurements to the comings and goings of my body, that it was all for design and fitting purposes. He grinned at me lustfully and snapped some more pictures of me just for the fuck of it, it seemed. I wonder till this day if that guy still has those pictures of me. Then the tailor stepped over to a wall where there was a panel of some kind. He opened the panel and pressed a couple of buttons that were inside it. I heard a whirring kind of sound and upon looking upwards I discovered a metal bar being lowered from above my head. Besides having chains extending back to the ceiling to support it the bar had a number of Velcro straps and pulleys attached to it. Once the bar was just above my head Dan pressed a button that stopped it from lowering. I simply stood there looking dumbly up at the contraption as Dan came back over to me and stepped up on the platform in front of me. He pulled down two cables with what looked like Velcro straps on each end. He attached those to my ankles and as he did so he instructed me to reach up and grasp the bar that was above my head. And guess what, I stupidly did as he told me to do. I thought all of this was still for the purposes of measurements for my custom made suit. DUH! Then, Dan stepped behind me and fastened two more of those Velcro straps around my wrists. By then I knew that this was not for the purposes of measurements but by then it was too late. I asked Dan, "What in the hell is all this for man?" feeling very confused as I said it. Dan chuckled and said, "Well, Timmy me boy, this is my tickle harness." My heart sank and I knew that I had been tricked by my brother yet again. "I yelled, "What!? Tickle harness? What the fuck am I being hooked up to a tickle harness for?" Dan said that he would have thought it was quite obvious that it was for tickling young naked businessmen and bankers. He chuckled again and told me with an affectionate tone in his voice that I fit the bill just perfectly. He left me strapped to that bar and stepped back to the wall panel. At the panel Dan began pushing a series of buttons and now the bar started back skyward, taking poor old me with it. I yelled, "Whoa! Wait a minute here!" Dan pressed a few more buttons and then not only was the bar pulling me up but the cables attached to my ankles suddenly pulled my feet up and out and oh yes, off the floor. I now sat in a sort of sitting down in the air position, hanging by my wrists with my poor feet moving upwards and toward my hands. I squirmed and wiggled and pulled like crazy, trying desperately to loosen myself from the grip of that infernal contraption, silently cursing my brother for having tricked me yet again. But all the squirming and wiggling just inflamed Dan's libido and had I been looking in that direction I would have seen the sizeable tent in the tailor's pleated pants. Instead I yelled at him things like, "Dan! Let me down right now! I mean it! There's not going to be any tickling! I'm not ticklish! (I thought that if I told the guy that I wasn't ticklish he would let me loose, no such luck however.) I went on though, saying, "Besides, this is illegal. This is like kidnapping, or unlawful imprisonment...or something, geez!" Dan laughed and said, "Well Timmy I will just have to judge for myself whether or not you're ticklish and I somehow get the feeling that you're going to have a very laughable weekend." As he said that my heart pounded in total fear and Dan looked at me lustfully, taking in the sight of the young handsome college boy about to turn businessman hanging there with his most ticklish spots exposed, including my goddamned cock and balls, and that little brown button of an asshole of mine. Oh how those spots would suffer tickle torments that weekend Ronald. I cried out, "Oh No! No, this can't be happening to me! Dan, Dan, don't do this! Please man... my brother is an asshole! You have no idea; you don't know wh-what this does to me... Please man; don't keep me here all weekend!" But Dan simply chuckled and said, "Oh yes Timmy, yes indeed, we are going to have a wonderfully fun weekend here, and I do plan on seeing what tickling does to you. Your brother assures me that you had no major plans to attend to this weekend so keeping you here won't hurt anyone." The tailor stood there and stroked a big stiff feather, where he had gotten it from I had no idea, as spittle pooled at the corners of his mouth. He was truly enjoying all this immensely and he hadn't even started on tickling me yet. He then said, "But first, since you are now naked, I don't think I'm quite properly dressed, or shall I say undressed, for your upcoming tickling." So without another word Dan began removing his tie, then his shirt and so on. He almost performed some sort of striptease right there in front of his captive, naked and strapped up customer, me. And surprisingly, even though I am fully straight my cock was responding. I mean, *fucking fucks*, I had been feeling hard in the cock as soon as the guy had stripped me down earlier, but now, strapped up tight and watching the tailor disrobe had somehow caused my cock to become nearly fully erect. It began to twitch and swell more and straighten. I hate to be tickled Ronald, you know that, I cannot stand it. But at the same time it makes me feel all sexy and horny. And even though I am straight, the fact that Dan had managed to get me naked, strapped up, and was now stripping his own clothes off and talking about tickling me, all of it just somehow enticed my libido and thus my cock was stiffening and tingling in anticipation of what I knew was to come. Now Ronald, that's come, c-o-m-e, not cum, c-u-m, hardy fucking har, har bud. I had been through some humiliatingly ticklish situations in my youth and in college as you already know, but this was looking like it could be one of the worst for me, but, maybe the best for Dan the tailor...

Dan the tailor, or should I say the S&M tailor stopped stripping once he had gotten down to what some might call underpants and a pair of calf length black sheer socks held up with garters. He looked comically sinister in a way. His underpants were actually some kind of Speedo brand thong. It was very little and was not much more than an elastic band around his waist with a little sheer stretchable pouch in the front that attached to the rear of the waistband via a single little elastic strap that went between his legs and up through the crack of his ass. He was already so aroused at getting poor me stripped down and dangling and ready for a sexy sort of tickling that his own cock was stiff and pushing against the already sheer material of his thong pouch. In fact, his big balls almost hung out of the sides of the pouch. For a man in his mid forties Dan was in terrific shape and was rather muscular. All of this added to the sexy picture of us two guys, one young and hunky and all strapped up in an apparatus and one older and hunky and stripped down to scanty panties and sheer socks with garters hooked to them, in the tailor shop... Dan then moved behind me and I turned my head back and forth, trying to keep track of what the guy was up to. I asked him where he was going, what he was going to do. But Dan was quiet. He moved up behind me and using that stiff feather he simply teased me as I hung there. He used that feather to tease the insides of my ears, then my neck. I started giggling softly and tried moving my head out of the way or in a manner to protect myself from that feather, but it was useless, being the position I was in I mean... He squealed meanly behind me and trailed that feather as deep into my ear as possible, then over the back of my neck again and into my other ear. I started laughing a little louder as he twirled the feather in my ear. The sound of his squealing was maniacal in a way and my laughter just combined with it, it seemed. Then, he stood behind me and he must have put the feather aside for the moment because he was then using his hands and very educated fingers on my sides and even upwards into my armpits. He squeezed his fingertips into my armpits and pressed hard, wriggling them around in there in a sadistic ticklish fashion. I began laughing louder as the cruel tailor tickled me. In my doubled up position Dan was even able to stand behind me and reach the soles of my feet. Then he used that blasted feather again, but this time he reached under me and stroked my ass with it, making sure to run the feather between the cheeks of my rear like a violin bow (Remember that my wrists and ankles were strapped together on the raised bar, making my sexy college boy ass the lowest portion of my body.) Tickling my ass crack really sent me into massive fits of laughter. Then, humiliating of all he stuck the tip of the feather into my ass crack and whirled it around in there, teasing my bunghole and making me fart a few times. I laughed crazily and swore all kinds of threats at him, up to and including how I would report him to the authorities for this. He simply went on tickling my asshole with that feather, making me fart loudly and real smelly... A few moments later Dan moved in front of me to a position where I could see him very well and where he was still able to work on my bare soles and even my armpits and sides. And as he tickled me from the front Dan was able to have his cock, that monster barely restrained in that little sheer pouch, bump against my own cock and balls and even my stretched little bum hole. I laughed loudly and Dan was really having tickling sexy fun and I was in tickle sexy hell once more...

Dan tickled me into an unbelievable frenzy Ronald. He alternated all over me with that damned stiff feather. He repeatedly tickled inside my ears, my neck area both back and front, ground his fingertips against my armpits and of course the soles of my bare feet. As the tailor tickled me I laughed and screamed and begged him to stop. But instead he unsnapped his thong and let it drop to the floor, leaving himself clad in just those black sheer socks he had on along with the garters clipped to them. The fucking naked guy was sporting an enormous erection and to me it really looked like it was pleading for release. Well, as he continued to tickle me in every imaginable way you can tickle a guy while he's hanging in the position I was in the fucking tailor reached between my upturned legs with his hand that was not presently tickling me. I let out a loud and guttural sounding breath as the tailor gripped my cock and balls and yanked them outward and let them dangle between my thighs, just over my ass crack. I screamed things like, "Let go of my manhood Dan! This is no way to measure a college boy for his first suit!" stupid things like that and laughing my head off all at the same time. But then, Dan began to rub his engorged meat against my cock and balls. His erection was oozing pre cum by the buckets it looked like and at this point the rubbing was stimulating the guy even more. He rubbed and rubbed his erection against my legs, my ass cheeks, my balls and even against my cock and my balls. I could do nothing but laugh and endure what the tailor was doing to me, but straight as I am I was being tickled beyond belief and the tickling had me sexually stimulated as well and my erect cock and low hanging balls just drove Dan on all the more. It drove him actually to the point that he succumbed to his own pleasures and squirted between my legs what would be his first load of ball juice for the weekend, most of his goo landing on my washboard belly. Through my tears I laughed and laughed and saw the thick gobs of sticky white goo splatter over my belly and some of it even dribbled down toward my crotch area and into my pubic hairs. This was total madness because my cock was rigid and still sticking out between my thighs and Dan was not going to give it any relief, at least not on Friday. We had the whole weekend ahead of us after all. Madness Ronald, totally laughable madness and I were thinking how I was going to laugh myself all the way to an asylum…"

A Boner Book

Chapter Twenty-Five

It had taken me a good while to tell my story to Ronald about Dan the sadistic tailor and how he had captured me for some tickle fun at his shop thanks to my conniving brother. It had taken long enough for both Ronald and I to digest our lunches and long enough for my stomach to have settled the food so that Ronald could resume tickling me. What I didn't know at that moment while I sat at the table across from my so called buddy with my socked feet locked in that wooden padlocked box was just how very soon I would be being tickled *yet again*... My latest tickle history story was done for the moment and Ronald stared at me across the table in awe...

"So uh, tell me Timmy, did you at least get your suit after all that?" Ronald chuckled.

"Yeah, actually I did," I said, running the palm of my hand over the table and looking at Ronald as I spoke. "Dan kept me there all weekend in tickle heaven/hell and while he wasn't serving customers he was either tickling me or working on my suit... By Sunday night when I left his shop I was a totally overly sensitized tickle mess of jello and goose bumps..."

"Good show though where Dan the tailor is concerned I have to say," Ronald laughed and picked up a remote control, holding it idly in one hand. "I'm sure that before your time here with me is done I'll want to hear more about your time spent with the sadistic tailor..."

I gulped hard as Ronald glanced up at a clock on the wall...

"But alas Timmy me ticklish laddy, its time to resume *our* own tickle business," Ronald said, sounding totally diabolical and somehow like a sinister child as he looked at me intently across the table. "And this time we won't have to go too far, not far at all buddy..."

B-but Ronald," I began to say as he held up his remote control device and pressed a button on it.

Suddenly, the wooden box that my socked feet were locked in began making a whirring sound.

"Wh-what the fucking fuck is that?" I prattled loudly and looked down at my trapped feet. "OH HOLY SHIT!"

Suddenly, from within the box it felt like thousands of vibrating round beads or something akin to them was grinding against every part of my feet in a spinning motion of what felt like thousands upon thousands of miles per hour...

"Dance for me Timmy boy," Ronald chuckled as I pressed my palms hard against the table and involuntarily stood up, my socked feet of course still trapped in that goddamned wooden box.

"Wha-what the fuck Ronald? Ha, ha, ha, ha, ha, ha, ha, ha, ha, ha, ha, ha, ha, ha, ha, ha, ha, ha, ha, ha!" I found myself suddenly laughing uncontrollably.

"That box is filled with miniature body massagers' buddy," Ronald said, getting to his feet as well, watching intently as I stupidly balanced myself in that box, my arms flailing at my sides every which way. "They are all attached to the ends of my famous spinning rods. In this case the rods are miniature versions of the ones you have seen already. Each rod has about ten massagers on the end of it and there are at least twenty rods in that box."

"OOOOOOOOOOOHHHHHHHHH OH MY GOD OF GODS! FUCKING FUCKS!" I squealed and doubled over as I felt the devices spinning against every goddamned part of my trapped feet. "HA, ha, ha, ha, ha, ha, ha, ha, ha, ha, ha, ha, ha, ha, ha, ha, ha, ha, ha, ha, ha! N-no wonder you had me blindfolded when you locked my goddamned feet in this contraption!"

My upper body was splayed on the table and I felt those spinning miniature monsters snaking their ways under my feet within the box. That sent me into a squealing and dancing frenzy let me tell you buds. I snapped myself back up to a standing position and again flailed my arms at my sides, starting to sweat as I danced in that box.

"Ronald, you prick what a twisted trick you played on me this time!" I reeled. "Ha, ha, ha, ha, ha, ha, ha, ha, ha, ha, ha, ha, ha, ha, ha, ha, ha, ha, ha, ha!"

I arched my upper body back a bit and with my arms now at my sides tried to balance myself in that box as I gyrated, danced and twisted my body from side to side…

"Ronald, turn it off man, ha, ha, ha, ha, ha, ha, ha, ha, ha, ha, ha, ha, ha, ha, t-turn it the fuck off!" I pleaded through my laughter.

I felt the massagers in the box snaking their way up my socked calves, practically licking at them while they tickled me into a further frenzy. The feeling of those devices against my nylon socked calves was maddening, more maddening I think than if my socks were not on me. As they tickled against my ankles I found myself dancing more speedily in the confines of that box. I pounded on the table in front of me, my hands clenched into fists, laughing my head off as I did so…

"Ronald, you are evil, ha, ha, ha, ha, ha, ha, ha, ha, ha, ha, ha, ha, ha, ha, ha, totally evil man!" I sputtered.

"What you need is some good music to dance to Timmy me laddy," Ronald chuckled. "And perhaps more freedom of movement to go with it…"

"F-freedom sounds nice b-buddy, real fucking nice, ha, ha, ha, ha, ha, ha, ha, ha, ha, ha, ha, ha, ha, ha, ha!" I laughed as I twisted my upper torso from side to side, looking ridiculous as I did so.

But what the fucking fuck was Ronald talking about now? Freedom to be able to move? And dance music? I quite honestly did not feel like dancing let me tell you… What the fuck did Ronald have in mind for me now?

"Ha, ha, ha, ha, ha, ha, ha, ha, ha, ha, ha, ha, ha, ha, ha, ha, ha, ha, ha, ha, ha!" I laughed louder and glanced down at the box, wishing I could somehow extract my poor feet from the imprisoning thing.

Unlike the shoe shine device that Ronald had secured my feet in the night before this thing was not pulling my socks down and off me. If anything it somehow loved the fact that it was tickling my feet with my nylon socks on me, making my feet all the more tickle sensitive. My hard cock wagged in front of me, droplets of pre cum oozing from the tip of it and flying off, landing on the table in front of me. My balls swung back and forth like a goddamned pendulum. As I danced and squirmed in the box Ronald sidled up behind me and trailed a stiff feather tip down my sweaty naked back.

"AAAAAAYYYYYYYYYYY!" I screeched. "OH GOD, ha, ha, ha, ha, ha, ha, ha, ha, ha, ha, ha, ha, ha, ha, ha, ha, ha, ha, ha, ha, ha, ha, ha! Hey no fair man, no fucking fair!"

"Ah Timmy, me ticklish laddy; *that* you certainly are," Ronald said mockingly.

Then, I made the mistake of again splaying my torso on the table as my socked feet suffered tickle hell in that box. Ronald took that as an opportunity to wedge the tip of his stiff feather into my gaping moist asshole. Like when Dan the tailor had me in his clutches and like when he tickled my bunghole with a feather I let rip with a few smelly farts. I laughed harder and felt totally beyond humiliated… Ronald strummed that feather as deeply as possible into my asshole and twirled it around in there, getting me laughing and cackling like a crazy man…

Next, Ronald put his feather aside, stepped up behind me and grabbed me under my armpits and pressed hard into them…

"HAR, HAR, HAR, HAR, HAR, HAR, HAR, HAR, HAR, HAR, HAR!" I chortled as I did my tickle dance in the box and suffered the awfulness of having my armpits tickle tortured at the same damned time. "L-let go of me, *let go of me Ronald!*"

I tried in vain to pull out of Ronald's grasp but he had his fingers hooked real tight in my deep, sweaty and randy armpits. As he jiggled his fingertips against my pits I again doubled over onto the table. Ronald leaned over me, his muscular body pressed against mine as he continued ribbing and razzing my armpits. I felt the hardness in his pants as he leaned his crotch against my rear end. He kept whispering the words, "Timmy me ticklish laddy" in my ear over and over…

"Ronald, ha, ha, ha, ha, ha, ha, ha, ha, ha, ha, ha, ha, ha, ha, ha, ha, ha, ha, ha, ha, ha, ha!" I screeched and squealed as I again found myself standing upright in the box, my arms flailing stupidly at my sides again after Ronald had let go of my armpits. "Ronald, those things in this box are makin' me crazy bud! Ha, ha, ha, ha, ha, ha, ha, ha, ha, ha, ha, ha, ha, ha, ha, ha, ha, ha!"

I found myself reaching under my pits with my own hands and scratching them, what a sight that was let me tell you. It seemed that after Ronald had tickle tortured the fuck out of my pits they felt all itchy, so I danced and scratched and danced and laughed and scratched…

"Hands up buddy," Ronald chided me from behind and pressed the tip of his infernal stiff feather against my lower back.

"YAYAYAYAYYYYYYYYYY!" I screamed and involuntarily raised my arms over my head for a moment.

While my arms were raised Ronald strummed his feather lengthwise into one of my pits and strummed it out quickly.

"HAR, HAR, HAR, HAR, HAR, HAR, HAR, HAR, HAR, HAR, HAR, HAR, HAR, HAR!" I laughed and quickly lowered my arms in an effort to protect my pits.

But Ronald would have his way. He again poked my lower back with the tip of his feather, causing me to again raise my arms above my head and flail my arms. As I did so, laughing stupidly at the same time Ronald strummed my other armpit.

"OOOHHHHHHHHHH you fucker, ha, ha, ha, ha, ha, ha, ha, ha, ha, ha, ha, ha, ha, ha, ha, ha, ha, ha, ha, ha, ha!" I laughed and quickly lowered my arms again, only to be back poked again by that feather and again made to raise my arms, and again have one of my armpits tickle tortured with that feather. "HA, ha, ha, ha, ha, ha, ha, ha, ha, ha, ha, ha, ha, ha, ha, ha, ha, ha, ha, ha, ha, ha, ha, ha, ha, ha, ha!"

So it seemed that Ronald was enjoying himself, getting me into a rhythm of sorts, making me raise my arms, tickle me under my pits with that feather and make me raise my arms again very quickly, all while my poor feet were being brutally tickle tortured in that box that they were trapped in…

"You know buddy, this is giving me another really great idea," Ronald mused, looking up at a ceiling rafter above where I was stupidly doing my tickle dance.

"Oh no, no, ha, ha, ha, ha, ha, ha, ha, ha, ha, ha, ha, ha, ha, ha, ha, ha, ha, you wouldn't, you wouldn't!" I chortled in a pleading tone of voice. "OH GOD MAN, you wouldn't!"

But a few moments later I found out (in total tickle misery) that he would, *oh God he would*…

With my socked feet still locked in that wooden cabinet/like box and still being tickled Ronald grabbed my arms from behind me, clasped my wrists together and roped them tight. Next, I found myself with my tied wrists yanked high above me and tied off to the rafter in the ceiling that Ronald had spied just moments before…

"OHHHHH GODDDDDDD!" I screamed, knowing the awfulness that was coming now.

As Ronald tied a blindfold over my eyes my cock jutted out long and stiff in front of me…

Chapter Twenty-Six

Ronald finished tying the blindfold over my eyes and then I felt his fingers trailing along my ribs and around my stomach and belly areas. He teased me in this fashion for a good while, running his fingers over me and even dancing the tips of them over my ticklish areas. Tied up the way I was now with my arms yanked above me and cinched at the wrists, tied off to a ceiling rafter and with my feet still locked in that box I was a pretty helpless ticklish Timmy let me tell you buds. Ronald then grabbed at my armpits as he stood behind me. I heed and hawed like an out of control banshee as the guy really gripped my sweaty and stinky pits, his hands and fingers feeling like a vise as he tickled the fuck out of me. The massagers in the box that my socked feet were in continued doing their dirty work in tickling me as well.

"HA, HA, HA, HA, HA, HA, HA, HA, HAW, HAW, HAW, HAW, HAW, HAW, HAW, HAW!" I laughed loudly, probably the loudest yet. "R-Ronald, th-this is a real dirty thing to be doin' to me here buddy! HAW, HAW, HAW, HAW, HAW, HAW, HAW, HAW, HAW, HAW!"

"Call it what you want Timmy me laddy, but from the sound of things and from that stalk between your legs I would have to say that you're truly enjoying yourself here," Ronald taunted me and I felt the tip of that stiff feather being slowly trailed down the center of my back. "You love this buddy boy…"

"AAAAYYYYYYYYYYYY, ha, ha, ha, ha, ha, ha, ha, ha, ha, ha, ha, ha, ha, ha, ha, ha, ha, ha!" I laughed crazily into the blindfolded darkness as that feather trailed along my back and my feet were tickle massaged in that damned box.

I arched my body a bit forward and my cock jutted out long and plumped up hard in front of me. God of gods, I had shot a few loads and I was hard and throbbing again, and *fucking fucks*, not to mention that my balls felt as if they were chock filled with sperm all over again. In my laugh filled haze I thought about the lunch I had just had, and fucking totally fucks, I knew that that food *had* to have been laced with Ronald's aphrodisiac. My pre cum oozing erection definitely attested to that let me tell you…

Ronald again danced his fingers over my ribs, grabbed at my armpits and tweaked his fingertips deep within them, grinding his fingertips in my armpits actually, agony, total fucking agony and my poor feet were *still* being relentlessly tickle tortured in that box.

"Haw, haw, haw, haw, haw, haw, haw, haw, haw, haw, haw, haw, haw, haw, haw, haw!" was all I could say at that point.

"Heard a good joke recently buddy?" Ronald teased me, now trailing his feather against the backs of my legs.

"Haw, haw, haw, haw, haw, haw, th-the fucking joke is on me, haw, haw, haw, haw, haw, haw, haw, haw!" I managed to say through my bouts of uncontrollable laughter.

Finally, Ronald stopped tickling me with that feather and with his fingertips.

He took the blindfold off me and I watched, still laughing, as he pushed a button on his ever-present remote control device. The massagers in the box slowed down and then came to a complete halt, and they stopped tickling my poor feet...

"Th-thank you man, oh fucking fucks, thank you," I hee hawed, heaving for breath at that point.

"You can call this a reprieve from dancing in that box buddy boy," Ronald said, holding up my sweat soaked blindfold as he spoke. "I want to hear more of your tickle history for now and then I'll have you really face the music..."

"F-face the music?" I asked, practically whimpering. "What, what do you mean, face the music?"

"That is presently for me to know and for you to find out Timmy me ticklish laddy," Ronald said and sat back down at the table where we had had lunch not all that long ago, leaving me in that awful position with my socked feet locked in the wooden box and my wrists cinched above me to the ceiling rafter. "That's what God invented blindfolds for buddy, so I know and you don't find out until I want you to know..."

I grimaced miserably, sweat pouring off me everywhere...

"Okay bud, now, here's the deal, if you want some time off from the massagers in that box tickling your cute sexy feet you'll tell me more about that wonderful device that Stephanie's friend Valerie gave you," Ronald began.

"The Spinning Chinaman," I said, finishing his sentence for him.

"Yes, the Spinning Chinaman, it sounds like an ingenious device," Ronald mused. "Next time I'm at your house for dinner with a date I'll want you to give me a firsthand demonstration buddy..."

"Ha, the next time you're at my house for dinner?" I said sarcastically. "It'll be freezing in Hell when that happens, *my so called buddy boy...*"

"Back to the business at hand," Ronald said and pointed down at my boxed up feet. "Again, if you want some time off from being tickled by the massagers in there you'll tell me more about the Spinning Chinaman, if not, I can easily turn the whirring little buggers right back on now..."

He held up his remote control and before he could press the button I heard myself saying, "No, no don't, I'll tell you, *I'll fucking tell you man!*"

"That's a good laddy," Ronald said and put the remote control down on the table in front of him. "Start talking..."

"Well, okay, obviously you remember that device "The Spinning Chinaman" that Stephanie's friend Valerie gave us as a goddamned present huh?" I asked Ronald and he nodded, a sinister look on his face as he did so. "Yeah, that fucking thing has been in my house ever since. Most of our guests don't even notice the thing and thank God. It's actually this big metal frame that sort of acts like a room divider in our big open living room and dining room areas. It has attachments so that the poor spinning victim can be secured safely into it at the wrists and ankles and around the waist in a spread-eagle position inside the frame. The overall frame has two inner frames that can be unlocked so that they spin on either a horizontal or vertical axis. Thus Ronald, my good buddy, the victim can either be spun round and round on his back looking upwards or facing forward and spun continuously head over heels. As you know Valerie has already put me through a spinning session down at her shop. Fucking fuck man, that spinning session also digressed into a tickling session as she had discovered through Stephanie my wife, that I was extremely ticklish, and Ronald you know that I mean it when I say that I am extremely ticklish. Well, that day Valerie got her jollies and really had some fun spinning and tickling me in her shop. But as you know, she also discovered that tickling me, and especially on my nipples was a real sexual turn-on for me. Anyway, I'm digressing too much here because you know all of this already. Anyway, when Timmy Junior was still a baby it was a January and Stephanie had taken him to visit with her mother. If you remember Ronald, my mother-in-law had not been able to come to our house for Christmas a few years back. I had banking work that required that I stay in town so I was "Home Alone" I guess you could say. No vacation time so early in the year for bankers that's for sure. Anyway, Stephanie was going to be gone for a few days so to break up the monotony I decided to invite two of my work buddies over for pizza and beer for dinner. It was a Wednesday night, the middle of the week and there was a minor postseason bowl that was on TV. So that evening me and two of my work buddies got together and had pizza and drank beer and thoroughly enjoyed each others company and the football game. It was halftime in the game and a good amount of beer had been consumed and we were jovial that our team was winning and we were just having a grand old fucking time. And, since the TV was in the living area of the house the spinning Chinaman was at the end of the room. I had not given the damned thing a thought until one of my buddies was over there inspecting the damned thing. Watching him looking the device over made me very nervous, needless to say. The dude asked me what the fucking fuck kind of room divider the thing was, imitating me in the way that I swear, hardy fucking har, and har. He said that he had never seen anything quite like it before in all his life. As he looked it over some more he asked me if it was Oriental. His name was Joe, just for the record and my other buddies name was Jeff. While Joe looked the spinning Chinaman over and asked questions Jeff and I was on the couch in front of the TV soaking up more beer. I quickly told Joe that it was a present from one of Stephanie's friends, and I also told him that yes, it was supposedly Chinese. As I reported back to Joe I had a nervous chuckle in my voice and to quickly cover it up I gulped down more beer. As I chugged some beer I then heard Joe say, "Hey, what are these things?" He said that they actually looked like wrist and leg restraints. I tried ignoring him but then he said, "And look here, there's a larger version here in the middle, more restraints looking things." Joe looked over at me with a sly grin on his face and asked if Stephanie and I were into some kinky stuff. We all laughed and chugged some more beer. I wiped my lips with the back of my hand and told Joe no, no way, that Stephanie was not that type of a girl and besides we had a child in the house as well. I added that on for good measure, as if Timmy Junior would be awake when we used that damned thing. My explanation seemed to satisfy my curious friend Joe and we all went back to watching the football game and drinking more beer. I stupidly thought I was safe. Ha, nice thought, because after the game Joe, being the curious guy that he is went back to take another look at the room divider AKA the Spinning Chinaman and encouraged my other buddy, Jeff, to take a look at it as well. I was pretty sloshed by now from all the beer I had consumed and I knew that very soon the need to piss like crazy would be setting in. The fact that I had been nervous earlier about Joe checking out the Spinning Chinaman had caused me to really chug down a lot more beer during the second half of the football game. I stupidly said, "Come on, you guys aren't interested in the Spinning Chinaman are you?" They both looked back at me as I sat on the couch and in unison said, "The Spinning Chinaman?" I knew then and there that I had blown it, that by calling the device by its proper name had just made their curiosity pique all the more. I quickly tried to recover by saying, "Uh, yeah, it's just a stupid something that my wife's friend gave us." As I spoke I tried to stay on the other side of the room, watching as my two work buddies were studiously mulling around the Spinning Chinaman. But then Joe called out, "Timmy, come here and show us how this thing works and why you call it "The Spinning Chinaman." Well, again, needless to say I was real reluctant but I didn't want my two work buddies to see my nervousness so I weaved my way across the room to where they were surveying the device with more and more interest. I figured that I should just tell them about the thing and how it worked. I told Joe that yeah, he had been right earlier, that those were restraints for the wrists, ankles and waist attached to the Spinning Chinaman. He laughed, clapped me on the back and said, "I knew it man, you and Stephanie *are* into some kinky stuff." I quickly said, "NO! NO! Nothing like that man." I told him how we only use the thing at parties and realized what a stupid thing that was to tell them, but alas, it was too late. Jeff piped up at that point by saying, "At parties Timmy? You use this thing at parties? I can just imagine what kind of parties you and Stephanie have. Okay man, we have to see how this thing works. I for one want to see firsthand." As Jeff spoke he took my beer out of my hand and looked at me with piercing eyes, saying, "Alright now, show us how this thing works." Again I was reluctant but at the same time I felt that I had no choice in the matter. I stood close to the device and showed Joe and Jeff the releases for the two inner frames and how they could be spun. But that wasn't enough for those two guys Ronald. They then demanded that I give them a real demonstration. I tried to say no, but my two buddies kept pushing their point and then they were literally pushing me toward the opening in the inner frame. I finally agreed, saying, "Okay, but just for a minute. Then you have to let me loose!" with a very stern look in my eyes as I said it. Joe and Jeff smiled at each other as I got myself situated in the Spinning Chinaman. Joe said, "Why of course we'll turn you loose Timmy, in just a minute or perhaps a few more." As I stood in the device in a spread eagle position Joe and Jeff worked quickly in getting me strapped in at the wrists, ankles and around my waist, saying things like "So the straps go around you like this?" I could tell that they were a bit tipsy as well, but as for me I was sloshed Ronald, but not so sloshed that my heart was hammering in my chest and I instantly regretted getting into the Spinning Chinaman as I was fastened good and tight. "Well yeah, the straps go around me, I mean, whoever, not just me, the straps go around whoever happens to be in the Spinning Chinaman when the game is being played," I said to them as they fastened me in some more. As I thought about it though I came to the realization that since Valerie had given me and Stephanie the goddamned device *I* was the only sap who had been spun in it. To try to just keep Joe and Jeff's attention on the device and not to hone in so much on spinning me I explained the rules of the Spinning Chinaman to those two clowns. I told them that the game works in the sense of that the person strapped into the device is asked questions, sort of like the game Trivial Pursuit. I also told them that the people doing the spinning of the person strapped into the device get to choose the subjects of the questions to be posed. If the person in the device answers the questions correctly he does not get spun. However, if he answers the questions incorrectly he gets spun. How he gets spun, rather head over heels in the vertical position or round and round on his back in a horizontal position was up to the people spinning the victim. Again, I realized in my beer haze that I had told Joe and Jeff too much. Instead of keeping my big yap shut about the device I was actually giving those two buddies of mine the ammunition they would need to spin me round and round. By then I was secured good and tight to the device and Joe did the honors of removing the round pin that prevented the Chinaman from spinning. The need to piss was setting in good and heavy at that point and when I saw Jeff pull the pin from the axis's of the device I quickly stifled a gulp of terror. I then said to them, "So now that you two know how this thing works and you've seen how the tickle victim is secured to it would you please let me loose?" Again, I had said too much, being that I had used the words "tickle victim." Jeff and Joe looked at each other, both of them grinning nearly maniacally at that point and said in unison "tickle victim?" Then they turned and looked at me. Joe said, "What the hell do you mean by that Timmy, what you mean by *tickle victim*? You said that the victim gets spun, you didn't say anything about being a tickle victim." As Joe spoke he was play-fully tugging at my pulled down necktie. As I said all this happened on a weeknight after work so we were all still wearing our business attire, our shirt sleeves rolled up, ties pulled down, suit jackets taken off, etc… I quickly tried to recover from my stupid state-ment about the tickle victim by adding more unneeded information. I said something like, "Well uh, you see, when I had gone to Valerie's shop to get Stephanie an anniver-sary present she showed me this thing, the Spinning Chinaman. And uh, I suppose you could say that she used her very sexy and feminine wiles to trick me into it, just the way you see me now." As I spoke Joe and Jeff again grinned at each other. Joe asked me, "What exactly did that bitch do to you buddy?" By now the need to piss was beyond heavy but I didn't want to tell Jeff and Joe that, although I think it was starting to become evident due to the piss hard-on that was starting to tent my suit trousers. With my lips now trembling I told them how Valerie had spun me and when I had landed with my face down by the floor and looking up in an upside down position how she had literally face fed me her sexy feet. I stupidly added, "And guys, that bitch has some sexy goddamned feet." By then I knew that I had said too much, by then I knew that my buddies were not going to let me out of the Spinning Chinaman all that quick-ly and by then the need to piss was increasing with each passing second, so much so that I was starting to sweat bullets… Jeff sidled up real close to me, gave my tie a grab and tug as well and teasingly asked me, "So you like feet huh Timmy?" I stammered out an answer that sounded totally stupid, something about how sexy women's toot-sies and toes drive me wild. Joe then announced, "Okay Timmy boy, seeing as you're presently hooked up in that thing and looking like you're in need of a game of "Spinning Chinaman" I vote that we play a game of questions and answers. We'll use work related stuff as the questions. If you answer correctly we'll spin you and if you answer incorrectly we'll spin you." Jeff laughed at Joe's twisted rules of the game and just for the fuck of it Joe gave the spinning Chinaman a good hard spin, sending me whirling round and round in the thing. I yelled out, "Hey *wait*, come on now Man! I'm not in need of a game in this thing, trust me on that! And what kind of fucking fucked up rules are those? If I answer the question correctly *I don't get spun!*" All this I said as I spun head over heels, head over heels, round and round and round. Joe said, "Yeah, that's all true enough Timmy boy, but you see, in this game, if you answer the questions correctly we'll still spin you, but we won't tickle you…" My heart sunk. I had been had and this time when had I needed to piss so badly that it was intoxicating somehow where my thoughts were concerned. I stopped spinning and was left at a position of a quarter to three with my body splayed in the Spinning Chinaman. Jeff then joined in the Spinning Chinaman fun by slowly turning me to an upside down position so that I was looking upwards at my two buddies. He started unlacing my wingtips and tauntingly asked me,

"So Timmy, are your feet ticklish?" I pleaded and begged the two of them to let me loose, even going so far as to tell them that I needed to piss, citing all the beer I had drunk during the football game. I told them that it was very important that they let me out of the Spinning Chinaman and let me go to the bathroom. As Jeff slid my wingtips off my feet Joe told me not to worry where my piss situation was concerned, that they would take care of that for me. What I did not know at that moment from my upside down perspective was that Joe was looking over at the coffee table where our empty beer mugs were and what a very kinky evening it was going to turn out to be for me and my two work buddies. By then Jeff had my shoes off my feet and my black silk dress socked feet were pointing up at the ceiling and instantly the musty scent from them was wafting around us. I garbled things like, "Come on guys, I don't know what you have in mind but I invited you here tonight for pizza, beer and the football game. Spinning me in this contraption was not on the agenda and taking my wingtips off my feet was *definitely not* in the game-plan either." My two buddies laughed and Joe gave me another good spin, sending me round and round and round. The scents wafting from my socked feet started to fill the room as I spun and spun. I yelled out, "Oh God, and off I go again!" as I spun and spun, seeing my two buddies faces as they laughed with each revolution I made. I saw that Jeff was holding one of my wingtips to his nose and mouth, sniffing at the inside of it. I heard him say to Joe "I wonder how his wife puts up with his foot odor," just as Joe gave the contraption another good shove, sending me spinning again. I chuckled a bit good naturedly and called out to Jeff, "That's a terrible way to be talking about a good buddies foot odor and how my wife tolerates it!" My two buddies laughed along with me and as the Spinning Chinaman started to slow down Joe quickly gave it another good whirl. I miserably yelled out, "Hey now wait a cotton pickin' minute here! You can't spin me yet, you haven't asked me any questions!" I stopped spinning, believe it or not in an upright position with my socked feet at the floor. The Chinaman swayed a bit and then Joe said, "Hey, he's right, we haven't asked him anything yet." And Jeff said, "So let's ask him questions. I say let the game begin" I looked at them, my eyes darting back and forth between them and moaned "I got to fucking piss you mugs!" Why I used the word mugs I'll never know, seeing as at the mention of it my two buddies again looked over at the coffee table where our empty beer mugs were. Jeff placed my wingtips on the floor as Joe threw me my first work related question. He asked, "How much money did the bank make last quarter on the merger with Swift Company?" I looked at him proudly and said, "One hundred million dollars exactly buddy boy of mine!" Joe laughed, said, "Very good Timmy my boy," and gave the Spinning Chinaman a whirl, sending me revolving round and round and round. "Oh God, Whoa!" I barked. My cock throbbed real piss hard in my pants and I could actually feel the first droplets of piss beading up at my slit and no doubt staining my under shorts. I heard Jeff say, "Looks like he doesn't get tickled with that question." As I spun my pulled down tie kept landing over my face each time I was upside down. Then Joe said to Jeff, "Your turn man, ask him a question before he stops spinning. That way when he answers he'll still be spinning and we'll send him round and round some more non-stops." I pursed my lips together in a mixture of anger and helplessness and said, "No, come on guys, if you do that I'll be dizzy as hell." Ignoring me it seemed Jeff called out, "Timmy, what's the name of the new girl in the accounting department? We hired her last week." I knew that it was either Jane or Jill but for some fucked up reason I could not remember. I figured that the beer, the overwhelming need to piss and being spun was clouding my memory. "Yeah, she's a real looker I'll say that," I began. "She's got real sexy feet too. Have you noticed those open toed shoes she wears? Oh man, heaven you guys, pure fucking heaven. Uh, yeah, her name, her name is, uh, I think, Jill. Yeah, that's it, Jill." Jeff laughed and called out, "Wrong!" and gave the Spinning Chinaman a real good shove, sending me spinning some more. I yelled out, "You fuckers" when I heard Jeff say, "I'll get his socks off him when he stops spinning and then we'll each tickle one of his bare feet." As I spun I called out, "No, there's no need for that! Don't take my socks off me, please guys!" To add to my upcoming tickle tortures Joe said, "I suggest we tickle his feet with these." With that said Joe reached into his shirt pocket and held up two ball point pens. I yelled out two words, "OH NO!" Jeff told me that the new girl's name in the accounting department was Donna. Fuck, I realized that both my guesses would have been incorrect so it looked like having my feet tickled was inevitable. But I was thinking woefully, not with ball point pens, God, not with those. When I stopped spinning Joe adjusted the Spinning Chinaman so that I was left in an upside down position. He quickly inserted the pin so the Chinaman wouldn't shift and then Jeff started pulling my socks off my feet, grabbing them at the toes section. He meanly and jokingly commented about how my socks were real moist and smelly, adding how it seemed so weird that a guy's regal looking dress socks could be so awfully smelly. Joe laughed at Jeff's comments about my damned socks and all I was able to do was look upwards as my socks left my feet. As I was desocked I begged and pleaded from my upside down position for them not to take my socks off me and not to tickle me. I even invited them to spin me some more, rather than tickle me. I was told that I would *indeed* be spun some more, after I was tickled. Jeff got my socks off my feet and from my upside down position looking upward I saw him cram those stinkers into his suit pants pocket. I called upwards, "Fucking fucks, stealing my stinky socks? What a fucked up thing man, to steal a poor guy's socks off his feet." We all laughed at my ridiculous comment and then the moment of awful truth arrived. Both Joe and Jeff took position with pens poised in their hands at one of my bare feet each. Over and over I said, "No, no, Oh God guys, no!" But then they were scrawling on my feet, writing letters, maybe numbers, who the fuck knew? I had started laughing, looking at their feet from my upside down view and somehow feeling my cock more than pulsing from the need to piss. I laughed crazily and utterly frantically as they scrawled on the bottoms of my feet and a few times I nearly lost my piss. I figured that the names they were writing on my tootsies were names of people we worked with at the bank. I just surmised that as I had been told that the subjects I would be asked about would be work related things. When I felt a squirly type of scrawl over my left heel I got the feeling that it was a letter "S" being written there. I somehow knew it was my wife's name that was being written. I laughed like a madman and then found myself spinning round and round again after they had written on my feet for a good ten to fifteen minutes or so. Joe called out the next question, asking me what computer system we used at the bank. I blurted out the word "Microsoft" and was spared some tickling. But I was not spared being spun. Even though I was still revolving like a clothes dryer Joe gave the Chinaman another good shove, sending me round and round and round and round. He mockingly said, "Round and Round Timmy goes, where he stops no one knows." My two buddies laughed meanly and when I stopped spinning I found myself again totally upside down and looking upwards at them. I hadn't been asked any questions so I fleetingly wondered where the game was headed now. As I looked straight outward though I was treated to the sight of my two buddies socked feet as they stood in front of me in the device. I quickly surmised that while I had been spinning and spinning they had each gotten their shoes off their feet. I glanced to where my wingtips were and saw a pair of burgundy loafers, Joe's and a second pair of black wingtips, Jeff's placed next to my shoes. Like most other guys out there in the world my two buddies socked feet really were musty and sweaty scented from the long day in their leather shoes. Joe was wearing brown nylon thinly ribbed socks and Jeff's feet were clothed in cotton wide ribbed navy blue socks. As I looked at and smelled their socked feet mere inches from my face I called out, "Wh-what now guys?" In response to my question Jeff asked me a question of his own, he said, "So Timmy, you really like feet eh?" Before I could reply Jeff reached up, grabbed my bare left foot with one hand for support, lifted one of his socked feet and placed the toes of it right under my nose, against my nose. I sniffed crazily, saying things like, "Oh you fucker," as he squeezed my bare written on foot. Jeff's foot smelled real funky and as I cursed and swore my lips grazed his socked toes. Involuntarily it seemed I stuck out my tongue and licked and lapped at his big toe under his sock, sniffing greedily at the same time. Joe watched in amazement and said, "Fuck, we were right, Timmy really is into some kinky shit. Look at him sniffing your goddamned smelly socked foot." Then it was Joe's turn to feed me some of his foot odor. Being that his socks were nylon they were more heavily scented and he wanted more than just to have his toes sniffed and licked. Like Valerie had done to me Joe fed me his toes and I found myself sucking the stink out of his socks, gulping it down as I hung upside down in that goddamned Spinning Chinaman. Then, after both of my buddies decided that their dress socks were cleaned enough I was asked another banking question, courtesy of Joe, he asked me, "Timmy, what's the secret function code in our computer system that only managers know?" He quickly gave the Chinaman a good whirl, sending me spinning round and round and round again and I quickly called out, "I can't answer that, goddamn it, it's top secret, and fucking FUCKS, I know I'm going to be tickled again!" As I hemmed and hawed and spun I saw my two buddies grinning faces as they anticipated tickling me. I begged them though, practically crying by then, for them not to tickle my feet with their ball point pens. When I stopped spinning I was in an upright position and facing them. Without a word they unbuttoned my dress shirt, got my tie off me and pushed the tails of my shirt behind me. My chest and stomach areas were now bared and totally accessible to them for tickle tortures. They drummed their fingertips over my sweaty stomach and chest areas and when they tickled my nipples they witnessed firsthand just what it does to me to have those man tits of mine worked over. Admittedly, as they bared my upper torso I thought of the sadistic tailor who had so brazenly stripped me down in his shop. Joe said, "Say Timmy, does Stephanie know just how ticklish your titties are?" holding one of my nipples by the tip and wagging it up and down at the same time, tickling the fucking fuck out of me. I laughed and laughed and told him yes, yes, Stephanie knew just how ticklish my man tits were. My two buddies laughed at my terminology of how I called my nipples my man tits. They finally stopped tickling me again and before they could ask me another question and send me spinning again I bellowed, "I got to fucking piss like a racehorse!" my voice having taken on a screeching sound at that point from being spun and meanly tickled. Jeff and Joe smiled at each other and it was Jeff who said, "I guess now's as good a time as any." I asked him what the fucking fuck he meant by that and in reply I saw Jeff pick up one of the empty beer mugs from the coffee table. I quickly and nervously said, "Oh no, oh fucking fuck, totally fucking fucks, you guys aren't going to do what I think you're going to do, are you?" Joe grinned at me and said something like, "Well buddy, seeing as you and Stephanie are into kinky stuff with that device you're presently in I suppose some beer recycling won't offend you too much huh?" My jaw dropped and a look of utter disbelief filled my face. All I managed to say was "Beer recycling? Fucking beer recycling? You have got to be fucking kidding me!" Just for the fuck of it, before letting me piss they spun me again. I cursed and swore and demanded to be released from the Chinaman, insisting that they let me use the bathroom in a normal type of fashion for a guy. If I remember correctly I think that I even told them that if they released me and allowed me to go to the bathroom that I would let them re-strap me into the Spinning Chinaman. That's how bad I had to piss Ronald, so bad that I was willing to submit to more spinning and tickle tortures. But oh man Ronald, they weren't kidding. They were not going to let me out of that thing anytime soon it seemed. And given the position I was in there wasn't much I could do to stop them. As Jeff got the beer mug it was Joe who brazenly undid my belt, pulled down my fly zipper, unfastened my suit pants and slid them down to just under the very bottom of the white boxer briefs I was wearing that day. My cock was mammoth sized and pressing erotically against the thin material of my under shorts, outlined in there along with my sweaty and juicy balls. Glancing down I saw that I had been right in my summation that beads of piss had stained my under shorts. And woe of fucking woes, not just beads of piss Ronald, but good thick droplets of sticky pre cum were there too. Fuck, what a thing for a business guy like me, to be seen this way in front of his two best office buddies. I had to think that it was all the beer we had drunk that had caused all this, not that we were really enjoying all this, nah, it was the beer doing the thinking for us. I was totally breathless and grunted like a marine as Joe reached into the top of my underpants, pushed them down under my low hanging balls, tucking them under there actually and then snagged my erect piss and cum filled manhood in his fist. I grunted things like, "Ohhhrrr Gawd, fucking fucks, leggo my cock man!" A few seconds later I was more than grunting, and totally gasping in a mixture of shock and forced ecstasy as Jeff held the beer mug under my cock and Joe was doing the fucked up honors of jacking me off, stroking my crank real hard and forcefully. My head spun from the beer and from the Chinaman and I could not believe what was happening, and in my own house no less... Joe said, "We need to soften up this cock of yours if you're going to piss and relieve yourself buddy boy, I don't know about you but I for one cannot piss with a steely hard-on." My eyes crossed in my head and I garbled, "Let me the fuck loose so I can take care of this, oh God, y-you bastard, you guys are goin' to get my creamy nut!" And with that I let fly with a good thick helping of creamy sperm, depositing it liberally into the beer mug as Joe jacked me off and Jeff held the mug under my spurting cock. The way Joe was holding my cock it felt as if he was siphoning and squeezing every possible drop of my sexy mess from me...

As I told Ronald about my exploits in the Spinning Chinaman at the hands of my two work buddies I was still standing with my socked feet encased in the wooden box prison, my arms still yanked above me and cinched at the wrists, tied off to a ceiling rafter, and from the telling of the story my cock was hard and sticking out like a flagpole in front of myself. Droplets of pre cum oozed from my wide sexy slit. As I glanced down at my manhood I heard Ronald say, "Please continue Timmy, I'm enjoying this immensely..."

I looked across at him miserably and went on with my sad, mortifying but erotic tale...

Chapter Twenty-Seven

After I had shot my load in the beer mug and as I was gasping for breath I was then pissing into the same beer mug. Joe held my now more flaccid cock in his fist as I pissed and pissed, relieving myself almost endlessly it seemed. With all the beer I had consumed during the football game it wasn't surprising to me that I should be pissing so liberally the way I was. Jeff said, "Oh man, that's real skuzzy Joe, us mixing his cum and piss with the leftover beer in that mug." Joe chuckled and said that it was real appetizing. The two men laughed. The sound of my hot frothy yellow stream mixing with my goopy cum and the still pretty cool beer in the mug was somehow hypnotic, not to mention the smell wafting up from there.... When I was done pissing I hung there in the Chinaman totally on display at that point, my feet bared, my upper torso bared and even my goddamned manhood and balls on display for my two perverted buddies...

Ronald looked at me in total amazement and asked, "At what point did they finally release you man?"

I told Ronald that if I remembered correctly it was a lot of hours later. Joe and Jeff had delighted in spinning me some more, tickling me a lot more and they had even managed to get another good cum from me into the beer mug along with yet another helping of my beer induced frothy piss. Unbelievably, between my cum and the amount of piss that they extracted from me I nearly filled that goddamned mug. What I remember most about it all though was that when I was showing Joe and Jeff to the door they both said something like, "Let's do this again some time soon huh buddy?" My latest tickle torture story done, Ronald looked me over in total amazement.

"It seems to me bud, that like I sort of said earlier, you've spent a good portion of time in your life being tickled by numerous people," Ronald said, holding the remote control for the massagers in the box encasing my feet in his hand, stepping over to me. "It would appear that I picked the right guy for the job here, would you agree?"

As Ronald spoke he tweaked one of my nipples and my cock dribbled a few droplets of pre cum down onto the box that my feet were in...

"Knowing what I've told you man, I would say you picked the wrong guy for the job here, thank you very much," I replied sarcastically. "I had hoped that after marrying Stephanie that my tickle torments would have come to an end, but it seems that wasn't to be the case..."

Ronald chuckled, held up his remote control and pressed a button on it...

"HA, HA, HA, HA, HA, HA, HA, HA, HA, HA, HA, HA, HA, HA, HA, HA, HA, HA, HA, HA!" I suddenly found myself screaming again as I laughed, the massagers in the box gliding and sliding all over my feet again...

I wriggled my muscular body in an erotic fashion, dancing stupidly as Ronald's device did its dirty work... My hard cock dribbled more and more pre cum and as I laughed and danced in that box Ronald enjoyed the show...

Chapter Twenty Eight

Ronald finally turned off the massagers in the box and as he helped me to step out of the wooden prison he said that I had really warmed up very well for what he had in mind for me next. Fucking fucks, *what he had in mind for me next*? After all I had already been through I couldn't even imagine anymore at that point. But Ronald was a relentless and generous buddy I'll say that for him, hardy fucking har, har. He was sparing no expense in making sure that I experienced every goddamned inch, every nook and cranny of his tickle torture palace. Once my socked feet were out of the box standing was nearly impossible and Ronald had to hold me balanced by my upper arms as my feet and legs readjusted to being out of the box-like prison. While I tried to stand normally Ronald managed to get my hands tied behind me and he blindfolded me again... I wobbled stupidly and because of being so unbalanced there really was no way for me to stop the guy from binding my hands behind me and blindfolding me yet again...

"Ronald, what the hell are you talking about man?" I asked him as he massaged my muscular legs and calves, pulling my socks up for me as well as he worked at getting the blood circulating properly for me. "What have you warmed me up for man? And what was that comment you made earlier about me facing the music?"

"You remember that huh Timmy me laddy?" Ronald asked me and I could feel him squatting in front of me as he massaged my legs and calves, playfully snapping the elastic in my socks against my calves, his face more than likely dangerously close to my erect and cum dribbling cock. "You really are a true blue silk socked executive I must say; you remember all the little yet important details. No wonder you've been so successful at the bank..."

"Never mind all that Ronald, just tell me what the fuck I'm in for next," I garbled, my upper muscular body jutted out as I managed to regain my sense of balance.

My jaw dropped and I was suddenly speechless when I felt, *my God*, it was unthinkable *wasn't it?* I grunted breathlessly as Ronald continued to massage the feeling back into my legs and calves, squeezing them good and tight at the same time all while he did what I'll just call the unthinkable. I grunted breathlessly again but felt it best not to comment on it as Ronald did what I call the unthinkable. Oh God, I was thinking that this really crosses the boundaries of friendship between two guys! Even as the ecstasy consumed me in the blindfolded darkness and my load was *again* extracted from me I tried not to focus on the *unthinkable*...

Then, when I was able to walk normally again Ronald got to his feet, took me by my upper arm and led me out of the room where we had just had lunch and where he had tickled my feet in that box-like device...

It was a short while later when I found myself standing next to my so called buddy Ronald in yet another of what seemed like endless rooms of tickle tortures. I was still clad in just those damned black socks of mine that seemed to be a major part of all of this for some reason. I got the distinct and definite feeling that besides tickling me and besides my feet Ronald had a severe fetish for seeing me in just those black dress socks. I would suppose that to a fetishist seeing a muscular guy in nothing but his black nylon dress socks would seem erotic somehow. Needless to say my hands were of course (still) tied behind me and, as mentioned I was blindfolded. The scent of my sweat mixed with the cum that had landed on me earlier when Ronald had forced me to shoot my load a few times filled the air.

"Fuck man, more tickle tortures now?" I asked Ronald miserably as he held my upper arm tight, standing me in place after we had entered the room, positioning me on a mark it actually felt like. "Ronald, what's the point of all this man? You've gone too far here buddy, making me shoot my load the way you did! I am a married guy after all..."

"Ha, coming up buddy, the very next and intense round of tickle torture and this time to some music," Ronald chuckled, holding my upper arm real tight.

"Music? *What do you mean music*?" I asked him, grimacing miserably and angrily behind my blindfold.

Fucking fucks, it was bad enough that the guy had kidnapped me, chloroformed me, restrained me, tickle tortured me and even forced me to cum a few times, but man, being blindfolded had to be the worst part of all this. I mean, lets face it buds, not being able to see what was coming next was maddening...

"Ronald, let me go already, this is totally humiliating man," I grunted, and unbelievably, after what Ronald had just done moments before, the unthinkable, I felt a sort of tingling in my cock as it started growing rigid and stiff yet again. "FUCK man, even after shooting all those loads my cock is getting hard again man... Fucking fucks Ronald, the least you could do is put my goddamned under shorts back on me! Shit, I'm feeling all sleazy and real sexy here buddy..."

"Looks to me Timmy me laddy that the aphrodisiac I've been administering to you via the chloroform and the food and drinks I gave you is still working its magic," Ronald snickered and gripped my arm tighter with one hand while with his other hand he squeezed one of my jutted up nipples.

"Ronald, you sick fuck, *again*, what's the point of all this man?" I asked him, sounding like a goddamned broken record. "Why are you doing this to me?"

"I've told you Timmy, for comedy, I absolutely love comedy and I love hearing a buddy laugh and laugh and laugh," Ronald replied and reached for my blindfold. "And laugh again you will buddy, *take a look*..."

That said Ronald whipped the blindfold off me...

My eyes adjusted to the light and at the sides of the room that we were now in I saw three long rectangular panels that stretched from the floor to the ceiling. Upon further observation I saw that the panels all had various holes in them and sticking out of each of those holes was one of Ronald's infamous furry cone shaped devices. I realized that he had positioned me to be standing dead center between all of those panels.

"H-holy fucking shit," I whispered as Ronald released his hold on my arm and took a few steps away from me.

My hard cock embarrassingly dribbled a few droplets of pre cum...

"There are thirty furries all pointed directly at you buddy, ten on each of those three panels," Ronald said, stepping behind me as I looked around miserably and helplessly. "They are all attached to long metal rods, or, if you would, stretchable arms.

Like the old telephone commercial used to say they're going to reach out and touch you buddy. They are going to spin real fast and touch you and tickle you *everywhere* on that ticklish body of yours! HA!"

My eyes opened wide in terror and I sweated and my feet stunk in my socks as Ronald quickly and efficiently hooked up some kind of harness behind me and under my arms.

"WH-what's that for?" I asked him.

"You'll find out soon enough buddy boy," Ronald laughed and walked toward a booth that was off to the side of the room that he presently had me in.

"My God, this place of yours is like something out of a goddamned twisted science fiction movie," I garbled as Ronald stepped into the booth.

In the booth Ronald sat behind a control panel that had buttons and dials all over it. He pushed a button and the room I was in was suddenly filled with soft thudding sounding disco music...

"Okay buddy, that's part one," Ronald said to me over an intercom speaker that was set up in the booth.

"Ronald, stop this!" I yelled over to him, while at the same time wondering at what it took to create this labyrinth that my so called buddy had me trapped in.

Suddenly, I saw the first panel of furries light up and the arms of the thing stretching the goddamned furries toward me, aimed firstly at my chest and mainly at my manly man tits. Now I knew what Ronald had meant about me facing the music and dancing...

"OH GAWD NO!" I screamed.

"Tickle and dance buddy, tickle and dance," Ronald chuckled.

As the disco music played I suddenly felt like John Travolta back in that old movie "Saturday Night Fever." The only differences being that good old John Travolta was clad in more than a pair of his black socks on that dance floor. And his hands weren't tied behind him and he didn't have three tickle panels surrounding him. And fucking fucks, he didn't have metal rods with cone shaped furries aimed at his man tits as he stood upon that dance floor. No, John Travolta didn't have those problems while he had been dancing, but I realized with twisted certainty that I did indeed have those problems. As the cone shaped fuzzies spun at a high speed and aimed at my chest, my poor man tits to be exact, I looked over at Ronald in the control booth.

"Ronald, what is this? My God, *what is this*?" I asked him, standing there and struggling to get my hands untied. "Look man, this isn't funny anymore!"

"Oh but Timmy boy, it's more than funny, in fact, it's about to become hilarious for you again," Ronald chuckled in the booth, me hearing his voice through the speakers that were in the walls.

Suddenly, the spinning fuzzies found their way to my man tits and spun meanly against them.

"HA, ha, ha, ha, ha, ha, ha, ha, ha, ha, ha, ha, ha, ha, ha! OH MY GAWD!" I laughed helplessly, dancing stupidly, just what Ronald wanted, as I was being tickled, and lo and behold my hard cock swung in the wind.

"There you go Timothy my ticklish laddy, your own private discothèque, dance for me buddy," Ronald spouted into his microphone and pressed another button on his control panel.

As I tried to back away from the fuzzies tickling my man tits, from behind me two more spinning fuzzies reached out from another panel and tickle tortured the backs of my legs and thighs.

"AAAAYYYYYYRRRRR!" I screamed crazily, jumping up and down in place almost to the music as my man tits and now the backs of my legs and thighs were tickle tortured. "G-got to get away from these infernal things, ha, ha, ha, ha, ha, ha, ha, ha, ha, ha, ha, ha, ha, ha, ha, ha, ha, ha, ha!"

I moved as quickly as possible to the side of the tickling devices only to be attacked by more of them at my ribs, sides and stomach.

"OOOOOOHHHHHHRRRR no fair Ronald! No fucking fair! HA, HA, HA, HA, HA, HA, HA, HA, HA, HA, HA, HA, HA, HA, HA, HA, HA, HA!" I screamed as the furry tickle torture devices seemed to come at me from all sides.

There was no escaping them, as I was broken heartedly learning. I jumped up and down, danced stupidly to the music and my cock dribbled pre cum as I was horribly and erotically tickle tortured. Then, I found myself almost involuntarily up on my socked toes as two of those blasted spinning fuzzies found their way from the panel that they were hooked up to, to under my scrotum...

"AAAAAAAAAAARRRRRRRR! HAR, HAR, HAR, HAR, HAR, HAR, HAR, HAR, HAR, HAR, HAR, HAR, HAR, HAR, HAR!" I blubbered crazily. "F-FUCKING THINGS ARE TICKLIN' and cookin' my damned nuts Ronald! HAR, HAR, HAR, HAR, HAR, HAR, HAR, HAR, HAR, HAR, HAR! OHHHHHH, GAWD man, what a twisted thing to do to a poor guy! HA, ha, ha, ha, ha, ha, ha, ha, ha, ha, ha, ha, ha, ha, ha!"

At that point, as I laughed and hardy harred I found myself standing with my back arched, surrounded by those goddamned spinning fuzzies. My legs and thighs were being tickled from behind, my man tits were being tickle roasted and my nuts were tingling and zinging as they were so meanly tickle tortured. My muscular chest bobbed up and down and I was sweating in my socks as I was tickled, tickled, *tickled*...

"Very soon I'll show you what the harness I put on your arms and shoulders is for Timmy me laddy," Ronald said into his microphone.

He then pressed a button on his control panel and two more fuzzies made their way toward my lower back, spinning like mad as they approached me...

"Ronald NO, ha, ha, ha, ha, ha, ha, ha, ha, ha, ha, ha, ha, ha, ha, ha, ha, ha! Please stop this, please!" I laughingly screamed.

"Oh come on Timmy, you know you're loving this, all of it," Ronald said meanly as the two new spinning fuzzies made their way tauntingly toward me, aimed at my very ticklish lower back. "I can see from that hard-on you're sporting again that you love this!"

God, it was bad enough that those twirling fuzzies were attacking my sides, my man tits, and my stomach area and to tell it bluntly the ones on my nuts were driving me stir crazy. But my cock man, my cock was again rock hard and dripping and dribbling pre cum like it was out of control. Fuck, I just wanted all this to stop already, but Ronald was insistent on driving me crazy it seemed...

"PLLLLLLEEEEAAAASSEEEE RONALD, ha, ha, ha, ha, ha, ha, ha, ha, ha, ha, ha, ha, ha" I chortled. "Please give a guy a break here..."

By then tears were running down my face from all the laughing. I could not believe that I was so hard in the cock and that I actually needed to cum again. Between all the tickling and Ronald's goddamned aphrodisiac I was like a seventeen year old guy on Viagra where my erections were concerned. Even Stephanie my wife, as sexy as she could get had never been able to get me all excited and erect like this. I was lucky sometimes if I came twice in one night with her and now Ronald had me hard again and ready to shoot what seemed like an umpteenth load from my nuts that were currently being tickled and tickled and tickled. I danced like an idiot to the disco music and gyrated as my nuts were roasted by those infernal fuzzies. I didn't know why I was so hot in the crotch over all this, I mean, fucking fucks man, I had been kidnapped from my own home in just my boxer briefs and black socks and that bastard Ronald had been tickling me and making me tell him of my tickle history ever since. I would never tell the guy how it seemed that some twisted and psycho-sexy part of me was loving it all so much and yeah, I wanted to shoot another load, but yet, of course I still wanted to be let go and taken back home to my house and wife and son. At that point I wasn't even sure how long Ronald had had me there. All I knew was that he wasn't stopping. He just kept tickling and tickling and tickling me, and now again, oh God, again, I needed him to help me shoot a load. How mortifying is that, to need your good buddy to touch your hard cock and jack you off so you could shoot the huge load that was building up in your balls while you were being tickled to death? Real mortifying I would have to say.

"Ronald, ha, ha, ha, ha, ha, ha, ha, ha, ha, ha, ha, ha, ha, ha, ha, ha, ha, ha, ha!" I screamed out. "Please buddy, you, you're making me all hot in the crotch here. HA, HA, HA, HA, HA, HA, HA, HA, HA, HA, HA, HA, HA, HA, HA, HA, HA, HA, HA! Please man, ha, ha, ha, ha, ha, ha, ha, ha, ha, it, it's looking like I need to cum again!"

I could not fucking believe that I had just said that but I couldn't help it. Ronald had me in a position where I was totally dependant upon him for all my needs. And at that moment I truly needed to cum, again. I needed to cum so bad and I needed that so called buddy of mine to do the honors of jacking me off. I needed him to jack me off but all he was doing was tickling and tickling and tickling me. Oh God, why the fuck, and what the fuck was he doing to me? Why was I thinking this way? I loved my wife!

"HAHAHAHAHAHAHAHAHAHAHAHAHAHAHAHAHAHAHAHAHAHAHAHAHA P-please Ronald, I need to cum…" I laughed insanely.

"Timmy, Timmy me ticklish laddy of lads, if you cum you are going to be *even more* tickle sensitive and the tickling feeling is going to be hundreds of times worse than it is now," Ronald said into his microphone as I danced and jigged while the spinning fuzzies did their dirty work. "You know that very well already from earlier buddy. Is that what you want?"

What I said next was unbelievable, even and mostly to my own ears…

"HAHAHAHAHAHAHAHAHHAHAHAHAHAHAHAHAHHAHAHAHA, jack me off Ronald, please jack me the FFFFFUUUCCCKKK, ha, ha, ha, ha, ha, ha, off!" I ranted.

"Ha, ha, yourself buddy boy, it looks to me like I have you right where I want you," Ronald laughed in his booth as he continued controlling the fuzzies attached to the long metal arms as they tickled me and tickled me relentlessly.

"R-Ronald, ha, ha, ha, ha, ha, ha, ha, ha, ha, ha, ha, ha, ha, ha, ha, ha, t-turn these things off man! I gotta cum buddy, please let me cum again!" I screamed out madly as the fuzzies now tickled my lower back, sending me into a laughing spiral and were still tickling my nipples, sides, ribs and scrotum.

As they glided over the backs of my legs and thighs I danced crazily to the disco music still playing and I laughed and laughed and laughed and laughed…

"Okay buddy, we'll get to that, but for now I want to show you why I have you hooked up with that harness over your arms and shoulders," Ronald said to me from within the booth.

He pressed another button and suddenly the harness on my shoulders hoisted me upwards a few inches off the floor.

"H-hey, what is this?" I garbled as I was lifted and the cone shaped fuzzies retreated back into the panels. P-put me down man! Put me down!"

I swung my black socked feet out in front of me and my hard cock swung back and forth as well, dripping pre cum.

"Oh I just need to lift you a tad higher for what I have in mind for you next bud," Ronald said jovially and pressed another button on the control panel.

Suddenly, my dangling socked feet were snared in two metal vise-like devices that shot out at blinding speed from one of the panels in front of me.

"H-HEY, fucking fucks man, those things have got my feet trapped Ronald, I can't dance like this buddy!" I shouted, sounding totally ridiculous.

"I don't need you to dance at the moment Timmy me laddy, I just need you to laugh for me," Ronald said and suddenly I saw two cone shaped fuzzies headed directly at the bottoms of my socked feet as I dangled helplessly.

"OH NO, NO, NO, NO, NO!" I ranted and then I was again laughing uncontrollably as the fuzzies made their way under my feet and started spinning against my soles. "HA, ha, ha, ha, ha, ha, ha, ha, ha, ha, ha, ha, ha, ha, ha, ha, ha, ha, ha, ha, ha, ha, ha, ha, ha, n-no fair again Ronald, no fucking fair!"

My hard cock dribbled more pre seed and the need to cum intensified even more…

"OH my God Ronald, PPPPLLLEEEEAAASEEEE NO, NO, NOOOOO, ha, ha, ha, ha, ha, ha, ha, ha, ha, ha, ha, ha, ha, ha, ha, ha, ha, ha!" I cackled. "I can't stand it buddy! Ha, ha, ha, ha, ha, ha, ha, ha, ha, ha, ha, ha, ha, ha, ha, ha, OH GOD!"

I was laughing like crazy by then and trying to breathe normally and trying (very unsuccessfully) not to think about my hard cock that was dripping pre cum all over the floor, all while I was hoisted up in that harness and while the bottoms of my socked feet were being tickled and tickled non-fucking-stop. Fucking fucks, I was also thinking how Ronald had to stop all this soon, or he was going to kill me with tickling me. I was starting to feel as if I would pass out from all the laughing I had done and all the laughing I was still doing.

"Wow Timmy, I can see that you really are enjoying yourself now," Ronald teased me meanly. "Look at how hard your cock is now, and not to mention those sensitive man tits of yours. They're really hard too and telling a story all their own, ha!"

"Ronald, ha, ha, ha, ha, ha, ha, ha, ha, ha, ha, ha, ha, ha, ha, ha, ha, ha, ha, ha, ha, ha, ha!" I chortled. "Please stop this, no more tickling, please man, please stop this! Ha, ha, ha, ha, ha, ha, ha, ha, ha, ha, ha, ha, ha, ha, fucking fucks, I need to shoot my load, Gawd!"

Ronald simply laughed at me from within the booth and much to my dismay I heard him say that he could not let me cum just yet, seeing that there was still more tickling that needed to be done to my socked feet. He went on to tell me that when I had been tickled long enough he would then help me out where shooting my load was concerned, but again, not until the bottoms of my feet had been tickled for a while longer. I didn't know how long I could stand it as my socked feet were relentlessly tickled; it was driving me crazy that was for sure. It wasn't as bad mind you, as when Ronald's psycho shoe shine machine had pulled my socks off me and then tickled my bare feet, but even with my black nylon socks on at the moment they were not providing much protection to my poor ticklish feet at all. I would think that was why Ronald wanted me in those silk stinkers when he captured me. By that point as the fuzzies twirled against the bottoms of my feet my cock was dripping pre cum like a faucet and throbbing almost painfully. I really needed to cum and didn't know if I could wait for Ronald to assist me in that area. But what choice did I have really? Fucking fucks, it felt like my balls were on fire and I knew that I could pump out a load again without even having my damned cock touched.

"Hey buddy," I heard Ronald call out to me. "I have a little surprise for you. Are you ready?"

I looked up at Ronald and he pressed a button on the control panel. Suddenly I saw a cone shaped fuzzy snake out of one of the three panels and it started moving toward my poor aching balls. This time it would not be under my scrotum, oh woe is fucking me, this time my balls would be tickled head-on. I screamed bloody murder...

"No Ronald, please, no, ha, ha, ha, ha, ha, ha, ha, ha, ha, ha, ha, ha, ha, not that!" I laughed. "HAHAHAHAHAHAHAHAHAHAHAHAHAHAHAHA please, not my balls, *please...*"

The cone shaped fuzzy headed right for my sexy ball sac and as soon as it touched my low hangers the bristles started to spin and tickle my helpless balls. The laughing that was coming out of my mouth was suddenly louder and louder as the tickling seemed to get worse and worse. My poor balls and socked feet (what a fucked up combination huh?) were now being tickled and tickled and my hard cock was throbbing out of control. I looked over at Ronald and through my teary laugh filled eyes I saw him laughing and smiling and turning a dial that caused those fuzzies to spin faster and faster. I screamed out my laughter by then...

Ronald's Journal
Dated February 1995

I've been dating a real hot little number that I met in a singles bar a few weeks ago. What a piece of ass she is. Her name is Marilyn, she's twenty six years old, comes from a family with money (she's proved that on our last three dates when I told her after the fact that I could not afford to pay for dinner; you would think that after that happened three times she would have stopped seeing me. But not this bitch. And to make it really clear, she loves my cock.) and she works only because she claims she needs something to do. She has blond hair, crystal blue eyes and a pair of tits that I could suck from now till doomsday. On a recent date we wound up back up at my place and what she did I could not believe. We sat down on the couch, a glass of red wine for each of us set out on the coffee table as we relaxed and Marilyn told me to lift my shoed feet up into her lap. I asked her what she had in mind, thinking she was into some kinky stuff and that was when she told me that she worked as a massage therapist and that she could tell from the way I walked that I could use a good foot massage. She went on to say how too many people don't pay attention to the needs of their feet and only take care of them after something has happened. My heart thudded in my chest at her choice of conversation and her choice of my body parts that she wanted at that night after our date. Here I had been trying to get thoughts of feet off my mind, let me rephrase that, I had been trying to get thoughts of Timothy Backman's (socked) feet off my mind and now this dimwitted blond I've been dating tells me she's a massage therapist and that she wants to massage *my feet*. Well, seeing as I had been out on a date that night I suppose it goes without saying that I was wearing dress shoes *and* dress socks, brown dress socks to be exact, so I guess I'll say it after all. I obediently hoisted my feet up off the floor, faced Marilyn on the couch and gently placed my feet in her lap. "So you're a massage therapist" I said to her. "Why didn't you tell me that sooner?" She smiled as she unlaced my brown Rockport shoes and slowly pulled them from my feet. She said that she was saving it for a surprise and how she wanted to show me how relaxing and stimulating it could feel to have my feet massaged. As she yanked my shoes off my feet she went on to say how very sensitive the feet are and that the nerve endings in them, when properly massaged and stimulated could lead to some real hot sex. I smiled back at her as she tossed my shoes one after the other to the floor. Now, my nylon brown socked feet were in her lap. She asked me if I preferred to have my socks on or off while she massaged my feet. I stifled a gulp and reached for my wine glass, my cock already getting hard in my khakis as thoughts of Timmy filled my head. I told her that either way was fine, socks on or socks off, it didn't matter. I think that it also needs mentioning here how this was the first time I was ever out on a date and my socks had become the topic of conversation. Who did I think I was after all, Timothy Backman? Hardy fucking har, har. As Marilyn began squeezing my left socked foot I told her about Tim and how his wife can't stand the scent of his socked feet after a long day in his shoes. Marilyn smiled and lifted the foot that she was squeezing to her nose. My heart pounded harder and my cock stiffened some more as she took a hearty sniff of my socked toes. As she squeezed my foot tighter with her fingers and thumbs she playfully told me that I did not have a stinky socks problem. I smiled a bit and told her that yeah, I knew that. But then, much to my own surprise I found myself telling her about Tim and how it seemed that his socks always stunk, even after a short time wearing his shoes. As Marilyn worked her magic massaging my socked feet I told her about the recent business trip I had gone on with Tim and how he had taken his shoes off in the train compartment we were in and how scented his socks were. Marilyn giggled, sounding real sexy and said that she got the feeling that Tim was a very nervous person, that would explain why he sweated so much and why his socks were so scented and she also added that he must be a very ticklish guy. When I heard that my heart thundered so loudly that I was thinking that Marilyn could actually hear it through my shirt. She said how most guys whose feet really sweat are very ticklish. Then, with a very sexy grin on her face she reached up and under my pants legs, found the tops of my calf length socks and quickly slid my socks off me and massaged my bare feet. It felt awesome and caused one of the hardest erections that I could recall. After she had massaged my feet for a good hour or so we both finished our wine and I found my blond beauty sitting on my lap facing me. I quickly got her dress off her and got her sexy bra undone. As she straddled my lap I sucked those big tits of hers like they were life support. My hard-on in my pants felt as if it would explode as I feasted and fed on her luscious tits. She groaned and moaned in passion and at one point I noticed that she had my brown socks clenched in her hand as she rocked on my lap... I sucked her nipples harder after seeing that. As I pounded the fuck out of her later in the bedroom, her screaming in passion of how much she loved my huge cock inside her I thought of Timmy and his socked feet and knew that I had to set up some kind of dinner date with him and his wife and me and Marilyn. Being that the horny bitch had just massaged my feet and we had talked about Timmy I felt it only right that she should meet him. With Valentines Day coming real soon I figured setting up a double date would be real easy...

Chapter Twenty-Nine

"OOOOHHHHRRRRR GOD NO, NO RONALD, don't tickle my balls too!" I screamed insanely through the bouts of uncontrolled laughter that were erupting from me as the cone shaped fuzzies pressed themselves most lovingly against my sweaty and cum filled ball sac. "HA, HA, HA, HA, HA, HA, HA, HA, HA, HA, HA, HA, HA, HA, HA!"

I swayed back and forth as I dangled from the straps secured around my shoulders, trying desperately to swing myself away from the cone shaped fuzzies tickling me, but it was no use. The way Ronald hit those control buttons in his booth kept those spinning devices right where he wanted them.

"HA, HA, HA, HA, HA, HA, HA, HA, HA, HA, HA, HA, HA, HA, HA, HA, HA!" I laughed madly as the damned fuzzies caressed my balls and once again the fuzzies that had been at my socked feet a few moments before were back again and doing their dirty work in earnest.

"Wow buddy boy, you really can dance, look at you there, a regular disco king if ever there was one," Ronald said to me from in the booth into the microphone as the beat of the music mixed with the sound of my raucous laughter.

"I-I hate disco! Ha, ha, ha, ha, ha, ha, ha, ha, ha, ha, ha, ha, ha, ha, ha, ha, ha, ha!" I seethed at my so called buddy boy. "I love rock and roll!"

"Well, for the moment you're a real disco duck buddy," Ronald laughed and as the fuzzies tickled my feet in front of me I suddenly felt two more of them sneak up behind me and they meanly slid under my socked heels and started tickling them as well.

"OOOOOHHHHHHHRRRRR GAWD, Ha, ha, ha, ha, ha, ha, ha, ha, ha, ha, ha, ha, ha, ha!" I squealed.

Now there were four of those goddamned fuzzies tickling and tickling my socked feet while my balls were tickled tortured as well as an added bonus. My cock jutted up big and fucking hard, dribbles upon dribbles of pre seed erupted from my wide sexy slit and my manhood twitched and danced from side to side along with the motion of my being tickled body…

"R-Ronald, this thing is driving my balls crazy, ha, ha, ha, ha, ha, ha, ha, ha, ha, ha, ha, ha, ha, ha!" I screamed out, looking across the room at Ronald's booth. "They feel all numb and tingly man!"

"Yeah, I would suppose that the time is coming for you to cum bud, and then after that you'll be even more tickling sensitive," Ronald said to me from within the booth.

"OHHHHHHH, NO, NO! HA, HA, HA, HA, HA, HA, HA, HA, HA, HA, HA, HA, HA, HA!" I laughed helplessly. "Ronald, ha, ha, ha, ha, ha, ha, just let me cum and stop tickling me already!" I ranted.

"Think about it Timmy me laddy, even more tickle sensitive than you are now," Ronald mused and made the fuzzies spin faster yet.

I screamed like mad…

"RONALD please, ha, ha, ha, ha, ha, ha, ha, ha, ha, ha, ha, ha, ha, ha, ha, ha, ha, ha, ha, ha, ha, ha, ha, ha! I can't stand it! I need to cum!" I screamed louder as the fuzzies tickled me more and more and faster and faster. "MY GAWD, my balls are going to explode man!"

Ronald had said that it would be soon enough for me to cum as he worked the controls and the dials in his booth. I could not believe that it could get any worse than it already was, but then, oh God then, I felt yet another twirling fuzzy at the bottom of my back, or to be more exact right above my stinking ass crack. I heard Ronald ask me, "Are you ready for this buddy? I know you're going to love it."

"NNNNNNOOOOOOOOOO RONALD, HAHAHAHAHAHAHAHAHAHHAHAHAHA HAHAHAHAHA I can't take anymore tickling!" I squealed.

"Oh sure you can buddy, just watch what happens when I start this fuzzie tickling your sweet and stinking asshole," Ronald chided me, sounding almost like a parent disciplining a child.

With that Ronald turned a dial this time and I felt that invasive fuzzie wiggling its way right in between my ass cheeks and it brazenly started tickling my asshole. It inched its way inside me, slowly at first, slithering, and then speeding up as it entered my warm confines back there. My teeth clenched involuntarily as that thing in my asshole started to spin. I could not believe the feeling at first and then the way I was being tickled I really could not stand it. Four fuzzies tickling my socked feet, another one tickling my cum filled balls and a fourth one wedged in my asshole and tickling me back there too, of all goddamned places. I was going to go insane for sure with laughter and with tears running down my face and my cock hard as a rock and dripping I screamed at Ronald, "SSSSSTTTTOPPPPPPPPPP! HAHAHAHAHA." I reeled like crazy "Ronald, I cannot stand this; I'm going to pass out man!"

My head was feeling very light and my cock and balls felt like they were going to explode for sure at any second. I was gasping and grunting for air as the fuzzies did their dirty work tickling my feet, balls and asshole and all I wanted was to cum and for the tickling to stop…

"We're almost there buddy, you just have to endure the tickling a bit more," Ronald said into the microphone.

I could not even respond at that point. All I was able to do was laugh and laugh and hee haw louder and louder…

Finally, Ronald turned off all the spinning fuzzies. I watched as the ones under my feet retreated away from me. The one under my balls retreated as well as Ronald pushed buttons in the control booth and the one that had been wedged up and spinning in my asshole came out with a popping like sound followed by an embarrassing fart from me. I stood in the center of the room where I had just danced and was tickled for my buddies' entertainment. Ronald had taken the harness off me and now I was standing blindfolded yet again with one of my hands being held in a tight grasp behind me by Ronald, while with my free hand I stroked my crank.

"AAAAHHHHHHH, yeah man, fucker you are Ronald," I grunted, all sweaty and still gasping from my tickle time just spent, every part of me tingling and alive it seemed. "Af-after this you have got to let me go man. I don't think that my wife will believe that my college fraternity buddies held onto me this long for tickle fun."

"Oh, I'm sure she will Timmy," Ronald said and held my arm tighter behind me as I stroked and choked my crank a tad faster.

I stroked my hardness and at the same time I felt totally helpless as Ronald held me tight in his strong vise-like grip. Being blindfolded of course only added to the feeling of helplessness.

"OHHHHHHRRRRR GAWD RONALD, I n-never thought that being tickle tortured would get me off so much man," I uttered breathlessly as I felt my sexy juices boiling in my balls. "S-Stephanie, my wife, she tickles me from time to time, as you know, but she never gets me so worked up to this point man..."

Ronald chuckled and bent my other arm further behind me, insuring that I was going nowhere...

"Just shoot that load Timmy me ticklish laddy, and trust me on this, after you do, you're going to be even more tickle sensitive," Ronald said directly into my ear as he pulled me closer to himself.

"OHHHHH GOD man, y-you can't mean what I think you mean," I babbled miserably, knowing that he was going to tickle torture me some more, but then I felt it. "OHHHHHH fucking fucks Ronald, I'm gonna cum buddy, I'm gonna fucking shoot a load like I cannot begin to fucking fucks tell you..."

I shook and shuddered as I stroked and choked my crank, and then Ronald whipped the blindfold off me. We both watched as thick ropes of my jelly-like sperm erupted from my wide sexy slit.

"OOOOOOHHHHHHHRRRRRRRRR!" I seethed loudly in a mixture of ecstasy, anger and fear. "FUCKING fucked up guy man, kidnapped my sexy ass and tickle tortures me..."

I swore like a marine as I seemed to cum and cum and cum...

When I was done and well spent I struggled a bit in Ronald's grasp but he managed to snag my other arm behind me and that done, he walked me on my black socked feet out of the room where I had danced for him... My flaccid cock swung in front of me as I walked and dripped the last remnants of my splooge...

"Time for the next tickle session bud..." Ronald said merrily as I struggled fruitlessly in his grasp.

As we walked down a hallway in Ronald's tickle torture palace my buddy held my wrists clasped together behind me with one hand and quickly produced a length of rope from one of his pockets. Being as exhausted as I was there wasn't all that much I could do as Ronald wound rope around my wrists behind me, securing them good and tight...

Next, I groaned miserably as he blindfolded me. Then I heard the door to the next room where I would be tickle tortured opening...

"Step inside buddy, it's time for you to stand tall and be tickled..." Ronald said, grabbing a handful of one of my sexy ass globes as he ushered me into the room.

"Stand tall and be tickled?" I asked him. "What the fucking fuck does that mean?"

"All in time buddy, all in time," Ronald chuckled.

Ronald's Journal
Lunch Before Valentines Day Dinner 1995

Well, getting Timmy to agree to double date with his wife and with me and Marilyn was easy pickings I would have to say. During the workweek while Tim and I were having lunch in a restaurant I told him about Marilyn and he said that she sounded absolutely lovely. He also said that he was glad to hear that for once I wasn't dating someone from the bank. It seems that Timmy had found out through the grape-vine about my in office romances, my love and leave 'em escapades if you would. God man, I don't care where you work; there's no fucking such thing as confidentiality these days. I let Timmy's comment slide and asked him about the four of us, me and Marilyn and him and Stephanie possibly hooking up and going out for Valentines Day drinks and dinner after work one night. Timmy said how since Tim Junior was born he and Stephanie didn't go out all that much anymore. He jokingly told me how the baby was basically in charge at home now. However, he did say how he and Stephanie would love to have me and Marilyn over for dinner. I kind of got the feeling that just like in the past Timmy was interested in meeting the current babe I was dating. The only differ-ence of course being that, like he said, since Tim Junior had been born it didn't give him and Stephanie too much leeway in going out anymore. We made it for Wednesday night, hump day as we suits in the business world call it. Timmy said that Stephanie would prepare one of her special meals for the four of us. I thanked him for the invita-tion and told him that Marilyn and I would be there an hour or so after work that eve-ning, adding how I would be glad to bring a couple of bottles of wine to go with dinner. Timmy said that sounded great. While we ate our lunch I decided to be a bit bold and I told Timmy of how on a recent date Marilyn had massaged my feet for me. I went so far as to tell the handsome laddy that I felt it in my cock as she massaged my damned feet. I could tell from the look on his face that Timmy was suddenly enraptured. After swallowing a mouthful of salad Timmy looked across at me, grinned, and said that that sounded awesome. I went on to tell him how she even took my dress socks (making sure to get the word "dress" in there when describing my socks) off for me and then massaged my bare feet. Timmy only commented by saying how he wished Stephanie would do that for him from time to time, but as I knew, because of the way his socks were scented after being in his shoed feet all day she was averse to them and not to mention how very tickle sensitive his feet are. I have come to realize how Timmy is the only buddy I know who I talk with about these things, his socks to be exact. (I mean, lets face it, how many of us guys talk with our buddies about our smelly socks of all things?) As we went on enjoying our healthy lunches I teased Timmy about how at the gym I had come to know how his dress socks were scented at the end of the day. (The gym story will be told soon at some point.) I told him how if he were to slip his loafers off that he was wearing at that moment how all the young executives in the restaurant would more than likely keel over. We both laughed and haw hawed at my comment, but Timmy, the good sport that he is, said that that was more than likely very true, very true indeed…

Needless to say I could not wait for Valentines Day dinner at Timmy's house. I've always loved going to Timmy and Stephanie's house for dinner, whether I am with a date or not. The reason for that is because Timmy always lounges around his house after work with his shoes off, padding around in his leftover dress socks from the workday… While Timmy and I ate lunch my heart thudded with the anticipation of Valentines Day dinner…

I thought of sexy Marilyn and Timmy's socked feet… I also thought about Timothy's fleeting comment about how very ticklish his feet are…

Chapter Thirty

Holding my muscular upper arms now in his steely grip Ronald walked me into the next room of his house of horrors where I was to be tickle tortured…yet again…yet some more… After all the tickling I had endured thus far it was beyond my comprehension how my buddy could want to force me through even more at that point. I have to say, that if it was me who had me trapped in that situation, I would have let me go at that point, hardy fucking har, har. But then again, Ronald is not me buds and I had the distinct feeling that he was going to hold onto me for as long as possible. The floor under my thin black socked feet felt like it was parquet, nice and sand blasted and cool feeling. As mentioned my hands were tied behind me and I was blindfolded. I was also a sweaty and stinking sexy mess from all the dancing I had done in the last room where I had been tickle tortured and capped off by shooting another potent load. And Gawd of Gawds man, after a guy shoots a load, (or a few like I had already) he becomes even more tickle sensitive. I could not imagine what I was now about to suffer. Then again, not being able to imagine it was part of the reason that that prick buddy of mine had me presently blindfolded.

"Okay buddy, here we are, you're about to experience yet another of my many ingenious and beyond clever inventions," Ronald mused from behind me as he led me into the room.

"Ronald, what the hell do you have in that twisted mind of yours for me now?" I asked as I felt myself being guided against what felt like some kind of flat panel or something.

"Good boy Timmy me laddy," Ronald said, gripping my arms tighter and pushing me forward. "Now, try to step forward, even though you really can't. The parts of your body that I want to have move *will* move."

Without knowing what the fucking fucks he was talking about I reluctantly or more to the point because I had no choice in the matter I did as he told me… I pressed my upper body forward against what felt like a wooden panel of some kind and I felt my muscular and brawny male cleavage both slip into what felt like some kind of openings in the panel.

"Wh-what the fuck is this?" I asked, grimacing behind my blindfold.

Ronald let go of my arms and I heard him step in front of me. It was obvious to me, even with the blindfold still tied over my eyes that I was standing and pressed up against some kind of wooden panel with two holes cut in it for my male cleavage and man tits to protrude through. Thinking about the ramifications of that was not all that pleasant let me tell you. I was about to take a step back to remove my cleavage from the two openings but it was then that I felt the wood around them tighten, as if there was a lever that would make the infernal device act like a pair of stocks, locking my upper bulk in.

"Okay, that looks good buddy boy, now for part two," Ronald said and I gasped real loud and audibly when I felt him grab my cock and balls.

"OOOOHHHHHHHHH, ea-easy with the family jewels you bastard," I grunted breathlessly and felt my pride and joy wedged through another opening in the panel I was standing against.

"Ronald, take this damned blindfold off me already and let me see what the fuck all this is about man," I demanded angrily.

"Heh, heh, can't wait for the unveiling huh Timmy me laddy?" Ronald chuckled. "Just a few more minor adjustments and then we'll get this show on the road..."

I felt the same deal at my cock and balls that I had felt at my upper torso as Ronald somehow locked my manhood in that opening in the panel. When I felt Ronald winding the rope around my upper body, securing me to whatever the fuck I was standing against I realized that somehow my man tits and my cock and balls were totally on display...

"UHHHHHHHHHHRRRHHH, fucker man," I seethed as my buddy tied me tight against the panel I was propped against.

When he finished tying my upper body he squatted down to tie my socked feet securely together as well.

"Okay buddy, now for the moment of truth," Ronald said and whipped my blindfold off me.

Looking down I saw that I had been right. I was tied up against a slab of wood that was bolted to the parquet floor in the room that Ronald now had me in. (Actually it was a lot like the hanging fiberglass panel that Ronald had tied me to earlier on my stomach and had poked my man tits and cock and balls through. The only difference this time was that I was standing up rather than lying down.) There were three openings in the slab, two for my hard male cleavage to protrude through and one smaller one for my semi hard cock and juicy balls to dangle through real sexily. (As I said just like that fiberglass slab I had been on earlier.) Looking downward and over the slab of wood, seeing as my neck was right above the top of it, I saw that I had been right again about there being a lever that would tighten the areas around my cleavage and my cock and balls, insuring that they were kept real secure within the holey prisons. All I could say as I took in the sight of myself now was "WHAT THE FUCKING FUCK IS THIS?" To answer me Ronald pointed to the device that was set up in front of the wooden panel that I was tied to. It was an electronic apparatus; from what I could decipher of it that is. It actually looked like some sort of gizmo that one would purchase at Ikea, something that you would need to assemble once you got it home. It was basically a square metal structure with three metal rods on it. And yep, you guessed it buds, on the ends of each of those metal rods was a stiff feather. And lo and fucking behold each feather was pointed at the areas of my body that were currently on display and wedged through the panel that I was propped against and tied up to...

"Ronald, you son of a bitch," I seethed softly through clenched teeth as my buddy stood a few feet beside me.

I was speaking softly on purpose, wanting to save my voice for the laughing that I knew was soon to come.

"Figured it out eh Timmy me laddy?" Ronald asked and held up his ever present remote control device from Hell. "As you can see those feathers are pointed directly and *very, very precisely* at the very, very tips of your succulent man tits and at the very, *very* tip of your cock, your piss slit to be exact."

I gulped hard in sheer terror and my cock seemed to stiffen some more and point straight out as Ronald spoke of my piss slit.

"RONALD, these are pretty fucked up areas to tickle on a poor guy!" I seethed some more, looking down at my ridiculous looking self tied to that panel with my man tits and cock and balls wedged through the damned thing. "You tickled my piss slit already man, and you saw what it did to me! How the hell can you want to put me through that again?"

"Well, seeing as you laughed all the way through it earlier I figured you would enjoy it a second time bud," Ronald mused.

Then with my eyes opened wide in sheer terror I watched helplessly as Ronald moved the apparatus with the feathers hooked up to it closer to me until the tips of the feathers were against the tips of my man tits and the lower one was against and almost wedged in my wide and sexy piss slit.

"OH GOD, oh fucking fucks, you're goin' to tickle my goddamned slit you bastard?" I grunted, barely able to get the words out.

"Sure as shit buddy, good thing I got you tied real tight and wedged good and securely into that panel eh?" Ronald asked me and looked at his remote control. "It's going to be a slow and torturous build-up to an orgasm that more than likely will never happen me laddy. But then again, you never know do you?"

"Ronald, no, please man, I'll do whatever you want, *anything*!" I pleaded, sweating in my socks like crazy.

"Oh, but you are already doing what I want Timmy, like I told you, I want you to laugh," Ronald said gleefully and then pressed a button on his remote control device.

Suddenly, the three rods with the feathers on the ends of them started spinning at a medium speed, rotating around and around against my man tit tips and inside my piss slit. The sound of soft whirring would actually have been soothing had it not been for the fact of what that whirring was causing...

"AAAAAYYYRRRRRRRRR, ha, ha, ha, ha, ha, ha, ha, ha, ha, ha, ha, ha, ha, ha, ha, ha, ha!" I suddenly cackled real loudly from down in my belly. "OHHHHHHHRRRR GAWD!"

Looking down I watched as my man tit tips were tickled and they jutted up even harder and my slit felt as if it was literally being fucked by that feather as it spun inside there. Actually, to put it bluntly my piss slit *was* being tickled and fucked by that feather...

"Stand and be tickled Timmy, stand and be tickled," Ronald chuckled, stepped in front of me and watched in delight as I suffered in throes of once more uncontrollable laughter. "The insidious device you're tied to is sort of like those new fangled stand-up MRI machines. The only difference is the few twists and turns that I added to make this my own creation. I would say that what you're tied to is more like a stall door in a men's room stall in a gay bar where those guys go glory holing, as they call it. Another difference in my creation obviously is the fact that unlike a glory hole set-up my creation has three holes wedged in it, rather than just the one for a guys' cock and balls..."

"Th-thanks for the most informative rampage, ha, ha, ha, ha, ha, ha, ha, ha, ha, ha, ha, ha, ha, ha, ha, ha, ha, ha, ha, ha, ha, ha, ha, ha, ha, ha, ha!" I laughed and laughed and laughed. "If you ever decide to market these horrid devices I expect some kind, ha, ha, ha, ha, ha, ha, ha, ha, ha, ha, ha, ha, of a commission! Ha, ha, ha, ha, ha, ha, ha, ha, ha, ha!"

As the feathers spun and did their work beads of piss and even droplets of pre cum formed at my being tickled slit. The sensations coursing through my entire body were electric and I was goose-bump riddled in what seemed like no time... All I could do was laugh and laugh and laugh and laugh..."

Ronald's Journal
Dated February 1995
Valentines Day Dinner with Timothy and Stephanie Backman

Marilyn and I arrived promptly at eight PM at Tim and Stephanie's house for our Valentines dinner date with them, two bottles of wine to go with dinner with us. I rang the bell and looked straight down; knowing that I would see Timmy's socked feet when he opened the door. But it was Stephanie who opened the door instead of Timmy. She greeted us warmly, her feet clad in a pair of slip-on low heeled sandal like shoes. As she told us to come in and as she closed and locked the door she said that Timmy would be joining us shortly, citing how he was at the moment putting his shoes out in the garage to air out *and* changing his socks at the same time. Marilyn looked quizzically at Stephanie and Stephanie quickly explained how Timmy always likes walking around the house in his socked feet after work, but like most men at the end of the day his socks were pretty musty scented. She said all this as if Marilyn totally understood and could relate. As Stephanie headed toward the kitchen, saying that she had to check on dinner she told me and Marilyn to make ourselves at home in the living room. I could not believe that upon entering Timmy's home his socks had already become the topic of conversation. It was uncanny really. But it would also prove to be an interesting evening conversation-wise. I whispered to Marilyn, "See what I mean?" She simply nodded as we walked slowly into the living room. The scents of cooking wafting from the kitchen were wonderful and besides the smells of Stephanie's cooking we heard the cooing and very sweet sounds of a baby. Obviously Stephanie had Tim Junior with her in the kitchen, in his infant seat no doubt. Stephanie called out to us to help ourselves to drinks in the bar. As I was pouring wine for me and Marilyn and setting aside glasses of wine for Stephanie and Tim as well Tim came into the living room, a smile on his face from ear to ear, calling out, "Hey there buddy, glad you could make it." Marilyn and I turned to greet our host, me shaking hands with him first and then I introduced him to Marilyn. I could see in her eyes that Marilyn most definitely found our host to be very handsome indeed. Over dinner Marilyn and I rehashed how we had met and how long we had been dating for. It seems that married couples like Tim and Stephanie like hearing about how their single friends all met their partners. While we ate Stephanie fed Tim Junior as he sat in his highchair. I have to say that he really is the cutest baby I have seen in a long time. He was very well behaved, barely cried and he smiled so cutely at me and Marilyn a few times. After dinner Stephanie put Tim Junior down for the night upstairs in his crib and the four of us relaxed in the living room with after dinner blackberry brandy. Marilyn and I sat on a loveseat for two while Tim got comfortable on a recliner, his socked feet elevated as he sipped his brandy. I have to mention that Timmy's socks were the same color of the brandy. When Stephanie came into the living room to join us she smirked at her handsome husband as he sat very comfortably in the recliner. She said, "Thank you for changing your socks after getting your wingtips off Timmy," and gave one of his big toes a squeeze as she past him by before stopping to pour herself a brandy and then getting comfortable in a living room chair. Timmy turned four different shades of red, obviously feeling very embarrassed over what Stephanie had just said to him. The conversation that emanated from that comment was one that I will never forget, if I live to be a hundred that is. Marilyn looked over at Tim and asked what the problem was where his socks were concerned.

He smiled stupidly and said how his socks sort of smelled when he would get home from work after a long day. Stephanie laughed sarcastically and said that her hubby's socks *more than* smelled when he got home. She said that before Marilyn and I had arrived for dinner that night she had begged Tim to leave his shoes on while we all had dinner. He flat-out refused, saying that he liked padding around in his socked feet after work. He looked to me for support where getting your shoes off after work feels great and really relaxes a guy. I grinned and told my buddy to leave me out of this where his socks were concerned. We all laughed good naturedly. Stephanie was adamant though about the fact that if he wanted to pad around the house in his socked feet when company was going to be there then he would have to at least change his socks after he got his shoes off. The compromise they reached was that Timmy would leave his wingtips out in the garage to air out *and* change his socks as well. I was sweating like crazy thinking of Tim's shoes out in the garage, his worn socks no doubt either crammed in them or perhaps reposing in a laundry hamper somewhere in the house. Tim laughed some more and asked if we could all talk about something other than his smelly socks, wiggling his toes under his fresh socks as he sat in his recliner. When Marilyn and I got back to my place that night she stayed over and again massaged my feet, both with my socks on and then with my socks off. She laughed about how all the talk over dinner about Tim's smelly socks made her want to really get to my feet again and massage them. Plus she remembered how while having my feet massaged really seemed to make me bulk up in the crotch for her. I'm learning a lot here lately where feet are concerned, both men's and women's at that. There seems to be some underlying unspoken about fetish and obsession where all this is concerned. When I fucked Marilyn's brains out after she had massaged my feet she rode my cock like it was a pony and held my socks in her hand as she swayed to the rhythm...

Chapter Thirty-One

"HA, ha, ha, ha, ha, ha, ha, ha, ha, ha, ha, ha, ha, ha, ha, ha, ha, son of a fucking bitch!" I hee hawed crazily as Ronald's latest mechanical device did it's work of tickling the very tips of my man tits and even worse my poor piss slit. "AAAAYYYYYYRRRRRRR! HAW, HAW, HAW, HAW, HAW, HAW, HAW, HAW, HAW, HAW, HAW!"

At that point my nipple tips were as hard as two bullets, sweat sheens coated my trapped male cleavage, and my cock was just as hard as my tits, sticking straight out, the veins in it truly plumped up all green and thick. As that damned feather tip whirled in my piss slit I felt as if I would be able to shoot yet another good load of goopy cum. I mean, after all, the way that feather was tickling me good and deep inside my slit was sending me over the boiling point... And like most guys, after I've cum once or twice my cock is really sensitized!

"R-Ronald, wh-what do I have to do to make you, ha, ha, ha, ha, ha, ha, ha, ha, ha, ha, ha, ha!" I screamed crazily. "What the fucking fuck do I have to do to get you to turn this thing off man?"

I arched my back a bit and looked up at the ceiling, without realizing at first that it would cause my male cleavage trapped in those wedges to stretch even more and cause my being tickled man tits to become even more sensitive to what was being done to them.

"HA, ha, ha, ha, ha, ha, ha, ha, ha, ha, ha, ha, ha, ha, ha, ha, ha, ha, ha, ha!" I reeled, quickly looking down and seeing those feathers whirling against my poor defenseless man tit tips.

"What you're doing is just great Timmy me laddy, most satisfactorily too I must say," Ronald said to me, standing nearby as I stood there and was tickled in the tight bondage.

"And as for turning the device off I really don't see the need for that at the moment." Ronald chuckled and held up his remote control for the feathers that were attached to the apparatus in front of me. He pressed a button on the remote and suddenly the feathers seemed to press harder yet against my man tits, the one at my piss slit seemed to burrow its way in further and all three of the feathers working me over were suddenly spinning faster yet.

"AAAAAAAAHHHHHHHHHH!" I screamed as the combination of having my tit tips tickled along with my piss slit sent me into a screaming fit combined with raucous laughter as well.

"HA, ha, ha, ha, ha, ha, ha, ha, ha, ha, ha, ha, ha, ha, ha, ha, ha, ha, ha, ha, ha, ha, ha, ha!" I laughed, feeling certifiably insane by then for sure...

"After a good helping of this device I'll have you tell me more about your ticklish past Timmy me laddy," Ronald said.

My lips trembled as I laughed and massive amounts of spittle flew from my mouth as beads of piss and pre cum emanated from my wide sexy piss slit... When

Ronald mentioned my ticklish past visions of that bitch Valerie danced in my head, I saw my two work buddies Joe and Jeff, and even a gay guy named Douglas who will be told about at some point as well. Gods' almighty but it seemed as if my whole (tickle) life was flashing before my eyes buds...

"OOOHHHHHRRRRRR, some, somehow, ha, ha, ha, ha, ha, ha, ha, ha, ha, ha, ha, ha, ha!" I guffawed crazily. "Somehow I think I'm cumming Ronald!"

"And somehow I doubt that buddy," Ronald chided me meanly.

It was actually what I'll call a false orgasm, and it was the worst form of teasing that I had experienced thus far. There was the feeling of an impending gusher, but when none came I simply laughed harder and harder in a mixture of frustration and non-control...

"OOHHHHHRRRRR, what an awful feeling!" I grunted in total frustration.

"Told you bud, you could very well be on the way to an impending gusher but I truly doubt you'll get off," Ronald teased me in a mocking tone.

"We, we'll, ha, ha, ha, ha, ha, ha, ha, ha, ha, ha, ha, ha, ha, ha, ha!" I began. "We'll FUCKING see! I still have a few ideas up my sleeve here, ha, ha, ha, ha, ha, ha, ha, ha, ha, ha, ha, or perhaps, more appropriately, down in my socks, ha, ha, ha, ha, ha, ha, ha, ha, ha, ha, ha, ha, ha, ha, ha, ha, ha! YOU FUCKER RONALD!"

I pursed my lips together and continued laughing. I hunched my broad sinewy shoulders up and continued laughing. I balled my tied hands behind me into a big fist and continued laughing. I looked downward toward my cock as the feather spun in my slit and I continued laughing, but I also tried my damned best to concentrate on my poor cock. Gods, my balls were dangling and they were receiving no action, and neither was my shaft for that matter. That was what had to be done buds. My rigid shaft and my balls needed some action here. I again felt the awful frustration inside me as another fake orgasm teased me awfully.

"OOOOHHHHHHRRRRR, th-there's that awful feeling again, ha, ha, ha, ha, ha, ha, ha, ha, ha, ha, ha, ha, ha, ha, ha, ha, ha!" I laughed crazily.

I concentrated intensely on my hard cock and then clenched my ass muscles. I tried to move my stiff and erect penis away from and off the feather that was tickling my piss slit. I figured that if I accomplished that and somehow got that feather whirling against my shaft it would somehow bring me off and cure that awful teasing feeling of the fake orgasms I was suffering.

"I'm not sure what you're up to buddy, but it will be fun to watch, that much I can say," Ronald said, stepping beside me and watching as I sweated and laughed through the latest tickle session he was subjecting me to.

I took a deep breath and with all I could I tried to move my cock backwards and off that feather. But all I succeeded in doing actually when I moved my tied up socked feet back a bit was to cause that feather to slither its way even further into my slit, if you can imagine such a thing...

"AAAAAAAAAYYYYRRRRR!" I screeched loudly and Ronald hooted and laughed over my unsuccessful attempt at finding some relief for myself.

"Ronald, ohhhhhhhhhhhhrrrr! Please man, please, ha, ha, ha, ha, ha, ha, ha, ha, ha, ha, ha, ha, ha, ha, ha, ha, ha!" I chortled crazily. "Please turn this thing off!"

But then, as I involuntarily twisted my bound up arms a bit the feather at my piss slit *did* fall away from my cock as it continued whirling.

"OOHHHHHHHHHHHH, oh God, oh yes, I did it, I fucking did it," I gasped and now that it was just my man tits being tickled I was no longer laughing so hard.

Ronald looked at me in disbelief, but then, my relief was short lived as the feather at my crotch started whirling against my rigid shaft.

"OOOOOOOOOOOOOOOOOO, ha, ha, ha, ha, ha, ha, ha, ha, ha, ha, ha, ha, ha, ha!" I laughed merrily and insanely some more.

The feather whirled around and around my shaft, slap, slapping it as it went, but just like when it was spinning around in my piss slit there would be no orgasm relief. I felt as if I was floating real high up with no net below me to break my fall if I were to suddenly plunge down…

"OOOOOOOOOOOOOOOO, m-my poor cock, ha, ha, ha, ha, ha, ha, ha, ha, ha, ha, ha, ha, ha, ha, ha, ha!" I screamed…

As I was tickled and tickled at the cock and my man tits I looked down over the wood I was tied to again and saw my piss slit seeming to be pulsing open and closed somehow. Suddenly, I involuntarily pissed a few droplets of a yellow stream onto the floor; all the while I was laughing and laughing and laughing and laughing. I supposed that all the whirling that feather had done in my slit had caused me to piss a bit involuntarily buds…

A Boner Book

Chapter Thirty-Two

Ronald finally turned off the spinning feathers after what seemed like a few hours later. From my very hazy estimations I guessed that it was early evening by then. Gawd, that buddy of mine had had me as his tickle captive for nearly an entire day at that point and not to mention the hours of the night before when he had first snagged me from my own home. He untied me from that infernal slab of wood, leaving my hands roped behind me and my feet tied. It felt like a rush of total relief as he pulled the lever that released my male cleavage from the wedges they had been in along with my cock and balls as well. Ronald lifted me like a groom carrying his bride and lugged me out of the latest room where I had been tickle tortured. As he carried me I commented of how my cock felt all tingly and numb, adding that my man tits felt the same way, a few giggles and chuckles escaping me as I spoke as well...

Ronald set me down at the table where we had eaten lunch earlier and held a bottle of cool mineral water to my trembling lips. I chugged the water down gratefully, seeing as I was thirsty as all hell. If the water was laced with Ronald's aphrodisiac I really didn't give a fuck at that point. I mean, by then I had gotten used to the feeling of being constantly horned up and I was so thirsty that I would drink gasoline, hardy fucking har, har, buds...

"Feeling okay bud?" Ronald asked me, tousling my hair as he fed me the mineral water.

I nodded my head up and down and simply gulped the water, my Adam's apple bobbing real sexily as I drank and drank. When I had consumed nearly half the large bottle of water Ronald sat down across from me and folded his arms, a mocking look on his face...

"What?" I asked him. "*What* do you want from me now man?"

"Years back when we were still working together you went on a business trip for the lawyers of the bank," Ronald said to me.

"Yeah, so what?" I asked him in an angry tone of voice. "I always went on business trips, I still do. What does the one I went on for the lawyers of the bank have to do with any of what's going on here?"

I of course knew exactly what it had to do with what was going on here, but at that moment I really didn't want to give Ronald the satisfaction, at least not yet.

"After you had returned from that trip I had asked you over lunch how the trip was, if you'd had a good time, things like that," Ronald reminded me and my heart pounded and my cock stiffened yet again. "Your response to me at that time was that you'd had a terrible business trip because some stuff had gotten all fucked up but overall you'd had a ticklish good time. I want to know what that meant all those years ago Timmy me laddy."

I leaned back in my chair, flexed my tied hands behind me a bit, looked down at my tied up socked feet and told Ronald to give me some more water and then I would tell him all about that ticklish business trip...

Ronald fed me some more mineral water and then I began yet another tirade from my ticklish past...

"I was about two to two and a half years into my job at the bank when I went on the business trip you're talking about Ronald," I said and just recalling that trip made my cock stiffen some more as I sat there tied up in front of my good buddy. "I had been summoned to Miami Florida by two of the bank's top lawyers to negotiate a contract for a client of theirs, a wholesale manufacturer of sexy women's lingerie. You can imagine how a young and studly executive such as myself would eat that up buddy. I proceeded to Miami on a flight the night before the meeting and for sample purposes the client had provided me with a suitcase of their products for me to use as samples the next day at the meeting for the contract negotiations. I had actually arrived early in Miami. I checked into my hotel, went to my room, opened the suitcase filled with lingerie, reviewed my notes and then went to dinner. Fucking fucks Ronald; it was when I returned to my room from dinner that my nightmare with two sexy maids began. Well, apparently, this hotel that the bank had set me up in had the customer service tradition of having a maid come around at eight PM to turn down the bed, adjust the lighting, and straighten up the room and to just generally make sure that everything was just right for the guest. And in my case as a bank executive they really went out of their way. When I got back to my room after dinner I walked in on, not one, but two Latin maids in my room. My first reaction was, "What the fucking fuck are you doing here?" I closed my hotel room door and took in the sight of the two maids as they were both standing at my queen-sized bed, the open suitcase of the client's lingerie on the bed below where they were standing and I saw that they were both holding up pieces of the lingerie against their maid's uniforms. At the sound of my voice they both jerked around and mumbled something in Spanish to each other. I did hear the word "chilendo" which I think in Spanish means cute. Well, I wasn't feeling very cute at that moment, I was actually pissed. With indignation, I marched into the room to get those two maids out of my business. But then, as I approached the two maids and really took in the sexy sight of them my indignation seemed to melt, but another part of me did not melt. The two maids were dressed in traditional hotel staff maid uniforms. Did I happen to mention that among other things where fetishes are concerned that I have a definite mania for sexy maids in those little uniforms, little white hats, button up the front simple black one-piece dresses that come to the knee, and comfortable white shoes, and oh God those silk white stockings. Well, these two maids in my hotel room were outfitted just the way that I described. But when I got an even closer look at them I could not believe what I was seeing. I uttered the word "Wow" when I realized that they both looked like two very famous and very sexy actresses. I'll only mention them by their first names, just so they can keep their anonymity, Rita and Jennifer. As I looked at their faces I stopped in my tracks, my mouth gaped open and I was staring fixedly at the two maids. They spoke again to each other in Spanish and were giggling at my reaction. Obviously they had gotten this kind of reaction before where their resemblances to two famous actresses were concerned. In fact Ronald, I think that it was my reaction that really emboldened the maid's actions. I mean, here they were, two hotel employees caught going through an executive customer's belongings, they should have been the intimidated ones in this scene. But, because I had stopped dead in my tracks and because I was gaping at them like the proverbial "deer in the headlights" they assumed that I had made the same connection that much other sex starved male hotel guests had made in the past. I think that they thought that I was under the impression that they really were Rita and Jennifer. Now I ask you, what man in his right mind would believe that two famous actresses would be dressed up like maids and working in this hotel that I was staying at on this particular business trip, even if it was a very, very expensive hotel. I knew that they really weren't Rita and Jennifer, but yet, my overwhelming lust got the better of me and I stupidly uttered "Rita? Jennifer?" as I just stood there. The Rita look-a-like said, "Why yes, and this is indeed Jennifer, and could you kindly tell us who you are?" I stuttered that my name was Timothy Backman, banker, there on a business trip at the instructions of the bank's lawyers. And then, holding up some of the lingerie the Jennifer look-a-like said to me, "And pray tell Mr. Backman, what is a man doing with all this lingerie in his suitcase? Can you tell us that? Are you one of what they call those kinks?" As the Jennifer look-a-like asked me those questions both of the maids were now slowly approaching me. Stuttering again I stupidly explained that those things belonged to a client of the bank that I worked for, trying to sound as insistent as possible as I said it. The Rita look-a-like said "Yeah sure, and we're really maids in this hotel." Then she said something in Spanish to Jennifer and they both laughed. What she said next really shocked me, she said, "Well, we think you should model some of this stuff for Jennifer and me." That said they both laughed again. I quickly told them that they did not understand. I explained that I was not one of those suit guys into wearing that stuff. With a stupid looking grin on my face I added how I was not a guy who wore his wife's underwear under his suit. I told them that all the lingerie was a customer's samples for a meeting the next day. I was doing my best to convince them that I was telling the truth. Suddenly, the two of them were on me and while conversing with each other in Spanish they began a dual attack on me, which I quickly determined was to undress me, Gawds! And Ronald, let me tell you man, these two maids seemed very adept at stripping a guy of his clothes, even if he was against the idea. One would struggle and grapple with me while the other made progress with an article of my clothing. They managed to get my tie off and as I prattled and bitched at them, threatening to tell the manager of the hotel about this they got my suit jacket off me by pulling it at the sleeves and over my head. They managed to get my shirt open and while one of them was working on my belt were when they discovered, woe of fucking woes and story of my fucking life, they discovered that I was ticklish... This discovery was now all that it took and now their attack was concentrated on tickling me, fucking fuck, they tickled me bare from the waist up, but that was only the beginning because you see the tickling had (as usual) rendered me defenseless and I was unable to ward them off. Being that as it was helped them to make short work of my belt and suit pants. As I was laughing and screaming for Rita to stop tickling my ribs Jennifer managed to get my belt off me. Then, they spun me a few times while still tickling me and threw me down on the queen sized bed to rid me of my wingtip shoes and finally my suit pants. I was chucking, giggling, laughing real loud and like in the past, hugging my sides and trying my best to fight them off, but Gawd of Gawds man, the tickling that they were doing to me had made me helpless. The two maids then looked at the laughing pile of man on the bed, me to be exact, stripped down to my tighty whities and my dark blue nylon dress socks. While I was trying to recover from having been so awfully tickled the maids spoke in Spanish yet again and then pulled me all the way up on the bed and holy fucking fucks, they began using the lingerie to tie my wrists up to the top part of the bed, the bed board to be exact. Much as I hated what they were doing to me there was something real hot and kinky about being tied up with women's frilly undergarments. They then proceeded to do the same thing with my ankles, tying them up real tight with the lingerie. My lame protests were thwarted by the least little rib or tummy tickle. So now, those bitches had me tied up and spread eagled on the bed. And now that they had me that way Rita and Jennifer began to strip off their maid uniforms. With no more tickling going on (at least not at the moment) I was not distracted from all that was happening and I have to admit that I was all-a-goggle as the two sexy maids stripped completely naked. And oh man Ronald, not only did their faces resemble the famous actresses Rita and Jennifer, but from my perspective, they had exactly the same bodies that I would have expected them to have. More and more I was thinking that this was some kind of crazy dream I was having. My mouth was once more agape, my eyes were bugging out of my head and now my cock was plumping up in my tight white underpants. But those two bitches didn't stay naked Ronald, oh no, not at all man. Instead they began trying on pieces of the lingerie that they hadn't used to tie me up with. Fuck, now they looked like Rita and Jennifer as Victoria's Secret models. When they got to the bottom of the suitcase they found a vibrating dildo and a bunch of feathers that must have been meant for one of the sexy and more provocative costumes. Holy fuck, but these finds just gave those two bitches more ideas, plus when they looked back at me tied to the bed they saw that I had a huge white cotton tent that I had pitched right in my goddamned underpants. Laughing real sexily and speaking to each other in Spanish they again approached me. Rita took some feathers and went to my head while Jennifer went to the end of the bed where my socked feet were. As Rita began toying with my ears, nose, neck and shoulders with the feathers Jennifer began to scribble her long fingernails on the soles of my socked feet. What began were giggles, chuckles and me saying, "No, no, now don't do that, stop that, quit it now!" and then turned into full, loud laughter, me screaming, "Ha, ha, ha, ha, ha, ha, ha, ha, ha, ha, ha, ha, ha, ha, ha, ha, ha, ha, ha, ha, HEE, HEE, HEE, HEE, HEE, HEE, D-DON'T, OHHHHH, ha, ha, ha, ha, ha, ha, ha, ha, ha, ha, ha, ha quit that, that fucking tickles!" I screamed all that as Jennifer went to town on my socked soles. Rita was distracted by my screams and laughing and she began to just watch as Jennifer then proceeded to peel my blue nylon dress socks off me. She bared my feet and toes to whatever she wanted to do to them. Both of those bitches were amazed that my laughing had actually increased an octave after Jennifer had bared my tootsies. So, after enjoying watching Jennifer tickle my bare feet with her long fingernails Rita told her to toss my socks over to her, which she used to muffle my volume. What an awful thing Ronald, Rita stuffed one of my own smelly blue nylon socks into my gaping mouth and then used a spare panty to tie around my head to keep that stinking sock in place. Fuck man, why do people do that to poor guys? Why gag a guy with his smelly socks? It truly sucks; I got to tell you Ronald. Then, Rita began to dibble the feathers in my armpits and my laughter, although muffled by the sock wedged in my mouth went up another octave. So Jennifer worked upwards from tickling my feet to my legs and Rita worked downward from the top and they both converged at my tight white underpants with the big tent in them. Jennifer then went to her cleaning cart and returned with a pair of scissors. I ranted and seethed behind that damned sock in my mouth as she proceeded to snip and cut my underpants clean off me. This rendered me completely naked and my cock was sticking straight up at the ceiling. This made an excellent target for Rita's feathers and she really worked my cock with those danged feathers, swishing them over my huge erection. Meanwhile, horror of all horrors, Jennifer had gotten the vibrating dildo that had been with the bank customer's samples. She checked the batteries to see if the dildo was working and lo and fucking behold it was. That bitch started working that vibrating fake cock at my ass lips. Now I was not only being tickled but I was on the fucking brink of an orgasm. But then, the two bitches stopped. Can you believe that shit Ronald? They saw that I was on the verge of shooting a whopper of a fucking load and they stopped. Rita came around to join Jennifer on the bed between my spread out and tied legs and they began to caress and kiss each other. They passed the vibrating dildo back and forth and diddled each others cunts and even slid that thing inside my chute a few times, just to tease the fucking fuck out of me. Those bitches brought each other off several times and just watching that sent my head spinning Ronald. While they both came a few times they seemed to ignore me. Then they returned their attention to poor tied up and gagged me and let's face it man, without being tickled I was no longer laughing. But the lesbian act right between my thighs had done nothing to reduce the swelling in my cock or my drive and need for an orgasm. But the girls decided that they wanted to tickle me some more, seeing as they saw how it really got me in motion, and that is exactly what the fuck they did. They alternated between tickling and teasing me to the fucking brink of orgasm all night long. Can you believe that Ronald? What a shitty and fucked up thing to do to an executive in his hotel room huh? They had forgotten about their jobs and by then I was in no frame of mind to think about anything except the tickling they were doing to me and the fact that I was trying to get them to make me cum. I was beside myself with laughter from the tickling and the sexual agony from the never-ending teasing. It continued all night Ronald, those bitches went at it all night and well into the next morning too. I finally shot my load around lunch time, of the next day, courtesy of those two bitches taking turns slowly jacking me off. After I shot a whopper of a load they untied me from the bed and left me lying there gasping and grunting for breath, still with my sock in my mouth. They loaded up their cart, put on their uniforms and when I finally took my sock out of my mouth I whispered the words, "Bitches, bitches you two are," as they walked sexily out of my hotel room. I angrily threw my rancid sock that had been my gag on the floor and it was at that moment that I realized I had missed my very important meeting with the bank's client. I quickly called Jerry, my direct manager and told him that I had gotten a bit tied up and asked if the client wouldn't mind rescheduling for that afternoon instead. Well, thank God the client was understanding and while we discussed his business contract over a late lunch he introduced me to his two associates as they sat down at the table, he said, "Timothy Backman, I want you to meet Jennifer and Rita." I stifled a gulp as the two maids sat down at our table, smiling coyly at me. They both said that it was a pleasure to meet me, calling me Mr. Backman.

Chapter Thirty-Three

"So there you have it Ronald, now you know how I almost lost a very important account for the bank," I said miserably, my tale of my business trip and the two maids complete at that point. "Looking back on it now I somehow get the feeling that the bank's client actually set me up for that experience with the two so-called maids."

"Do you think so Timmy?" Ronald asked me, sounding totally sarcastic, and then glancing at his watch.

"What?" I asked him, sounding totally miserable. "Is it time already for my next tickle torture session?"

"No, actually I think its time to drive you home buddy boy," Ronald said and got to his feet.

"WH-what?" I asked Ronald, my lips trembling as I said it. "D-do you mean it? You're going to bring me home?"

"Of course Timmy me laddy," Ronald stated happily, stepping behind me and untying my hands for me. "I mean, after all, I can't keep you here forever now can I?"

"Of course not man, fucking fucks, I am so glad you've finally come to your senses bud," I said after my hands were untied, kneading them together, massaging the numbness out of them as Ronald sat back down across from me.

"What'll I wear though man?" I asked him, sounding very confused over this sudden revelation that I was going home. "I mean, lets face it buddy, when you brought me here all I had on were my boxer shorts and black socks."

As I said that I glanced down at my still tied black socked feet and wiggled my toes in my socks.

"Well, for being such a good sport about all this I have a surprise for you bud," Ronald said. "I had a suit custom made for you by your old buddy Dan the tailor. When I was at your house one night with one of my many dates I managed to peek in your wardrobe when I had excused myself to the bathroom. I got your exact measurements and had Dan make you a beautiful suit for your ride home. You can wear the same socks and boxer shorts you had on at the time that I nabbed you though."

"Now that's real sleazy man," I chuckled.

"Hey, I even got a shirt and tie to go with the suit, wait till you see it," Ronald said to me, smiling. "Look at it this way bud, at least you got a suit out of all this, and a custom made one at that..."

"Yeah, it reminds of me the time my sinister brother got me my first suit when I was starting out," I said and smiled back at Ronald. "Is, is it okay if I untie my feet man? I'd like to shower and maybe shave before you drive me home, if that's okay."

"Sure thing man," Ronald replied. "You can leave your socks with me while you shower. I'll put them with the suit I have for you..."

"Sounds like a plan to me buddy," I said and with a feeling of euphoria engulfing me I reached down and untied my feet.

Without a word I peeled my moist black socks off my feet and handed them to Ronald.

"Please don't blame me if I don't thank you for a wonderful time," I said with a grin as we both got to our feet.

"Listen man, I really hope you're not too pissed off at me because of all this," Ronald said as we stepped from our perspective places at the table and stood facing each other a few inches apart, Ronald fully clothed and me naked as a jaybird with a steel like erection pointing straight up at the heavens.

"Well, I suppose I should be pissed off huh?" I asked Ronald. "I mean, you did kidnap me after all and what you put me through here, oh God, fucking fucks, *what you put me through man! Hardy fucking har and har!*" But, all in all it was all in sleazy fun I will suppose. It's not like I was kidnapped for ransom or anything like that… And thanks to that phone call you had me make to Stephanie she at least has some sort of explanation for my absence."

"Good man Timmy me laddy," Ronald said to me and suddenly without warning he grabbed my erect cock.

"OHHHHHHHRRRRR fuck, fucking fucks," I gasped breathlessly.

With a look of total determination etched on his face Ronald tugged my cock upwards a few times, tightening his hold on it with each tug and crank he gave it.

"OOOOOOOOOOOOOOOO," I swooned and swayed on my bare feet.

I crossed my hands up behind my head and my head spun as Ronald did the honors…

"OHHHHHRRRRRRRRR, goddamn man," I seethed. "Fucking guy…"

Droplets of pre cum erupted from my erect member and slithered down the shaft, under Ronald's fisted hand, acting like a lubricant of sorts as he stroked and choked my meat pole some more…

"FUCKING totally FUCKS," I grunted as Ronald reached forward and gave one of my man tits a good hard squeeze, mashing it tight. "OHHHHHHHHH fucking fuck, that just did it man!"

I clenched my teeth and snarled as my cock erupted my sexy man juices, splattering all over my muscular chest. Ronald stroked me like I was plugged up in the cock, forcing every goddamned possible drop of my good stuff from me.

"OOOOOOOOOHHHHHH man, oh yeah, time to go home," I breathed heavily.

When I was done spewing my load it slithered down my robust chest, over my nipples and stomach area. Ronald let go of my cock, we looked at each other blankly and then he said, "Follow me, the bathroom is this way where you can take your shower and shave."

I walked slowly behind my buddy, running my fingers through the sticky mess on my chest. My black socks were sticking out of the back pocket of Ronald's pants. For some reason seeing them like that my cock started to stiffen again…if you can believe that buds.

"I suppose it's good to juice my cock a bit huh buddy?" I asked stupidly. "Seeing as you filled me with that aphrodisiac after all…"

At the door to the bathroom Ronald looked at me and said, "Sure thing buddy, just make sure to save some for that pretty wife of yours…"

We both chuckled and as I reached for the doorknob of the bathroom Ronald reached again for my semi hard cock.

"OHHHHHHHHHHHHHH!" I grunted in total surprise as my buddy again had me by the cock.

"Looks like you got enough there for Stephanie and for one more good siphoning here buddy boy," Ronald laughed as I slammed my back up against the still closed bathroom door.

"OHHHHRRRRRR you fucking fucker," I garbled and clenched my hands into fists at my sides as Ronald did the honors of working at squeezing another load of ball juice out of me. "GAAAAWWWDDDDDDD!"

It seemed that after all the times he had dosed me with the aphrodisiac laced chloroform and after all the ways he had fed it to me and after all the sexually teasing based tickling Ronald had forced me to endure and after all the ways he had made me tell him of my tickle past I truly was worked up real well in the area of my cock and balls. As my buddy stroked and choked my newly erect cock I slammed my head against the bathroom door, grunted, sweated and curled my naked toes back. I suffered erotically as I felt my balls cooking up another batch of Timmy juices... But through it all I didn't once try to get Ronald to let go of my cock...

"FUCCCKKKK!" I snarled as a few moments later Ronald squeezed one of my man tits and I let fly with another super sized load of thick creamy slop. "AAAARRHHHHHHHHHH!"

Once again my load splattered all over my chest, mixing real well with the load from just a few moments ago...

I heaved, grunted and gasped and as Ronald let go of my cock for the second time I reached for the doorknob of the bathroom. I let the door open behind me and still heaving for breath, still in sheer ecstasy I stumbled naked into one of the most beautiful and luxurious bathrooms I had ever seen, closing the door slowly behind me. I heard Ronald call out for me to take all the time I needed in the bathroom as I took in the sight of the immaculate room, the huge shower-stall with the showerhead attachments hanging from it, the bidet next to the toilet, the Jacuzzi tub, the gold sink.

"How the fuck does he afford this?" I whispered as I slinked over to the toilet and sat down on it.

As the first fart escaped me I heard Ronald chuckle from outside the bathroom...

"Go ahead and laugh all you want me laddy!" I called out sarcastically loud enough so that my buddy could hear me outside the bathroom and I deliberately farted again. "But you really do need to face the fact that since you captured me I haven't taken one good dump..."

Ronald laughed again and said that he was well aware of that...

When I was done relieving myself I took advantage of the bidet before I stepped into the spray of the shower. I slathered myself with liquid soap, caressed my tickled and very sensitized body with the various shower attachments and when I sprayed the jettisoning water over my chest and nipples my cock was again erect and at full mast.

"Gawds," I whispered as I washed that special spot under my balls.

As I washed I realized as I cleansed each spot how Ronald hadn't left out one area when it came to tickling and teasing me. I grabbed my cock and tugged it a few times. Under the spray of the water I was sure that Ronald didn't hear me grunting as I shot load number three, or maybe he did hear me. I wondered how many more times I would cum before I left my buddies' sinister lair. I knew I wanted to have some stored up for Stephanie, but somehow I did not think it would be a problem rising to the occasion for her once we were back together again. God, just the thought of my beautiful Stephanie sent chills through me. I suppose that old saying is true after all how about absence making the heart grow fonder. It sure made my cock grow fonder, hardy fucking har and har buds. After I washed my hair I applied a goodly amount of shaving cream to my face and slowly shaved away the day's growth of beard that had accumulated during my captivity. Ronald's shower stall came complete with a fogless mirror and an array of shaving utensils. Fucking fucks, it seemed that the guy had spared no expense when it came to creating this lair of his. When I finished in the shower I looked longingly at the Jacuzzi, wanting to sit and bathe in it for a while and let the jets of water at the bottom caress me in what I call those special places, but thoughts of being at home overpowered the desire for the Jacuzzi. I wrapped a towel around my waist and stepped to the sink to brush my teeth, floss and use mouthwash, all supplied by my good tickle buddy, Ronald. When I was done I towel dried my hair and combed it into my usual banker's style. I checked my reflection in the mirror and decided I was ready to head home. I slapped some aftershave lotion on my cheeks and chin and exited the bathroom. Ronald was standing there waiting for me.

"I'm ready bud," I said to him, sounding both excited and for some reason fearful at the same time.

"I have your clothes set up in here," Ronald said, taking me by my upper arm and walking me into a room right next to the bathroom I had just enjoyed.

"I have to say man, I was just thinking out here while you showered how you did real well," Ronald said to me as we walked into what looked like an oversized tailor's fitting room. "You sure can take it when it comes to being tickled Timmy…"

Hanging on a hanger was one of the most debonair and dapper looking suits I had ever seen. On the floor was a well shined pair of black wingtips with my own black socks sticking out of them. On a chair were hung a silk gray tie and a white shirt. Also on the chair were my boxer briefs and a white tee shirt.

"Wow, I'm really going to be going home in style huh?" I asked Ronald as I stepped over to where the suit was hanging and ran my fingertips up and down the lapels of it. "This feels like silk almost…"

"Yeah, I spared no expense for you bud," Ronald said and brazenly took the towel off my waist.

"Get dressed so we can be on our way me laddy," Ronald said as I got my underpants on very quickly.

It felt great just to be wearing my underpants, I mean after having been kept just about fully naked (except for my socks from time to time) for the last day or so it really was great to finally be putting clothes on.

"How will I explain this new suit to my wife?" I asked Ronald as I sat to get my black socks on.

The scent wafting from my socks was musty and kinky at the same time… I pulled on my white tee shirt…

"That's up to you buddy," Ronald replied. "Maybe you should just tell her that your fraternity buddies bought it for you as a way of saying thanks for the great time you all had."

"Yeah, that's a thought, I suppose," I said as I stood up to climb into the suit pants.

"So I guess you're really glad that you're going home huh?" Ronald asked me as I pulled on the white shirt and buttoned it, followed by slipping the silk tie under the collar of the shirt.

"Sure I'm glad to be heading home man, no more tickle torture, no more being kept tied up, no more chloroform, God, that stuff was awful Ronald," I said as I did the knot in my new tie. "God, back to my beautiful wife and my kid, back to the security of my home, back to peacefulness...back to normalcy buddy..."

A short while later I was standing in front of a full length mirror, beautifully decked out in the new suit as Ronald straightened my tie for me.

"So you're not pissed at me at all huh bud? You're not planning to call the police about all this?" Ronald asked me.

"Well, in all honesty, sure I'm pissed, I mean, its not every night that a poor guy is kidnapped out of his own bathroom and tickle tortured for hours on end," I said as Ronald finished straightening my tie for me. "But, in time I'm sure I'll get over it, just like I did years ago where Linda and my college buddies were concerned, but man, I won't be turning my back on you any time soon..."

We both laughed...

"But as for the police, nah, who would believe me anyway man?" I asked Ronald.

Ronald clapped me on the back, told me that I truly was a good sport and then we walked out to his car together. I saw that it was a beautiful mini Cadillac with dark tinted windows, the kind a lot of companies use to transport their traveling employees around for business.

"Where's the van you brought me here in?" I asked my buddy as I sat down in the passenger seat.

Ronald closed the door for me once I was seated and comfortable.

"It's in the garage," Ronald replied. "I only use the van when I have stuff to ship."

Ronald climbed into the driver's seat, started the car and joy of joys I was then being driven toward home. As we plowed down the highway and a couple of hours later as things started to look familiar tears of happiness welled up in my eyes.

"So, you told Stephanie that you had been abducted by your college buddies, what have you decided to tell her happened to you for the rest of the time that you were missing?" Ronald asked me and I saw the nervousness in his eyes as we stole a glance at each other.

"I guess I'll just tell her that I partied a bit too hard and fell down and hit my head and had temporary amnesia," I said to Ronald, sounding as sarcastic as possible. "Fuck man, there's no way I can tell her what *you* did to me man, its too goddamned humiliating...I mean, she knows that my buddies tickled me, but I can't tell her that *you* did that to me as well..."

"Thanks again man..." Ronald said, sounding totally relieved.

A long while later, more than a couple of hours actually, Ronald slowly drove down my block. The sight of my neighbor's houses filled me with an almost childlike glee.

"Oh man, I'm home, fucking fucks, *I'm home*," I said breathlessly, smiling from ear to ear, looking out the tinted window of the passenger side of the car.

I pressed my hands against the window and had to choke back tears as the familiar sights surrounded me. As Ronald pulled up in front of my house I saw my son, ten year old Timothy junior playing with some of his toys on the front porch. He glanced up to spy the car with the tinted windows pulling up in front of the house, but of course he couldn't see his dad for the dark glass.

"Oh man Ronald, I just want to run over there and tell him daddy's home!" I said jovially, looking at Ronald and then looking back out the window at my son.

I reached for the door handle on my side of the car and found that there wasn't one there.

"Hey, what's up Ronald?" I asked, sounding a bit alarmed. "There's no door handle here."

"Damn, I keep forgetting to get that fixed buddy," Ronald replied and reached for the door handle on his side of the car. "I'll have to open it from the outside for you. Sit tight…"

Ronald stepped out of the car on the driver's side, slammed the door shut and quickly scooted around to my side of the vehicle. He opened the door for me and said, "Welcome home Timmy me laddy." I looked up at him, said, "Thank you, thank you, thank you so much Ronald," and slid one leg out of the car, placing one sexy wing-tipped foot on the pavement. But, then, as I was preparing to slide my other leg out of the car and as I looked at the beautiful sight of my son on the porch Ronald reached down toward me, and before my son even saw me Ronald slammed the ever-present chloroform soaked cloth against my face, very firmly over my nose and mouth.

"GGGGRRRRRRMMMFFFFFFF!" I snarled in more than total shock.

Ronald thrust forward, pushing me hard till I was fully back in the car. He kept the cloth pressed tight over my nose and mouth. My feet kicked involuntarily against the floor of the car as I tried to pry Ronald's hands off my face, to get that chloroform soaked cloth away from my nose and mouth before sleep claimed me *yet* again.

"R-RONALD, MMMMMMFFFFFFF…wh-*what*…" I gasped and then my head was spinning in a reverse orbit as a sleepy stupor claimed me.

I leaned my head back against the headrest, my poor mind awhirl, wondering what the fucking fuck was going on now and Ronald slammed the car door shut on me…

"Hey there Stephanie," I then heard Ronald calling out to my wife.

"H-huh?" I asked stupidly and slowly turned my head and through hazy vision saw my beautiful wife as she just happened to be coming out of the house and onto the porch to see about our son.

"Any word on Tim?" Ronald asked my wife. "I called him at work today and they said he was out on some business or other."

"That's right Ronald, he's uh, out on business," I heard Stephanie reply as she waved at my buddy. "When he gets back lets all do dinner…"

I supposed that Stephanie wasn't about to blab to anyone about the stupid explanation I had given her for my absence and what Tim junior had seen the night when Ronald captured me, the story of course being that my college fraternity buddies had playfully abducted me.

"St-Stephanie, I-I'm here," I mumbled as my eyes closed.

"Sure thing," Ronald said to my wife. "I'll bring my new girlfriend!"

"You always have a new girlfriend," Stephanie laughed. "See you soon."

"Yeah, see you soon Stephanie," Ronald said and got back in the driver's seat.

As he settled in the driver's seat I managed to open my eyes slightly. I looked out the tinted window at my wife and son…

"Steph, oh God Steph, *Timmy*," I gasped and pressed my hands against the window in desperation. "H-he's got me here..."

I saw that they were looking at Ronald's car but of course because of the tinted windows they could not see poor me. From behind me Ronald dosed me with another nose and mouth full of chloroform before driving off...

"MMMMFFFF..." I whimpered as my buddy held me close to him, the chloroform soaked cloth held tight against my nose and mouth.

I could have sworn that I felt Ronald's lips peck me on the cheek and then the car was moving away from my house as I dozed off in the passenger seat...

Most Definitely Not The End...

About the Author

Christopher Trevor was born in July 1963 and grew up in New York City. As soon as he was old enough to know how he began writing fiction and has been writing gay erotic/fetish stories for the past ten to twelve years at this point. He became an avid reader as well from the time he knew how and reads everything from fiction, to non-fiction to biographies of interesting and unusual people, people who have made a difference or who have paved the way for others. Christopher attributes his writing artistic inspiration to artists such as Etienne, Tom of Finland, Tagame, The Hun, and most notably Joe T, who Christopher has had the pleasure of speaking with and even meeting over the last few years. Christopher states, "Joe T encouraged me to write about my fetish because I was embarrassed about it at the time. Joe T said that when we are embarrassed about something that makes it even more enticing somehow." Christopher totally agreed and never stopped writing in this genre. Erotic writers who inspired Christopher Trevor were: Tom Shaw (author of "That Day at the Quarry), C.S. White (author of Big Sur), Larry Townsend (author of countless erotic novels), and Mason Powell (author of the classic story "The Brig.")

Christopher discovered that not only did he enjoy writing erotic tales but that after his first bondage experience he had a genuine flair for it. Writing to erotic oriented magazines about his first bondage experience truly opened the floodgates for Christopher where this style of writing is concerned. Christopher thanks the handsome and muscular "Greg" for that experience way back in time. Christopher took "Creative Writing" courses every semester during his high school years and while other friends of his stopped writing what they loved to write about as time went on Christopher never let a day go by when he didn't write something… "I feel that if I don't write every day I will die," Christopher has said many times over.

Foot fetish stories and all things related; spanking fetish, erotic shaving, muscle bondage, tickle torture, and hardcore stories are just a few of the areas of gay eroticism that Christopher enjoys writing about and inspiring in others as well. As one internet buddy said to Christopher where the black socks fetish is concerned, "Until I started talking with you I never gave a thought to my socks when I got dressed for work in the morning. Now when I pull my dress socks on every morning I get a chill up my spine."

Christopher is proud of the erotic effect he has on people…
Christopher Trevor is also the author of:

The Executive Guide to Foot Fetishism and Office Discipline
1-887895-36-1

Executive Ties That Bind
1-887895-37-X

Don't! Stop! That Tickles!
    1-887895-31-0

The Taming of Dominick
    1-887895-45-0

Timmy and The Hong Kong Tailor
    1-887895-30-2

Love, Torture and Redemption
    1-887895-32-9

Many More on the way...

Look for them where you found this book or Amazon.com.